LORELEI JAMES

BOUND

The Mastered Series

 New American Library

New American Library
Published by the Penguin Group
Penguin Group (USA) LLC, 375 Hudson Street,
New York, New York 10014

USA | Canada | UK | Ireland | Australia | New Zealand | India | South Africa | China
penguin.com
A Penguin Random House Company

First published by New American Library,
a division of Penguin Group (USA) LLC

First Printing, February 2014

 REGISTERED TRADEMARK—MARCA REGISTRADA

LIBRARY OF CONGRESS CATALOGING-IN-PUBLICATION DATA:

James, Lorelei.
    Bound/Lorelei James.
        p.   cm.—(The mastered series)
    ISBN 978-0-451-46730-0 (pbk.)
    1. Graphic artists—Fiction.   2. Martial artists—Fiction.   3. Bondage (Sexual
behavior)—Fiction.   I. Title.
    PS3610.A4475B68   2014
    813'.6—dc23   2013035275

Printed in the United States of America
10   9   8   7   6   5

Set in Bembo
Designed by Spring Hoteling

yum!   *P.*

PRAISE FOR THE NOVELS
OF LORELEI JAMES

"Lorelei James knows how to write fun, sexy, and hot stories."
—Joyfully Reviewed

"Lorelei James excels at creating new and evocative fantasies."
—TwoLips Reviews

"Incredibly hot." —The Romance Studio

"Beware: Before you read this hot erotic from Lorelei James, get a glass of ice. You are going to need it." —Fallen Angel Reviews

"Think it's impossible to combine extremely erotic and sweet? Not if James is writing." —*Romantic Times*

"Plenty of steamy love scenes that will have you reaching for your own hottie!" —Just Erotic Romance Reviews

"I honestly do not know how . . . Lorelei James keeps doing it, but every new book is a masterpiece." —Guilty Pleasures Book Reviews

BOUND

CHAPTER ONE

"SO this is where you're learning to kick some ass."

Amery scrutinized the front of the restored historic brick building. At six stories it was the tallest structure on this end of the block. On the street level, iron bars covered the few windows that hadn't been bricked over. The signage on the glass door read BLACK ARTS with a phone number below it.

She craned her neck to look up. Had to be a killer view of the river and the city from the top floor.

"Uh, Amery? What are we waiting for?"

"A welcoming party of ninjas to rappel down from the roof? Any less than a dozen masked killers brandishing swords and I'll be sorely disappointed."

Molly laughed nervously. "Um . . . well, maybe next time. But we should go in. Class starts in five minutes and we were warned to be on time."

Amery bit back a sigh. She really didn't want to be here, but she'd suck it up and do it, even if only out of solidarity.

Her stomach twisted into a vicious knot every time she remembered the phone call from the police last month, after her sweet-natured employee, Molly, had been attacked by homeless guys in downtown Denver. Poor Molly had defined introverted even before the incident; the attack had pushed her further into her shell. So when Molly asked Amery to accompany her to a women's self-defense class, Amery had agreed.

But looking around this sketchy neighborhood, she'd be surprised if they weren't jumped after class. Maybe that was part of the training. Seeing if students put the moves they learned to good use as they fought their way back to their car after dark.

Amery must've seemed reluctant, because Molly said, "If you don't want to do this . . ."

She plastered on a smile. "I don't know about you, but I can't *wait* to be in an enclosed space with a bunch of macho martial arts guys who like to beat the crap out of each other for fun."

Molly's eyes narrowed.

"Kidding, Mol. Let's hit it. Wouldn't want you to be late for your first day."

Inside the building, the entryway split into two hallways, one that pointed to the men's and women's locker rooms and the other to the classrooms. They headed to the main entrance.

A bald-headed, heavily tattooed guy in what resembled white pajamas manned a small cubby that looked like a cross between a ticket booth and a coat check.

"Good evening, ladies. How may I help you?"

Molly cleared her throat. "I'm here for the women's self-defense class."

He picked up a clipboard. "Name?"

"Molly Calloway."

Mr. Tattoos had to be bald by choice since he appeared to be under twenty-five. He checked the list, marked off Molly's name, and looked at Amery. "Ma'am? Your name?"

"Amery Hardwick."

He frowned. "You're not on the list. You signed up for the class?"

"Technically? No. I'm here as a bench warmer to support my buddy Molly."

"I'm sorry, that's against our policy."

"Excuse me?"

"You're only allowed into the dojo if you're a participant in the classes. We do not allow spectators. Or supporters."

"Ever?"

"Ever."

Amery looked at Molly. The poor girl blushed crimson. Then Amery focused on the bald-headed gatekeeper. "You don't allow parents or guardians inside to watch their kids beat each other to a pulp?"

"No, ma'am."

Well, that was stupid. And she said so.

"It's all right, Amery," Molly whispered. "This was a dumb idea. We can just go." She grabbed on to Amery's arm.

"Hang on a second." Amery pulled her black-and-white cowhide wallet out of her purse. "How much is the class?"

"This isn't a movie theater where you can just show up and buy tickets at the door. You have to be approved in advance before you can even register for the class. Those are the rules. I don't make them. I just enforce them."

Amery tapped her fingers on the counter. "I understand. But these are extenuating circumstances."

He scowled.

"Maybe you oughta just get your supervisor, because I'm not leaving."

He hesitated about ten seconds before he reached for the phone. He turned his back so they couldn't hear the conversation. Then he faced them again. "If you'll have a seat, someone will be right out."

Molly looked mortified, which made Amery more determined to make sure she took this class.

Less than two minutes later a big blond guy, about mid-thirties, dressed in what resembled black pajamas, stopped in front of them. He offered Amery his hand. "I'm Knox Lofgren, the dojo general manager. How can I help you?"

Amery explained the situation, adding, "I would've officially signed up for the class ahead of time had I known that was required. It's not fair to penalize Molly." She leaned closer and whispered, "Ever since the attack . . . she's jumpy and avoiding all social situations where she doesn't know anyone. She won't start the class if I'm not here. You don't want that on your conscience, do you, Mr. Lofgren?"

The man studied Amery as if she was lying. Just as she was about to crack and back off, he said, "Fine. I'll squeeze you in. But understand that you two will not always be paired together in class. You'll both be expected to train with others." He focused on Molly. "Will that be a problem for you?"

"No, sir."

"Good." Then Knox handed Amery a clipboard. "Also, we alternate Tuesdays and Thursdays for this class. Next week class will be Thursday night. The following week Tuesday evening, and so on."

Don't ask why, Amery.

"Just fill in the basic details on the application. Will you be paying by credit card or check?"

"How much is the class?"

"One hundred and fifty dollars."

Seemed high but she'd pay it. She slid her credit card from her wallet and handed it to him.

"I'll get your receipt."

"Thank you." Soon as she finished scrawling her information, she glanced up at him. This Knox guy could intimidate on size alone. He had to be at least six foot four. Although he had the rugged all-American-boy-next-door good looks, he was . . . just slightly scary.

"I've included a description of the class and the schedule. Make sure you follow all the rules—"

A teenaged boy raced in. "Shihan? We've got blood in the fourth ring."

Shihan or Knox or whoever he was bailed immediately.

Tattooed Bald Guy said, "Ladies, step through the far door. Put your bags on the conveyor belt. If you're bringing weapons to class, I need them out of the bag. If not, you can proceed through the metal detector."

Metal detector? Amery was having a hard time wrapping her head around this much security in a place that should be swarming with killer ninjas.

"Problem?"

She just about let it lie, but curiosity had always been her downfall. "Level with me. Is this some secret military training camp?"

"No. Why?"

"Why the extra security for a teaching facility?"

The guy shrugged. "Weapons are part of the training. Swords, knives, sticks. We have to check and approve all weapons that are brought in."

"Oh."

Molly nudged her toward the door.

After they were cleared through security—still sounded bizarre—he pointed to a stocky guy, and that guy waved them over.

As they approached him, Amery checked out the joint. The place had clean lines and neutral colors: gray carpet and white walls—where there were walls. Some of the training rooms were separated by Plexiglas. Since there weren't any windows along the entire side, the walls were mirrored, creating a fun-house effect. In the center of the room was a guard tower that overlooked the entire space.

The stocky guy did a quick bow to them and offered his hand. "I'm your instructor for the women's self-defense class. We do use formal titles at Black Arts, so you can call me either Sandan or Sandan Zach."

Molly introduced herself first.

When Amery gave her name, he frowned. "I don't remember your application."

"That's because I'm a last-minute addition." She nudged Molly. "I was supposed to be here for support only, but that somehow violates the dojo rules."

"The rules are . . . precisely the way Sensei wants them." Zach gestured to the area behind them. "There's nearly fourteen thousand square feet of training space on two floors, so we can have all student levels training at the same time if we choose. Some of the rooms are open like these. And some on the backside, for the more advanced students, are semiprivate."

Molly pointed to the watchtower in the midst of everything. "What's that?"

"The Crow's Nest. Sensei Black can observe the classes."

Amery had an image of a grizzled but wise and agile Asian man sitting up there muttering to himself about the lack of discipline in today's youth.

"We're happy to have you both at Black Arts," Sandan Zach said, without looking away from Molly. "Your class is over here. Set your bags along the back wall."

Their fifteen classmates ranged in age from younger than Molly to a woman in her mid-sixties and all sizes and ethnicities.

One other thing Amery noticed? All the women wore white shirts and black sweatpants or yoga pants. A few stared at her jeans and short-sleeved white blouse.

Sandan Zach clapped his hands. "Listen up, ladies. I'll do a brief overview of the class, but first everyone needs to remove socks and shoes."

Amery shot Molly a look, but she'd already started untying her laces. She unzipped her black riding boots and tossed them on top of her purse.

"This class is more involved than the typical women's self-defense class you take at the Y. Taking charge of your safety is the first step since most violent acts happen one on one. But during this class you will learn together, and part of that is being supportive of each other and helping each other learn."

Good philosophy.

"We'll warm up. Nothing like the rigorous jujitsu warm-ups you're seeing in other classes, I promise you. So spread out, arm's length on each side."

Molly headed for the back row, but Amery snagged her hand. "No hiding, remember?"

"You're bossy even outside of work."

Amery grinned.

But it seemed everyone wanted to be in the front row, so they ended up in the back anyway.

Sandan Zach walked a circle around the class members as he gave directions for gentle stretches. Amery wished she had on yoga pants—the jeans were cutting into her every time she moved.

Molly leaned over and puffed. "I thought he said this wouldn't be a rigorous workout. I didn't sign up for aerobics."

"No doubt." Amery felt a little out of breath herself. "And if he tries to make me run? Sorry, I'm making a break for the door."

Molly snickered, but she stopped abruptly when Sandan Zach stared at her.

"Before we get started, are there any questions?"

"Yes. Why isn't she wearing the required uniform?"

Amery froze. The commanding voice sent a chill through her. Like a hot breeze blowing across wet skin and resulting in head-to-toe goose bumps. Before she could turn around and determine if his face matched his sensual voice, her instructor piped in.

"I apologize, Sensei. Would you prefer that I excuse her from class?"

Excuse her from the class? Bullshit. Seemed Mr. Tattooed Bald Gatekeeper up front had neglected to remind her about the dress code, but that wasn't her fault. She'd paid the fee; she wasn't going anywhere. And why wasn't either of these men, Mr. Dangerous and Delicious Voice or Drill Instructor Zach, addressing her directly?

"*She* can speak for herself." Amery whirled around to face the sensei.

Holy hell. Good thing she'd locked her knees or else she might've fallen to them. The man's face more than matched the seductive voice; he was quite simply the most stunning man she'd ever seen. High cheekbones and a wide, chiseled jawline courtesy of Germanic or Nordic genes in his lineage. His full lower lip bowed at the corners, giving his mouth a sensual curve. The slight bend in his nose added interest to his otherwise perfect features. And his eyes. She'd never seen eyes that hue—a light golden brown the color of topaz. The corners of his eyes tilted upward, indicating his family tree also included an Asian branch. His black hair nearly brushed his shoulders. Everything about this man, from his face to his posture, announced his commanding presence.

Sensei definitely wasn't the decrepit man she'd imagined.

"Are you done?" he asked in that velvet voice, but his tone was decidedly clipped.

Amery blushed when she realized she'd been staring at him practically slack-jawed.

"Why isn't your student wearing the required uniform?" he asked Sandan Zach again, while maintaining an intense eye lock with her.

"Why are you chewing him out? It's not his fault I'm not wearing the right clothing," she snapped.

And that whole *could've heard a pin drop* saying? Now Amery knew exactly what that meant. Seemed everyone in the entire building—not just in the vicinity—had gone silent and was gaping at her.

Then Mr. Sexy Sensei leaned forward, placing his mouth right next to her ear. "I don't allow open defiance in my dojo. Ever."

The warmth of his breath flowed across her neck and she suppressed a shiver.

"Is that clear?"

"Uh-huh."

" 'Yes, sir,' 'Yes, Sensei,' or 'Yes, Master Black' is an acceptable response. 'Uh-huh' is not."

"Got it, uh, Master Black."

"If you hope to stay in this class, I'd suggest you wear the proper clothing without argument."

"Since I was a last-minute addition to this class, I don't have the proper clothing."

He said, "We'll remedy that now. Follow me."

His tenor demanded that she obey. She trailed after him, feeling every eye in the place on them. Her focus remained on the broad back in front of her.

Maybe it bothered her that he hadn't turned around even once to see if she'd obeyed—he just assumed she had.

Because you aren't exactly a rule breaker, Amery.

But "you can call me sir, Sensei, or Master Black" didn't know that. Maybe since she'd mouthed off, he thought she was some kind of troublemaker. She swore she'd be as meek as a kitten from here on out—if only for Molly's sake.

They cut down a short hallway.

He opened a door and Amery followed him into a storage area. On the far back wall were stacks of uniforms she'd seen everyone wearing. Some white, some black.

Sensei eyed her from the waist down, turned, and shoved his hand into a stack. Then he held out a pair of black pants.

"What are those? They look like pajama bottoms."

"It's called a gi and beggars cannot be choosers, can they, Mrs. . . . ?"

"Ms. Hardwick," she retorted.

"Feel free to change in the bathroom across the hall as long as it doesn't take you all night."

Amery's rarely seen rebellious side appeared again. Although she could count on one hand the number of men who'd seen her half-naked, something about this man pushed her buttons and she wanted to push back. "Not necessary. I'll just change here." She unbuttoned and unzipped her jeans before pushing the denim off. Kicking them aside, she snatched the pants from his fingertips.

And Master Black didn't pretend he wasn't looking at her bare legs as she fumbled with the drawstrings. When his perusal of her lower half ended at her lavender bikini panties, he glanced up at her.

The blast of heat from those liquid gold eyes reminded her that her boldness was only an act.

His was not.

So not.

Was it possible to be burned by a look and frozen in place by it? At the same time?

Yep, if it was coming from Sensei's laser eyes.

Why are you stalling? Get dressed and go.

Amery dragged the cotton pants up her legs and fled.

Or she tried to flee. But that sinfully compelling voice stopped her before she made it halfway down the hall. "Forgetting something, Ms. Hardwick?"

She faced him, feeling the rush of emotions that ran the gamut from annoyance to awe to alarm . . . and annoyance won out. "What?"

He held up her discarded jeans. "Don't you want these?"

"Keep them as collateral," she tossed over her shoulder, and hustled away.

And surprise, surprise, the man didn't follow her.

In class, Sandan Zach didn't pause in his lecture as she slid into her spot in the back row. "For most women, it goes against your natural response to fight back. So our aim isn't to teach you how to start a fight, but how to defend yourself, which is a far cry from being the aggressor. Any questions?"

Amery had a ton of them, but she kept her mouth shut. Wouldn't want to be known as the problem pupil any more than she already was.

"I'm sure questions will arise over the next few weeks. But right now we'll do the most basic self-defense technique for an attack without a weapon. This is Shihan Knox. He'll be assisting me in class."

Shihan Knox came up behind Zach and snaked an arm around his neck.

"Three things to be aware of in this situation. How much head movement you have, where the person is behind you, and where your arms are. It'd be difficult in this position to try a reverse head butt to connect with the attacker's nose. You might first try turning your head and biting the attacker's arm. We're not talking a little love bite, ladies. I'm talking about opening your mouth wide like you're gnawing on a turkey leg and biting down like you're trying to reach the bone."

Other class members giggled.

Which didn't amuse Sandan Zach at all.

"If your head is too immobilized for that, remember where your hands are. Usually right up here." He wrapped his hands around Knox's arm, trying to pull it away. "That is a wasted motion. Use your hands elsewhere. If your attacker is a man, ladies, you've got one shot to grab on to his junk and try to twist it off. That said, that's a pretty risky move because a guy's automatic response is to protect the family jewels. So you've got to assume he'll anticipate where you plan to attack. Your best option is stomp on his foot."

"But what if she's wearing flip-flops and I'm wearing combat boots?" Shihan Knox asked.

"Good point. That won't work. In that case, kick out and aim for the knee. Even connecting with the shin with just the back of the heel is painful and a hard-placed kick will often loosen up the attacker's hold enough that you can escape." Zach kicked out at Knox and he released him from the choke hold. "Let's call this a victory for now. The goal has been achieved—to break the attacker's hold."

After fifteen more minutes of demonstrations, during which Amery's eyes had sort of glazed over, Molly scooted closer and whispered, "Could you ever bite someone like that?"

"Hard enough to break the skin?"

She nodded.

"It'd depend." Her eyes searched Molly's. "Could you have bitten your attacker if you knew it would've stopped him?"

"When you put it that way . . . yes. I'm tired of being scared of my own shadow."

Amery squeezed her hand. "I know. Let's focus on turning you into a badass no one wants to mess with."

"Are you talking during class because you've already got all the answers?" Master Black asked behind her.

She jumped. When she spun around he took her wrists in one hand and lightly wrapped his hand around the base of her throat.

"Hey!"

"See how easy it is to get into trouble when you're unaware?"

Damn him.

"You are here to learn."

"I know that," she retorted. Then when his stony face remained that way, she tacked on "Sir."

"Prove it." He did some fancy twisting maneuver and then he was behind her, dragging her off the mat. "Remember what to do if you're put in a choke hold? Or were you too busy talking to listen to your instructor?"

"I can multitask."

An arm snaked around her throat and he pinned her left arm behind her back. "Show me how to get out of this hold."

Her heart rate zoomed. Her free hand came up to claw at his arm, but that did nothing to loosen his grip.

"Try again."

She turned her head and opened her mouth over his meaty biceps, intending to sink her teeth into the marrow of his bones.

Master Black released her.

Score one for her. But Amery's victory was short-lived. Then he wrapped his other arm around her neck but left both her arms free. "Again. Make me release you."

She swung her elbow into his gut and attempted to scratch his eye out.

He let her go.

But he wasn't done. She'd barely get him to release her and then he had her immobilized again.

The man was relentless in his drills.

During a short break, Amery noticed the rest of the class was working with partners too—just not instructors—and they were on the far side of the room, giving Amery and Master Black a wide berth. She'd give anything if she could just pick him up and throw him over her head on his ass.

She was fantasizing about the look of shock on his too-perfect face, not paying attention, and that's when he wrapped his hands around her neck and stayed back, not in close proximity to her body. "Free yourself."

Shoot, she didn't remember this one. She tried to kick out at his knee, but he dodged. She tried to twist away, risking a neck injury, but he held fast.

"Come on, think," he said evenly.

"I can't. You're choking me."

"That's the point."

She attempted to gouge his forearms.

"Better, but not enough. Try again."

"I don't know! Let me go. I can't breathe."

Master Black released her and moved directly in front of her. "Calm down."

"I am fucking calm." Amery inhaled several deep breaths. His gaze never wavered from hers, which was disconcerting . . . and yet not.

Once she'd settled, he gave her a quick nod. "You try choking me."

This would be fun because she didn't intend to hold back. Amery stepped behind him, noticing for the first time that he'd pulled his hair into a stubby ponytail. Why in the hell did that look so sexy? And why did she have the overwhelming urge to slide the elastic band free and plunge her hands into those gorgeous black tresses?

"Problem?" he asked in that rumbling rasp.

"No, sir." Amery tried to get her hands around his neck, but it was so muscular that she had to slide her hands up and down to find a decent position. Her hands on his warm skin released a heavenly scent.

Dammit. Why did he smell so nice? Shouldn't he reek like sweat and suppressed anger?

"Are you finished fitting me for a necklace?"

Cocky man. "Maybe I'm fitting you for a noose."

"Then you'd need a better grip."

She dug her fingernails into his flesh.

"I still have my hands free." He raked his fingers up the back of her arms and pinched the skin on the underside—not hard enough to bruise but with enough pressure she released him. "With that move you will definitely get your attacker's attention."

"Then what should I do? Because pinching someone that hard will piss him off."

He studied her. "You should run."

"And what if I'm caught again?"

"Then you'll fight. The goal of this class is to make your reactions instinctive. To give you a tool and a solid mind-set to deal with a physical crisis situation where you don't have time to think—you just react."

Master Black had gotten close to her again, and spoke in the deep timbre that rolled over her like warm honey. "Since you're short a partner, next week I'll show you more options."

They stared at each other, locked in an eye-fuck that was better than any sex she'd ever had.

"Sensei, if I may interrupt, you're needed in the black belt class," someone said behind him.

Master Black backed up and gave her a small bow. "Until next time, Ms. Hardwick."

She returned his bow, not as smoothly. "Thank you for the instruction, Sensei."

After class ended, some students were giving her suspicious looks. Including Molly.

"What?"

"It's just strange, the fact that Master Black took interest in you and—"

"All but made me wear a dunce's cap and sit in the corner when he wasn't beating the crap out of me in front of everyone?"

"Um, that's not how I saw it at all."

Amery was moving her boots off her purse when she felt her phone vibrating. She picked it up but didn't recognize the caller ID. "Hello?"

"Is this Amery Hardwick?"

"Yes, who's this?"

"Officer Stickney, Denver Police. We received a call from your alarm company regarding a possible break-in. We arrived on-scene and discovered the front window is shattered. We've done a sweep of the main floor and the upstairs. Are you able to return to the property to verify if anything is missing?"

Amery's heart hammered. Someone had broken into her building? *Damn, damn, damn.* Her computer with all her client files was on the desk in her office, right in plain sight.

"Ma'am?"

"Sorry. Yes, I'm on my way." She jammed her feet into her boots.

Molly sidled up as Amery retrieved her keys. "What's wrong?"

"Someone vandalized my building. The cops are there. I've got to go."

"Since I rode here with you, I'm coming too."

Amery shouldered her bag, Molly close on her heels as they exited the building a lot easier than they'd gotten in.

The dojo was across the Platte River, which separated Platte Valley from Lodo—a nickname for lower downtown Denver. With one-way streets and dead-end alleys, the trip took fifteen minutes. On the drive she spoke with the alarm company and then she called an after-hours window repair company to temporarily board up the window until the new glass could be installed.

Parking was nearly impossible to find—especially with all the cop cars blocking the street. She didn't get the full impact of the damage until she stood in front of the building.

The front window wasn't just shattered; it was completely gone.

Spots danced in front of her eyes. She had to bend at the waist to keep the bile rising in her throat from exiting her mouth. Had she been robbed too? Had they done damage to Emmylou's side? What about her loft? Had that been ransacked?

Keep it together.

A cop moved toward her. "You'll have to move along—"

"I'm Amery Hardwick. This is my building."

"Need to see some ID."

Her hand shook when she removed her driver's license from her wallet and handed it over.

"Okay, ma'am, you can go in. Officer Stickney is waiting inside."

The beat cop tried to keep Molly back, but she snarled at him—very un-Molly-like—and he let her go with Amery.

She stepped over the glass to take a better look at the damage inside the building. Two officers paced in her office. She just about fell to her knees when she saw her computer on her desk intact.

Molly squeezed her hand. "I'll go check and see if anything is missing at my desk."

The African-American cop approached her while the other cop, a young Hispanic woman, talked on a phone.

"Ms. Hardwick? I'm Officer Stickney."

"Do you have any idea what happened?"

"It doesn't appear that anything was taken, so we doubt robbery was a motive. It's sad to say, but there've been random acts of vandalism like this across the Denver metro area in the last six months."

Amery slumped against the wall. "So it's just my bad luck?"

"Possibly. Or it might be some freak accident where a car spins its tires, dislodging a rock that hits the window at just the right speed and shatters it. Sounds weird, but I've seen it happen. We weren't able to find any evidence of what was used to break the window inside the store."

"Am I still supposed to check upstairs to see if anything is missing in my loft?"

"Yes, and we'll need Officer Gomez to accompany you."

Molly looked up from her desk. "Nothing missing or out of place on my side."

"Thank god."

Amery led Officer Gomez through the rear door that led from her office into the small back area with a steel door that led into the alley. A circular staircase dominated the space and opened up into the second-floor loft apartment where she lived. In true loft fashion the only room walled off was the bathroom. This was the first place that was completely hers, and it put an extra twist in her gut to imagine her safe haven had been violated.

But nothing had been disturbed in her oversized bedroom, or the large eat-in kitchen, or the great room with the funky windows that overlooked the street.

"Anything missing or destroyed, Ms. Hardwick?" Officer Gomez asked.

"No. I can't even blame the mess on the counters on anyone but myself."

The female cop smiled. "I can relate. I'm relieved this wasn't a B and E, but I will offer you some advice." She pointed to the businesses across the street with the drop-down steel cages covering the storefronts. "Those might be ugly, but they are effective; those cages do deter crime. And it's an especially smart add-on since you're a single woman living alone above your business. I'd also suggest you install a heftier door with a dead bolt between your business area and your living space. Once that's done, have the alarm company add a trigger to that door, so if someone does get in from the business side, it'll alert you."

"Thank you so much. I appreciate your advice."

The cops didn't stick around after that.

Amery and Molly sat in their office chairs facing the gaping hole.

"I can't believe it," Molly said.

"Me either." As grateful as Amery was that nothing had been stolen, she worried about how much the repairs would run. Yes, she had insurance, but she'd have out-of-pocket expenses. She was running a much smaller profit so far this year and had been cutting corners and pinching pennies everywhere she could.

The window replacement company arrived and off-loaded pieces of plywood.

As they heard hammers banging, saws going, and an electric drill screeching, Molly said, "Amery, you're awful quiet. Are you really okay?"

"No. I'm wired. There's no way I'll be able to sleep tonight. Especially not when all that'll be separating me from the street is a sheet of plywood." Amery offered Molly a wan smile. "I'll probably be all caught up on my backlog of filing and stuff by the time you get here tomorrow."

Molly frowned. "Get here? Where do you think I'm going?"

"Home where you belong." *Where it's safe.*

"Huh-uh. I'm staying right here with you."

"I'll be—"

"No, you aren't fine. Which is why I will be right there, on that couch. I'm used to pulling all-nighters. So suck it up and grab me a pillow."

"Man, I didn't know you had such a bossy streak," Amery grumbled.

"And I never would've thought you'd be so antagonistic toward a man who could probably kill you with a look," Molly retorted. "So it looks like we're both full of surprises."

"Let's hope we done with all surprises—good or bad—for the rest of the night."

CHAPTER TWO

GROGGY from lack of sleep, Amery released a little scream the next morning when her best buddy, Chaz, enveloped her in a gigantic bear hug from behind. "Girl, I'd ask how you're doing but the scream pretty much gave it away."

"You surprised me," she said defensively. "Can you blame me for being a little shaken?"

"No." Then Chaz curled his hands around her biceps and helped her to her feet, demanding, "Why didn't you call me last night?"

"Because I didn't want to freak you out. There wasn't anything you could've done anyway."

"Except be there for you. That's what friends do for each other, hon."

"Chewing her out after the fact won't make her feel better," Emmylou intoned dryly from the doorway that separated their two businesses.

"Did she call you and your lesbian Mafia connections for help?" Chaz asked snottily.

"They could protect her better than that gay brotherhood you hang around with," she shot back.

Although their jabs were meant in good fun, given her mood,

her two best pals would drive her crazy with their dicks-versus-chicks bickering.

"I stayed with her," Molly piped in. "Which is why I'm still wearing the same clothes that I had on yesterday." She scowled. "Not that Amery let me do anything but sleep on the couch down here while she made sure no one tried to get in."

"Just knowing you were here eased my mind." Amery had managed to tie up a few projects during the wee small hours, keeping a wary eye on the big chunk of plywood where her front window used to be. She hadn't needed caffeine either; adrenaline had kept her up all night. But now? Talk about exhausted. She was dangerously close to face-planting if she didn't keep the liquid energy flowing, so she poured herself another cup of coffee.

"What did the cops say?" Chaz asked.

"They're calling it a random act of vandalism since nothing was taken. Which just shows how lucky I am as well as how stupid I am."

"Sweetie. You're the victim here," Emmylou said gently.

Amery twisted her ponytail, a nervous habit from childhood she'd yet to break. "For the random act? Yes. But believing a sheet of glass is adequate protection between the outside world and my business does make me naive."

"You have plans to rectify that?"

"The glass place is installing thicker panes this time. They're also replacing the glass on your side," she said to Emmylou. "Once that's done, I'll have them mount drop-down chain fencing outside both windows. I know they're ugly, but they'll offer another layer of protection. Half the businesses on this block already have them anyway." She closed her eyes. "I don't ever want to relive what I went through last night after the cops called. Where I envisioned my computers with all my client information and projects being ripped off or smashed to bits. And that doesn't include how guilty I'd feel as your landlord if something had happened to either of your workspaces."

She'd been lax in her responsibilities as the building owner because her tenants were her friends. Emmylou rented out the left half of the bottom floor space for her massage studio. Chaz rented the tiny center section for his various artistic enterprises. Amery's graphic design business was on the right bottom half and she lived in the loft that spanned the length of the two-story building.

Emmylou crossed the room and put her arms around Amery. "What can I do? You need a massage?"

"Thanks for the offer, but those magic hands of yours would put me right to sleep. And I have to be alert for the insurance adjuster and the glass repair place to show up."

"As soon as you've signed off on the paperwork, I'll stay until everything is done. It's the least I can do, especially after last night," Molly said.

"Speaking of last night, Molly, how did your self-defense class go?" Chaz asked.

"Great except Amery had to take the class too. She wasn't allowed to be there just for support."

"I wondered how you planned to get past that 'no observation' rule at Black Arts," Emmylou said.

Amery frowned at her. "You knew?"

"Honey, everyone knows that rule," she drawled in her thick Oklahoma accent.

"Then why did you send Molly there?"

"Because it's the best dojo in Denver. My clients can't speak highly enough of the place, even when they're intimidated by the owner. He's, like, a hundredth-degree black belt or something."

"Amery wasn't intimidated," Molly threw out. "Master Black hauled her out of class first thing. Made her change her pants. Then he worked with her one-on-one for half the class."

Worked with. Ha. The man had picked on her endlessly. "Someone should've told me there was a dress code," Amery mumbled.

She'd been so scrambled last night she'd left wearing the borrowed gi pants.

Emmylou's mouth fell open. "You had a run-in with Master Black on your first night?"

"Yeah. Why?"

"Because he doesn't bother with the lower-belt classes. To hear my clients talk, he's some kind of super-samurai throwback. Dangerous. Stealthy. Deadly. Evidently he can sneak up behind you and you'd never know he was there until it was too late."

That wasn't entirely true. Amery had known where Master Black had been at all times last night. She'd felt the weight of his gaze on her—even from the Crow's Nest.

"I'd have to disagree with that statement."

Amery spun around. Holy shit. Master Black lingered just inside the main doorway. A very hot looking Master Black, casually outfitted in jeans and a long-sleeved white T-shirt that set off his coloring to perfection. The ends of his untamed hair brushed his shoulders, giving the impression of wildness lurking beneath his controlled demeanor.

Faced with the devastatingly powerful and sexy whole of him, she was having difficulty breathing. Not only hadn't she ever experienced such a visceral reaction to a man, she couldn't look away from him. But she had the oddest feeling she should drop her gaze, so she did.

After she'd broken the intense eye-fuck, he sauntered forward and offered his hand to Emmylou. "Seems my reputation has preceded me once again, Ms. . . . ?"

"Simmons. But, darlin', you can call me Emmylou. I'm pleased to meet you, Master Black. I have several clients who train at your facility, and they can't speak highly enough of your training programs."

"Your clients?"

Emmylou pointed to the door to her massage studio. "I'm a

masseuse. With my background in sports medicine I deal mostly with professional athletes. That's how Amery and I met."

"I'm sure Master Black isn't interested in how we met." Amery gave him a cool once-over, trying to gain some equilibrium. "What do you want?"

He moved with alarming speed, stopping directly in front of her. "You forgot your jeans at my place last night."

He'd phrased that so intimately her cheeks burned.

"Then you left so abruptly after . . . well, afterward."

Making it sound as if they'd had a fuck-and-run encounter. He seemed to enjoy flustering her.

He turned and pointed to the plywood. "Did that have something to do with your rapid departure?"

"Yeah, I tend to drop everything when the cops call and tell me about a break-in."

His eyes narrowed. "Has this happened before?"

"No. We weren't robbed either. It seems to be just a random act of vandalism. But it's shaken us all up, as you can imagine."

Chaz sashayed over and offered his hand. "Chaz Graylind. Nice to meet you, Master Black."

He shook Chaz's hand. "Please call me Ronin."

Ronin. The sexy, mysterious name fit him perfectly.

Then he returned that laser focus to her again.

Amery was acutely aware how awful she looked. She fought the urge to smooth the wrinkles from her shirt, the same one she'd worn to class last night. In fact, she still wore the black pants he'd forced her to change into.

"Is there anything I can do to help?" he asked.

"Not unless you own a glass company and can have this fixed in the next hour."

"I can make some calls, if you like. See if I can speed up the process."

"Why would you do that?"

"Because you're a beautiful woman in distress and it's in the samurai code of honor that I help you."

Her friends scattered. Traitors. But they probably assumed given the sparks flying between her and Master Black that she wanted to be alone with him.

Don't you?

Amery backed up. "Are you so concerned with *all* your new students that you stop in to check on them?"

"Only you, apparently."

She found her back against the brick wall. He hadn't caged her in with his arms or blocked her in with his body. He even kept a respectable distance, not touching her at all, but something about him held her in place. "What do you want from me, Master Black?"

"Ronin," he corrected. "When we're outside the dojo like this, you can call me Ronin. As for what I want from you . . ."

Butterflies danced in her stomach as she waited for him to answer his own question.

Those sun-warmed topaz eyes locked on to hers. "Guess."

"Ah, you want your pants back?" *Brilliant comeback, Amery.*

"I want much more than that from you, and I think you know it."

Gulp. She feared her swallow was audible.

He smiled.

Holy crap. Ronin Black smiled and she swore the heavens opened up and a chorus of angels started singing. Oddly enough, she worried they were humming "The Strip."

Man, she was punchy when she was sleep-deprived.

"But getting you out of those pants is a good place to start."

Amery glanced down. "You want them off right now?"

"I didn't bring your jeans with me, so we'll wait to swap. Time and place to be determined."

Her eyes met his. "Not before class next week?"

He shook his head.

"You are freaking me out."

"But you're not scared of me, are you?"

"No." It came out of her mouth before the logic center of her brain weighed in with a solid *hell yes*.

"Good."

"Is that why you singled me out last night?"

"No."

"Then why?" she pressed.

"You were out of uniform."

"But if I'd been in proper clothing . . . ?"

"I still would've singled you out."

His cryptic answers were sort of pissing her off. "Why?" she asked, slightly exasperated.

Ronin reached out to stroke the edge of her cheek. "Your attitude . . . intrigues me."

"What attitude?"

"Defiance. Especially since I don't think that's a natural reaction for you."

She raised an eyebrow. "Or maybe you're intrigued by the fact that I took my pants off within a few minutes of meeting you?"

"Which you did by your own choice, so you can understand my interest in a woman who blushes as she's tossing her jeans at me."

Amery blinked at him. This had to be the most bizarre conversation she'd ever had. Wait, maybe this was a dream.

Then he edged closer. "Where'd you go?"

"Maybe the better question is where am I? I'm out of it and don't even know what I'm saying. I need to go to bed."

"I'd be happy to take you to bed," he murmured.

"Ronin." God, just saying his name made her heart race. "We're getting past my comfort zone."

His eyes searched hers. "Now you're getting it. From the minute I watched you walk into my dojo, this has been past my comfort zone."

Holy hell.

"Hello?" echoed from the doorway.

Grateful for the reprieve, Amery sidestepped the formidable Ronin Black and headed toward the man with the clipboard.

"You're Ms. Hardwick?"

"I am."

"I'm Dennis Harris from Schmidt Insurance. I'll just poke around and be out of your hair before you know it." He returned outside.

She turned around to see Master Black studying the projects she'd framed and hung on the wall.

His movements were measured and deliberate even when it appeared he was wandering. His profile was well proportioned—both rugged and classic.

"You do great work," he said without looking at her. "Very original when so much graphic art seems like a rehash."

"Thank you."

"Have you been in the business long?"

She opened her mouth to answer, but instead she yawned so widely her jaw cracked. All of a sudden everything went fuzzy and she swayed.

"Sit down before you fall down." He rolled Molly's wheeled office chair over and held it steady as she dropped into it. Then he crouched in front of her. "You're fading fast."

"I just need more coffee." Amery started to stand, but two strong hands on her thighs kept her in place.

"You need sleep, not coffee."

"But that one guy is here, doing that one thing." She frowned because she couldn't remember. "What's his name?"

"Harris," the man said from somewhere. "I've finished."

"Already? That was fast."

"Expediency is our motto." He handed her a clipboard. "So I'll just need you to sign off on this and I'll get it filed."

Amery held the pen poised at the bottom of the paper, and then the next second the clipboard was gone. She glared up at Master Black, who'd gotten way too close. "Hey, what're you doing?"

"You're just signing this without reading it?"

She fought another yawn and the temptation to rest her head on his broad shoulder. She muttered, "I'm exhausted and just want to be done with this."

"Which is all the more reason for you to wait until you're coherent to sign a legally binding document." He shoved the clipboard back at the agent. "You've done the preliminary work. She'll be in touch about finalizing it."

"She's already called the window replacement company. We won't pay the claim without her signature. And most of the companies expect COD in these situations."

"Amery, which glass company did you call?"

Her fuzzy brain rallied and she said, "Bet Your Glass, on Colfax."

"I've dealt with them. They owe me a favor. They'll waive the COD fee and I can get them here within the hour."

More male bickering. Amery closed her eyes and tuned them out.

That wonderful darkness beckoned only to be yanked away when someone poked her shoulder. "What?"

"Chaz is taking me home. I have class in an hour."

She opened a bleary eye and squinted at Molly. "But I thought you were going to stay until the glass guys were done?"

Molly's gaze darted to the right. "Master Black said he'd be happy to handle it for you. That's okay, isn't it?"

"Of course it's okay," Chaz inserted. He squeezed Amery's shoulder. "She's exhausted and who better to trust her safety with than her self-defense instructor?"

Ronin flashed Amery a wolfish grin that no one else saw.

"Besides, Emmylou is here and she promised to lock up after the new windows are installed. So we're heading out, okay, sweets?"

Amery was too tired to argue. She closed her eyes when Chaz

kissed her forehead. Her mind blanked out the hushed voices until they faded completely and sleep teased the edges of her consciousness.

Ronin's deep voice roused her again. "You can't sleep in the chair."

Dammit. Why wouldn't everyone just leave her alone? "Fine. I'll go sleep in my bed." She mustered the will to push upright. Her feet seemed to be encased in cement blocks as she trudged to the back door that led to her loft. After nearly tripping, she slapped herself in the face to stay focused. Seeing the twisty metal staircase leading to her living space put an extra spring in her step.

A hard hand landed on her shoulder. "Slow down. Don't want this pretty face of yours smacking into the concrete."

She wheeled around. "What are you still doing here?"

"Helping you."

"Why?"

"I don't know."

"Seriously."

"Seriously. I don't know." He encroached on her space, coming chest-to-chest with her. "So will you please cut me a break and let me make sure you fall face-first in your bed and not on the floor?"

Something . . . oddly sweet flickered in his penetrating stare, and her flip comment dried up. "Thank you, Ronin."

He smoothed her hair from her cheek. "My pleasure."

Why didn't it bother her that he touched her with such familiarity? Amery turned away before she did something stupid like face-plant into that amazing chest of his.

He followed her closely up the stairs. That breathing-down-her-neck proximity didn't change when she cut toward her bedroom. She crawled into the unmade bed and wrapped her arms around the closest pillow with an enormous sigh.

A soft laugh sounded behind her.

Then she felt him unzipping her boots. She wiggled her toes and sighed again.

"Need my help with the rest of your clothes?"

She cracked one eye open and looked at him. "Nice try."

"I could point out half of what you're wearing belongs to me and it's within my rights to demand you return it."

"Go away, Ronin."

"I will." He covered her with her comforter. "But I'll be back."

That's the last thing Amery remembered.

CHAPTER THREE

THE following day Amery felt Ronin Black's eyes on her before she knew he'd entered her office. No lie, the man had that stealthy approach down. She spun her chair toward him and her belly cartwheeled at the heated way he looked at her.

She continued her phone conversation, but her focus remained on him. "No. That isn't a problem at all. Absolutely. I can have the changes to you by tomorrow. Thank you." She hung up. "I assume Molly sent you back?"

Ronin leaned against the doorjamb, looking delectable and dangerous in a short-sleeved black polo, dark jeans, and modified combat boots. "Yes. She said to tell you she was going to lunch."

"So, Master Black, why are you here?"

"Ronin," he corrected.

"Okay, Ronin. What brings you by today?"

"I want to hire you."

She hadn't been expecting that—and maybe she felt a tiny kernel of disappointment that he wasn't here because he intended to act on this undeniable attraction between them.

Maybe he's disappointed that you haven't acknowledged how much he helped you out yesterday.

Guilt for her oversight caused her to blurt out, "Thank you for sticking around and dealing with the glass installers yesterday morning after I went comatose."

"You're welcome. The workers didn't milk the installation time with me watching them."

She suspected Master Black's displeased glare was hot enough to melt glass.

"Besides, it gave me a chance to look at your graphic art work more closely and decide to hire you."

"Hire me for what?"

"To create a new logo for Black Arts. I'd like to scrap what we've got and start from scratch. Is that a project you'd be interested in tackling?"

I'd rather tackle you.

She fought the pull of this man's incredible magnetism and put a lid on those *I want to jump you* thoughts that were so unlike her. "I'm always interested in taking on new projects."

"Good. Because I brought this." Ronin sauntered into her office and handed her a rolled-up sheaf of papers. "Our current logo. Black Arts has always kept a low profile, which suits me. But my instructors have pointed out that we need an updated official logo that can be screen-printed on the back of gis and used for patches so Black Arts students are more recognizable when they compete in tournaments."

"You don't seem very enthusiastic about that prospect."

His eyes never strayed from her face. "I'm enthusiastic about the prospect of working with you."

Amery's pulse leaped.

"Are you free so we can discuss it over lunch?"

"When?"

"Now."

She didn't have anything scheduled, but part of her wanted to lie and claim she did. Lunch with the sexy sensei . . . she wasn't sure she'd honed the feminine skills to cope with a man like him. But if she kept it focused on business? Business she could do. Amery smiled. "I'd love to have lunch with you. There's a great bistro a few blocks away."

"Maybe next time. I've already made reservations for us at Dillinger's."

Normally she'd bristle at such presumptive behavior. But Amery liked that he hadn't stopped by as an afterthought, that he'd planned it. "Sounds good."

"I'll drive. I'm parked out front."

"I'll grab my purse and meet you."

She quickly peeked in the bathroom mirror to check her hair and makeup. Thankfully her meeting with a new client earlier meant she'd put extra effort into her appearance today. One thing she loved about her job and owning her business? She didn't have to dress to the nines every day. So donning a feminine business suit always bolstered her self-confidence. She'd need an extra boost in dealing with an enigmatic man like Ronin Black.

After locking the front door, she scanned the cars parallel-parked on the tree-lined block. No sign of him. She turned and her heart stopped. Ronin stood in front of a motorcycle.

His gaze moved over her, from the tips of her gray peep-toe pumps to the hem of her pink and gray tweed pencil skirt. His lips quirked. "Nice suit. Good thing the restaurant is only twelve blocks from here."

"You don't seriously expect me to climb on the back of that thing in this outfit?"

"Of course. I even brought you a helmet."

"I don't see how a helmet will keep my skirt from riding up and showing everyone in downtown Denver the color of my panties."

"Then I guess you'd better sit real close to me to keep it a secret."

"Maybe I should—"

He loomed over her. "It's twelve blocks. If you hate the ride over, I'll call a cab to bring you back here after lunch. But you've got to at least try it. You know you want to."

How had he known that? "I'm putting myself in your hands, Ronin."

"You have no idea how much that appeals to me," he murmured.

His words flowed across her as potent as a caress.

"Hold still." He slipped the helmet on and flipped the visor up. "Is it pinching anywhere?"

"No."

Ronin swept her hair over her shoulders. He draped her long purse strap over her head, positioning her purse against her hip. "Let's go." He closed the visor and dug the keys out of his pocket before he climbed onto the bike.

Talk about a nice butt. Good thing the visor hid her lustful eyes—not good to be drooling over a new client.

And she might've pulled off her silent reminder to keep it professional, if she hadn't been forced to sit so close to him on the bike seat that angled down, smashing her crotch against that nice ass. All professional thoughts vanished when she wrapped her arms around his hard muscular core as they zoomed through city traffic.

The ride didn't take long and Amery was sort of sad to see it end.

Ronin held the bike steady as she quickly dismounted. She pulled the helmet off, shaking her hair free before she straightened her skirt.

"Want me to carry your helmet?" he asked.

"Nope. Holding it makes me feel a like a badass biker chick."

"You're a little too wholesome looking to pull that off."

Amery faced him. "Did you mean wholesome as an insult?"

Ronin invaded her space. "Not at all. It just requires more patience convincing a wholesome woman like you to take a walk on the wild side. But once you're there . . ." His eyes were glued to her mouth. "I bet you'd put badass biker chicks to shame."

Her entire body heated, but she managed a droll, "I'm wondering who you see when you're looking at me, because I don't see that at all."

"You should look deeper, because it's right there in your eyes."

Amery placed her hand on his chest and leaned in, catching a whiff of his exotic cologne. "You are dangerous, and not because you've got mad martial arts skills."

"Why?"

"Because you almost make me believe you can read me that well." Amery sidestepped him and walked through the open door to the restaurant. She paused at the hostess stand, inhaling several deep breaths to try and calm down.

A warm body pressed against her back, and soft lips brushed her ear. "Pink."

She turned her head and his lips moved to her cheek. "What?"

"The only person who saw your underwear was me. And they're pink."

The host approached and bowed. "Master Black."

Ronin returned the bow. "Michael. You're looking good. How's the family?"

"Wonderful. Angelina and I are so proud our Christina graduated with honors in May."

"Congratulations. You have every right to be proud."

"If not for your help . . . our Christina might not be . . ."

"Please." Ronin held up his hand in a *say no more* gesture. "Give my best to your wife and daughter."

"I will. Francis will show you to your table."

After they were seated upstairs on the patio, in the corner table with an amazing view, Amery said, "Best seat in the house, Master Black. I'm impressed."

"Don't be. Michael is too shrewd a businessman to hold a special table for me during lunch rush. I chalk it up to my good luck today."

Amery didn't buy that, but she let it go. She scanned the menu. "I've heard the food is fantastic. What do you recommend?"

"The salmon quinoa salad. Or the roasted vegetable pasta." She must've frowned because he said, "Is something wrong?"

"Just wondering if you're a vegetarian."

"Because I suggested vegetarian dishes? No. I'm very much a carnivore. In fact, I've decided on the buffalo burger."

"I was looking at that too."

Once the waiter took their order, Amery handed over the menu and felt Ronin's eyes on her again. "You're staring at me. Do I have helmet hair or something?"

"No. I just like looking at you."

"Well, it makes me uncomfortable."

He shrugged, as if to say *too bad*.

"So that guy you talked to up front. What did he mean when he said if not for you? Did you save his daughter's life or something?"

The change in his face was subtle, from relaxed to guarded, but she caught it. By the stiff way he held himself, she suspected he wouldn't answer. Finally he said, "His only daughter was attacked at college her freshman year. She closed herself off from everyone and was failing all her classes. Michael signed her up for a self-defense class with me at the dojo and she worked through her issues."

"Do you teach self-defenses often?"

"Almost never anymore." He took a long drink of water. "Your accent . . . I can't put a finger on it. Where are you from originally?"

Talk about changing the subject. "North Dakota."

"I've seen the movie *Fargo*."

She rolled her eyes. "We're not all like that, doncha know?"

A small smile curled the corners of his mouth. "So noted. Tell me why you left the cold climes of North Dakota."

"Because of the cold climes of North Dakota," she said dryly.

"Why Denver? Why not California or Florida to escape the cold and snow?"

"After I graduated from the University of North Dakota with a graphic arts degree, my boyfriend at the time had a tryout with the Colorado Rockies, so I followed him. We broke up and I loved it here, so I stayed."

"You stayed because you already owned your own business?"

What was up with the twenty questions?

He's entitled to your background information since he's already hired you.

"No. I worked for DeeDee Lewis of DDL Designs for three years. Then both her parents had health problems, forcing her to move back to Boston. I took out a loan for her business and the building and I've been working for myself ever since. Luckily I kept most of DDL's clients and added a few of my own. Molly works for me part-time while she's getting her master's degree."

"And Emmylou? Was she already renting space there?"

Amery shook her head. "When DDL owned the building the entire first floor belonged to the company. But I don't need that much space, especially since I downscaled to being a one-woman operation. Around that same time Emmylou, who I'd met through my ex, was looking for a permanent place for her massage clients. We erected a wall between the two businesses and it works." She didn't want to admit that without Emmylou's rent, she might not be able to swing the mortgage payment.

"What about Chaz? Where does he fit in?"

"Chaz worked for DeeDee when I first started. Then his free-lance work started paying better, so he quit. Anyway, after my ex and I broke up, I moved in with Chaz. I didn't know anyone in Denver besides the group my ex and I ran around with, and he got custody of them in the split. Chaz took me under his wing. After I assumed ownership of the building and company, he asked to rent the tiny room, which was the employee break room before the remodel. He doesn't like working alone in his apartment all the time."

When Ronin continued to stare at her, she bristled. "So, did I pass the Sensei Ronin Black business qualifications test?"

He leaned forward. "That wasn't a business test. Have I not made myself clear that it will be more than self-defense training and business between us?"

"Why me?" she blurted. "To hear people talk, you're some kind of martial arts god. You have that whole scary, mysterious Zen thing going on. And you are one of the hottest guys I've ever met."

"One of?" he repeated.

"Okay, *the* hottest guy I've ever met, but I didn't want to admit that because I didn't want you to get a swelled head."

Ronin smiled. "Thank you for the compliment. But I'm just a guy, Amery. A guy who works too hard and plays too little. And after meeting you?" His heated gaze roamed over her face. "I'm more than ready to play."

His deep velvety voice dripped with promises of sweaty, combustible sex. And her panties started getting very, very warm.

"Are you seeing anyone?"

"No. I have a hard time finding a date." Now, why had she admitted that to the hottest guy she'd ever met?

"You are a beautiful woman. But I'd venture a guess to say if you're hanging out in gay bars with your friends, then you're batting zero on the dating front because of your choice of venues."

Since both Chaz and Emmylou wore their sexual orientation like a banner, his insight about them wasn't shocking after one meeting. But his supposed insight into her was wrong. Dead wrong. And she told him so.

"I'm never wrong." Ronin cocked his head. "I'll prove it to you."

"How?"

"Pick a bar around here where young urban professionals hang out after work. I'll bet you get hit on at least six times. In an hour."

"There's no way to prove it," she argued. "I could just tell you I didn't get hit on at all and you'd never know."

He picked up her hand. "But I will know because I plan to be in the same bar. I'll keep track of how many men hit on you. You just have to be your beautiful, charming self."

His thumb was drawing tiny circles on the base of her hand. Sexy circles. Gentle, yet insistent. Would Ronin kiss that way? Starting out slow and then unleashing the heat that burned in his eyes?

"What were you thinking about just now?"

She guzzled half her glass of water. "What's in this bar experiment for you?"

Ronin brought her hand to his mouth, pressing soft kisses from the edge of her wrist to the fleshy skin below her thumb. "I get to look at you for an hour, which you know I like. And when the time is up, I get to be the guy you'll leave the bar with."

Amery gave him a skeptical look. "You won't have a bunch of your friends there as ringers, pretending to be interested in me?"

"First of all, I wouldn't do something so dishonorable. Second, I want *you* to see all the men that flock to you when you're not surrounded by gay camouflage."

She laughed. "Okay. You're on. But I have two conditions."

"Which I'll allow you to mention but I do not have to abide by, since the experiment was my idea and the rules are mine to make." He smiled serenely. "But please, go ahead and tell me your conditions."

"I want to hear your backstory."

"Didn't you read my bio on the Web site?"

She had, despite the fact that she'd only read it to see if he'd listed any personal information. "Yes. But that's your official bio. It's not the same. So tell me."

The food arrived, putting an end to the discussion.

While they ate Amery wondered if Ronin would skirt the subject again.

But he started talking without prompting after he finished his burger. "My father was stationed in Japan when he met my mother. They married, against my grandfather's wishes. Since my father was in the air force, we moved a lot. My dad trained in jujitsu and started taking me to class with him when I was three. Long story short, after my father died, we moved to Japan."

"How old were you?"

"Eight. Even though I'm a quarter Japanese on my mother's side, I didn't fit in anywhere besides the dojo. By age twelve I'd enrolled in a school where the main focus was jujitsu. By age sixteen I knew I'd found my calling. My grandfather refused to pay for advanced training, so I found an old master who agreed to swap training for my help with his business."

"That's very *Karate Kid*."

"I swear I'm not making this up. I trained with him for two years. When I turned eighteen I joined a . . ." He said a Japanese phrase. "There's no word for it in English. The closest description is a sort of monastery."

Her eyes widened. "Are you freakin' kidding me?"

"No. I spent four years there. It was a humbling and inspiring opportunity that I'm grateful for to this day. Upon my return to the real world at age twenty-two, I had to choose citizenship since Japan doesn't allow duality. I chose the U.S. Within four years of living here, I'd earned the money and built the reputation to start my own dojo."

"Wow. That's way more exciting than my story."

"It is what it is. Now what's the second condition?"

"I want to know if you're serious about hiring me or if it was just a way to get me to go out on a lunch date with you."

"I'm serious about having you design a new logo. But I also wanted a lunch date with you."

"Do you always get what you want?"

"Always." Ronin bent his head closer to hers. "As far as the logo is concerned, I'd like a bolder design that speaks of Japanese jujitsu, not the Brazilian method that's become so popular."

An edge had crept into his voice. "I take it you don't approve of that method?"

"Brazilian jujitsu is the preferred form for MMA fighters and I have no issue with the method. Just the guys who claim to have training in it. Few of the dojos around here have a qualified leader. They add the term 'Gracie method' and students flock to their classes. I'm traditional in that I train students to master techniques and learn control, not only to fight."

Everything about his physical charisma compelled her. Even when he wasn't looking directly at her, she could see the fire dancing in his eyes. She watched the agitated muscle popping in his jaw and how his full lips flattened into a thin line. All subtle movements that she might've missed if she hadn't allowed his magnetism to pull her in. A section of hair fell across his cheek and she had to curl her fingers into her palms to keep from brushing it aside. "Were you a good fighter?"

"I don't have TKO stats, or an official win-loss record, or a medal or a winner's belt. But I did make a whole bunch of money fighting, and that allowed me to start Black Arts."

"And that was the endgame for you? The only reason you fought?"

Ronin seemed surprised she'd moved so close. He reached out and followed a section of her hair from her scalp to the end where it rested against her breast. "You're the first person to ask me that in a very long time. It'd be tempting now, even fourteen years later, to say I only fought to earn my place so I didn't have to fight anymore."

He stroked her hair again and the blunt edge of his fingertip grazed her cheek. "But the truth is, I like fighting. I like matching my skill against another opponent. In class, we work the techniques, but we're always careful not to hurt the students. But on the mat during a match? Pain isn't a concern. The fighting is raw."

The gentle way he touched her hair as he spoke so nonchalantly about violence gave her a surprisingly intimate peek into this complex man. "Do you still fight?"

"Four years ago a Brazilian jujitsu practitioner publicly questioned my credentials and openly mocked me for claiming I'd studied in Japan and that I was part Japanese. Normally I don't bother with martial arts politics, but when he brought it into my house? Making those claims in front of my students? I couldn't let it slide."

"Is that why you've got security at the front door?"

"Partially. He did just walk in with twenty of his students and disrupt my classes. I had no idea if they'd brought weapons, so I took preventive measures after that incident to provide better security for my students."

"What happened? Was him showing up on your turf like he'd declared war?"

Ronin smiled. "He said he'd meet me anytime, anyplace, so I suggested a time and a place. He bragged near and far about the public beat-down he was about to dish out."

"And?"

"I lost."

Her mouth fell open. "Are you serious?"

"No. But telling you the truth will put me in a different light in your eyes, and I'm not ready for that. I'm liking the way you're looking at me now, Amery."

She blushed. "Tell me anyway."

He kept absentmindedly running his fingers down that same section of hair. "I wiped the floor with him. He wanted it real—I gave him real. I broke his arm and his nose. I dislocated his shoulder. I cracked his ribs. All within five minutes."

Amery fought a shiver. "Did he do any damage to you?"

Their eyes met. "He dislocated my finger and gave me a deep bruise on my hip." He tugged on the end of her hair. "How did we get so far off topic?"

"It's not off topic. It's stuff I need to know if you and I are . . . ah, working together."

He seemed amused that she'd kept her answer professional.

"I'll work up some design ideas for the logo."

"Perfect. But on the personal side of us *working together*, mark your calendar tomorrow night for the 'hot chick getting hit on in a bar' challenge."

"Ronin—"

He held up his hand, forestalling her argument, and took his phone out of his pocket. "What's your number?"

Amery recited the digits, watching him plug the numbers in. Then her phone buzzed with a text message.

"Now you have mine. You decide on the destination at the last minute so you know it's not rigged." Ronin scowled at his phone buzzing in his hand. "Excuse me, I need to take this." He left the table and walked to the far edge of the balcony.

She stood and straightened her skirt. She picked up the helmet. Ronin's conversation drifted to her—so odd to hear him speaking in Japanese.

That reiterated her misgivings. What did she really know about this man? Besides that he fired her blood? No doubt he embodied sexy, exotic, and mysterious—but she reminded herself his life was devoted to teaching the finer points of violence.

He returned. "I'm so sorry, but I will have to send you back to your office in a cab. Something came up that I need to deal with right away."

She placed her hand on his chest. "Are you okay?"

Ronin dipped his head and brushed his cheek against hers. "Yes. But I appreciate your concern because that shows me you know this is more than just business between us." He kept his hand on the middle of her back as they walked downstairs.

At the hostess stand he spoke to Michael and discreetly palmed him cash. He paused in the doorway and looked at Amery. He mouthed, *Tomorrow,* and then he was gone.

CHAPTER FOUR

"IS this seat taken?"

Amery glanced up at the tall, lanky man with sandy brown hair. Cute in that geeky sort of way. "No. It's open."

"Great. Thanks." He picked up the chair and carried it to his table of friends.

So much for him offering to buy her a drink.

But she'd suspected that's how this hour-long social experiment would play out. She feigned interest in the TV in the corner, trying not to devour the bowl of snack mix placed in front of her.

This was a cool bar. Why had she walked by the place dozens of times but hadn't stopped in? The vibe here was relaxed despite the upbeat music. Great ambience with the brightly colored pendant lights hanging from the high ceiling. Like in so many old warehouses in Lodo, the rafters had been left exposed, as had the brick walls. She'd checked out the scarred wide-planked oak as she'd walked in, wondering if she'd find similar flooring beneath the carpet in her loft.

As she'd prepped herself for a night at the meat market, she considered Ronin's observation—maybe she hadn't been looking in the right places to meet eligible men. She chatted with the same guys at the gym, but they'd never asked her out. No men attended her yoga classes. She'd smile at guys at the grocery store, or the bank, keeping it friendly, but it hadn't made a difference. She went to the movies alone. She ate out by herself frequently and it didn't bother her, but other patrons avoided making eye contact, pitying her as a single diner.

Amery admitted she'd fallen into a rut—relying on Emmylou and Chaz to entertain her. Molly had pulled into her shell completely after the attack and they hadn't done anything together outside of work for ages. In recent months if her pals were busy, she'd stay home and watch movies or TV or read.

Nothing wrong with liking her own company . . . was there?

A man sidled up next to her and smiled. "Hey. I haven't seen you in here before."

"First time. I thought I'd swing in and have a drink."

"If you're thirsty I could buy the next one."

"That's sweet. Thank you, but I'm meeting a friend."

His eyes filled with regret. "Shame. Enjoy." He took off.

After that, Amery fended off advances from several other guys as she nursed her drink. If she hadn't made plans with Ronin, she might've given her number to a couple of them.

Where was Ronin anyway?

Then she felt his eyes on her, even though she couldn't see him. Calming her even as he assessed her. Thankfully this demonstration or whatever it was ended in ten minutes. She ordered another martini. As the clock wound down, she felt a tap on her shoulder. She faced the guy. He looked familiar.

"Amery? It's Will Aberle. Do you remember me? I'm friends with Chaz."

"Will! Of course I remember you. Chaz dragged us to that laser tag place last fall. We froze our butts off."

"I haven't seen Chaz for a while. How is he?"

"Good. He's in a relationship now. Well, as much as Chaz can be in a relationship, which means—"

"He's still on the prowl," Will finished.

"God, don't we sound like bitchy queens dissing on our friend?"

"That's the problem with always being the straight man."

She laughed. Will was funny and had the blond-haired, blue-eyed look Amery found so appealing. So why hadn't she ever let him know she was available?

Because no matter how nice he seems, he reminds you of your ex.

"How've you been?" Will asked.

"I can't complain. I've kept up with new business and haven't lost much of my old business. What about you? You're in insurance, right?"

"Yes, I'm in the actuary department, which sounds incredibly stuffy every time I say it."

"So, is this your usual hangout?"

"I'm usually in one night a week. I never see you here."

"My first time."

"I ought to buy you a drink to celebrate."

A hand landed on her shoulder and Ronin's smooth cheek brushed hers as he inserted himself between them. "Sorry I'm late. I know how much you hate waiting." Then he offered his hand to Will. "Ronin. And you are?"

"Will."

"Thanks, Will, for keeping my girl company."

What was up with Ronin acting as if they were a couple?

"My pleasure." Will smiled at Amery. "Good seeing you again." Then he moved to the other side of the bar.

"You ready?" Ronin asked.

"For you to explain to me exactly what the hell that was? Yes. Start talking."

Ronin squeezed her shoulder. "A friendly reminder that you're off the market."

"Like I'm a slab of meat?" she asked sharply.

"You are Grade-A prime cut all the way, baby."

"Ronin. That's not funny."

"No, it's not."

His eyes were so . . . penetrating that her heart sped up. "What's wrong?"

"You're a beautiful woman, who just rejected eight offers from strangers who wanted to buy you drinks." He traced the edge of her cheek and tipped her chin up. "Watching you was a special kind of torture for me because I willingly devised it."

"Why?"

"I wanted you to see the truth about yourself. Then I realized you would've let some of those guys buy you a drink or maybe even left with them had the situation been different."

"Do you want me to admit you were right?"

"About letting any one of them buy you a drink? No." Ronin's thumb slowly followed the curve of her lower lip. When she trembled, he seemed to take great pleasure in treating her to another leisurely pass, ensuring that she trembled from his touch again. "Was I right about you being the sexiest woman in this bar? Yes. So say *I'm unaware of my own beauty and you were irrevocably right, Ronin.*"

Somehow Amery eased back from his enthralling touch. "Fat chance. So, where were you sitting while I was proving your point?"

"In the corner."

"Watching my back?"

He gestured to the front of the bar. "I didn't want to watch your back; I wanted to watch your face." He plucked up her restless hand. "Since I won, I get to pick what we do tonight. Have any idea what that might be?"

Please say hours of hot, raunchy sex.

Ronin's eyes narrowed. "Did you say something?"

"Uh. No." Thank god she hadn't said that out loud, but she half suspected he'd read her mind. "What are we doing?" she asked quickly. "I hope it involves food."

"Isn't it fortunate I planned to cook for you at my place?"

So maybe hot sex was on the menu for tonight. She smiled. "Sounds delicious."

"Let's go."

Amery upended her drink and took his hand as he led her outside. No worries about driving since she'd walked to the bar. She'd even worn jeans in case Ronin had driven his motorcycle.

But out on the street he stopped beside a black Lexus SUV. He opened the passenger door. "You look disappointed."

"I kind of like the bike."

"Next time."

Once they were tooling down the road, she said, "I don't know where you live."

"Same as you: where I work."

She frowned. "You live in the dojo?"

"On the top floor. And also like you, I own the building."

"What else is in the building?"

"Dojo offices and additional training areas take up the second and part of the third floor. I rent out the fourth floor to businesses that don't have much walk-in traffic but needed office space."

"How long have you owned the building?"

"Bought it ten years ago. Needed a ton of work. My priority was the dojo. Then my living space. It's just in the last six years the middle floors were updated and ready to rent out."

"So, do you have instructors and students just pop into your place to say howdy?"

Ronin shook his head. "It's no secret I live on the top floor, but access is limited." He circled the area twice. "The downside to this area is the lack of parking."

"Sucks when you have to haul groceries, doesn't it?"

"That's why I don't have a membership at Costco."

He had a better sense of humor than Amery had credited him for. She headed for the front entrance, but he snagged her hand and led her to the alley. "Back door."

"Afraid you'll get waylaid and need to show a technique or ten to some poor struggling white belt?" she teased.

"No." They stopped in front of a rusty steel door. He unlocked a small metal box, which housed a keypad, punched in a code, and the locks popped.

"Fancy."

"Safe," he corrected.

Amery could hear the sounds of the dojo as they cut down a narrow hallway. They stopped at another door, which also required a key card for the code box. Through that door was an elevator bay with two elevators. They rode in silence to the fifth floor and got off.

She followed him down a short carpeted hallway and he stopped in front of a set of double doors. Another swipe of the key card, another code.

"I'm starting to feel like I'm in a spy movie."

Ronin held the door open for her. "Almost there."

Before her was another elevator. She faced him, her mouth open. "You have a private elevator to your apartment?"

"Keeps the riffraff out."

She laughed.

"It's no different than standard high-rises. The top floor always has a separate elevator."

With all the security measures, how would she get out if she had to? Her heart raced at the sudden thought and she studied the pattern in the fake-wood paneling as Ronin messed with another keypad.

The elevator started to go up.

He didn't speak until the door opened. "After you."

Amery stepped onto a tiled entryway and stopped.

Then Ronin was in her face. "What's wrong?"

"This . . . private elevator, super-secret security stuff. What if there's a fire and I can't get out because I don't have the key card or the codes? Or what if I just want to leave?"

His rapt gaze remained on hers. "If you want to leave, I'll take you home right now. No questions asked."

That mollified her some.

"This is a no-pressure situation, Amery. I won't drag you into my bedroom and tie you to my bed." He smiled devilishly. "Well, not at first."

Her quick laugh held a trace of nerves.

"We'll have dinner, conversation, see if there's something between us worth pursuing."

"And if there isn't?"

The look on his face said he didn't believe that was a possibility. "Do you want to be here?"

"Yes."

"Good." Ronin crowded her against the wall and curled his hands around her face. "I've wanted to kiss you since the moment you threw your pants at me."

Amery couldn't think of a witty retort; she couldn't think period. Then he teased her mouth with his. A glide of his lips, followed by an exchange of heated breath. She trembled with heart-pounding, body-tingling anticipation.

His tongue lightly swept across the seam of her lips and she automatically opened her mouth wider. Wanting more.

Ronin slowly licked his way inside. First a taste. Another lick. A soft suck. His thumbs feathered across her cheeks as he held her face. Then he angled her head and consumed her mouth in a blistering kiss.

Oh god. Could the man kiss. No holds barred, he poured passion and skill and need into the kiss until Amery returned his fire with her own. She closed her eyes and her fingers curled into his chest, holding on to him even as she gave him control.

He took it as if it were his due.

By the time he ended the kiss, her body vibrated. Her head was muzzy and her lips buzzed.

"Still want to go?" he murmured.

"No."

"You sure?" he asked, his lips trilling down her throat.

"Yes, I'm sure."

"I'm glad. Do you want a tour? Or are you starved?"

"A tour would be good."

Ronin placed one last, lingering kiss on her lips and took her hand. He led her through a curved archway. "This is the living room. Feel free to look around while I see to dinner."

Maybe austere was a Japanese thing. Or maybe his décor choice reflected his bachelor status. The furnishings weren't scaled to the size of the room. Just two simple couches, long and low-backed, covered in plain neutral brown fabric. Two tan chairs sat opposite each other in front of a fireplace. A coffee table, end tables, a leather bench, and several floor lamps finished the space.

He hadn't scattered personal items on the horizontal surfaces. No family pictures. No accolades from his jujitsu career.

Art hung here and there. One picture contained a graphic scene—a fat Japanese man opened his robe, exposing his exaggerated genitalia to a disheveled geisha cowering on the ground. Two more similar in theme hung next to it. One with a long-haired samurai wielding a sword at a snarling tiger standing in front of massacred bodies. The last picture featured a crouching Japanese man, naked, his oversized genitalia resting on the ground. In front of him was a half-clothed woman, tied to a post in some fancy rope configuration, and the man held her foot, licking the sole with an enlarged tongue.

From behind her, Ronin said, "Those are shunga prints."

"Interesting decorating choice."

"They're heavy with symbolism, not at all what they appear to be on the surface."

Ironic that description could also be applied to him?

They skirted a wall that divided the living spaces but didn't reach the ceiling or the other two walls and left a large gap by the floor. Gave the illusion of a floating wall, which was cool.

A dining room and kitchen area took up the entire side.

She frowned. For the size of the building, the main living spaces seemed off.

"Something wrong?" Ronin asked in that deep and sexy voice.

"I just was trying to grasp the area spatially. The dojo, for being divided into smaller training areas, seems much bigger than this open space. Since I know the building is the same dimension on the bottom as it is on the top, it's throwing me off."

Ronin took her hand. "Very astute observation. As a single man, I don't need seven thousand square feet of living space. The remodel chopped the top floor in half. So this is roughly four thousand square feet."

"So you don't use the other half of this floor for offices or anything?"

"No." He skirted another long floating wall that created a corridor between the living areas. He opened the first door. "Guest bedroom."

Amery wasn't sure if he expected her to nod and move on, but she wanted to see the space because it actually had personality. Two bright red club-type chairs were arranged in front of a window, creating a small sitting area. A queen-sized bed with an ornately carved headboard with red lacquered accents took up the far wall. The floors were wood. Sisal rugs with red borders were scattered throughout. She wandered to the open doorway in the corner and stepped into a large bathroom. The shower stall walls looked like rice paper; the bathroom sink was a polished teak bowl atop a black lacquered cabinet. All the accents were red. "Great room, but does it make your guests want to stay longer?"

"I discourage that."

She laughed.

Between the guest bedroom and the next room was the main bathroom, which also carried the wood, black, and red theme. The next room housed an enormous blank wall for what looked like a projection-screen TV, a pool table, and floor-to-ceiling bookshelves on one wall that were filled with DVDs and CDs. No snapshots or funky kitschy things either. Just out of curiosity she approached the shelf. Yep. The titles were alphabetized. That made her smile.

"Do you spend much time in here?" she asked.

"Not as much as one would think."

Cryptic.

Ronin took her hand and she knew the next stop would be his bedroom. He bypassed the next door, which had a lock on it.

"What's that room?"

"Storage."

"Got valuables locked up in there?"

"A few things." Ronin opened the last door. "This is my bedroom."

Her face flushed.

He led her inside and released her hand.

The white carpet in this room was so plush she swore she sank to her ankles. The focal point of the room was a king-sized bed on a raised platform with two steps leading to the mattress. The head-board, easily ten feet tall, had been crafted out of twisted black metal and smooth chunks of thick wood. A beautiful, luxurious-looking turquoise silk covered the bed. Were his sheets silk too? Or simple cotton?

Why don't you dive in and find out?

Ronin came up behind her. She closed her eyes against the surge of want when the hard wall of his chest connected with her shoulders. She breathed in his intoxicating scent.

"What are you thinking about?"

You and me naked, rolling around in silk. "How much I want to jump on your bed to see if it's as puffy as it looks."

"Know what I was thinking about?" His warm lips moved down the side of her neck.

She sighed and angled her head, giving him full access to wherever he wanted. "What?"

He lifted her hair, wrapping it in his fist as he kissed the sweep of her shoulder. "I want to see how you'll look spread out on my bed." His mouth stopped at the ball of her shoulder and he lightly sank his teeth down. "Will you indulge me?"

Amery twisted away from him and climbed up the platform, facing him. Something spiked her daring side and she taunted him. "How were you imagining me in your bed, Ronin? Like this?" She fell back onto the mattress and threw her arms above her head.

Was it her imagination or had Ronin just . . . growled? She lifted her head. Wasn't her imagination that he'd inched closer.

"Or maybe you want me like this." She turned and dropped to her hands and knees. She arched her back, canted her hips, and wiggled her ass, emitting a soft moan.

The bed dipped and Ronin was on her. His big, hard body caging hers, his mouth at her ear. "I definitely want you like this. Not for the first go-round, though. For that, we'll be like this." Ronin smoothly flipped her onto her back and pinned her arms above her head, settling his groin against hers. His mouth landed on hers hard. His tongue plunged into her mouth and he turned her inside out with a kiss that wasn't careful and exploratory but packed with pure hunger. He rocked his hips, transferring her wrists to one hand, and followed the outside curve of her body from her forearm down to her hip.

Amery arched into him, lost in him.

But Ronin slowed the kiss. He released her wrist and offered that side of her body a thorough caress before he rolled to his knees and gazed down at her.

She pushed up on her elbows, trying to play it cool even though her body had gone haywire. Her chest was heaving; her panties were damp. Her breasts ached for his touch—his mouth, his hand, his chest, she didn't care. She also tuned out the voice in her head warning her not to sleep with him on the first date. She'd played it safe, always been a good girl—yet something about Ronin Black made her want to throw caution to the wind for the first time . . . ever.

Ronin stared at her. His breathing was equally labored. "As much as I'd like to strip you and fuck you until we knock this mattress off the platform, I didn't bring you into my home for this." He angled close enough to curl his hands around her face. "This will happen between us, but not now. Not even tonight." Then he kissed her once more.

His kiss was a promise, a tease and completely . . . sweet.

Ronin Black . . . sweet? Totally unexpected.

He stood and waited for her at the edge of the platform.

Feeling free, she laughed and leaped to her feet, bouncing in the center of the bed. "This is a springy mattress. I bet when I'm under you I won't even feel the mattress coils digging into my spine."

Another growling noise. "Tempting the beast while still in the cage might not be the wisest course of action for you."

Ooh. A philosophical threat. "I'll stop." Amery bounced once more before landing on her feet.

"Let's eat." Ronin held her hand and towed her back to the kitchen.

"So, did you really cook for me?"

"I really did." He pointed to the place settings at the counter. "Have a seat."

Amery studied the space. The kitchen, like every other area in this enormous loft, was spacious and uncluttered. But he did have a few whimsical pieces in here. Ceramic salt and pepper shakers shaped like samurai warriors. A fruit bowl entwined with dragons.

Ronin poured her a glass of white wine. "Poached salmon okay?"

"Sounds perfect." She squinted at the double oven. "Are you cooking it right now?"

"It's done. Why?"

"It doesn't reek like fish in here. That's the thing I hate about cooking fish at home. Takes a day to get the smell out."

"These ovens have exceptional ventilation, or like you, I'd rarely cook fish."

She sipped the wine. Very dry. Maybe she could choke down one glass. She'd seem unsophisticated if she admitted she preferred wine coolers to actual wine.

Ronin didn't bustle around the kitchen. No wasted movements as he removed the pan from the oven. He scooped out a piece of salmon, arranged it on a square red plate, and doused it with a spoonful of yellow sauce. He added a scoop of risotto from a pan on the stove and slid the plate onto the bamboo place mat. He plated his own food before he grabbed two bowls from the fridge and set one beside her.

"Ronin. This is amazing."

"Maybe you should taste it first before you say that," he said dryly.

Amery sliced a chunk of the flaky fish and popped it into her mouth. The sauce wasn't lemony as she'd expected, but orange and mint. "I stand by what I said. This is amazing."

He nudged the bowl of greens toward her. "Spinach, kale, and bok choy salad with a spicy peanut yogurt dressing."

She bumped her shoulder into his. "This is an incredibly healthy meal, isn't it?"

"It's a staple in my cooking repertoire."

"Good. I was afraid maybe this was your way of telling me to lay off the Keebler fudge-striped cookies."

Then her chin was in his hand and Ronin was right in her face. "You are beautiful. Every inch of you. I'd never presume to change you, Amery, only enhance what I know is already there. And if eating Keebler fudge-striped cookies makes you happy, eat them."

Okay. His intensity even when he was trying to be cute was a little scary. So why was she tempted to kiss him? Nibble on his lips, wanting his flavor on her tongue along with the food?

"You are trouble," he murmured, "although I do like that you look as if you'd rather take a bite out of me than the food."

"You caught me."

Ronin lightly kissed her lips and returned to his meal.

The silence lingering between them wasn't awkward. If Ronin had something to say, he'd say it; she appreciated that he wasn't the type of guy who yammered on because he had a wealth of knowledge to share. Besides, she preferred a quiet dinner to the dinners she'd suffered through growing up, where her parents grilled her about everything and would lecture her endlessly on mistakes that would put a mark against the entire family.

"You're picking at the salad. My feelings won't be hurt if you don't like it."

"No, it's not that. This is delicious. I was just thinking it's refreshing we don't have to talk all the time. It's like people are afraid of silence."

"And you're not?" he asked.

Amery shrugged and swigged her wine. "I work alone seventy percent of the time. I don't have music playing in the background. I don't call people and spend hours on the phone. To be honest, I think being content with silence is out of the norm. Chaz can't work without his iPod blaring in his ears. Every thirty minutes he has to wander around and see what everyone else is doing. Even Molly wears earbuds most of the time she's in the office."

"What about Emmylou?"

"She has soothing music playing, and she only holds a minimal amount of conversation with her clients during her sessions. But as soon as she's done, she's talking a mile a minute on her cell or surfing online." Amery shrugged. "Or maybe there's something wrong with me."

"Then it's wrong with me also. I'd prefer a quiet dojo with students working on mastering techniques without distractions. But my supervisory belts disagree with me. They claim music inspires the students to work harder. And since I trust their judgment, I've left it their choice on how to run their classes. But if I'm teaching? No music."

"Did your stance on that come from your monastery years?"

"I learned many skills there, including finding the balance between what I need and what the world requires from me."

Amery sighed. When he said Zen stuff like that, she wanted to curl into him and absorb his strength and wisdom, while surrounding herself with his enticing scent.

She managed to eat half of her meal and felt guilty when Ronin asked, "Are you finished?"

"Yes. Thank you. It was delicious." She excused herself to freshen up in the bathroom. After rinsing her mouth and popping a mint, she ran her fingers through her hair and double-checked her makeup. Then she turned away from the mirror—it was a rare day when she was happy with the reflection.

Ronin was staring out the windows in the space separating the living area from the kitchen. There seemed to be no rhyme or reason to his mood changes. He could switch from hot to cold literally in the blink of an eye.

Maybe he's decided this isn't worth pursuing after all.

She approached him cautiously. "Ronin?"

He didn't turn around.

"Is everything all right?"

"Not really."

"What's wrong?"

"I'm a liar."

She froze. "About what?"

"I told you I didn't invite you here for dinner because I intended to take you to bed. But that's a total fucking lie. I want you in my bed in the worst way, Amery. All I can think about is stripping you bare and feasting on every part of you before I bend you over the back of the couch and fuck you. Then I'd fuck you on the chair or on the rug before dragging you to my bed and starting all over again."

That was his *I'm a liar* confession? Amery nestled her cheek against the heat and hardness between his shoulder blades. She couldn't help it; she smiled against his back.

"You find that amusing?" he said a bit testily.

"Somewhat." She snaked her arms around his waist. "Because when I saw you standing in front of this window, I half expected to see your keys in your hand. Like you'd changed your mind and couldn't wait to get rid of me."

"Why would you think that?"

"Maybe I'm not what you expected? We're different when it's just you and me, rather than in the dojo, or talking business, or when we're having lunch in a crowded restaurant or a drink in a crowded bar."

He spun around and cradled her head in his hands, keeping their bodies close. "No, baby, it's better when we're alone like this. I'm the one who feels like . . ." He pressed his lips to her forehead. "I don't want to go fast, and yet everything inside me races when I see you."

The man had all the right words. "So take the pressure off yourself and off me. I didn't come here tonight expecting to get laid." Amery turned her head, letting her mouth whisper across his jaw. "In fact, I wore crappy, mismatched lingerie so I'd be too embarrassed to take my clothes off in front of you."

He laughed softly. "You are such a breath of fresh air in my life."

Amery looked at him. "I don't want to scare you off, but I haven't done the whole dating thing in quite a while."

"I know that."

"How?"

"Because you're not completely jaded. You weren't sizing up my assets."

"Well, yes, actually I was sizing up one asset in particular." Her palms slid up his chest. So firm and defined. She wished she could feel the warmth of his solid muscles beneath her hands.

"Amery," he warned. "I'm a little on edge, so tread lightly."

"That commanding tone is so sexy."

"It's who I am." He fastened his mouth to hers. The kiss started out slow but didn't stay that way for long. His heat, his passion bowled her over. His hot, wet, demanding tongue warred with hers. He gathered her hair in his hand, pulling until she angled her neck exactly how he wanted it.

Her skin was electrified from his openmouthed kisses. Each nuzzle, below her ear, on the pulse point of her throat, the arc of her shoulder, the underside of her jaw, sent her senses reeling. "Ronin."

"Your skin is like a drug." He planted kisses to the top button on her shirt. He released her hair and ran his hands down the sides of her face and her neck. His fingers circled her wrists and he brushed his mouth across her ear. "Beautiful girl, I'd better get you home before I come up with one hundred more reasons why I shouldn't take you home."

Ronin placed another kiss on her temple and stepped back.

Amery noticed the bulge in the crotch of his jeans.

His rough-tipped fingers were under her chin, forcing her focus higher. "Eyes off my asset."

After he'd driven her home, he insisted on walking her to the door in the alley she used to reach her loft. "I had an amazing time tonight, Ronin."

"Same here." He kissed her fingertips. "Unfortunately I've got things scheduled, so we can't do it again this weekend."

She masked her disappointment and chastised herself for expecting to spend more time with him over the weekend anyway. They'd had one date. *One.* She needed to keep her enthusiasm in check. "I've got plans myself."

"Doing what?"

"Catching up on work. Dinner with friends. Hitting the movies. The usual. How about you?"

"Nothing as enticing as what you're doing," he said with a smile. "Would that work have anything to do with designing a new logo for Black Arts?"

"Could be. A few drafts are almost done and ready for you to look at."

"Would Monday work for you to meet with me and a couple instructors to show us what you've got?"

She did a mental check of her schedule next week. "Sure. What time?"

"Ten. The dojo offices are on the second floor."

"Any crazy security measures I need to be aware of?"

"No." His mouth landed on hers hard for a quick kiss. "See you Monday."

CHAPTER FIVE

"SO, you're having a nooner with Master Black?" Chaz asked with a straight face.

"Why are you here bugging me? You never work on Mondays."

"Because you didn't fill me in on what happened over the weekend. I knew if I asked you about it over the phone, and something did happen, you could lie and I wouldn't know. Face-to-face, I can always tell when you're lying, so spill the deets, *ma chérie*."

Amery refilled her coffee. "We went to a bar after work Friday night, he fixed me dinner at his place, and I came home. No mattress mambo for us, if you're wondering—but not because the chemistry's not there. I worked on Saturday until Emmylou dragged me to this truly horrible piece of performance art at some dive bar." She shuddered.

Chaz tsk-tsked. "I warned you about that weird shit she's into. I won't be surprised the day she comes in here wearing a collar and chains. She's destined to be somebody's bitch."

"Funny, Emmylou said the same thing about you," Amery shot back.

"Please. I own up to being anyone's bitch, anytime, anyplace. I'm not in denial." He wandered back to his work area.

Amery followed him. "What masterpieces are you creating now?"

"Three actually. This one is for a gay manga collection." He shuffled through the papers and pulled out a sheet.

She examined it closely. Yes, it was over-the-top erotic, but the artwork was phenomenal and incredibly detailed. "This is fabulous."

"I know. Which is why they're in negotiations with my agent for another big project."

"Why didn't you tell me? I'm so proud of you!" She hugged him. "What else?"

"In addition to the straight manga contracts I already have? This guy I know has written a gay superhero series and he's asked me to illustrate it. He wants to present the finished package to a new, edgier comic book line that's building some good buzz."

"This guy . . . do I know him?"

Chaz spun in his chair. "Nope."

Then she knew. "Dammit, Chaz, you're sleeping with him already?"

"Yep."

"What about Andre?"

"What about him?" Chaz said breezily. "I'd be up for a three-some, but as it stands, boy A don't know about boy B and maybe I'd like to keep it that way."

Then maybe you should keep it in your pants.

Chaz glared at her, even though she hadn't said a word. "About to go all holier-than-thou on me? No wonder you didn't get laid this weekend."

"Really? I get that snap judgment snark from other people, Chaz; I don't need it from you, so piss off."

Amery stormed into her office and slammed the door.

She hated that Chaz could be so mean. He knew about her screwed up her childhood as the daughter of a fundamentalist Christian minister. She'd been shamed by her body, shamed by her need for physical intimacy, shamed for just about everything. Threatened by eternal punishment from God for every little transgression, but the punishments from her dad were always way worse. And her mother had just stood by and let the man of the house rule. Watching as her husband belittled and shamed Amery until the day Amery left for college.

So it wasn't any surprise the first real relationship after she'd dated casually for a couple of years had been fucked up from the start. Tyler, star athlete, self-professed Christian boy, had played on her insecurities, manipulated her, and used her until he hadn't needed her anymore.

Chaz had been the one to pick up the pieces. He'd always been there to bolster her when she needed it. And for him to be so harsh toward her now? She didn't deserve it from him. She wasn't judging him. She just wanted him to be careful. Mixing business with pleasure wasn't a good idea.

And yet here you are, about to do a presentation for a man that you hope to get naked with very soon. Maybe you *were* pulling an attitude on *Chaz.*

But there was nothing she could do about it now—she didn't think she had anything to apologize for. Besides, they both needed to cool off.

Amery grabbed her portfolio and her laptop and left through the back door.

Parking wasn't any easier to find around the dojo during the day. She ended up hoofing it three blocks, so she was sweaty and wrinkled when she entered the main entrance ten minutes late.

The elevator dumped her on the second floor into one long corridor. No reception area. She followed the hallway midway down until she came to a door. BLACK ARTS was etched in the frosted glass, along with *by appointment only.*

Did she knock? Or walk in? Was the door locked?

After thirty seconds of indecision, Amery knocked rapidly four times and opened the door. "Sensei Black?" she said loudly as she stepped into an empty waiting area.

The big blond instructor exited from a door halfway down the hall. He beckoned her closer. "We're in here, Ms. Hardwick."

Amery plastered on a smile. Her heels clicked loudly on the tile floors and she wished she'd worn different shoes.

He bowed slightly and offered his hand. "I'm Knox Lofgren. We met briefly the night you signed up for the self-defense class."

"I'm hoping you won't hold my behavior that night against me, Shihan."

"No. But you did manage to get under Sensei's skin, which is as rare as it is amusing." He pushed open the door. "Come in and get settled. Ronin is on a conference call and he'll be in shortly. Would you care for coffee? Tea? A soda?"

"I'm good, thank you." They'd entered a large meeting room lined with windows and a U-shaped conference table in the center. Another guy stood when she came in.

He looked . . . mean. Bald head. Tattoos decorating his arm from wrists to elbows. Tattoos peeking out from the V in his T-shirt. His eyes were the lightest blue—almost translucent. He wasn't tall—not as big as Ronin and definitely not as big as Knox—but he was built like a cement block. Solid. Probably solid muscle. She guessed he was somewhere around her age.

"Ms. Hardwick, this is Deacon McConnell."

Deacon also offered her a slight bow before extending his hand. "Ms. Hardwick, it is a pleasure."

Oh, wow, he had a honey-thick Southern drawl that softened his I'm-a-badass vibe. She smiled at him. "Please, both of you, call me Amery. And I have to ask, what is your official title, Deacon?"

"Yondan. Fourth-degree black belt."

"Technically my official title is Godan, which is fifth degree black belt," Knox said. "Students call me Shihan as a sign of respect since I'm the second-highest belt rank in the dojo."

She pointed to the screen on the wall. "I hope you're not expecting a PowerPoint presentation?"

"To be honest, we weren't sure what to expect."

"So neither of you knows why I'm here?"

They shook their heads.

"Sensei Black approached me last week about creating a new logo for the dojo. He indicated he's needed to do that for some time."

Knox grinned. "Hot damn. I'm happy to hear that."

Deacon nodded.

"Bear in mind I have limited ideas because I am waiting for more input."

"Which they'll be happy to provide," Ronin said behind her.

She jumped and whirled around. "You have *got* to stop doing that to me, Master Black."

"Ronin," he murmured.

"But we're in the dojo, aren't we?" she murmured back.

"Technically? No. So relax."

Knox and Deacon seemed to be watching them very closely.

"I see you've met Knox, my second-in-command, for lack of a better term. And Deacon, my third-in-command."

Amery seized the chance to learn more about Ronin. She looked at Knox. "How long have you been associated with Black Arts, Shihan?"

"Since I was discharged from the service five years ago."

"And you, Yondan?"

"Three years."

From what she'd read about dojos and the student's loyalty to train with one master for years, and sometimes decades, she'd expected both of these men to have been with Sensei longer.

"While we're informal, please call us by our first names," Knox said.

Ronin pulled out a chair for her. Then he parked himself right beside her.

Damn hard not to get flustered. Especially since the man wasn't giving her any space. He was dressed like Knox and Deacon in a white T-shirt and white gi pants. None of them wore shoes. What had they been doing before she showed up? Working out? Sparring? Rolling around on the mats beating on each other? Why did that image make her heart pound?

"Problem?" Ronin prompted.

Her cheeks flamed. Stupid lily-white skin. She fake-coughed. "I might need some water after all."

Amery expected Ronin to appoint either of these guys to get her a drink. But he grabbed a bottle of water from the minibar fridge and handed it to her.

She really wanted to roll the plastic bottle over her hot face, but she uncapped it and drank. Then she smiled. "You guys will want to come down here because my ideas are on the computer."

Knox and Deacon crowded behind her. At some point Ronin had draped his arm over the back of her chair. Now he was so close she could smell his scent: sweat and laundry soap. She could feel the heat of his thigh muscle pressing against the outside of her leg. Then his fingers would absentmindedly drift across her shoulder.

The man had thrown her completely off her game.

Take control. You don't want to look incompetent.

"I'll run through it once as a slide show and then we can stop on individual images to see if anything pops out at you."

She wasn't expecting them to chatter, but their absolute silence unnerved her.

Knox spoke first. "I like images three and seven."

"Those are polar opposites. One has clean lines. The other has Japanese influences."

"Probably why I like them both. Any chance you could marry those two styles into something bolder?"

Amery started clicking on the keys, designing on the fly. Taking suggestions. Adding, discarding.

An hour of collaboration later, Black Arts had a great new logo. They were so pleased with it even Deacon said, "Fine job."

Then Knox and Deacon left the conference room.

"You are very good at what you do, Amery. I'm impressed."

"Thank you."

"But I'll confess I hoped it'd take a lot longer. That way we would have excuses for long lunches."

She gave Ronin an arch look. "So you need an excuse to see me?"

Annoyance flashed in his eyes. "No."

"Good to know. Do you want to give me a list of all the promotional items you'll need updated? I can set up the orders with the printer and make sure everything fits—"

Ronin grabbed her by the back of the neck and stopped her jabbering with a long, deep, wet kiss. By the time he pulled back, her body shook. Inwardly. Outwardly. And Ronin took great satisfaction in his effect on her. He didn't say a word; he didn't have to. He just leaned in to kiss her again.

The next kiss was lazy. A sensual exploration. He caressed the side of her face while he fed her kiss after kiss. Then he cranked up the intensity. She finally understood what it meant to be weak-kneed—and she was sitting down. If Ronin kept this up she'd slide into a big puddle on the floor.

The door opened and Knox said, "Ronin, do we have—oh, shit. Sorry. Didn't mean to barge in." Then he was gone.

Amery turned her head and rested her cheek on his. "Guess your second-in-command knows we're . . ." *Whatever this is.* She'd wait to hear what term he used to explain it.

"I won't hide the fact that we're seeing each other. The only place it might be an issue is in the dojo during class."

"I'm not dropping out," she warned. "Molly needs this class, and the only way she'll stay in it is if I'm around."

He gently tilted her head back. "I wouldn't ask you to quit."

"Then I think you should let Sandan Zach teach me."

"No. *I'm* teaching you."

She did not understand why it was so important to him, but he had that *don't argue with Sensei Black* look in his eyes, so she let it slide.

"But I don't want to wait until class to see you. What are you doing tonight?"

"A Bikram yoga class. I'm exhausted afterward. Don't you teach tonight?"

"Yes." He sucked her lower lip and gently bit down. "Since I can't see you tonight, have lunch with me."

"Did you already make reservations someplace like last time?" she teased.

"No." Ronin lifted her hand and kissed her palm. "I ordered in a light lunch and thought we'd eat upstairs at my place."

Amery had opened her mouth to say yes when Knox walked in and headed to the minifridge for a bottle of water. He drank deeply and addressed Ronin. "Are you coming back to finish our training session?"

"No. Amery and I are having lunch upstairs."

Knox's jaw tightened and his gaze winged between Amery and Ronin. "I'll remind you that you called this training session. If you're leaving halfway through, Deacon and I won't be around when you're done."

Ronin carefully placed Amery's hand on her lap and stood. He said, "A word please," to Knox before he brushed past him.

Might make her snoopy, but given the tension between the two macho men, something was going on and she wanted to know what. She hopped up and stood by the door. And she heard way more than she bargained for.

"Lose the attitude, Knox."

"Or what? You gonna discipline me?"

"Maybe I need to," Ronin said evenly. "Regardless of our friendship, I'm still your sensei and your boss."

"What is it about that woman?" Knox demanded. "You've been off your game since the moment she walked into this dojo."

Her heart skipped a beat.

"I can't explain it."

"You mean you won't explain it," Knox said hotly. "Is she why you were wandering around aimlessly at the club Saturday night?"

Amery frowned. Club? What club?

"That is none of your fucking business."

"Bullshit, Ronin. I was fucking there after Naomi, remember? And this goddamn situation has Naomi written all over it again."

Who the hell was Naomi?

"We are not discussing this. You and Deacon are done for the day. I'll finish up the paperwork on the job proposal for Stanislovsky after lunch."

Amery practically ran to her seat. She didn't want to get caught eavesdropping. She shut down her computer and looked up when Ronin reentered the room.

"Sorry about that. So about lunch?"

"Sure, if it's not a long lunch. I always have a ton to do on Mondays."

"Standard hour. No more."

Amery shouldered her laptop bag and picked up her portfolio. She watched as Ronin snagged a plastic deli bag from the fridge.

"Let's go."

She followed him down the corridor and was momentarily confused as to why they were heading away from the elevators. They passed an enormous room that had more workout equipment than a commercial gym. She stopped and looked through the glass partition that stretched to the far wall. In one corner were stacks of mats. And standing on a mat were Knox and Deacon. They appeared to be beating the shit out of each other.

Ronin noticed she'd stopped. He backtracked and followed her gaze to the men throwing each other everywhere. "What?"

"Shouldn't you intervene before one of them gets hurt?"

"No. They're training."

"For what?"

"Mixed martial arts. Deacon is a professional MMA fighter. Knox and I train him. We're trying to build a training program, but most fighters want Brazilian jujitsu instruction as well as Muay Thai. We also train others, but Deacon is our highest-ranked fighter."

"You train him because . . . you're his sensei?"

"Partially. Mostly I train him because I fought in combat sports before there was MMA and I know what it takes to win."

"Do you still fight?"

"Thirty-eight is too old to compete with twenty-something guys in their prime."

His world was so different from hers—was that why he'd deflected the question? "So this is a separate training area for MMA competitors?"

He shook his head. "This is the training gym for all students. It's open to them anytime during class hours. But when Knox and Deacon and I are working on techniques, we train up here, simply because it's closer to the offices where we spend our business hours." He tucked a strand of hair behind her ear. "How can this possibly interest you?"

Impulsively, she stood on her tiptoes and kissed him. "If it has to do with you, it interests me."

Ronin wrapped his hand around the back of her neck and kissed her with breathtaking passion. It felt completely natural to lean into him and press her hands against his chest. When she shifted even closer, her laptop bag swung and connected with the bag of food, forcing her to step back. "Sorry."

"Don't be. I like your hands on me, Amery."

They stared at each other, the attraction between them getting stronger each time they were together.

"You think it's a good idea for us to be alone in your penthouse?"

"Yes. Because the first time I fuck you I'll need more than an hour."

Oh. My. God. Amery just about came right then.

"Come on. Let's eat."

Once they were on the elevator, she said, "I don't want to seem obsessed, but I've never known anyone with a private elevator. My inner eight-year-old girl is squealing with happiness at being in a real-life Barbie Dreamhouse."

He laughed softly. "It was a cargo elevator at one time and I had it revamped. It's key-coded after the second floor since it's mostly used for the students to get to the gym."

Inside Ronin's apartment, first thing she did was ditch her heels—she noticed he didn't wear shoes in his place. They trooped into the kitchen and he emptied the contents of the deli bag. "The plates are directly behind me. If you'd grab two small bowls too, that'd be great."

He sliced the sandwich and put half on each plate. He divided up a container of salad into the two square bowls. Then he grabbed a fruit plate from the fridge and set it on the counter. "What would you like to drink?"

"Water is fine."

"Sit. I'll get it."

This domestic side of Ronin surprised her. And pleased her because she doubted he showed this side to many people.

As she checked out the food, Ronin said, "It's Thai chicken salad on rye. The salad is quinoa, lentils, and alfalfa sprouts in balsamic lime vinaigrette."

"Looks delicious. And healthy."

Ronin shrugged. "It's how I eat."

Amery scooped strawberries, honeydew melon, and canta-
loupe onto her plate. "Is there any food you won't eat?"

"Sushi."

That floored her. "But . . . isn't it, like, a law in Japan you have
to love sushi?"

"I can't stomach the stuff. And to further alienate my kind, I
don't drink tea either. Doesn't matter if it's hot, cold, green, orange,
or some flowery shit. I pass."

"Sake?"

"Sometimes. Has to be good sake, and there is a difference. We'll
do a taste test sometime."

"It'd probably be wasted on me. I'm not much of a wine drinker."
Amery tucked in to her sandwich, which was probably the best
chicken salad she'd ever had. And she must've been starving because
she finished it in record time. She shot Ronin a sideways glance; he'd
finished his and had moved on to his salad.

"What about you? Any ethnic type foods you won't eat?"

"Lutefisk, which is a nasty dish that's served around Christ-
mastime. My dad is Norwegian, so we had it every year. My mother
is of Scottish descent, so we had haggis. If I had to pick the lesser of
two evils? I'd say the stuffed sheep's intestine."

"Haven't had the pleasure of either and I'll avoid such delicacies
in the future."

"Wise choice."

Amery finished her salad and decided this healthy eating wasn't
all bad. She forked in a couple of bites of fruit and wondered how
often Ronin brought women to his penthouse for meals. Had he
brought Naomi here?

"Something on your mind?"

"Yeah. Who's Naomi?" She glanced up to catch his reaction as
soon as she'd said it.

Not a single change in his demeanor. "Where'd you hear that name?"

"I overheard part of your conversation with Knox. He indicated I'm like Naomi—or at least the situation between us is similar? So I think I have a right to know who she is, especially since it sounded bad."

"You are nothing like Naomi. Knox was talking out of turn and talking out his ass."

Amery took a drink of water. "Which is fine, but who was she to you?"

Ronin picked up the plates and carried them to the sink. After he took a long time rinsing them, he stared out the window and Amery thought she'd stepped over the line.

When he skirted the island, she wondered if he was headed to the bar and what it meant if he needed a drink to talk about Naomi. But Ronin detoured to the windows in the living area and opened them, letting the breeze wash over him.

She studied his profile. His stiff stance. Everything about this man screamed *back off*, but she couldn't seem to stay away from him. She moved in behind him, wrapping her arms around his waist and nestling her cheek between his shoulder blades. "We haven't talked about exes, have we?"

"No."

"I'll tell you about mine if you tell me about yours. And just think, this can't drag on for hours because we have limited time today."

"There's a silver lining."

"So tell me about her."

His voice was tinged with reluctance. "Naomi and I met at a . . . club. We seemed to have a lot in common. We dated. It became serious, meaning exclusive. Then things went to hell, like really went to hell, and it ended."

Talk about a short and not sweet explanation. "How long were you together?"

"Almost three years."

"How long ago did it end?"

"About that long ago."

Ronin turned around and held her face in his hands. "You're only the second woman I've brought up here, Amery. No other women have been here since Naomi."

Was that his way of telling her she was special?

He must've read the question in her eyes, because he said, "Yes, that makes you—that makes this—different." Then Ronin kissed her with bone-melting intensity, as if kissing her, giving her pleasure was his sole purpose. It was a kiss unlike any she'd ever experienced. Thrilling, scary, consuming. She wound up twisting her hands in his T-shirt, needing something to hold on to.

Ronin slowed the kiss to a soft glide of wet lips and soft smooches before releasing her. "She's in my past."

"I get that. But our past can seriously fuck up the present."

His mouth brushed hers again. "Your turn. Your ex . . . ?"

"Tyler," she supplied.

"He still live around here?"

"I'm not sure. After he dumped me four years ago, there was no further communication. I blocked him from social media. Any of our so-called friends were his friends. So it's not like I'm having drinks with them getting status updates on his life." Thank god.

Ronin led her to the couch. But when she tried to sit beside him, he settled her on his lap.

"Whoa. What's this?"

"We have twenty minutes left of our lunch. I want my hands on you while you're telling me about the douche bag dumb enough to dump you."

Amery ran her hands through Ronin's hair. "Fine. As long as you keep it PG. No touching below the waist."

His hands slid to her ass. "So I can't do this?"

She said, "No," primarily because if Ronin kept doing that she'd end up pantsless. "You didn't look me in the face when we talked about Naomi, so this is highly unfair."

"I've got a solution." He started kissing her neck. Soft nibbles and sucks, rubbing his smooth cheeks across her skin. "I'll do this. You talk."

As if she'd be able to concentrate now. When his warm mouth connected with the skin below her ear, she broke out in goose bumps and released a soft moan.

"This won't work." Ronin spun her around, facing her forward. "You make that sexy noise again and I'll have you naked in less than three seconds," he growled in her ear.

Amery couldn't resist wiggling her ass against his erection.

Ronin pulled her hair. "Stop that and talk."

"I met Tyler at a frat party our junior year in college. We were the only sober ones and hid out in the kitchen, talking all night." She would stick to the basics, just as he did. "We dated, and he said he wanted to marry me after college once his baseball career was on track. When he got a tryout with the Rockies and ended up on the farm team, I decided to move to Denver."

"Did you live with him?" Ronin brushed his fingers up and down her bare arms.

"No. At the time it was too ingrained that I'd be living in sin. If I had a ring on my finger, it would've been different. So we lived in the same apartment complex. Not quite a year after I moved here, I caught him screwing some skank. He said a bunch of horrible stuff, blamed his cheating on me, and I broke it off. I moved in with Chaz. Focused on my career."

"Any other men?"

Her face flamed. "I've been out on a few dates, but it hasn't progressed past that."

Ronin kissed her neck. "He did a number on you, didn't he?"

"Between him and my parents . . . I wonder if I'll ever have a normal relationship."

His hands slid up to her shoulders. The deep timbre of his voice caused her skin to vibrate when he spoke into her ear. "No such thing as normal, baby."

Baby. Why did she like that he called her baby? Why did she get the sense he wasn't the guy who called every woman babe or baby? Why did it make her feel special?

His hand coasted over her breasts, stopping to cup them, weigh the heft in his palms as his thumbs stroked her nipples.

Even through the cotton shirt and bra, her nipples responded. Puckering into rigid points. Making her ache.

His hot mouth skimmed over the side of her neck. "How many guys have touched you like this?"

None. But that wasn't what he wanted to know. The demand made her bristle. "Are you willing to give me a running tally of the number of woman you've touched like this?"

Ronin lightly bit her neck. "Answer. The. Question."

Amery shuddered at the eroticism of his teeth. She'd never considered biting sexy, but everything seemed new and exciting when Ronin did it to her.

"Stubborn," he whispered in her ear. "I don't have a scorecard. But I do have ten years agewise on you, so my tally of past dalliances will be higher by default." He licked the shell of her ear while his hands teased her breasts. "Tell. Me."

"Four guys," she breathed. "Guy in my hometown who popped my cherry, a random hookup at a party my sophomore year in college, Tyler, and another random hookup last year. Happy now?"

"Very. Because with that few it'll be easier erasing the memory of any man's touch but mine."

She groaned. "If you're trying to turn me into a pile of goo, it's working."

"Not goo, baby. Just want you trembling in my arms."

"I already am."

Ronin ran his hands down her abdomen and thighs, stopping at her knees. "So you are." He nuzzled the back of her head. "Will you come over tomorrow night? I'll have a surprise to show you. And no, it's not what's in my pants."

"I wasn't thinking that."

He bumped his hips up. "Our lunch hour is running out."

Amery set her feet on the floor and stood. Then she offered him her hand to help him up. She grabbed her laptop bag and slipped on her shoes before they got onto the elevator.

Once they reached the main entrance, Ronin said, "I'm done tomorrow about eight. Can you come by?"

"Sure. I'll text you if something changes."

"Same goes." Then Ronin pushed her against the wall and kissed the holy hell out of her. By the time he let her go, her mind was scrambled and she wondered if she could walk.

All that. From just a kiss.

He murmured something in Japanese to her and retreated.

Before she asked what it meant, Knox strode down the corridor. "We've got an issue. You able to handle this now?"

"Yes." Ronin offered Amery a quick bow and then he was gone.

CHAPTER SIX

THE next night Ronin whisked Amery into the elevator within thirty seconds of her walking in the building.

He didn't touch her until they were in his penthouse, herding her against the wall with the soft command "Hold still."

Not only did she hold still, but Amery held her breath.

Ronin's lips glided across hers. His mouth imparted softness and heat. And patience. Lord, he had such patience. He didn't dive in. His lips moved with erotic precision, as if memorizing the shape of her mouth.

One of Ronin's hands cradled the back of her head; the other lightly circled her neck. He held her entirely in his thrall: her body and her will.

"So warm. So soft. I could eat at his mouth for hours," he murmured, taking his own sweet time.

Amery clenched her fists by her sides, wanting so much to touch him. To feel the hard planes and the curves of his muscles beneath her hands. But she wanted his kiss—his whole kiss. Wanted to feel his tongue invade her mouth. Wanted him to consume her however aggressively or sweetly he desired.

His thumb swept across the pulse point at the base of her

jaw—a lazy counterpoint to how fast her heart beat. And still he teased. Stealing her breath with every leisurely slide of his lower lip over hers.

Finally he said, "Open and let me taste you, Amery."

Her lips parted and he sealed his mouth to hers. His tongue slipping past her teeth to stroke and lick.

The man knew how to kiss. Gradually cranking the power until she felt the change in him and his passion, his hunger rolling over her in a storm of need.

Amery returned his kiss with equal greed. Losing herself in his taste, letting him lead, but also showing him she'd follow wherever he opted to take them.

The kiss reached the combustible stage. She wanted to claw at his clothes to get to bare skin, reach down and undo his fly.

Ronin broke the kiss and pressed his cheek to hers, murmuring, "Hands at your sides."

She let her hands fall down.

His ragged breathing ruffled her hair. He remained like that until she relaxed. Then his fingers started caressing her neck. He rubbed his lips across the top of her ear. "It's humbling the way you just hand yourself over to me without question. That act of trust is a drug to someone like me."

"Someone like you?" she repeated.

"Someone who not only wants a beautiful woman on his arm and in his bed, but a woman who can truly surrender herself to a man who will give her what she wants."

"Which is what?"

"Pleasure without apology."

Amery found herself leaning into him again. "Are you taking me to bed, Ronin?"

"Soon, but not tonight."

She knew he sensed her disappointment.

"While I want you twined around me in every possible configuration, there's no rush." Ronin kissed her temple, then her forehead, and placed a chaste kiss on her lips. His hands fell away. "I promised you a drink."

"You said you had a surprise for me."

"I do. Let's figure out what we're drinking first." Ronin threaded their fingers together and led her to the bar in the corner of the dining room.

She loved the mix of old and new in this cozy corner bar. It had such personality she didn't know how she'd missed it the night he'd given her the penthouse tour. Exposed red clay brick walls, bright blue neon lighting beneath the teak bar top. Track lighting hanging from the rafters highlighted the glass shelves holding the liquor bottles on the bar-back and cast muted light over the entire area. She slid onto a sleek leather and chrome barstool.

"What'll it be?"

Her eyes scanned the liquor bottles. "Do you have every kind of booze there is?"

"I like a variety."

"What do you usually drink?"

"Depends on my mood. I'm leaning toward a gin and tonic."

"I'll have the same."

Ronin smiled. "Coming right up."

Amery bit back a girlie sigh at seeing his rare smile. With her, away from the dojo, he seemed to have a softer side. Ronin in action as eighth-degree black belt and hard-ass owner of Black Arts had a cool veneer as well as an aura of power. Everything about him screamed *discipline*.

With that cool veneer stripped away, the man oozed sex. From his unruly black hair, to his liquid brown eyes that changed from ice to fire in one quick blink, to the fullness of his sensual mouth. And don't get her started on the strength in his body. The measured way he walked—a combination of purpose and grace. The deliberateness as his hands performed a task even as simple as making a drink—no wasted movement. The man was an erotic enigma.

So . . . why was he interested in her?

She'd been so lost in thoughts of him she jumped when he slid a drink across the bar.

"See if that tastes okay."

Amery sucked in a mouthful and swallowed. Crisp, tangy, limey. She smacked her lips. "It's perfect. Is there anything you don't do well?"

Ronin thought about it a bit before he shook his head. "If it's worth doing, it's worth doing right."

"You're intimidating as hell, Ronin Black."

He offered a slight bow. "Thank you."

Yeah, she was in way over her head with this man.

"Come on."

Amery followed him inside the elevator.

He opened a small panel above the main controls and punched in a code.

The elevator moved up.

Wait. Up? Weren't they on the top floor?

Before Amery could ask what was going on, the doors opened and a breeze blew in.

Ronin took her hand.

They stepped out of a small alcove onto the roof. As soon as they turned the corner, she gasped.

Ronin said, "Surprise."

This wasn't an ordinary roof in the city with vents sticking up and razor wire strung across the roof supports. This was an urban oasis with a view of the Rocky Mountains, the Denver skyline, and the Platte River Valley. And with the added height of brick walls around the entire perimeter, none of it was visible from street level. She said, "Heckuva surprise, Ronin," and set her drink on the closest table.

The forward space had been transformed into a Japanese garden, complete with full-sized junipers shaped into bonsai trees and a rock garden with a trickling waterfall. Pots of blooming flowers were scattered everywhere. Long strips of green grass were interspersed with raised beds filled with sand and stones.

Amery looked to the right to where an eight-foot wall bisected the space. The pattern in the brick was eye-catching, as was the curved door in the center, crafted out of ornate metal. She glanced at Ronin over her shoulder. "What's through there?"

"Take a peek."

She crossed the decking, giving the thickly padded cushions on the chaise lounges a longing look. Somehow she tore her gaze from the relaxing garden and paused in front of the doorway.

That's when she caught a whiff of chlorine. "No way." She pushed through the gate and found herself in front of a big swimming pool with underwater lighting. This side had the same concealing brick walls. Tables and chairs lined the outside of the pool with seating for at least a dozen people. Torches were jammed in planters at various intervals. She squinted at the far back corner and noticed a structure with a grass-thatched roof. Tiki bar?

Amery closed her eyes and listened. She could barely hear the city noise up here. She felt him move in behind her, and her pulse quickened.

He didn't touch her even when he spoke directly into her ear. "You're quiet."

"Stunned into silence. This whole rooftop thing you've got going on is beyond fabulous. I feel like I stumbled onto an episode of *Cribs*."

"I'll admit I indulged myself. Urban living has rewards, but I need that daily communal with nature in my life, so making the rooftop into usable outdoor space was the logical choice. Maybe not the cheapest or the most practical solution, but this garden is my haven."

"How many people know about this place?"

"Not many. I guard my private space militantly. This is the tallest structure for several blocks. The only people who can see it are flying in the air above us. And even if they pinpoint the location, if they were standing on the street level they'd never find it."

She tipped her head back, intending to look at the night sky, but Ronin was right there, gazing into her eyes, his face completely unreadable.

"Thank you for sharing this with me."

"You're welcome."

"I promise I won't tell anyone."

"I'd appreciate that." Ronin pressed his lips to the pulse point at the base of her throat.

Amery wanted to curl herself into him. Beg him to strip her and take her right here on the sun-warmed cement. But the nice-girls-don't-do-that voice popped up in her head and took control of her mouth, keeping it firmly closed.

"Would you prefer to sit on the garden side or the pool side?"

"Pool side."

He kissed the area below her ear. "Pick a spot and I'll grab your drink."

She wandered around the pool, choosing a chair with an ottoman. After sinking into the plush cushion, she propped up her feet. A soft breeze drifted over her and she closed her eyes. She heard Ronin wandering around and opened her eyes to see him lighting a candle on the table.

"I feel like I'm in some tropical paradise far from the mountains of Denver, Colorado." She sipped her drink. "Do you spend much time up here?"

"As much as I can. I swim most mornings. I don't bring work up here. I keep it . . . pure, for lack of a better term."

"The sand and rocks portions on the other side . . . part of a Zen garden?"

"On a small scale. It is gratifying and mind clearing to draw images in the sand and attempt to stack rocks. Humbling to witness the resilience in nature's elements and understand that no matter how much we fight against it, we can't control it."

His mind fascinated her; he had such a unique outlook. "I hope you don't take this question the wrong way, but is a Japanese garden a family tradition?"

Ronin looked at the wall as if he were looking through it. "I never thought about the garden being a household tradition. But there's been one in every place I lived growing up, even for the few years we lived in the U.S."

That was the most he'd ever said about his family beyond the basics. "Do my questions bother you?"

Those sharp eyes were on her. "You ask me questions most people don't, which is probably why I answer them."

"I wasn't allowed to ask too many questions growing up, so I made up for it after I escaped to college."

His thoughtful gaze remained on her as he sipped his drink. "We had that in common."

Silence lingered between them.

Amery let her head fall back and closed her eyes. She couldn't remember the last time she'd been so content.

Yet she felt Ronin's eyes on her, moving across her body with as much power as an actual caress. She knew Ronin wanted her. They were adults; they should feel free to act on those desires. What was the holdup?

"What are you thinking about that's put that furrow in your brow?"

She didn't respond immediately.

"Don't try to craft a plausible lie; I'll know if you're telling the truth."

"How? Ninja mind tricks or something?"

He laughed softly. "No tricks. I can tell by your eyes. You have very expressive eyes, Amery. Your emotions are right there."

Feeling a little reckless, she opened her eyes and leaned closer to him. "So tell me what I'm feeling, Ronin."

He reached out and ran his knuckles down the side of her face, his gaze locked on hers. "You're frustrated with me. You wonder why we're not in my bedroom or even going at it right here on a chaise. You wonder if the problem is you. If you're acting too desperate for sex and if it's a turnoff for me. You also wonder if it's me. If I have some kind of sexual dysfunction."

Could he tell, even in the darkness, that she was blushing? She picked up her drink and drained it. Then she hopped up from her chair and walked around the edge of the pool. The concrete had retained some of the day's warmth as she crossed to the steps on the far end. She dipped her toe into the water before she dropped both feet onto the first step.

She sighed. Of course the water was the ideal temperature. What would it feel like to have the warm caress of water over every inch of her bare skin? To float in the void where all her senses were dulled?

"You're welcome to swim," he said from across the patio.

"I don't have a swimsuit."

"So swim naked."

Amery choked back a laugh. Right. She'd just strip and dive right in as if being naked in public was no big deal. It was a very big deal to her, and she hated that it was.

That sense of panic seized her. How had she ever believed she could get naked with Ronin Black? A man who probably had zero inhibitions and acres of muscles beneath his golden skin. Whereas she . . . had pasty white skin everywhere, the majority of it never having been exposed to the sun, or to very many men.

Right then she suspected this would be the last time she'd be alone with Master Black. She couldn't risk—

Rough-skinned hands curled around her face and tipped her head back. Ronin said, "Lose that forlorn look, Amery. And don't even think about leaving," before smashing his mouth to hers in a consuming kiss.

If she hadn't gripped the handrail tightly, she would've lost her balance and tipped them both into the pool. Her knees were feeling as weak as her will. Her head buzzed and she didn't know if this was from slamming her drink or from his powerful kiss.

When she shifted toward him, he made a low sound in the back of his throat and scooped her into his arms.

Okay. The buzzing in her brain and the zinging in her blood were definitely from this man.

Ronin sat, keeping her sideways across his lap, continuing to kiss her. A hot, wet kiss that deleted all thoughts beyond *more*. The hard ridge of his cock digging into the outside of her thigh erased her doubts about his attraction to her.

Finally he broke their lip-lock and rested his forehead to hers. "You are beautiful. Get it out of your head I don't want you because I haven't pinned you to the ground and fucked you until my knees are raw."

"Ronin—"

"Listen to me."

That tone immediately had her mouth snapping shut.

"What were you thinking when you were standing in the pool?" He eased back to look into her eyes. "Truth."

"That for all my bold talk I'm not brave enough to strip my clothes off in front of you and dive naked into the deep end of the pool."

"Why?" His eyes darkened. "Do I scare you?"

"*I* scare me. I'm not a casual nudist."

"And yet . . ." His fingers traced the seam of her capris up the inside of her thigh. "You tore off your pants and threw them at me the first night we met. Seeing those purple bikini panties? Every professional thought vanished from my head."

She buried her face in his neck. "I don't know what possessed me to do that. I've never done anything like that before in my life. I was just so . . . mad at you."

"I've been told I have that effect on people," he said dryly. "But most people throw punches at me, not clothing."

"Did you think I was crazy? Or just easy?"

"Neither. I thought you were fiery and sexy. You were real, Amery. Because of who I am . . . I receive deference, not defiance. Your response intrigued me." His lips brushed her ear. "You intrigue me. The proper girl who balks at casual nudity, yet I sense your desire to be bold. You can see yourself as the woman who strips bare to skinny-dip because it makes you feel rebellious. You want that rebel to break free."

How had he read her so easily?

"Am I wrong?"

"No. I want to be freed from the moral shackles that've weighed me down my entire life. Not in a *Girls Gone Wild* way, but like you said, to show myself that I can let go and not feel guilty about it."

"I'll help you to let go."

Her belly flipped. "How?"

"You have to trust me to find out."

But I don't really know you.

That realization didn't bother her as much as the thought of saying no to him. Amery inhaled a deep breath and said, "Okay."

"Hang on." Ronin stood and deposited her on the chair. He scooted the ottoman closer to her and sat on it. He claimed her mouth in a sensual kiss. While his tongue tangled and teased, he began to unbutton her blouse.

She lifted her hands to touch him.

He took her hands and peered into her face so deeply she swore his gaze had brushed her soul. He kissed the tips of her fingers. "I touch. You let me."

"But how is sitting here doing nothing teaching me to be bold?"

"Bold is not only an action. Bold is an attitude. Bold is a state of mind." Ronin rubbed her knuckles across his jaw. "Sometimes the boldest choice is to let go. It takes more courage to trust someone else to give you what you need than it does to just rely on getting it yourself."

"I never thought of it that way."

Ronin smiled. "Which is the perfect time for me to point out I don't want you to think. I want you to feel."

Amery had the oddest feeling of . . . surrender? Or was it power?

"I see it in your eyes, Amery. Let me show you how bold you can be." He kissed her again, his mouth coaxing hers to respond.

And respond she did. She stopped worrying where her hands should be and concentrated on the placement of *his* hands. Of the dexterity in his fingers as the rough tips brushed her skin. She let his pace—sometimes fast, sometimes slow—roll over her. Feed her. Soothe her. Incite her.

Then his callused hands were sliding beneath her collar. He pushed the shirt off her shoulders and down her arms until the fabric caught in the bend in her elbows. Rather than tugging it free, he murmured, "Perfect," and pressed an openmouthed kiss to the center of her chest. "Lean back and rest on your hands."

In this wanton position, she couldn't help arching her spine, offering him total access to whatever he wanted.

Ronin's fingers danced over her. Following the edges of her collarbones, the cords in her neck. The curve of her shoulders. "Your skin tone is amazing. So pure."

Not pure, her anti-goddess side chimed in, *pasty white*.

For once she told that voice to shut up.

He twisted the front clasp of her bra and the cups separated. Although her eyes were closed, she felt his greedy gaze on her breasts as he slid her bra down to meet her shirt.

She tried to slide her palms out, but there wasn't any give in her shirt and she couldn't move.

Not a terrifying thought; an exhilarating one, the new goddess inside her purred.

"That's it. Just you and me out here. No one knows what we're doing but us." Ronin's hands cupped her breasts. He circled his thumb across her areola, almost brushing her nipple but not quite. His hands squeezed and plumped her flesh. Her breasts weren't large, but they'd always been sensitive. Former lovers hadn't paid much attention to her chest, and she'd assumed men preferred a big rack.

But Ronin worshipped her, first with his hands. Then with his mouth. Light flicks of his tongue. Soft sucks increasing in intensity until she swore he'd sucked her whole breast into the wet heat.

He said, "I want to hear you if you like how I'm touching you."

Amery opened her eyes and met his gaze. "You think I'm being quiet because we're outside and I'm afraid someone will hear me?"

"Are you?" he asked, and blew a stream of air over the damp tip.

"No. I'm just in shock because no man has ever given so much attention to my"—*just say the word, don't be PC*—"tits before."

Ronin said, "Pity, because these tits are perfection. Soft, creamy white flesh, big pink nipples. And they're so responsive." Keeping his eyes on hers, he bit down just shy of the point of pain. "Can you come just from nipple play?"

"I—I don't know. I've never tried it."

He continued to pluck the rigid points while he moved his mouth and face across the upper swells. "Would I find your cunt wet if I slipped my hand into your pants right now?"

"Yes."

"I want to make you come. But I want to do it my way, Amery. You still feeling bold?"

"Yes."

"Say, *Make me come, Ronin. I don't care how you do it.*"

Amery repeated, "Make me come, Ronin. I don't care how you do it, but make me come now."

She felt him smile against her chest at her added plea. "Close your eyes. No matter what, keep them closed. Arch your back and spread your legs."

Ronin's voice had become velvet coercion—soft and sexy wrapped around a steely command.

He curled his hands around her face and he kissed her with the single-minded concentration that left her breathless. Helpless. Delirious. He eased back on the kiss, and one hand fell away as the other stroked her cheekbone.

He said, "Hold still," and a second later something landed directly on her nipple. Molten at first and she almost cried out from the quick pain, but then it was gone, leaving warmth in its wake. Then his mouth was on hers again, for a long, slow kiss.

She whimpered when he pulled away and whimpered louder when a splash of heat seared her other nipple. That spark of pain lasted longer and was immediately followed by another one on the top of her left breast.

Before Amery could open her eyes, Ronin was there again, his fingers on her jaw, holding her in place as he kissed her stupid.

"So bold," he murmured in her ear after he broke the kiss. "A little more and I promise I'll make you come."

More spikes of fierce pain. More intoxicating kisses. Just when she thought she couldn't take any more, and considered jumping into the pool to ease the fiery heat spreading across her skin, a breeze wafted over her, cooling her off. Along with that came Ronin's scent; she let that male musk soothe her senses, even as her heart picked up speed whenever that scent came closer. And beneath that she caught a whiff of citronella. Her mind cleared enough to realize Ronin was dripping candle wax on her.

Ronin didn't kiss her after the next pinpricks heated her flesh. His hand moved between her legs to rub the seam of her capris against her clit.

"Oh god."

Then his assault was relentless. Hot wax spattered on her chest, running down the valley of her cleavage—hot enough to steal her breath. Then Ronin's hungry mouth was licking and biting her neck, turning her skin into a mass of gooseflesh. She swore the man had three hands and two mouths with the way he touched her and teased her.

"My bold Amery," he whispered against her throat. "Are you ready to come?"

"Yes, please." She canted her hips up, wanting his hand on the zipper of her pants, wanting his fingers testing her wetness and pushing deep inside her.

"Look at yourself."

Amery opened her eyes and looked at her chest. Spots of wax dotted her skin. Her nipples were completely coated. A few rivulets ran down the plane of her belly. Seeing what it looked like, knowing she'd let him do that to her, caused her face to flame.

Ronin tipped her chin up. "Are you embarrassed?"

"I don't know. It looks like . . ."

"Like I came on your chest. Like I marked you."

She nodded.

"My way of letting you know I intend to mark you this way sometime."

Be bold. Amery cocked her head. "And if you had? If my hands were free I'd swipe my finger across that big spot above my nipple and lick it."

Ronin snarled and seized her mouth, one hand on the back of her head as he angled her backward, his other hand diving between her thighs, the heel of his hand grinding side to side, rubbing the seam directly over her clit.

The ferocious kiss ended abruptly. She kept her eyes closed as his teeth enclosed her nipple and bit down until the wax cracked and fell away. Then he suckled the tip strongly.

Amery was off balance. Entirely at Ronin's mercy. She couldn't move; she couldn't control anything except accepting that she had no control.

Ronin moved his mouth to her other breast. The wax pulled at the tender tip as he removed it with his mouth. Then he groaned and his focus was on her nipple.

The grinding rub of his hand, his sucking mouth, his labored breathing, and the intense attention he lavished on her coalesced into that perfect moment. The orgasm hit her from all sides, setting off a throbbing in her nipples, clenching in her pussy. Even him pulling a fistful of her hair added to the erotic sensations bombarding her.

She couldn't quit gasping until that moment when the pulses ended, the roaring in her ears faded to a dull whoosh, and her body quit trembling violently.

Stu-fucking-pendous. She'd never come like that. Not in twenty-eight years. She never knew she could come that powerfully. She'd begun to believe the awe-inspiring orgasm claims women made were a myth.

Not a myth with Ronin Black. He'd made her come that hard without his mouth or his cock, or even his fingers directly on her pussy.

The man had ninja sex skills too.

"I like that smile," he said with amusement.

"You put it there."

Ronin teased her lips and dragged his fingertips across her lower belly. "So I did. Hang tight for a second." He brought her upright and disappeared into the tiki hut bar.

Amery watched his movements as he crossed the deck of the pool. He grabbed something off the counter and turned around.

That's when she noticed the bulge in his pants. A big bulge. She kept her eyes on it as he settled across from her. Then she met his eyes.

"Yes, my cock is doing a steel post impression right now. That's how you affect me." He followed her jawline from side to side with the tips of his fingers.

"Do you want me to do something about that?"

"No. It'll pass." He kissed her again. "We'll test your boldness with that another night."

She laughed, mostly because this sexual teasing felt right between them. "Okay."

He bent forward and breathed on her chest, a hot wash of air that made her skin tingle. His touch as he peeled the wax away wasn't clinical, but highly sensual. His fingers stroking her skin and his soft mouth placing a tender kiss in the spot before moving to the next dot.

Amery closed her eyes, turned upside down by this man. Maybe part of her worried this was a practiced routine with him, but if he'd wanted something in return, he would've taken her up on her offer to alleviate his hard-on.

Then he said, "Done." He kissed her again while he slipped her bra back into place and as he adjusted her shirt and rebuttoned it. He rested his forehead to hers. "You know I want you to stay tonight, right?"

"I do. And you know I would if you asked me. But I understand that's not in the cards." She didn't push—for some reason he was sending her home. If he wanted her to know why, he'd tell her.

Maybe this Zen thing was contagious.

"I'll walk you down to your car."

He'd do it regardless of whether she argued with him, so she didn't bother.

Ronin rose to his feet and helped her up. "You'll be in class tomorrow night."

Not exactly a question. "I imagine." She cocked her head and looked at him. "Unless Sensei says otherwise?"

"No. You will be in class tomorrow night," he repeated. But he said nothing about what happened after class.

Amery took one last look around the garden before they got on the elevator.

"Don't worry. You'll be here again. Sooner, rather than later."

That was enough for her, for now.

CHAPTER SEVEN

GOING through the security checkpoint at the dojo still seemed weird even after Ronin had explained the reason for it. Molly had seemed more nervous for the second class than for the first.

Amery took her aside before they joined their classmates. "Mol, what's going on?"

"I feel like such a klutz in this class. Everyone else got the basics last week. I know we're moving on to more advanced things, and what if I can't do them?"

This constant reassurance was exhausting, and frustrating for Amery, because it never seemed to stick with Molly. Still, she wouldn't give up on her. "What if you can do every technique on the first try and everyone in class is jealous of you?" she countered.

Molly bit her lip. "I never thought of that."

"We're here to learn. You're wrong if you think this stuff comes easily for everyone else."

Sandan Zach clapped his hands. "Okay, ladies, let's get lined up and warmed up." He checked out Amery's attire. She couldn't help giving him a little wave that she was in the proper uniform tonight. She wasn't sure, but he might've rolled his eyes.

She'd forgotten to ask Ronin why he required this class to wear uniforms. Made more sense if they wore street clothes to learn the defensive techniques since they wouldn't always be in nonrestrictive clothing in the real world.

Amery and Molly ended up in the back of the class again. The warm-up consisted of kickboxing moves, focused on keeping a defensive stance while throwing punches. A few push-ups, jumping jacks—which surprised her because they were old school—side stretches, and a minute of running in place.

Before they could catch their breath, Sandan Zach said, "Everyone grab a partner, not the same partner you had last week. We'll drill what we learned last class."

Amery didn't have to look at Molly to feel her panic. Luckily the young woman in front of her, around Molly's age, snagged Molly for her partner. Amery watched as her classmates partnered up. With the odd number of students, she was left without a partner.

Then she sensed him behind her. How could she be so attuned to him in such a short amount of time? Yet she felt his power—the strength of his presence and how strongly he was drawn to her. Amery allowed a deep cleansing breath, but her lungs were filled with his scent.

As she waited for him to speak, she glanced at her classmates, who were unaffected by his appearance. Only Sandan Zach noticed. He bowed quickly to the man behind her and returned his focus to his other students.

Did that mean he was washing his hands of her?

"Face me," Sensei said curtly.

When Amery turned around, she swallowed a stab of longing. The man before her was not the man who'd dripped candle wax on her breasts and scraped it off with his teeth while giving her an explosive orgasm that caused her sex to clench in remembrance. He wore black gi pants and a black tunic-like top. Red lettering in Japanese and red embroidery started at the knot of his black belt and stopped at the fringed ends.

His voice was so low she strained to hear it. "Get into position and show me what you learned last week."

Fuck me. That bossy tone of his did it for her in a bad way. As soon as she assumed the position, he shook his head.

"Defensive stance. I can knock you over with little effort." Master Black put two fingers in the center of her chest and pushed.

Amery tumbled back a step. The movement hadn't hurt anything but her pride. "Why'd you do that?"

"To show you that type of balance has no place here. Again."

She resituated herself. This time he pushed his shoulder into hers and knocked her back a step.

"You are still fighting the form."

"I've been practicing yoga for eight years. The concept of balance is pretty ingrained."

"Watch me." Master Black moved into a squat position. "Push me."

She did and he immediately lost his balance.

"Watch how a small adjustment changes this into a defensive stance." He dropped into a semi-squat but turned his right foot in, keeping his shoulders in line. "Now try and push me over."

Amery placed her hand on his chest and shoved him. He didn't budge. "Oh. Now I get it."

"Face forward."

As soon as she was in position, Master Black slipped in behind her. When his hands curled around her hips, she jumped.

"Relax. Concentrate."

His heat and strength overwhelmed her. Amery wanted to turn her head and rest her face in the curve of his neck. Feel his pulse against her lips to see if he was as deeply affected by the touch of their bodies as she was.

"Stop."

I can't.

Master Black retreated.

Okay. So he wasn't bothered by being in such close proximity to her.

His voice, so even toned and precise, melted into her ear. "Here you are the student. I am the teacher. That is all we are. Understand?"

She needed to pull herself together. "Yes, Sensei."

"Return to position."

The position she wanted to be in? Naked, on her hands and knees on the mat. Ronin would have one hand fisted in her hair, holding her head upright as he fucked her from behind. His lean hips powering into her. His fingers digging into her skin, holding her in place for his sexual blitz on all her senses.

Amery could feel the give of the mat beneath her knees. She could hear the slap of his groin against the flesh of her ass as he thrust into her. Would Ronin come in silence? Would he roar?

Rough-skinned hands latched on to her chin, forcing her head up to meet his gaze. The dark pools of his eyes held no amusement. "Were my expectations unclear?"

"No, Master Black."

"Resume the position."

She moved her feet and threw her shoulders back. He pushed her, but she didn't wobble as easily.

"Better. Now find the stance again."

Amery shook it off and found the place between balance and aggression. He couldn't knock her over, but he came up behind her and put her in a headlock. Her hands went up to claw at his arm.

"Remember the training," he suggested as he calmly tried to choke the life out of her.

Fuck, fuck, fuck bounced in her brain. *Think, Amery.* She kicked out behind her and connected with his knee. That caused him to loosen the hold.

But he didn't let go, which meant she still didn't have it right.

She reached behind her and cupped his groin. His cock was completely hard. In class.

"Let go," he said in that deadly quiet, yet demanding tone.

Feeling bold, she managed to rasp out, "Maybe you should show me how you get out of this hold."

In hindsight, she probably deserved to get thrown on her ass.

One second she'd had a loose hold on his groin; the next he'd twisted her arm behind her back, knocked her to her knees, and placed his elbow on the base of her neck while pushing her face into the mat.

Ninja skills: 1.

Amery: 0.

The position didn't hurt anything but her pride. Although the man had her pinned down—when had he grown an additional pair of arms?—he still had the flexibility to put his mouth on her ear. "Smart responses will always get you in trouble. A challenge will always get answered. Understand?"

"Yes, Sensei."

He released her and said, "Stand."

Amery didn't bother to look around and see if anyone was watching them. Being dumb enough to taunt Master Black was humiliating enough.

Then the man wrapped his arm around her neck again. "Free yourself."

She raised her arms and grabbed two handfuls of his hair. Before she could pull hard, he let her go.

"That wouldn't work if I were a bald man."

She faced him. "Isn't self-defense all about adapting? I would've tried another move on a bald guy."

"Show me."

Dammit. She'd fallen right into that one.

His muscled arm snaked around her throat. This time she reached for his ears, intending to tear them off his head, but he dodged her. Same thing when she attempted to scratch his face or gouge at his eyes.

"Think."

"There isn't an automatic **response** for me yet, like there is for you," she choked out. "This is only the second class. I don't think I've even learned some of the maneuvers you expect me to know."

"Then next class you'd better pay closer attention because there will be a test afterward."

Yippee.

Master Black dropped his arm and stood in front of her, blocking her from the room. "I will push you, Amery, because I have a personal interest in your safety."

Sandan Zach clapped his hands and said, "Everyone line up."

Sensei offered her a bow and disappeared around the corner.

And she still found it really hard to concentrate for the remainder of class even when he wasn't in the room.

AFTER class, Molly was quieter than usual. Amery should've let it go, but that wasn't her way. "Something wrong?"

Molly whirled on her. "How is it fair that you get Sensei Black's personal attention? *I* was the one who was traumatized after being attacked by a homeless thug, not you. I'm the one who needs to know how to defend myself. But this class is just like everything else in my life."

"What do you mean like everything else in your life?"

"Forget it."

Count to ten. "No, Molly, you started it. Tell me."

"You won't understand. You're so pretty that everyone is drawn to you. And it's stupid for me to be jealous of the attention you're getting from Master Black, because even if you weren't there, he wouldn't be focusing that attention on me. I don't shine like you do. I'm just a bland blob that everyone overlooks."

Amery was shocked and a little pissed off by this conversation. "Why did you ask me to attend this class with you?"

"Because I didn't want to go by myself."

"So by having me there as your crutch, you don't have to mingle with other students, you don't have to step out of your comfort zone. That's what this all boils down to, Molly."

"No, it boils down to I'm a freak who's having a hard time making friends here. Then it seems I've been on the outside looking in my whole life."

And whose fault is that? Amery didn't voice that, but she certainly thought it. She'd been raised that way and she'd overcome it. Molly could overcome it too. But she wasn't even trying. "You can change that."

"I don't know how."

"Getting ticked off at me isn't the way to do it."

"So how did you meet people after you moved to Denver?"

"I made sure I was open to it. I introduced myself to my neighbors. I've tried to get to know some of the people who live on this block, whether they're working at the coffee shop or they own the business across the street. I've had smoothies with a couple women in my yoga class. I'm sure there are people in your master's program who'd love to hang out with you. Do you know anyone in your apartment complex?"

"I've met a few people." Molly sighed. "When I act bold it doesn't feel right."

I know how that goes. "Take it one step at a time. Tell yourself you're going to connect with one person each week who is out of your normal realm."

"Okay."

She pulled up to Molly's apartment building.

Molly faced her. "Thanks, Amery. And sorry for . . ."

"No worries. It gets easier. But, sweetie, you've gotta try."

"I will. I promise."

AN hour later Amery stood at the front window in her living room, watching the rare summer rain. She'd opened the windows to let the scent of warm, wet concrete fill the room. The curtains billowed in the damp breeze and droplets spattered against the floor.

There was something so cleansing about rain. Something soothing.

Her phone buzzed on the coffee table. Tempting to ignore it and wallow in the fresh air, letting the rain wash away her troubles for one night.

But she picked it up and felt that little twist in her stomach when she saw Ronin's name. She answered, "Yes?"

"I'm in back, soaked to the bone. I've been beating on the door for five minutes. Will you please let me in?"

She'd been so lost in thought she hadn't heard him. Ironic that most of her thoughts had been about him.

After ending the call, she made her way down the spiral staircase. She swung open the heavy door and momentarily lost the ability to breathe.

The streetlamp bathed Ronin in a silvery glow. Water dripped off the ends of his hair and ran in rivulets down the planes and angles of his face. Droplets sparkled like liquid diamonds and flowed down his black leather coat.

He stared at her, equally mesmerized. In that moment she knew what would happen if she let him in. But he didn't push. Didn't speak. He left the decision up to her.

Was she ready to be Ronin Black's lover?

And the answer came quickly in a mental shout. *Yes.*

Amery stepped aside.

He scaled the step and stood before her.

A cold blast of air gusted in as she closed the door, sending a shiver through her.

Her shivers intensified when she looked at him. Larger than life but so deadly still. A predator poised to pounce.

"If you get the coat dried off, the leather will probably be fine."

She continued to babble. "You can use my blow-dryer on the lining so it doesn't get moldy. There are towels in the bathroom upstairs—"

"Amery."

Just the way he said her name shut her up immediately.

He stepped forward, full of grace and purpose.

She stayed frozen, letting him come to her. Watching the rise and fall of his chest. His strong jaw was set, as was his mouth. When he got close enough she could see his face, the searing heat in his eyes had her backing up a step. Then another.

"Stop."

She stopped.

"Yes or no."

Still giving her a choice. Amery barely whispered, "Yes," and Ronin was on her, his hands on her cheeks, holding her head steady for the onslaught of his kiss.

Her mouth opened to welcome him. She tugged him closer, desperate for body to body contact, craving his passion. But he continued kissing her, holding her head hostage while the rest of her body clamored for more.

Ronin's kiss was all-consuming. Controlling. Fiery hot.

She slipped her hands inside his coat, digging her fingernails into his pectorals. Wanting to rip the material free so she could feel his heated skin beneath her hands. His mouth dragged her deeper into the kiss, deeper into him. Her pussy grew slick. Her nipples hard. Her desire greater.

He released her mouth, and whispered, "What you do to me," against her throat. "Need you now. Fast and hard. The rest can come after."

"Yes."

Ronin's coat hit the concrete floor with a wet splat. He ditched his T-shirt and unbuckled his belt.

She hooked her fingers into the elastic band of her sweatpants, shedding the sweats and panties. Next came her shirt, and lastly her sports bra.

How she'd managed to get undressed with Ronin mere inches from her surprised her as much as the fact that he was naked too.

"I see you've got ninja clothes-removal skills," she said with a soft purr, finally getting her hands on his bare skin.

"You should've seen how fast I put on a condom."

She stared at him. "You've already got a condom on?"

"Yes, because I don't want to wait. I don't think I can." He slapped his hands on her ass and lifted.

Amery wrapped her leg around his hip and he hoisted her up until both legs circled his waist. She clutched his neck as he walked backward. How could he see where they were going with his mouth doing such wickedly naughty things to her ear?

He stopped, pressing her back against the circular staircase. "Reach above you and grab on to the railing."

"But I want to touch you."

"You will. But for now, baby, I need you to hang on."

Her palms bit into the metal as she wrapped her fingers around the thin hand railing. She wasn't supporting her weight—Ronin's body bore every bit of that. Seeing the lustful expression as his golden-eyed gaze started at her breasts and tracked upward, her sex clenched.

He whispered, "Beautiful," and dragged an openmouthed kiss from the inside of her arm above her armpit to the bend in her elbow.

Amery had no idea that tender section of flesh was an erogenous zone. A soft moan escaped. Each nibble and lick sent a bolt of electricity straight to her pussy. "Ronin. Please."

One of his hands slipped between their bodies. He positioned his cock at her entrance, swirling the head through the thick cream pouring from her. "You're so ready for me."

He didn't have to tell her to keep her gaze locked on his; she couldn't look away from him. He pushed inside her on a slow, slow, slow glide until his cock was fully seated.

Amery fought the urge to close her eyes, wanting to savor the connection. The feeling of fullness. The heat and hardness of him finally inside her.

Then his mouth was on hers in a soft kiss as he withdrew. And just as slow as the first thrust was, the second thrust was fast and deep.

She gasped in his mouth as he began to fuck her with hard, steady strokes. Each time he bottomed out, tingles broke out across her body. Her nipples tightened. Her toes curled. She squeezed her pussy muscles around his shaft after every upward thrust.

Ronin broke the kiss to demand, "More."

He'd moved his hands to protect her lower back from slamming into the metal framing of the staircase. His strength was such he kept her from hitting it even as his hips jackhammered into her.

She did close her eyes then and let the reality of the situation sink in. The hottest man she'd ever met was all up in her, driving her to the point of no return, making her body quake.

"I've wanted you like this since the moment I saw you," he growled against her throat. "Sexy spitfire, throwing her pants at me."

"Ronin."

"Sassy with a side of sweet obedience." He nipped her earlobe. "I never had a prayer of staying away from you."

His words, coupled with the grinding of his pelvis on her clit, worked magic on her and she whimpered.

"You ready to come?"

"Yes."

"And if I said I wanted you to wait?" he said against her lips as he stared into her eyes, without missing a single hard stroke.

Amery was so primed, her body so super-sensitized that one more hot kiss below her ear would ignite the fire he'd started inside her. But something in his glimmering eyes offered assurance that any delay he decided she needed would be worth it. "Then I'd wait," she said softly.

That must've been the right answer, because his mouth was on hers, kissing her voraciously. He rolled his pelvis, keeping the contact on her clit continuous.

Her orgasm blasted through her and she fought the urge to let it send her spinning into cyberspace. With as hard as her cunt was contracting, Ronin would be coming right behind her. She wanted to see his face when he lost control.

Then it happened. His head fell back. His body kept pumping at the same pace, but it was as if everything had switched into slow motion. A bead of sweat rolled down the cord straining in his neck. She bent forward and licked it, which made his entire body tremble.

She whispered, "Such a beautiful man," and brushed her lips across his rigid jaw.

After he stopped moving, she let go of the railing and twined her arms around his neck, threading her hands through his hair, craving closeness from this sometimes aloof man.

"Hang on. We're not even close to done." His cock slipped out of her and he hoisted her higher on his waist.

CHAPTER EIGHT

IT was the most marvelous thing ever, being in Ronin's arms as he carried her upstairs. She pressed her lips to the side of his throat, breathing him in. The scents of man, sweat, and rain completely filled her senses.

"I like that little hum you just made."

"That's because you smell divine and it's romantic how you're whisking me off to bed."

He laughed softly.

Then they were in her bedroom.

"Last time I was up here, you had on way too many clothes."

"Not the case now, is it?"

"No." Ronin set her on the bed. He covered her mouth with a languorous kiss. She melted deeper into the mattress and tried to tug him down with her. He pulled away and said, "Be right back."

Amery was too sated to ask questions. She stretched. The sheets were cool and a little damp from the open window. Pushing the pillows aside, she rolled over onto her belly, spreading her arms and legs into an X. She loved the decadent feeling of nakedness. Although she lived alone, she rarely slept in the raw—just another weird taboo lingering from her restrictive childhood.

The bed dipped—no surprise she hadn't heard his approach—and she started to face him, but his hand on the middle of her back stayed the motion.

"Let me look at you." He swept her hair aside and placed a kiss at the base of her neck. "I'll start at the top and work my way down."

Ronin kissed and licked and caressed the nape of her neck. Her shoulders. Her arms. Her spine. Provoking her body to the point she might come again if his soft lips and rough fingers continued to trail over her skin.

Then his hot mouth found the dimples above her butt and she felt him groan. His breath drifted past those spots as he rubbed his lips across the dents. Over and over. "Your hair is strawberry blond here too. It's so fucking sexy I just want to take a bite out of you."

The image of him marking her with his teeth caused her to shiver.

He said, "You'd like that," a beat before she felt the nip of his teeth on her right butt cheek and then her left. The pointed end of his wet tongue flicked across the spot.

"You . . ." She started over. "Your mouth and your hands should be registered as lethal weapons."

"Technically they are." His fingertips floated over the back of her thighs. "Right now I want to use my lethal tongue on your cunt." He moved and said, "Turn over."

When Amery faced him, his eyes held a gleam, his mouth a smirk, and a long scarf dangled from his fingertips.

Holy. Shit. "Ah. What are you doing with that?"

"Teasing you." He snapped the end and the soft material floated across her skin in a serpentine curve from her neck to her pubic bone.

She shivered from the sensation.

Ronin twirled her scarf around her breasts, left, then right, and her nipples hardened. He trailed the fabric up and down her thighs. "Spread your legs."

As soon as she complied he teased her pussy with tiny swirls light as butterfly wings but as effective as the flick of a whip. She moaned and arched her back, wanting more.

"Amery."

Her gaze zipped back to his.

"Do you want my mouth here?" He fluttered the scarf over her sex.

"Yes. Please."

"Arms above your head."

She didn't hesitate. Why didn't she hesitate?

Because this man's touch sets you on fire.

"Beautiful. Cross your wrists."

Ronin twined the scarf around her left arm and slowly tugged it upward until the fabric brushed the back of her hand. He secured her wrists together and then looped the scarf through the slats in her headboard.

Amery couldn't take her eyes off his face. A sort of serenity had settled over him that absolutely entranced her. And those wonderfully rough fingertips trailed over every inch of her arms with lazy sensuality.

Then he grabbed another scarf from her dresser, the one with fringed ends. He dragged the fringe over both breasts, a smile curling the corners of his mouth as her nipples peaked. He twisted the scarf before he slipped it underneath her, crisscrossing the silky material above her left breast and below her right breast. He created a knot in the valley of her cleavage, and pulled the roped scarf taut beneath her between her shoulder blades.

She glanced down at his handiwork. Her small breasts did look good—maybe even tempting—highlighted with the silk scarves he'd twisted and wrapped around her.

Ronin lowered his mouth to her right nipple. He sucked. Vigorously. Then softly. Opening his mouth wider to bring more of her flesh inside. When she started to wiggle, he placed the heel of his hand on the rise of her mound and pushed her hips down.

His control of the situation, of her, ratcheted her need higher.

Amery bit her lip when he positioned himself on the bed between her thighs and planted kisses in a straight line over her belly button, her lower abdomen, stopping when he reached the start of her bikini line.

He glanced up at her. "How many times should I make you come with my mouth before I fuck you again?" He nudged her thighs open wider with his shoulders. He ran the pads of his thumbs up the inside of her pussy lips and opened her like a flower.

"Um . . . twice?"

"Good answer. Even if you'd said once, I would've made you come twice."

Ronin licked her. Delicately at first. Then he flattened his tongue and dragged it up her slit. He drew circles around her clit. Tiny, barely there circles before he pushed through her tissues and jammed his tongue inside her pussy completely.

She wanted to arch up. Dig her heels into the mattress and grind her pussy into his face. But she feared if she tried to take control, he'd remind her he was in charge by withholding her orgasms.

So Amery focused on the strength of his shoulders pushing her thighs apart and the velvety softness of his tongue. His alternating use of tender licks and brutal sucks. The soft silk of his hair tickling the crease of her thighs. He flicked her clit with a firm tongue. Once he started that, Amery knew she wouldn't last. Her legs trembled. She clenched her fists. So close. God, she could feel that pulsing need hovering just out of reach.

He made a growling noise against her sensitive flesh. Then he rapidly sucked her clit as his thumbs gently stroked the inner folds of her pussy.

The combination of relentlessness and gentleness sent her off like a rocket. She couldn't help thrashing. The scarf around her wrists tightened and she could feel the blood pulsing beneath the bindings in the same cadence as the spasms in her sex. Spasms that intensified with every hard pull of his mouth.

Then it was over and she felt strangely bereft as Ronin eased back, still nuzzling and stroking her inner thighs, kissing the skin between her hip bones.

Why did Amery have the overwhelming urge to curl into a ball and cry? Because he'd just shown her that she wasn't a cold bitch in bed? He'd proven that she could burn hot and fast with a man who took the time to find her fuse before he prematurely lit the match.

Those hard-skinned hands traveled up her sides. Ronin stroked the skin below the scarf crisscrossing her breasts. He crawled up her body, his hands pressing into the mattress beneath her shoulders, his warm mouth connecting with the skin below her ear. "Sweet baby. Has no man ever made you come like that?"

"No. It's only been like this with you. The time with the candle wax and before downstairs and now . . . this."

He dragged an openmouthed kiss down to her collarbone, the move so possessively erotic she knew he'd left a mark on more than just her skin. "I will make you come like that all the time. You're beautiful all the time. But you're especially beautiful when you unravel from my touch."

"I want you to unravel for me too, Ronin." She angled her chin and brushed a kiss across his forehead. "I want my hands in your hair, scratching your back, clutching your ass when you're fucking me this time. Please untie me."

Without a word he reached up and untied her. He checked her wrists for marks and rubbed her palms. "Any numbness?"

"No."

"Tell me if you get strange tingling, okay?"

"Okay."

Ronin snagged a condom off the nightstand.

Amery pushed up on her elbows. "Huh-uh. Hand it over. I get

to do that this time." She plucked the package from his fingers. "I'm glad you remembered them, because I'm fresh out." She laughed. "Fresh out. Right. I haven't needed them for several years."

When Ronin cupped her chin and swept the pad of his thumb across her bottom lip, she darted her tongue out to taste herself on him. She'd never dared do that before.

He murmured, "Again."

On the second pass she licked all the way around it and suckled the tip.

"Do you like that? Does it feel dirty?"

"Not dirty. Just naughty. And new."

"Next time I eat your pussy I'm going to kiss you with a mouthful of your juices so you'll know how delectable you taste."

Her pulse jumped. She looked at the condom package clutched in her hand and ripped it open.

Ronin watched as she tentatively cupped his balls. He didn't have much pubic hair. Her fingers drifted up his fully erect shaft, even longer and thicker than she'd imagined. She slid her hand up and down, seeing a milky dot of precome beading on the tip. She'd had this thickness inside her, so it seemed strange this was the first time she'd touched him like this.

That's because he's a control freak. The only reason you're touching him now is that he's letting you.

Amery didn't care. She wanted him any way she could get him. If she'd had any sexual self-confidence at all, she'd attempt to roll the condom on with her mouth. Instead she enclosed the shaft in her fist and pushed it down until that male hardness was encased in latex.

Ronin tipped her face up. Then he crushed his lips to hers and dove in for a blistering kiss as he rolled her onto her back.

Her thighs gripped his as she waited for that first hard thrust. But Ronin slipped into her carefully, slowing the kiss down to match the speed of his movements. She threaded her fingers through his hair and held on.

He broke the kiss to say, "Cant your hips."

Amery crossed her ankles behind his back, giving him a deeper angle. She arched but couldn't feel the press of his chest against hers through the binding around her breasts.

She traced the muscles in his left biceps with her tongue while she curled her hands around his hips. Her thumbs slid into the deep groove of muscle running along both sides of his lower abdomen.

"Amery."

Hearing her name as a demand, she turned her head and let his mouth reclaim hers.

This was such sweet heat. Bodies in motion. That crescendo building with every pump of his hips. She never wanted it to end.

Ronin grabbed her left knee, pushing it up and out. Then he twisted his pelvis, hitting her clitoris on every upward thrust, and his balls swung against her anus on each downward pass.

"Omigod." She'd never felt anything so deliciously dirty.

"Like that, do you?"

Amery answered in a soft moan as he did it again.

And again.

And again.

And again until she came undone again.

His stamina, whether from martial arts discipline or just from practice between the sheets, was something to behold. Something to celebrate because she'd never felt like this before. Sexy. Freed. Wanted. The way he touched her stole her breath.

He pounded into her harder. "Hold on to me."

She gripped the back of his neck.

"Look at me."

Amery tilted her head down and met his gaze.

"Beautiful."

Ronin arched back and came in silence even as his body moved frantically. He didn't slow; he just shoved in deep and stayed there.

She licked another rivulet of sweat, rubbing her face in his damp flesh, marking herself with his scent. She might never shower again.

When he came back to himself, he nuzzled her cheek. Then he stroked her skin as he undid the scarf.

"That was . . ." She fought a yawn. "Incredible. But you wore me out in bed and in class, so I'm tired."

"So sleep."

"Will you stay?"

"Yes. Let me ditch the condom."

Amery heard him in the bathroom. When he returned to bed, he snugged himself against her back and placed his palm flat on her belly, pulling her closer.

Maybe it made her weird, but she liked that he said nothing as they floated off to sleep together.

THE next morning Amery found herself alone in an empty bed and had a pang of disappointment that Ronin had left in the middle of the night.

No, he had his wicked way with you in the middle of the night.

She'd awoken from a deep sleep to his hands on her everywhere. Her breasts, her ass, her hair as he pulled her nipples into hard points. He'd slipped a finger into her pussy, then two, whispering, "You're already wet for me." He'd taken her like that, spooned to her back, her right leg draped over his as he entered her from behind. His breath hot in her ear. His fingers rubbing her clit. His cock driving into her until they both exploded. They'd even fallen asleep like that for a while.

Amery heard the shower shut off the same time "Wake up, sleepyhead" echoed up the stairs. "I brought you a cup of your favorite mocha java blend."

She didn't have time to straighten her hair, or put clothes on—she barely had time to clutch the sheet across her naked breasts before Chaz bounded into her bedroom. She really needed to remember to lock the door between her work and living space.

"You must be tired this morning if you're still lying in bed." Chaz paused at the end of the bed. "Wait. Are you sick or something?"

"No. But this isn't really—"

"'Or something' applies this morning," Ronin said from the doorway.

Chaz gasped.

So did Amery, but not for the same reason. Ronin Black was a vision of male perfection: water beading on his well-defined chest, his wet hair falling around his unshaven face, giving him that dangerously sexy look. The small towel wrapped around his lean hips above his washboard abs left little to the imagination.

"Oh. Oh, damn. I'm so sorry. I didn't realize you had company because you never have overnight guests." Chaz cranked his head around quickly. "I apologize, Master Black, for barging in. I'll just set this coffee down and go."

Then Chaz was gone.

Amery sighed. "I believe that's the first time I've ever seen Chaz flustered."

"Why? Because you're using your bed for something besides sleeping?"

She grabbed the coffee and took a big swig. "No. Because you're half-naked and that's enough to make anyone flustered, faced first thing in the morning with"—she gestured to his body—"all that."

Ronin smiled. "Keep piling on the flattery, and I'll have you pinned to the bed flustering you again."

Amery poked him on his bare chest when he perched next to her. "No fair flashing that smile at me first thing this morning either."

He swiped her coffee, swallowed a mouthful, and set the cup aside. Then he pounced on her.

"Ronin!" she shrieked.

"Ssh, you wouldn't want the people downstairs to hear you screaming my name. They might get the wrong idea."

She twined her arms around his neck. "Close enough to the truth of last night."

"And what an amazing night it was." He nipped her neck and then lifted his head to stare into her eyes. "I don't care if your friends know we're sleeping together, but I do care if you give them a play-by-play."

"I won't."

"I have to go." He kissed her. "My sweet, bold Amery . . . I'll call you later tonight, okay?"

By the time she left the bathroom five minutes later, there wasn't any sign of him.

CHAZ avoided Amery all day. Molly seemed chattier than usual. How much of that was due to their conversation after class last night?

God. Had that only been last night?

How much things could change in a few short hours.

She had a productive day, including a few new client calls.

At five o'clock, Chaz approached her desk. "It's officially the weekend and we're kicking it off with happy hour."

"First drink is on me. I'll grab my purse."

After she'd locked the front door, she dropped the metal screens in front of the windows.

"They really don't look too bad," Chaz offered. He looped his arm through hers. "Let's head to Tracks."

She stopped. "No."

"No?"

After the advice she'd given Molly, she stood her ground. "While I love hanging out with you, I'm tired of you and Emmylou only taking me to gay bars."

Chaz raised that imperious eyebrow. "What's gotten into you?"

"Common sense maybe. In three years I haven't once complained. I'm complaining now. I want to go someplace else. Someplace mainstream."

"Oh, so you've finally got a man in your bed and you selfishly want to be the only one? I'd like a man in my bed too, Amery."

"How can you throw that in my face?"

"Because you should've said something before now if you hated hanging out with me so much," he sniped.

"I don't hate it! For the last year you've harped on the fact that I don't date." She poked him in the chest. "Did it ever occur to you that the places you and Emmylou drag me to aren't the right demographics for me?"

That shut down whatever smart retort he'd been about to make.

"Admit there are lots of awesome bars around here that we never go to and that's just lazy on our part. I want to go someplace new. Be adventurous, Chaz."

He rolled his eyes. "Why can't you go to these bars with your straight friends?"

"I want to go with you. You're my BFF," she cooed.

"Girl. You are a totally different animal after you've gotten laid. Fine. We'll both widen our horizons. I know just the place. I've heard their tapas are to die for." They headed up the street, arm in arm. "I guess I should seize the chance to spend time with you because that'll change soon enough."

"Why do you say that?"

"Now that you're doing the nasty with—omigod, could Ronin Black have a more banging body?—your free time will be at a premium. And the way he looked at you today?" Chaz sighed. "He wanted to karate chop me in the face for even being in the same room with you when you were naked."

"Karate chop. Right. He's a jujitsu master, not karate."

He waved his hand. "Whatever. The point is, he didn't even notice me drooling over his arms, his chest, and his abs. Most straight guys freak out about gays eyeing the goodies. He didn't want me to get an eyeful of you."

Amery rested her head on Chaz's shoulder. "I love you. You make me feel better. Ronin is . . . enigmatic. I don't know how long he'll find me interesting."

"Sugar cube, you've got enough baggage to keep him interested for a long time."

"Oh, shut up. And for that, you're buying the first round."

PROBABLY a good thing she had a decent buzz when she got home and her cell rang. She needed a buffer for this call. "Hello, Mom."

"Amery. How are you?"

"I'm fine. How are you?"

"Oh, you know. Busy, busy. We start summer session of vacation Bible school next week. Lots of prepreparation. I swear these women who volunteer are just there as a way for God to test my patience."

She made a noncommittal noise.

"Have you heard from Aiden?"

"No. I think he's lacking basic services in Afghanistan, not just phone service."

"You don't need to get snippy with me. I was just curious. He doesn't keep in contact any better than you do."

Don't take the bait.

"It's hard to answer members of the congregation about how Aiden is doing when we, his parents, don't even know. To top it off, he doesn't acknowledge the care packages the congregation sends him, which also makes your father and me look like we raised him to act ungrateful."

Yes, it was always about appearances with her parents. Not the scary fact that Aiden was in hostile territory getting his ass shot off every damn day. And knowing her mother, she'd played that "my only son is fighting for our country" card just to get sympathy from members of her father's flock anyway. Amery shipped Aiden a package once a month and he always thanked her. She suspected he didn't want the guilt and "Jesus Saves" pamphlets in with baby wipes and lip balm from the church members, and no response would be the fastest way to put an end to it. Not so, apparently.

"Enough about your brother. I'm surprised you're home on a Friday night."

Amery wanted to beat her head into the wall. Either she was a whore out at the bars sinning, or being at home on a Friday night made her pitiable. She grabbed a bottle from the fridge and twisted off the cap. "I went out earlier."

"With a man?"

"With Chaz." Amery gulped down a mouthful of beer.

Her mother snorted a sound of disgust. "Spending so much time with a man like him will keep decent men away from you."

"What's a decent man?" slipped out before she could stop it.

"Honestly, Amery, you don't have to be so snotty. Decent men see Chaz's lifestyle for the perversion it is."

"I don't see why you care. Chaz's lifestyle isn't affecting you at all."

"It is if being friends with him is preventing you from finding a decent man, getting married, and having children. Most of your friends are already married. Quite a few have babies. As a matter of fact, I saw Jillian in church last Sunday. Her little girl, Parlay, is adorable."

Parlay? Who the fuck picked such a dumb name for a kid? "I'm sure she is cute. Jillian and Tommy got divorced, right?"

"Yes, such a sad thing. He likes to drink."

"I heard that Candy and Billy-John called it quits too. Didn't he smack her around and she finally had enough?"

Her mother got quiet on the other end of the line.

"Seems your definition of *decent* men and mine vary, because neither Tommy nor Billy-John is a decent man in my mind. So I'll stick to hanging out with Chaz."

Her mother chuffed out the noise that reminded Amery of an annoyed bull. "I see you're impossible to talk to as usual. Lord, help me; I don't know why I bothered."

She hated the quick sting those words still gave her. "Then why did you call?"

"Two reasons. First, I wondered if your business was in some sort of financial trouble. I received a phone call this week from a very rude woman who demanded details on your business practices and your personal life. "

What the hell?

"No need to curse, Amery."

Shit. She'd said that out loud?

"Anyway, I set her straight and hung up on her after she refused to tell me why she needed the information."

"I appreciate that. And I'm not having business problems, but even if I was I don't understand why you'd get a phone call."

"Which is why I mentioned it. Your father doesn't need it to get out that his daughter is under some kind of investigation."

And there it was . . . the concern wasn't about her but about the pastor's sterling reputation.

"The other reason I called was to remind you of your father's anniversary party. Thirty-five years serving the Lord is a very big occasion in his life, and we expect you to be here to help celebrate it."

Since she worked for herself she couldn't claim her boss wouldn't give her the time off. "If I come I'll probably stay at the Super 8."

"Aren't you staying with us?" her mother asked sharply.

Hell no. "I assumed you'd save beds for out-of-town guests so they didn't have to book a hotel room."

"Oh. That's probably a good idea."

"I'll let you know after I've made my reservation what day I'm flying in."

"Flying in? That seems a little frivolous when you've got a nice car."

Ten hours in the car one way? Uh. No.

"It would be nice if you'd get here a few days early to help with the cooking and cleaning."

Maybe you should guilt Dad's parishioners into doing it. She really needed to get off the phone before the snarky comebacks in her head started popping out of her mouth. "I'll let you know about my, uh, schedule."

Her mother's disapproval hummed across the line. "I'll be in touch. God bless." She hung up.

"And bless your heart too." She refused to let her mother ruin her good day and happy buzz. She popped a huge bowl of popcorn and settled in for a marathon night of bad TV until Ronin called.

CHAPTER NINE

BUT Amery didn't hear from Ronin that night.

Or the next day.

Or the next night.

And she'd be damned if she'd call him first. It wasn't a childish thing, but rather an adult thing. Accepting that she could have casual sex and not feel guilty. Granted it'd been amazing sex, best sex of her life. Now that she knew firsthand she wasn't an iceberg in the sack, maybe she could jump back into the dating pool.

Over the past three years she'd been focused on building her business, and not wanting the distraction of a relationship was a valid reason for remaining single. But she could admit part of her reluctance had been fear. Tyler's parting shot scared her. *"You're fucked up, Amery. You'll never be normal because you're afraid your daddy will find out you like sex. The only time you get on your knees is to pray, and what man wants to live like that?"*

Well, fuck that and fuck him. She didn't want to be normal. She wanted to be outstanding. She had friends. She had a good life. She had lots of things to be thankful for. And she'd damn well celebrate it and not wait for a man to swoop in and make her life complete.

So early Sunday morning she showed up for the yoga in the park class she'd always wanted to attend. Afterward she walked around, savoring the gorgeous summer day. Happy families, happy singles, happy dogs. On the way home she decided she'd throw a dinner party. After she invited her friends and tallied up the number of guests plus more for last minute add-ons, she stopped at her favorite market to load up on food. Fresh pasta, ingredients for a basil cream sauce, loaves of French bread, the makings for a salad, and double chocolate brownies.

Amery quickly cleaned her house and cranked the tunes while she prepared the food. As she was trying to figure out where everyone would eat without ending up in the office space downstairs, she had a crazy idea. She had roof access through a narrow staircase.

She checked it out. It'd be cooler up here once the sun dropped. And there was a decent view of the city blocks to the north. The space wasn't in the same league as Ronin's, but it'd do for tonight.

Emmylou and her latest squeeze—a big-breasted blonde with a Marilyn Monroe vibe—showed up early and helped her. They dragged two conference tables up to the roof, covering them with sheets of brown paper and scattering mismatched candles in funky containers. Wrapping clear Christmas lights around the ductwork added a little chic to their shabby. Galvanized garbage cans packed with ice served as coolers for the BYOB party. Then they hung a sign on the alley door directing partygoers upstairs to the roof. She made sure to arm the system and lock access to the office space. Still, it felt weird leaving the back door unlocked, especially after the recent break-in.

After checking her watch, she scaled the stairs and cut to her bedroom to get ready.

By the time she'd piled her hair into a messy bun, fixed her makeup, and changed into her party sundress with the floral poppy print, her guests were arriving.

Chaz brought his latest friend with bennies, a sweet musician named Andre. He'd also invited his neighbors, two straight guys named Jake and Lucas. Rich and Larry, a couple she'd met through Chaz, arrived with booze. Emmylou's friends Roz and Josie, also Amery's clients, showed up next. Suze and Mark, the married couple that lived in the loft next door, came and brought Suze's parents, who were visiting from Seattle.

A lot of people. Good thing she'd made a ton of food.

Molly, always so punctual, showed up last with her date, Sandan Zach from the dojo. Amery hid her shock, and resisted asking if Zach had seen Ronin. She discreetly gave Molly two thumbs-up. Ronin must not have an issue with teachers and students dating— since he was the one who'd initiated things with them.

Things. Just say it. Sex. *You had rocking sex with the man, no regrets, no promises.*

As she was slicing bread in the kitchen, Chaz's arms came around her and he squeezed. "Great idea. Perfect night, great company, the food smells amazing, and you've created your own rooftop nightclub, which is so fantastic I may sleep up there tonight."

"Thanks."

"Where'd you get the idea to host this shindig on the roof?"

She couldn't tell him about being inspired by Ronin's secret rooftop garden, so she hedged, "It's been a long time since I had a par-tay, and I wanted to do something different. Isn't it fun to see who our friends bring?"

"Or who doesn't show up." He swiped a slice of bread and dipped it in the garlic butter before she could swat him. "So, where's your hunkalicious Master Black tonight?"

"No clue. And he's not my Master Black. We banged the headboard a couple of times and that's it."

Chaz forced her to look at him. "What's really going on, North Dakota?"

He called her that when he wanted her attention. "Nothing." She smiled. "It's all good. I promise. Now, do you think we should haul the food to the roof? Or serve it down here?"

"Down here. Definitely."

"Would you be so kind as to ring the dinner bell?"

After everyone had gone through the chow line, Amery fixed herself a plate and headed to the roof.

Applause greeted her. Then Emmylou raised her wine cooler. "A toast to the excellent hostess, Amery Hardwick, for arranging such an awesome dinner party. For feeding us and for welcoming old friends and new."

Amery blushed when everyone toasted her. "I'm just glad you all came and brought friends, or I'd be eating pasta for the next three weeks."

Laughter.

She seated herself across from Larry and Rich.

Larry patted her arm. "We missed you this week. Chaz said you dragged him to a different bar for happy hour Friday night."

"Dragged? Please. Chaz put up a token protest. He's been forcing me to go to Tracks for years. And as much as I love hanging out with you guys . . ."

"Trust me, sweets, I understand. Finding a straight guy who regularly hangs out in gay bars usually means he's not entirely straight. I don't blame you for casting a wider net."

"Did you meet anyone at the bar Friday night? Or did Chaz scare them all away?"

Amery laughed. "He scared them away. You should've seen the pants he was wearing." She kept an eye on her guests while Larry and Rich bickered good-naturedly over a TV show, their cockapoo, Fritzie, and Larry's pesky mother. She shoved her plate aside.

Chaz's neighbors, Jake and Lucas, sat on either side of her with their dessert. She gestured to Larry and Rich. "Have you guys met?"

"Yes. Chaz is acting as your cohost tonight if you hadn't noticed," Rich said.

"I'm fine with that. I'm flying solo anyway."

"Beautiful woman like you?" Jake said. "How's that possible?"

She turned her head to study him. Tall. Good looking. Dark hair and dark eyes. Sweet smile. But he did nothing for her. Not the way Ronin did.

Stop thinking about him.

"So, Jake, I admit I've got a total mental blank about what you do for a living."

"We bankers are either villains or ghosts."

"Now I remember. Investment banking."

"Specializing in small businesses," he added.

She smiled at Lucas. Equally attractive. Sandy brown hair, green eyes, freckles, and dimples, but she felt no zing of attraction. "And how about you?"

"Professional mud wrestler. This is the cleanest I've been in weeks." He paused and grinned. "Just kidding. I run an at-risk management system for kids with a history of truancy."

"That's noble. Does the program keep them in school?"

"Our attendance numbers have gone up significantly, which is encouraging, and they increased our budget this year. Not to bring up business at a social event, but we're looking at upgrading our existing pamphlets with a hipper design to appeal to our demographic. The kids complain what we've got is lame and straight out of the 80s. Since you own a graphic design business, would you be interested in pitching an idea?"

Amery never turned down the possibility for new work. "I'd love to. Can you get me copies of the existing brochures and all your promotional materials?"

Lucas said, "Hey, Chaz, buddy, can you come here and bring your murse?"

Jake snorted. "Watch him get bent out of shape about his man purse."

"It's not a murse, you moron. And you don't get to make fun of my *messenger bag* since you asked me to put something in it," Chaz sniped. He lightly whapped Lucas on the back of the head with it before dropping it on the table.

"Sorry." Lucas turned and grinned at Amery. "Just because it doesn't have flowers and rhinestones on it doesn't mean it's not a purse."

Amery bit her cheek to keep from laughing.

"Anyone need anything from the kitchen?" Chaz asked. When no one answered he disappeared into the roof-access doorway.

Lucas slid the envelope in front of her. "It's all right here, including my contact info. Take a look and let me know either way if it's something you'd be interested in. We could discuss specifics over lunch."

"Thank you. I will." They discussed national ad campaigns, arguing good-naturedly about the impact of social media versus traditional media outlets.

Jake made the time-out sign. "The truth is no one knows what works." He beamed at Amery. "I'd be happy to discuss what does work in the business world—having your banker as a partner. I'd love the chance to pitch to you on why you should switch your business banking to Western National."

What was up with these two tonight? They'd hung out a few times the last year and they'd never come on this strong.

Maybe after being with Ronin Black you have sexual confidence you've been lacking and men take notice.

"Look who I found wandering around downstairs," Chaz said.

Amery turned around and Ronin stepped into view.

Speak of the devil.

"Chaz invited me up," he said to Amery.

Of course he didn't ask permission to join the party or explain what he'd been doing wandering around in her alley in the first place. Or why she hadn't heard from him at all in the last two freakin' days.

Immediately Sandan Zach stood, offering Ronin a slight bow. "I wasn't expecting you to be here tonight, sir."

"You're not the only one." He shot Amery a slightly sheepish smile. "I'm glad to see everyone is enjoying Amery's hospitality." Ronin moved to stand behind her. Keeping a proprietary hand on her shoulder, he offered his hand to Jake. "I'm Ronin Black. And you are?"

Jake seemed flustered as he introduced himself. As did Lucas. Amery saw Rich and Larry exchange a smirk as Ronin shook hands with Lucas.

Pissed off that he'd crashed her party, she stood. "Excuse me." She sidestepped Ronin and headed to the other table.

Emmylou had her arms draped over her date's shoulders as they chatted with Josie and Roz. Suze from next door leaped up, intercepting her. "Amery, thanks so much for the party. My parents are having a great time."

"I'm glad. Hey, I just wanted to say I'm sorry for not stopping over and reassuring you guys after the break-in that even the cops think it was a random incident. But then again . . . I haven't seen much of you and Mark lately. Are you both traveling a lot for work?"

"Mark is. I've backed way off on my travel schedule." She smiled serenely and touched her stomach. "You'll see a lot more of me after the baby comes."

"You're pregnant?"

Suze laughed. "Five months already."

"How exciting! I am so happy for you guys. I know you've wanted this for a while."

"Thanks." Her gaze drifted to someone who'd stepped behind Amery. One guess who it was.

Ronin slipped his hand across Amery's lower back. "Didn't mean to eavesdrop, but it sounds like congratulations are in order."

"Thank you." Just as Suze was about to ask his name, her husband, Mark, approached. As did Suze's parents. Ronin introduced himself and made small talk.

Would wonders never cease? Ronin Black was indulging in

cocktail party chitchat—with complete charm and none of that haughty sensei demeanor.

Amery murmured about checking on something and dislodged Ronin's hand from her hip. She headed for the drink station and checked the ice supply.

Footsteps sounded behind her. "Amery? Are you okay?"

"I'm fine." She adjusted the beer bottles in the ice. She kept her voice low as Molly moved in beside her. "So, you and Zach, huh?"

Molly blushed. "You told me to stop waiting for life to happen to me and go out and grab it. So I did. My knees were knocking when I asked Zach out, but I did it anyway."

"That's great! I'm so proud of you."

"Thanks. I'm proud of myself for bucking up and taking that first step." She grabbed a bottle of hard cider. "So, what's going on between you and Master Black?"

"Nothing," she answered honestly.

"I was really surprised to see him show up here."

"Me too."

"You didn't invite him?" Molly asked skeptically.

"No. Evidently he's above following societal norms like—"

"Making a phone call and keeping in touch about future plans?" Ronin intoned directly behind her.

Amery jumped at the sound of his voice and spun to face him. "Would you stop doing that?"

"No. You need to be more in tune to what goes on around you."

"You need to be more in tune when someone is pissed off at you," she snapped.

Ronin's eyes never wavered from Amery's when he said, "Will you please excuse us?" to Molly. He didn't wait for Molly's response; he steered Amery to the edge of the roof behind the duct.

Might be petulant to twist out of his hold, but she tried it anyway. No surprise she couldn't make the man budge. "What are you doing?"

"Getting you alone so I have a chance to explain—"

"Why I haven't heard from you since you rolled out of my bed Friday morning? Or explain why you feel entitled to crash a party I'm hosting?"

"Both."

Silence.

"So? If you wanted to explain you'd better start talking."

"I should've called you. But I promise you were on my mind all damn weekend."

Amery got right in his face. "Not a good enough apology, Master Black. Try again."

"Such a hardass," he murmured. "I like this side of you."

Her belly fluttered, she felt herself softening toward him, but somehow she rallied to keep her backbone up. "I liked the side of you that promised me no games between us. You told me you'd call; I expected to hear from you. And don't give me some lame excuse like your cell phone died or you were out of service range."

Ronin's eyes changed then, from cool and detached to contrite. "The truth is I owed someone a favor and he collected on it this weekend. I wasn't expecting it and it sapped every bit of energy out of me. You deserved better than to deal with that, especially since you're so used to my extremely engaging and chatty side." He brushed his mouth across her knuckles.

Even though his answer was more cryptic than she liked, she believed him, especially since he'd just proven that he could poke fun at himself.

"I *am* sorry." Curling his hand around the nape of her neck, he pulled her closer.

"Ronin—"

"Ssh. Just let me apologize like this too." He kissed her with the mix of tenderness and passion that fogged up her brain.

She intended to keep her hands by her sides, but they crept up his chest of their own accord. Within fifteen seconds of his mouth mastering hers, Amery forgot her anger with him. She forgot everything but the way kissing Ronin consumed her.

Somehow her sanity clawed to the surface, urging her to break the kiss. "Stop mauling me at my own dinner party. A dinner party you weren't invited to."

"I'll behave if you let me stay."

Amery realized he still held her hands, except he wasn't looking at her, but across the roof. That caused her to bristle up again. "I know it's not as nice as yours—"

He shut her up with a kiss. Then he pressed his forehead to hers. "Right now this place far exceeds the beauty of mine because it's filled with people who care about you. My place may be twice as big, but that only makes it feel emptier when it's just me up there. Which it almost always is."

His vulnerability in that moment spoke to her on the most basic human level. Ronin was lonely. Maybe not always, but often enough that he understood that visceral fear that it might never change.

"Fine. You can stay. Come on. I need to see if anyone needs anything."

"I need something first."

Amery's gaze snagged his. "What?"

"Your promise that I can stay with you tonight."

"Sure. Be warned; you'll have plenty of dishes to wash."

Ronin flashed her a quick, boyish grin. "Had plenty of experience with that at the monastery."

For the rest of the party, he remained at her side, being charming in his understated way. As she watched him, she noticed he kept his guard up among people, not only when he was at the dojo.

But he lowers it around you.

Now she realized what a big deal that was for him.

As the party wound down, Amery promised Lucas she'd get back to him quickly on her project proposal. Jake didn't suggest they set up a lunch date when Ronin kept a hand on her at all times.

Since Emmylou and Marilyn, aka Sasha, were the last to leave, they offered to stay and help clean up, but Amery shooed them out.

Leaving her and Ronin alone.

First thing he did was back her against the wall. The kiss started out slow. A lazy twining of tongues. But it picked up steam and soon they were kissing like maniacs. He stopped kissing her long enough to say, "Need you naked."

"Which is an awesome idea, but we have to clean up and put this food away first."

"Can't it wait an hour?"

"No. Because once I hit the sheets with you, I won't want to crawl back out. And the thought of facing this mess on a Monday morning is crazy-making enough that I won't enjoy getting naked with you if it's not done."

"Fine." Ronin backed up. "What do you want me to do?"

"Be my pack mule. Take the tables and chairs from the roof back down into the office."

He made a braying sound before he disappeared up the stairs.

CHAPTER TEN

AFTER she'd finished setting the kitchen to rights, Amery drained the remnants of her wine cooler and tossed the bottle in the recycling bin. When she turned around, Ronin was so close she bumped into him. "Hey there, ninja."

"You really had no idea I was behind you?"

"No. You are just too damn good at that stealth thing."

"Years of practice." Ronin tucked a tendril of her hair behind her ear, then ran his finger down the arch of her neck. "This is so pretty and tempting, but I'll admit I like your hair worn down."

"Why?"

"Because a true strawberry blond is such a unique color. It complements your beautiful face so well and gives it an extra glow."

"You say the sweetest things sometimes, Ronin."

"The other reason I like your hair down is that I've fantasized about having these silken tresses wrapped around my fist as I'm fucking you."

A curl of need unfurled in her belly.

"You'd like that, wouldn't you?"

"I like everything you do to me." Amery pressed her palms

against his pectorals and rubbed the heels of her hands against his nipples. "But that brings up a point I wanted to talk to you about."

He said nothing. Some of the warmth bled from his eyes.

"Thursday night was amazing." She raised her chin a notch. "You've been stingy on giving me equal time in touching you. So if you're staying with me tonight? I demand full access to your body. I expect you'll let me touch and kiss and play with it as much as I want."

Ronin placed his hand on the side of her face, letting his thumb trace the lower curve of her lip. "Demanding something that intimate from me when you've got a pretty red blush heating your cheeks is enough to make a man lose his head entirely."

"But not you."

"Don't get me wrong. I want your hands on me." His gaze dropped to her lips. "I've imagined my cock buried in your mouth many times. Dreamed of your hair teasing my skin as you're jacking me off. So, beautiful, you can drag me to your bed right now and do what you will with me."

"Really?"

"With one exception."

His thumb made those gentle sweeps on the inside of her lip, and her blood heated as she remembered him stroking her pussy the exact same way.

"I direct how you use this mouth when you blow me."

Amery didn't bristle. In fact, his demand for control took the pressure off her. She wouldn't have to worry if she was doing a good job, because truth was, her experience in that area was pretty slim. "Okay."

"You humble me." Ronin kissed her. "Is everything locked downstairs? Because once we're in your bed we're not leaving until morning."

"All locked, including the door between my office and my loft to keep Chaz out."

"Good." He let his mouth drift over her ear and whispered, "Take me to your bed, Amery."

She threaded their fingers together and led him to her bedroom. *No nerves,* she sternly told herself. *No holding back either.* She'd touch and taste to her heart's content.

Normally she'd only leave on one lamp for softer light, but tonight she flipped on the overhead track lighting. She wanted to see every inch of him.

Before she could command him to start stripping, he said, "You look gorgeous in this dress. I believe it's my privilege to take it off." He tugged at the sash tied in the back; then he unzipped her. The sound seemed so loud in the expectant silence between them. The material slipped down her arms, clearing her breasts and hips before the dress pooled on the floor.

His fingertip followed the waistband of her poppy-colored panties. Goose bumps broke out across her skin when he traced the back band of her bra. "Pretty."

"I like my bra and panties to match."

His breath teased her ear. "I was talking about your skin."

"Oh." Amery stepped out of the full skirt at her feet and bent over to pick it up. She draped the dress over the ladder-back chair and faced him.

When she started to remove her bra, he shook his head. "Leave your sexy lingerie on for a bit." He swept the back of his knuckles down the swell of her scant cleavage. "It'll serve as a barrier to keep me from fucking you blind." That intense black gaze locked on hers. "For a little while anyway."

She gestured to his dark brown polo. "Off."

Ronin yanked it over his head and threw it on the floor.

"Pants."

He pushed the tan-and-brown-flecked linen trousers down his legs and draped them over the back of the chair.

A pair of light tan boxer briefs was the last barrier. She didn't even have to say off; he did it automatically.

What an absolute feast this man's body was. Hard, sinewy muscles covered with tawny skin. He wasn't bulky, which didn't mean he wasn't completely ripped. His pectorals? Incredible. His six-pack abs were completely lickable. As was his cock, jutting up from a closely trimmed thatch of black hair. She motioned for him to turn around.

Ronin raised both eyebrows but followed her instructions.

The rear side was just as yummy. Powerful shoulders and defined back musculature that tapered into slim hips. Oh. And then there was that perfectly round butt. The hair on his thighs and calves was much lighter than on his head—not that he had an abundance of it on his legs.

Her heart thundered as she approached him. She placed a kiss between his shoulder blades and snaked her arms around his chest. Amery wanted to wax poetic about his physique, but that sort of fawning seemed to put him on edge, so she said, "On the bed and get comfy because I intend to take my time."

"You are going to milk this for all it's worth, aren't you?"

Amery slid her hands down, cupping his balls with one hand and squeezing his shaft with the other. "I'll be milking something all right."

He hissed in a breath.

"On the bed." She lightly slapped his ass.

"Baby, whatever you do to me I'll do right back to you, understand?"

"Nope."

She thought maybe he'd crawl across her bed with his animal grace and give her the molten look that made her pussy weep with want. But Ronin sat on the bed, scooted into the middle, and stretched out as if waiting for a medical exam.

That stung a little. Okay, more than a little. Wasn't he looking forward to this?

Ignore his attitude.

No, call him on it.

"How about if we just skip this? You can put your clothes on and go home."

Ronin jackknifed. "What are you talking about?"

"You could act somewhat enthusiastic at the idea of me touching you. Right now you're acting like I'm about to give you a prostate exam." She turned away, intending to leave the bedroom.

Before she made it two steps, Ronin was on her. Banding his arms over her chest, immobilizing her completely. "I'm very enthusiastic, Amery. It's just I'm used to being in control and I don't know how to act if I'm not." He kissed the side of her neck. "So the fact that I'm willing to give up that control to you? Says a lot, don't you think?"

"Maybe." She turned and twined her arms around him, plastering her lips to his. Kissing him as though she wanted to swallow him whole. As she controlled the kiss—only because he let her—she herded him back toward the bed.

Ronin lowered them to the mattress, ending up flat on his back with her on top.

Amery kissed him for a good long while. The man was such a good kisser that kissing him was an erotic experience in itself. She gradually slowed the kisses from deep to soft. Fleeting. Flirty. "You have the most sensual mouth," she murmured against his lips.

Then she pushed his arms out to the side and began kissing his throat.

"Can I have my hand in your hair?"

"As long as you don't use it to direct me."

"I won't." He paused and added, "This time."

Ignoring his warning, she nuzzled his neck and her mouth moved along the top of his shoulder. He was so strong here. The muscles had hardly any give. Her tongue traced the ridge of his collarbone. When she hit a bump, she stopped and eased back to look at the scar. "What happened?"

"You'll find a lot of marks and bumps like that. Martial arts training leaves its mark. My fighting years were hell on my body too."

Amery looked up at him. "Is that why you didn't want me to—"

"Inspect every inch of my naked body? Partially." He kept smoothing her hair with his hand.

"Partially?"

"The other reason is I don't like to be out of control, and your touch does that to me."

She leaned in to softly kiss him. "I'll be gentle. I promise."

His scars didn't matter. Didn't change anything except for the fact that she knew a couple of them had to have hurt. She kissed each one and moved on, losing herself in touching this strong man so intimately.

His lower abdomen trembled beneath her stroking fingers. His nipples—probably the most perfect set of male nipples she'd ever seen—were a dark brown and flat. Until she licked them. Kissed them. Sucked on them. Bit them. Ronin's whole body quaked and he hissed in a breath with every flick of her tongue.

So . . . sensitive nipples. Check.

Amery mapped the muscles in his arms with her fingertips and followed that same path with her tongue. As much as she drooled over his biceps and triceps, his forearms captured her attention. She'd never seen forearms muscled like that. She ran her tongue up the deep groove, pausing when she reached the crease in his elbow. And on the inside of each of his forearms were the only tattoos on his body.

She outlined the dark Japanese symbols on his left forearm with her thumb. "Does this have special meaning for you?"

"It means remember the tenets of jujitsu and embody them every day."

"Japanese in written form is so pretty."

"It's a bitch to learn to write. And speak."

"You do both fluently?"

"Yes."

She turned his right arm over and traced those symbols. "And this one?"

Ronin pointed to the top symbol. "This means birth." He pointed to the symbol closest to the crease of his elbow. "This means death." Then his finger swept over the blank space between the symbols. "It's a reminder to make the time between birth and death count."

Amery kissed all the marks. "That is so lovely. So Zen, Master Black."

"I don't know about Zen, but both are daily reminders to live my life as I wish." His hand was back in her hair. "Are you finished with your explorations?"

"Uh, no. I haven't gotten to your legs or even to your back. Why?"

"Because I've reached my limit." He wrapped his hand around her jaw and brought her mouth to his for a mind-scrambling kiss.

Stretched out on top of him as she was, his hard cock pressed into her belly. She started to grind into him, but a hand slapped her ass.

She gasped and broke the kiss. "Why'd you do that?"

He held her chin and looked into her eyes. "I don't want you grinding on me so I come on my belly." He swept his thumb across her lips. "When I'd much rather come in this mouth."

His words sent a flush through her entire body.

"I want you naked." He kissed her quick and hard. "Now."

Amery didn't hesitate. She rolled off him and ditched her underwear and bra.

Ronin sat on the edge of the bed with his thighs splayed.

Her gaze dropped to his cock. A clear drop of precome beaded on the slit. She'd never wanted a taste so much in her life.

"Turn around. Arms behind your back."

He was fully back into control mode.

As soon as she faced away from him, he caressed her arms from her shoulders to the base of her wrists. Up and down, alternating from using his fingertips to using his rough knuckles. She closed her eyes. How could a touch so simple feel so electric?

Then Ronin held her wrists together and wound a scarf up to her elbows. He didn't speak. Didn't give an explanation of why he'd bound her hands again. And she didn't question why she liked it. Or why it shot her anticipation through the roof.

"Beautiful. Turn around and drop to your knees."

Her mouth dried and her pulse sped up. She kept her balance—thank you, yoga—and lowered to the carpet.

"Graceful too. Slide forward."

She inched closer until she was directly between Ronin's thighs.

His hand cupped the side of her face, forcing her to look at him. "Suck me." Then his other hand circled his cock and he brought it to her mouth. He ran the wet tip across her bottom lip.

Amery's tongue darted out to lick it. Circling the thick head, first directly across the slit and then on the ridge.

"Open," he said hoarsely.

As soon as she'd parted her lips, the head slipped into her mouth. She sucked, taking his shaft in as she sought a more complete taste of him.

"That's it, baby. Hands just get in the way of your hot mouth. How deep can you take me?"

She shrugged.

His hand moved to the back of her head and he pushed more of his cock across her tongue. Another couple of inches. Another couple more.

"So good, but I'm stopping here." He twined his fingers in her hair. "Work me. Make me fucking crazy like you did when you were touching me."

That made him crazy? He'd hardly uttered a peep. Her competitive nature surfaced and she aimed to give him the best hands-free blow job ever.

Amery sucked him all the way to her soft palate, pulled her head back, and let the tip of his cock rest on the rim of her bottom lip before drawing the shaft in fully again.

If Ronin enjoyed it he didn't verbalize it besides the heavy breathing and the occasional tightening of his fingers in her hair.

She kept the pace steady. Without the worry that her hand was pinching his shaft too hard, her mind drifted to the sensuality of his cock plunging in and out of her mouth. Such a rigid muscle but so hot and silky gliding across her tongue. Teasing the fat head with her teeth and little whips of her tongue could make his entire cock jerk. The flavor and scent of him would be forever imprinted on her taste buds.

The slickness spilling from the corners of her mouth had nothing on the slickness between her thighs. Amery swore the pulse running on the underside of his dick matched the pulses throbbing in her swollen clit. Knowing Ronin wouldn't leave her hanging, she sped up her pace, not taking him deeper but using the suctioning power of her mouth to propel him to the point of no return.

Then Ronin's hands were on her cheeks, tilting her head. "As much as I want to feel your tongue flicking the sweet spot on my dick while you suck down my seed, I want to be balls deep in your pussy when I come." His greedy gaze watched his finger follow the circle of her lips almost pressed against the root of his cock. "If I reach between your legs, will I find you wet?"

She nodded.

"You need to come just as bad as I do." Ronin held her head in place as he eased out. "Stand up and bend over the bed, baby, because I'm coming at you hard." Gripping her biceps, he hoisted her to her feet. He set her completely off balance by kissing her with such passion before he lowered her chest to the mattress.

Amery was still reeling so much from the kiss, from the surge of self-satisfaction she'd gotten driving Ronin Black to the brink of orgasm, that she'd forgotten he'd immobilized her arms.

A condom wrapper crinkled. He sucked in a sharp breath after he reached between her legs and found her drenched. Then he opened her, aimed his cock, and impaled her to the hilt.

She gasped. She was already so close. And the rapid-fire pistoning of his hips only increased that pressure. That need. She squirmed against the mattress, searching for some relief for her aching clit.

"Don't make me guess, tell me what you need."

"Push my clit into the mattress when you . . ." And just like that he changed the angle of penetration, so every single drive gave her the friction she needed.

But he went a step further, latching on to her hips and sliding them against the sheet so the contact was constant as he slammed his cock in and out.

Pulling and pushing . . . Amery couldn't hold back the surprised yelp when she started to come. Heat and friction and throbbing and tightening. Her mind shut down to everything but the pleasure.

When the whoosh of consciousness roused her, she tried to push upright, but her arms didn't work and she panicked.

Ronin's body covered hers and he kissed her temple. "You're okay. You blissed out there for a second."

"Oh."

His heated breath drifted over her ear. "That was incredible. Thank you."

"So I zoned out while you . . . ?"

"Came like a wild man?" he teased. "Yes. But, baby, that is the ultimate compliment." He kissed the corner of her mouth. "Stay still and I'll undo your hands."

The way he untied her was as erotic as the way he tied them. With almost a loving touch.

You're reaching. This isn't love, just a case of supersized lust.

Then Ronin brought her onto the mattress and caressed her back. Not just with his fingertips, but with his whole hand. As if he couldn't get enough of the curve of her spine, the edges of her shoulder blades, the breadth of her neck, the flare of her hips, and the roundness of her ass.

And Amery was so sated she didn't ever want to move.

"Your skin is remarkable," he murmured, and bent to kiss her shoulder. "Like ivory."

"You mean sickly looking pasty white."

"No, I mean like ivory. There aren't many moles or freckles to mar the perfection."

"That's because I've spent most of my life avoiding the sun. I've had to slather on sunscreen every day since I was a little girl or else my skin turns cherry red. Then it blisters. Some of the kids I went to school with called me an albino."

It'd bothered her during junior high, when everyone was at the city pool, playing in the water and soaking up the sun. On the rare occasions her parents had allowed her go to the pool, she'd had to sit in the shade, covered in SPF 75, which had been bad enough. But add to it that she had to wear a T-shirt over her one-piece swimming suit because of the congregation's stance on modesty, and by age fifteen she'd stopped asking to go swimming with her friends.

"You tensed up. Why?" Ronin asked, zigzagging his fingertips across her lower back.

"Thinking about all the rules my parents set for me still has an impact on me, sad to say."

"Why?"

"My dad is a minister. I grew up in a hard-core fundamentalist household. Anything fun was considered a sin and would be punished by God—or my father. My mom's goal in life was to be the perfect minister's wife. Her job was to make sure the minister's children were examples of godly perfection in the eyes of the congregation and the community."

"Were you the rebellious minister's child?"

"No. I followed the rules, even when I didn't agree with them, because it was easier than fighting with my parents. By age sixteen I counted down the days until I could be free of that life and that small town. I kept my grades up because I knew college would save me. And it did. My parents weren't happy with my choice because I'd opted for a state school instead of a private Christian college. Even now I still struggle with acting bold, acting how I want to, when the girl inside me who abided by the rules for so many years tells me my actions and thoughts are morally wrong." She wanted to hide her face after that confession. Would Ronin believe, as Tyler did, that she'd never be able to tackle those demons from her past?

"Seems family expectations can bog us down no matter how old we get."

Tears sparked her eyes; he did understand.

"How's your relationship with them now?"

She inhaled and exhaled slowly. "Strained. I almost never go home. They repeatedly subject me to the *I've forgotten all my family and Christian values* lecture. You'd think they'd clue in that their shaming attitude about how I've chosen to live my life isn't making me want to come home. But the kicker is, they've never visited me in Denver. Not once in six years. I rarely hear from my father directly—which isn't all bad. My mother calls me maybe once a month, mostly to see if I've had a 'come back to Jesus' moment or if I've met a decent man. I always need a stiff drink after that conversation. Or during it."

Ronin kissed her temple. "That's got to be hard."

"It is. But I don't miss anything about that life or who I was expected to be."

"You don't seem to be carrying much baggage from the way you were raised."

She laughed. "Wrong. I just hide it well. Or try to. As I'm sure you've noticed, I'm still really modest." She looked at him over her shoulder. "Which is probably hard to believe since I'm lying here naked with you."

"And we've sinned twice too."

"My parents are probably holding a prayer vigil for me even as we speak."

He laughed.

"Sorry about the weird pillow talk."

"Don't apologize. I want to know everything about you. Even the stuff that makes you uncomfortable to talk about."

But that wasn't a two-way street. He talked, but didn't reveal much personally, only in the context of how it affected her. In response, she reverted to that "don't ask questions" girl, because she feared if she pushed him to open up, he'd just walk away.

Do you really want to be involved with a man who keeps so much of himself to himself?

Yes. She'd take Ronin Black any way she could get him.

"This is totally off topic, but are you busy next Saturday night?"

"Not that I know of. Why?"

"There's this Colorado Sports Banquet I'm supposed to go to." He smoothed his hand over her hair. "I intended to skip it, but it might be tolerable if you went with me."

Amery drew circles on his chest but didn't look up. "As your date?"

"Are you surprised I want people to know we're seeing each other?"

"Well, I wasn't sure . . . what this thing is. If we're just having fun or whatever."

Ronin lifted her chin. "Should I be insulted you think I'm some fuck-around playboy?"

"I didn't say that."

"You didn't have to. I'm not involved with any woman, Amery, besides you. I haven't been involved for quite some time."

"Why not? You're . . . perfect. Gorgeous, with a killer body, and you're amazing in bed."

He stared at her for so long she feared she'd said the wrong thing. "Because I don't do this sort of thing."

Was this his way of warning her this wouldn't last? "What sort of thing?"

"Dating. And before you get all indignant, I said that because I want to continue this with you. It doesn't feel casual to me." His eyes searched hers. "Does it to you?"

"No. But if we're going to be involved . . . or whatever . . . I need to know how long you've been enjoying casual sex. A guy doesn't get to be an expert at anything without practice. Knowing what a sexual man you are, I doubt you've gone long without a woman in your bed."

He rolled over to stare at the ceiling. "I've been selective as far as partners go. No woman lasted beyond two nights at the most. I've always worn condoms. I got a clean bill of health six months ago, but if it'll make you feel better, I'll get tested again."

That was more information than she'd expected. "I'm on the pill, but I'll get tested so we can ditch the condoms. But if we're together, I want to make sure we're exclusive." *For however long it lasts.*

"You have my word." Ronin rolled on top of her. "I'll set up the appointments for Monday afternoon. We should have the results the next day."

"That fast?"

"A guy owes me a favor."

Wasn't the first time he'd said that, and she wondered what Sensei Black had done to garner such a vast array of favors. "How far is this testing place from downtown Denver?"

"Across the river, over by me."

"Okay. But . . . I've never done anything like this before."

"I know, baby. It's necessary, but a bit of a buzzkill. Would it help if we went together?"

"Yes."

He kissed her. "So, is that a yes on the banquet date?"

"Of course it's yes. What's the dress code for this banquet?"

"Formal. I'm required to wear a suit and tie."

"I can't wait to see you in a suit." Her hands trailed down his muscular back. "Then again, it'd be hard to beat how you look in your birthday suit."

CHAPTER ELEVEN

"YOU'RE shitting me, right?"

Amery looked at Emmylou over the rim of her coffee cup and frowned. "What did I say?"

Emmylou stalked over. "We're having normal Monday morning conversation and you just happen to let it slip that Ronin Black asked you to be his date for the Colorado Sports Banquet?"

"Yeah. Why? Is that a big deal?"

"Yes! It's only the most exclusive event of the year. All the biggest, hottest names in the Colorado sports world, including current and former Broncos players, Rockies players, Nuggets players, Avalanche players, and Olympic trainers, are involved. Million-dollar deals are made at this event. They choose an athlete of the year and give an award for most philanthropic work. Not only is it huge that Ronin is invited, but it's huge that he asked you to be his date."

"I guess he's been invited in years past but he's never gone."

Emmylou jokingly beat her head on the wooden support post. That's when Chaz breezed in. *"Bonjour, mesdemoiselles."*

"Chaz, you're absolutely gonna flip when I tell you this news."

"The cast from *Magic Mike* is making a sequel and this time it's all gay porn?"

She rolled her eyes. "No, pervert. Amery is going to the Colorado Sports Banquet this Saturday as Ronin Black's date."

"Shut. Up."

"I'm dead-ass serious." Emmylou leaned forward and mock-whispered, "She had no idea it's a big deal."

Chaz put his hand on his stomach. "I might actually have to sit down."

Amery narrowed her eyes at her overly dramatic friend. "How do you know about this event? You are the least sporty guy I know."

"I know about it because everyone who's anyone in Denver goes to this event. It's not only about sports; the event is elbow to elbow with philanthropists. This event is so exclusive the catering staff and servers are subjected to serious military-style background checks."

"Why have I never heard of it?"

"Because you live under a rock?" Chaz suggested sweetly.

Emmylou swatted him. "Be nice, because you know what Amery attending this event means . . ."

"What does it mean?" Amery demanded.

"Shopping trip," they said simultaneously.

Then Chaz said, "Girl, I'm on this. This is what I live for."

"This isn't a costume party," Emmylou drawled. "Amery needs to look classy."

Chaz gave Emmylou's outfit—a floral chiffon baby doll dress, worn over ripped pink leggings, and her Doc Martens with flames on the toes—a sneering once-over. "I guess that leaves you out of the shopping excursion."

"I swear if you two don't knock it off, I will buy a dress at Kmart and call it good."

They both gasped. "No, no, no. We'll work together, we promise, won't we, Emmylou, my love?"

"Absolutely, Chaz, my turtledove," she cooed back.

Amery made gagging noises.

"Wait, it's Monday, right?" Chaz said. "You know what's open today?"

"Natasha's."

"At the risk of being outed as ignorant again, what is Natasha's?" Amery asked.

"A vintage and designer clothing boutique. She owns stores in ten states and only takes the highest-quality pieces in exchange for store credit—no cash. But the kicker is, if you drop off your item here in Denver, it won't be resold in Denver. It'll be shipped to one of the other nine stores. And it's only open two days a week."

"She moves that much merchandise?"

"That, I'm not sure of. I do know it adds another layer of exclusivity."

"So it's a Goodwill for rich people. Except with fewer store hours."

"Exactly."

Chaz didn't recognize her sarcasm.

"Go on." He shooed her toward the stairs. "Since this is a fashion emergency, we'll close up shop."

Emmylou said, "I'll grab my purse and my keys."

TWO hours later, Amery stared at the rack of dresses, more than a little discouraged. She must've tried on two dozen outfits, from funky to chic. A couple looked good, but none looked great, or gave her that *wow* factor she wanted.

Emmylou and Chaz had ganged up on her with the help of Niles, the nattily dressed salesman. They brought her long dresses, short dresses, even a couple of Halston pantsuits from the 70s that were retro enough to be hip.

Since they were convinced they knew what style suited her better than she did, Amery hadn't checked the merchandise. But while Niles and Chaz were advising Emmylou on professional outfits, Amery snuck out of the dressing room.

She'd been a bargain shopper all her life and immediately headed for the sales rack. Rather than sticking to her size, she checked the selection a size smaller and a size larger. Sometimes clothes were mismarked, and other times tiny adjustments fixed fitting issues.

Her friends were overly hung up on designer labels and tended to overlook design, while Amery gravitated toward simple styles. The pieces they'd brought to her were anything but simple. One dress had feathers around the hemline. *Feathers,* for god's sake. Feathers reminded her of being forced to gather eggs on her grandparents' farm—she'd had enough flying feathers to last her a lifetime, thank you very much.

She flipped through hangers slowly, weighing the pros and cons of each piece, while keeping an eye on the price. She spied a dress half dangling off the hanger. It was a black silk sheath, simple looking at first glance, but then she noticed the fabric overlay was threaded with silver. When she tilted the dress, it gave the illusion of movement like lightning. The beaded hem made a cool clicking sound as the clear round beads connected with the silver tube beads around the bottom edge. Although it was shorter than she normally wore, she figured the extra weight of the beads would keep the dress from riding up.

The woman next to her eyed the dress and Amery draped it over her arm and returned to the dressing room.

Even before she'd zipped it up she knew it was "the" dress. She didn't care if Emmylou or Chaz didn't like it; she felt glamorous. As if she might not embarrass herself on Ronin's arm, because, guaranteed, the striking-looking man would turn heads in whatever he wore.

"Amery, darling, I've found . . ." Chaz's eyes raked over her.

"Hey, could you zip me up?"

"Where did you get this?"

"Pawing through the sales rack." When he continued to stare at her, she turned defensive. "I didn't like anything I tried on and I don't care if you don't like this; I love it."

"I love it too. It's perfect. You are a goddess in that, Amery. A goddess." Then he yelled for Emmylou.

She poked her head in, took one look at Amery, and said, "Holy shit."

"I know, right? Our little North Dakota farm girl is all fancied up for her trip to town for the annual pie-and-ice-cream social."

"Fuck off," Amery said to Chaz. "I *can* dress myself."

"Oh, really? What shoes would you wear with that?" he demanded.

"Heels."

He rolled his eyes. "You gotta be more specific than that."

"I don't suppose you could find me a pair of silver Louboutin spike heels or black Manolo sling-backs in my size?" Amery spun and checked out her rearview. "Maybe I need something funkier. Check to see if there's a pair of Jimmy Choo booties. Or better yet, chunky Alexander McQueen platforms or wedges would be perfect for this dress."

Chaz got right in her face. "How is it that a woman who professes to care nothing about fashion can rattle off the top footwear designers?"

"I never claimed I didn't care, as my subscriptions to a dozen fashion and beauty magazines can attest. Just because I can't afford haute couture doesn't mean I'm unaware of it."

"I feel like I don't even know you. You never want to discuss fashion trends with me," he said with an exaggerated pout.

"Because then that'd be all we'd ever talk about," she pointed out. "Besides, I'm more interested in the layout and design of the ads in those magazines because it's my job to stay on top of advertising trends. I can't help it if specific fashion brands make a better impression than others."

"But—"

"Chaz, leave her alone," Emmylou warned. Then she smiled at

Niles brightly. "So, sugar, you fixin' to show us some fancier shoes for our girl?"

Amery tuned them out as they debated shoe choices. The truth was, it wouldn't matter if she picked a pair from Payless. No one would be checking out her feet in this hot little number. Wow. She was smokin'. She couldn't wait to see Ronin's reaction.

TUESDAY night she showed up at the dojo at nine when Ronin was almost finished teaching class. As much as she would've loved to see him in action, his "no observation" rule applied to girl-friends as well. She waited in the reception area for either Ronin or Knox to escort her to the elevator.

Knox showed up ten minutes later. "Amery. Sorry to keep you waiting. Sensei has been detained, so I'm escorting you upstairs."

"But . . . Alone?" She wouldn't feel comfortable just roaming around his place without him there.

"He insisted. You don't want to get me in trouble by refusing a direct order, do you?"

"I suppose blindly following orders is why you're Master Black's second-in-command ninja badass, huh, Shihan?"

Knox grinned. "It helps."

They didn't make small talk as they rode the elevator to the fifth floor. She expected he'd put her in the next elevator and then leave. But he swiped the card and punched in the code for the roof.

When Amery gave him a challenging look, he smiled again. "I know about it because I'm his second-in-command ninja badass. But that doesn't mean he lets me wander around up there by myself as he's allowing you to. He's a very private man for a reason." *Don't fuck that up for him* went unsaid.

The doors slid open. She faced Knox before they closed again. "Thank you. I promise not to run off with the silverware."

The stress of her day vanished when she entered the garden. She wandered through the tree canopy, running her hands along the smooth bark. The garden designer had created a bonsai look with the trees without all the years it took to groom a tree to that size. Pots of flowers were tucked between the trees and ringed the perimeter. She loved the riot of colored blooms, from azalea bushes to bird-of-paradise and anthurium. How often did he have to replace these plants that weren't native to this area? She paused at the sand garden and looked at the zigzag pattern. Different than the last time she'd been up here. What had Ronin been thinking when he'd drawn that pattern?

Amery stretched out on a chaise and stared at the purple twilight sky. A breeze stirred, bringing the sun-warmed scent of petunias.

Time truly lost all meaning when she was nestled in Ronin's rooftop paradise. Closing her eyes, she let herself drift into that place as relaxing as *savasana*.

Even in that dreamy state, she sensed his presence. She smiled without opening her eyes. "How long have you been standing there?"

"Long enough to plan what I intend to do to you first."

Amery didn't bother dressing to impress when she came to Ronin. She wore yoga pants, no underwear, and an athletic tank top—all clothes that could be easily stripped away. Just hearing him say he had plans for her made her wet with anticipation. Made her arch and purr because he was about to pet and stroke her until she yowled.

"Did you get the test results today?" he asked.

"Yes. I'm clean. You?"

"Clean. So I plan to get very, very dirty with you tonight. Take off your pants."

She did as he bade and waited for further instruction.

"Lower the chaise completely and remove your shirt for me."

Her blood began to pump faster as soon as she was naked. But she didn't feel bare, or exposed, just anxious for his touch.

"Your skin glows. You like being out here, naked in my garden, waiting for me, knowing I'm as drawn to you as the bees are drawn to the brightest, sweetest blooms."

Hearing the scrape of his bare feet across the cement as he erased the distance between them, Amery felt her stomach pitch.

"I can smell that honey you're making just for me. A full bouquet that's sweet and creamy on my tongue."

How could just his words turn her on this much? She squirmed, rubbing her thighs together.

"No cheating. I will take you there."

She opened her eyes. Ronin was less than a foot away, and his eyes were molten. Hungry. Assessing. He still wore his gi.

He touched her then. A single fingertip down the center of her body, from the hollow of her throat to the rise of her pubic bone. "Yes, I came here straight from class because I couldn't stay away from you another moment."

"Ronin—"

He placed his fingers over her mouth. "Do you trust me?"

She nodded.

"Drop your hands to the ground. Palms flat, press the inside of your arms against the support posts of the chaise."

Amery had to scoot down to stretch out her shoulders.

"Good. Now stay still." Ronin dropped to his knees. His hard-skinned hands caressed her forearm, from the bend in her elbow to her wrist. Goose bumps spread across the right side of her body from that simple touch.

The long strings from the chaise cushions tickled as he untied them. Then she felt the ties crisscrossing her forearm as he tied her to the support post. It didn't hurt, but she couldn't move. Then he switched sides and secured her other arm. His hands followed the length of her arms up to her shoulders and down to her breasts.

"You okay? Not cutting into you?"

"Not unless I move."

Ronin stood and straddled the chair. "Then you'd better hold still, hadn't you?"

"What do you plan to do to me?"

He drew lazy circles around her nipples. "Anything I want."

Amery's mouth dried at seeing the heat in his eyes.

More lazy circles. "Does that scare you?" He leaned forward and curled his tongue around her nipple. "Or excite you?"

Her nipple puckered into a rigid point. She wanted more of his touch, his mouth, more of him.

"Answer me," he said in that velvet rasp, sending his warm breath across the nipple he'd wet with his mouth.

"It excites me." She felt him smile against the lower curve of her breast.

He suckled her nipples long enough to make her squirm and arch up. Then he pushed upright.

Amery watched as he unknotted the embroidered black belt he wore with his gi. When he snapped the ends together, a loud pop echoed.

"I want my mouth on you. I want to lick and suck your pussy until your honey pours down my throat. I don't want to miss a single, fucking drop." Ronin dragged his middle finger up her slit and popped the digit into his mouth. "Mmm. But with the way you wiggle . . ." He snapped the belt together again. "I'd better make sure you can't get away from me." He pushed the bottom of the cushion up so it raised her pelvis. Then he placed her heels on the edge of the chair, which in turn spread her knees wide. "Such a pretty, wet cunt."

Whenever Ronin said such blatantly sexual things, she blushed from the roots of her hair to her toenails. He looped his belt beneath the underside of the chair and brought the ends up to tie a knot directly over her belly button.

With the cushion lodged under her butt, her midsection secured, and her arms immobilized, Amery was completely at his mercy.

"Every part of you is mine to touch." He put his mouth on the inside of her knee and sucked. "Mine to taste." He swept his fingers alongside the edge of his belt tying her to the chair. "Mine to tease."

When he settled himself on the end of the chaise, Amery knew why he'd pushed up the cushion; it put her pussy at his mouth level. A wave of want nearly swamped her.

"You're always speaking of balance. Let's see if you can keep your balance when I'm doing this." He licked her from the opening of her pussy to her clit.

She tried to arch up to meet his mouth, but if she moved her lower half, her heels slid off the chair.

His mean little chuckle was unnecessary.

"Did you think of me today, Amery?"

"Yes."

"When you thought of me did you imagine my tongue licking you from the inside out? Like this?" He burrowed his tongue into her channel.

She released a long moan.

When he came up for air, he eased back and nibbled the inside of her thighs until her legs quivered. His hands skated up the tops of her legs, pausing to squeeze her hips, and up farther yet to span her rib cage. "Breathe. If you pass out I might get a swelled head that I made you come so hard you lost consciousness."

Amery sucked in a deep, slow breath.

While she did that Ronin licked her clit. Then softly kissed her intimate flesh. A tender swirl of his tongue followed by gentle sucking. Kissing and exploring her pussy in the same unyielding way as when he first kissed her mouth.

And she got that same dizzying sensation—except it seemed more acute. She didn't have to push and move to get to that sweet spot where she unraveled; she knew it was coming. The buzz started behind her tailbone and spread upward. Making her belly muscles quiver, her nipples hard. She didn't stiffen up; she just let Ronin coax her to the detonation point. She hovered on the brink as he lit the match.

The wait for the explosion was sweet torture. But when that first shock wave hit, Amery might've actually screamed. Then another one blasted her. And another. And each subsequent pulse built on the last one and the skill of Ronin's mouth.

After the waves ebbed, she found herself blinking at the dark sky, wondering if she was still being tossed about in that spinning vortex. Her gaze fell on the dark head between her legs.

Their eyes met. Ronin murmured, "Again," and slipped two fingers in her drenched pussy. Those fingers expertly stroked her to another shuddering orgasm so quickly she did cry out. She'd never been so in tune with every nuance of her body's response—even with her inability to move. Maybe it was because she couldn't move and she'd given control of her pleasure to him. She didn't have to think; just feel.

Her thoughts scattered again when his hands were stroking her belly and a hot mouth brushed her breast. Then she was looking into that sigh-worthy face.

"You're beautiful," he said. "Every inch of you."

"Ronin. Untie me. I want to touch you."

He brushed a soft kiss across her mouth. "Not this time. This time it's all about you."

"But . . ." *It's always about me.* How could she complain about that? She watched as he stripped off his gi. "You don't plan on fucking me?"

"I plan on fucking you. But even then, it's still about you." Ronin balanced on his knees and slowly fed his cock into her. Once his shaft was fully buried, his hands landed on the armrests beside her and he began to move. "Wrap your legs around me up high. That's it. I want to feel your heels digging into my shoulder blades."

That changed the angle and she moaned. "That's so good."

Ronin kissed her. But it was a different kiss than usual. He kept his eyes open. He teased her lips with his; then he sank his teeth into her bottom lip. Their breath mingling, breathing each other in, staring into each other's eyes further enclosed them in a bubble where the world outside this one ceased to exist.

He quickened his pace; his thrusts became shallower.

"How long are you going to hold off?"

He nuzzled her neck. "Until I feel this hot cunt clamping down on my cock."

"Say that again."

His breath warmed her ear as his hard shaft stroked inside her. "You're so wet, so hot, so fucking tight I could spend every waking moment slamming my cock into you. Feeling this pussy milking every drop of seed from my dick. Make it happen, Amery. Make me come."

Amery turned her head and scraped her teeth up and down the tendons straining his neck. "Anything you want from me. Anytime. Anyplace. It's yours. I'm yours." She squeezed him with her cunt muscles. "Let go of that control."

Ronin emitted a growling noise and fucked her harder. Rolling his hips so the chaise bounced with his effort to get inside her as deeply as possible. A dozen nearly brutal strokes later, he stilled as his cock emptied into her.

She felt the burst of heat as he came inside her without a condom for the first time. Each time she bore down on that thick shaft filling her up, a throbbing pulse zipped from her G-spot to her clit.

He buried his face in her neck, panting as she'd never heard from him. Ronin stayed like that a long while before he whispered, "Thank you," and pushed away from her.

First thing he removed his belt. His fingers and mouth soothed the tiny red lines on her belly. Two quick tugs and he freed her hands. He immediately brought her upright and massaged her forearms to get the blood flowing. He examined her closely, tracing the marks. "Any pain or numbness?"

"None."

"You sure?"

"Positive."

Ronin continued to sweep his hands everywhere across her body. "Every time I touch you . . . I want more of you. I want you in ways that you can't even imagine."

Now that she could touch his face without restriction, she mapped the planes and angles that made him so beautifully masculine. "It's a rush that a man like you wants me like that."

"Amery."

"I'm serious, Ronin. I know we agreed that what came before this doesn't matter. But it does, because I've never had this kind of . . . freedom before. I've never had any man look at me the way you do. I've never had any man want me the way you do." *I've never been obsessed with a man the way I am with you.*

"Does that frighten you?"

"Only in that I'll disappoint you." When he started to protest she pressed her fingers over his lips. "So promise me you'll let me be whatever you need. *Whatever* you need," she repeated. "Because you've given me things I didn't even know I needed."

He closed his eyes. His whole body trembled. "I promise" was barely audible as he breathed it through parted lips, but Amery heard it, and that's all that mattered.

CHAPTER TWELVE

"I didn't spend this much time getting ready for prom," Amery complained.

"This is much bigger than prom," Emmylou said, unwinding the curling iron from Amery's hair.

Sasha, the blonde Amery secretly called Marilyn, swept powder over Amery's face. Maybe she'd lucked out that Sasha made her living as a makeup artist, but to be honest, she was half-afraid to look in the mirror. What did it mean when Sasha swore Amery would look "glamorous yet natural?"

"I still can't believe you're going to this. I'll bet John Elway is there."

"If he is he'll be mobbed. He's on equal footing with the Messiah in this town," Amery said.

"As he deserves to be."

Amery fought the urge to roll her eyes. Emmylou was a jock through and through—sports heroes were the only heroes in her eyes.

"How much longer?"

"Just your lipstick, sweets, so pucker up." Sasha started painting her lips with a thin sponge.

"Better make it the kiss-proof kind. The way Ronin looks at her . . . I think he might actually eat her up."

"Emmylou, you are such a romantic," Sasha said with a sigh.

"Back atcha, babe," Emmylou cooed.

Amery looked away as they pawed at each other and kissed noisily. When the grab-ass session continued, she slipped from the barstool and went into her bedroom. She picked up her shoes and her beaded handbag and headed downstairs. She texted Ronin: *R you picking me up in the alley or out front?*

Ten seconds later her phone vibrated.

RB: I'm parking out front right now.

She slipped on her shoes and reached the front door the same time Ronin walked in.

He stopped dead. His gaze started at the tips of her toes and wandered up her body, lingering on her hips and breasts before locking on her eyes. "You are absolutely exquisite."

Amery blushed. "Thank you."

"But . . ."

Her stomach pitched. "But what?"

"But here's a warning; I swear to Christ, if we get five minutes alone in a dark corner, I'll have my hands and my mouth all over you."

The emphatic way he growled that caused her girl parts to tingle. As much as he kept eyeing her hungrily, she returned the favor. The man could rock a suit. In black, of course, a modern cut worn with a white shirt and a subtly patterned tie. Ronin hadn't done anything to his hair, like pull it back into a ponytail when he was in the dojo, so the casual messiness of those dark, thick locks and the formality of the suit made her mouth dry and her panties wet. Amery's lust-filled gaze hooked his. "Same goes, Master Black."

Chaz exited the bathroom and marched up between them.

"The two of you will turn heads at this gala." His gaze flicked over Ronin from head to loafer. Then he said, "Tom Ford?"

"Yes."

"Sharp. Always an excellent choice. So, did you pick up my gorgeous BFF in a limo, Mr. Class Act?"

"No. I hate having someone else drive me."

"In charge in all aspects. Gotta respect that. Can I snap a picture of you two to commemorate this occasion?"

Just as she'd been about to say *yes*, Ronin said *no*.

Why didn't he want a picture of them?

Because this isn't prom, Amery. Don't act like a North Dakota rube.

Ronin held out his hand. "Let's hit it."

Amery air-kissed Chaz. "Don't wait up, Mom."

He swatted her butt. "I'm more like your fairy godmother and I'm here to lock up, so you don't have to worry about coming home at midnight, Cinderella."

"Thank you."

As she and Ronin clipped down the sidewalk, the sun's intensity had faded but retained enough brightness that she needed her shades. She didn't see his Lexus and for a brief moment she feared he'd ridden his bike. But he stopped beside a sleek black sports car parked at the curb.

"This is yours?"

"Yes. I don't drive her very often."

"This is a Corvette?"

"Corvette ZR-1. She can haul serious ass, but I'll drive with utmost caution tonight, I promise."

Amery moved in close enough so their chests were touching. "Oh, I don't know. Might be fun to go fast."

"There is that . . . thrill," he said in the silken timbre that caused her pulse to zing. "To see how much she can take when I push her to her limits."

A funny tickle started low in her belly. "Do you do that a lot?"

"Push boundaries? All. The. Damn. Time. And especially with you." Ronin tugged her against his body. "Before you slide in and torture me with those legs for the next half hour, gimme this mouth."

Ronin took her mouth; there was no other way to describe the kiss. He owned her in that moment, his warring tongue stroking and teasing hers. His passion for her was barely contained. On the outside he might look like a sophisticated gentleman, but on the inside Ronin Black was pure sexual beast.

His mouth brushed her ear. "Good thing your friends were at your place. Because if we'd been alone? I would've hiked up this dress and fucked you on your desk. And then I would've bent you over the back of the couch and fucked you again."

She trembled. "Ronin."

"And you would've said yes. Both times." His mouth meandered down her throat. "Will you spread your legs for me in the front seat of my Corvette? Let me slide my fingers into your pussy and finger-fuck you until you come?"

Her next shudder was more pronounced. "Yes."

Ronin made that low rumble in the back of his throat, and it vibrated against her skin. "At some point tonight I will have my hand up your dress and you will come for me. Anything I want, any time I want was a very dangerous promise to make to me, Amery," he whispered against her jaw, "because you have no idea what I want from you."

"I don't care," she breathed, "it's yours."

Someone yelled, "Get a room!"

Amery blinked out of the sexual fog and realized they were still standing on the sidewalk.

He placed one soft kiss on her lips. "I lose my head every time I'm around you."

But will you ever lose your heart?

Where had *that* thought come from?

Then he stepped back and opened her car door.

The Corvette practically hugged the ground and she was glad the dress wasn't any shorter.

Ronin slid behind the wheel and the car made a throaty purr as he started it. He smiled. "Hang on."

So much for him driving with utmost caution.

After a few minutes of enjoying the ride, she said, "I'm surprised you have a sports car."

"I don't seem like the Vette-driving type?"

"You have a nice car, and a nice bike, and an awesome penthouse, but you don't strike me as the kind of guy who cares about owning expensive toys to impress others."

"I don't." He picked up her hand and kissed it. "But I do like things that go fast, and buying a Ferrari or Lamborghini seemed indulgent."

Her mouth fell open. He could afford to buy those?

"Kidding. A guy I know got in over his head with this car and I took it off his hands before the bank re-poed it."

"That explains the purple fuzzy dice hanging from the rearview mirror," she said.

"Those are mine. Needed to pimp it out a little."

She laughed.

A few minutes later, Ronin said, "You're quiet."

"Nerves. This gala is a big deal to you—"

"The gala isn't a big deal to me. The fact that you're going with me is all I care about. And right now if you said let's blow this off and have an intimate dinner, just the two of us, I'd do it in a fucking heartbeat."

"You just want to get me out of this dress."

Ronin flashed her a predatory smile.

They drove through a wooded area. Before she saw the venue where the event was being held, they joined a long line of cars waiting for the valet.

"Will you know very many people?"

"I'll guess we'll see."

Amery watched attendees alighting from cars ahead of them. The women were wearing everything from full-length ball gowns to glitzy cocktail dresses. She tugged on the hem of her dress.

Ronin's hand stopped the motion. "Don't."

"I'm nervous."

"You're with me. Doesn't matter who else is here or what they're wearing. We're here to have a good time. And if it sucks, we'll leave."

"Okay."

"That said, don't be surprised if the women glare at you and the men lust after you since you're stunningly beautiful." He kissed the inside of her wrist. "And the dress isn't bad either."

It was starting to scare her how crazy she was about this man.

Ronin rolled down the window when the valet approached. "Good evening, sir. May I have your name?"

"Ronin Black."

"Welcome to the Hidden Hills Resort, Mr. Black. I will need to trouble you for a picture ID."

This event did have tight security.

He pulled out his driver's license. The valet checked the picture on it against Ronin's face and then he scanned it to make sure the ID wasn't a fake.

Really tight security.

The valet smiled. "You're good to go, Mr. Black. Brian is your assigned valet for the evening." He handed over two tickets. "This is what will gain you admittance to the event, so take care not to lose them between your car and the front door."

"Thank you."

Ronin rolled up the window and muttered, "Jesus." He looked over at Amery. "I can pull a U-turn. It's not too late to get out of here."

"I'll hold the tickets." Grinning, she snatched them from his hand and shoved them in her bra. "See? Perfectly safe."

It took another ten minutes before they reached the valet stand,

and Amery was getting antsy, but Ronin stayed calm. She wished his calm demeanor would settle her down. Immediately after he put it in park, both doors were opened. He said, "Stay put, I'll help you out," and exited the car.

What was that about? She heard him instructing the valet and then he skirted the front end of the car. He offered her his hand. Once they were on the sidewalk, a person with a clipboard approached them. "Good evening and welcome. May I please see your tickets?"

Ronin's eyes were on Amery's as he traced the line of her throat from her chin to her cleavage. A devilish smile lit his eyes as his fingers deftly slipped inside her bra cup and fished the tickets out. "Here you go."

That flustered the girl with the clipboard. "Ah, thanks I just needed to see them. The tickets are actually being taken at the door."

Ronin kept his hand on the small of Amery's back and guided her to the main doors. The ticket taker scanned the tickets—as if checking for forgeries?—before smiling and granting them access.

"I think it would be easier to crash a White House party than this one," Ronin murmured.

"So if we get the standard shitty rubberized banquet chicken, overcooked green beans, and warm cheesecake, I'll be pissed."

"That'll make two of us. For the price of these tickets we should be served Kobe beef and Russian caviar for every course."

The wide hallway teemed with people. Some of the dresses bordered on spectacular, and Amery wanted a closer peek, but it'd be a faux pas to gawk, so she feigned aloofness.

He slid his arm around her back and settled his hand on her hip. "Would you like a drink?"

"No, I'd like five drinks."

"How about we start with one?" Ronin steered her out of the room and down the opposite hallway. He nodded to several people but didn't stop to speak to anyone. A waiter held a tray of champagne.

"Ooh, I'd like some of that."

He snagged two glasses and handed one to her. "May tonight be full of welcome surprises."

Amery clinked the crystal flute against his and drank. Okay, that was really good. "This is not Brut champagne."

"No, but don't ask me what it is because I'm not a wine connoisseur." His molten gaze drifted over her. "But looking at you, I know I have the absolute finest taste in women."

Amery blushed.

"I'd like nothing better than to taste you right now. Suck the champagne from your tongue. Lick it from your lips. Pour it down the center of your body and lap it from between your thighs."

Her belly swooped.

"I like that all I have to do is look in your eyes and I see what you're feeling."

"So you know what I'm feeling right now?" she countered.

Ronin let his knuckles follow the curve of her jaw. "You're turned on but you don't want to be. You're trying hard to fit in, but you outshine them all. And you're wondering why I'm saying all this now when we're in public. Maybe someone will overhear. But I don't give a good goddamn if that happens."

"Does that drummer in your head always do his own thing?"

"Always."

She drained her champagne and grabbed another glass before hooking her arm through his. "Let's mingle. I want to spot some celebrities."

"Anyone in particular?"

"The only mover and shaker I know in Denver is Alexis Carrington."

He shook his head. "Fictional TV character. Try again."

"I was so hoping for a catfight between her and Krystle—a hair-pulling, clothes-ripping, shoe-throwing beat-down."

"Aren't you a little young to have grown up watching *Dynasty*?"

"I watched reruns every day after school. My mother, for being a self-professed happy homemaker, wasn't happy when school dismissed for the day. She let me and my brother watch whatever we wanted. Yes, we did make fun of it, but it was an eye-opener as to how the really rich lived. Not a lot of billionaires in North Dakota." She laughed. "I wouldn't know how to act if I ever met a billionaire anyway."

"I'm sure you'd do just fine. Nothing special about them, trust me."

They'd almost crossed into the banquet hall when a voice boomed, "Ronin Black." Then an African-American guy about six foot five and three hundred and fifty pounds blocked their path. "I thought my eyes were playing tricks on me. Sensei Black. In the flesh. At a party. But here you are." He offered a formal bow, which Ronin returned. Then he thrust out his hand. "Man, it's good to see you."

"Same goes." Ronin drew her forward. "Tegs Green, meet Amery Hardwick."

"Pleased to meet you," Amery said.

"You too." Tegs grinned. "Got you a real foxy one, eh? She know about the time I whipped up on the unbeatable Master Black?"

"You sitting on me and squashing me like a bug hardly qualifies as a true victory, Tegs. And I choked you out after you let me up, so no whipping up on me there either."

"I always forget that you wrapped those lethal fingers around my throat until I passed the motherfuck out."

"Which is why I always remind you."

"Such a hardass." Tegs addressed Amery. "This psycho fucker made me run three miles on a treadmill. Three miles," he repeated.

"Look at this body. Do you think it fucking *enjoys* running? Hell no. But I did it. Puked like a frat boy on the first weekend of college afterward, but I goddamn did it."

Amery had heard Ronin acted as a personal trainer, but this was the first evidence she'd seen of it. "Good for you. I keep trying to convince him to teach me a shoulder throw."

Tegs laughed. "Little-bitty sprite like you throwing grown men around? You go, sister." He held out his knuckles for a fist bump. "I hope the first guy you throw on his ass is that sadistic fucker Deacon, 'cause I'd pay good money to see that."

"Deacon didn't like it any better than I did when you sat on him," Ronin said.

"Don't matter. S'what I get paid to do." He clapped Ronin on back. "Really great to see you out and about, old-timer."

After Tegs left, Amery said, "He's some kind of sports guy, right?"

"Tegs plays offensive tackle for the Broncos."

"Should I have recognized him?"

"Only if you're a football fan."

"Are you a die-hard sports fan?"

He shrugged. "I'll watch a game if it's on. I try to keep up with what's going on locally. But I'm not a fanatic."

A shadow fell over them again.

Ronin faced Tegs. "What now?"

Tegs's hands came up in surrender. "Whoa. Don't shoot the messenger. Krueger wants to talk to you."

"About?"

"How the fuck do I know? He heard you were here, said you've been ditching his calls, and he told me to ask you for five minutes of your time." Tegs shot Amery an apologetic smile. "Quick business thing, pretty lady. I'll bring him right back."

She watched as the Master Black mask dropped back into place. Ronin said, "Amery, don't wander off. This won't take long."

The man didn't even crack a smile when she saluted.

None of the people milling about were friendly, except for a pervert or two she caught eyeing her ass. In lieu of starting a conversation with a stranger, she downed another glass of champagne, wondering how she'd ended up ditched at a cocktail party within fifteen minutes of arrival. This was what had kept her up last night: Ronin knowing everyone. Her knowing no one. Him leaving her alone while he roamed around.

What she wouldn't give to see one familiar face.

That's when she heard, "Amery?"

She froze. Goddammit. The one time in her life she'd gotten what she'd wished for, she'd ended up with the one person she'd hoped never to see again. Maybe if she ignored him he'd think he was mistaken and walk away.

Please let him walk away.

Before she could vanish into the crowd, Tyler stepped in front of her.

He wore an expression of shock. "Amery Hardwick. It is you." Tyler pulled her into his arms. "My god, it's been what? Four years since we've seen each other?"

"Yes," she said, trying to disentangle from his embrace.

But Tyler wasn't letting her go. He scrutinized her face. "You look fantastic. Like really fantastic."

"Thanks. I need to—"

"Stay and talk with me. We've got a lot of catching up to do."

No, they didn't. But if she didn't act as if she wanted to escape, then maybe she'd satisfy his curiosity and he'd move on. Quickly. "I didn't realize you were still in Denver."

"Left for about a year to oversee the Rockies feeder teams. When I returned management promoted me. And I also work with the pitching staff, so I've got the best of both worlds."

"Sounds great." Amery tried not to stand on tiptoe and peer over his shoulder for a glimpse of Ronin.

"I'm living in Cherry Creek now."

"That's nice."

"One of the perks of being upper-level management is I get to attend this event every year."

"Lucky you."

Tyler went on to tell how awesome his life was and never stopped to take a breath or to ask about her. He hadn't changed a bit. How had she ever found the me-me-me aspect to him attractive? Yes, he was a good-looking guy, but as she stood in front of him, trapped by his gigantic ego, she couldn't remember what she'd ever seen in him.

Confidence. He had it; you lacked it.

That was the one good thing that'd come out of their relationship. In trying to emulate him she'd learned to act more confident—even if she had to fake it.

He was frowning at her. Oops. Had he noticed she'd tuned him out? "Sorry, I didn't catch that last part."

"I'm here with Chantal."

"You two are still together?"

"We've had a breakup or two over the years, which is why I'm dragging my feet on giving her the engagement ring she's been nagging me about."

Yeah, Chantal and Tyler deserved each other.

"Who are you here with?" Tyler asked.

"She's with me," Ronin said, sliding his arm around her waist.

Tyler's eyes widened so fast she almost heard a cartoonish *sproing.*

Then Ronin offered his hand. "Ronin Black. And you are?"

"I know who you are, Sensei Black. I'm Tyler Pessac. I'm with the Rockies management team."

"How do you know Amery? Or did you just see a beautiful woman standing alone and decide to hit on her?"

Tyler shot her a grin. At one time she would've considered it the cutest thing ever. Now it came across as super-cheesy.

"Amery and I were involved for a few years before and after we moved to Denver." When Tyler's gaze scanned her thoroughly, Amery felt as if she'd been slimed. "Damn, Ame, you're a knockout tonight."

Ronin's demeanor didn't change. "Yes, she is. And she's all mine. So if you'll excuse us . . ." And Ronin steered her away.

Once they were far enough away, Amery spun in front of him, forcing him to stop. "Mine? What was that?"

"A friendly reminder that your past with him is just that, long past." He pressed his lips against her temple. "Shall we track down the dining area?"

Just like that he changed the subject and led her away.

CHAPTER THIRTEEN

THE dining room defined opulence. Forty-foot-high ceilings with mahogany crown molding, a preponderance of sparkly crystal chandeliers, silk-covered walls, carpeting that mimicked a pricey Persian rug.

The already beautiful space had been further transformed. Each table had different jewel-toned linen. From the back of the room, the hundred or so colored tables spread out like a rainbow, darkest to lightest. The glassware on each table was clear, reflecting the individual color, creating the illusion that each table had customized glassware. The centerpiece on each table initially looked tacky—artificial flowers with color-changing LED lights on the edges of the leaves and flowers. But as Amery watched the lights morphing from one shade of the rainbow to the next, she noticed the effect sent tiny shards of light outward, so it looked as if diamonds had been sprinkled across the table.

This was one of the coolest decorating themes she'd ever seen.

And the Hidden Hills Resort didn't allow its members to sit on padded metal conference chairs. No, every chair was draped in the same fabric as the table.

A female server intercepted them as they tried to cut through the tables. "One of the staff members with the clipboard will have your seat assignments."

"I'd forgotten about that. Thank you."

Assigned seating felt a little junior high-ish. Were the attendees deemed more important seated at a better table with other bigwigs? Maybe it was the champagne, but Amery could give a shit where she and Ronin ended up. In her mind he remained the most interesting person in the room—regardless of how many people filled the space.

After they were properly seated, she snuck a look at him and bit back a feminine sigh.

Ronin's mouth brushed her ear. "What's the smirk for?"

"Just thinking about how sexy you look in that suit. But as nice as the wrapper is, it's the body beneath that gets me all hot and bothered."

"You always so flirty and flattering when you drink champagne?"

She laughed softly. "I'm serious."

"I know." He placed a kiss below her ear. "Which is why I'll make sure the champagne keeps flowing."

"Maybe that's not the best idea. I do all sorts of crazy things when I'm tipsy."

"If this shindig gets dull, I have ideas on how we can liven things up." Ronin's hand slid up her leg.

"Ronin. Behave."

"No." His teeth enclosed her earlobe and he tugged. "And don't pretend you want me to be the gentleman in the suit. You prefer the master in the gi."

To anyone else it would appear that she and Ronin were having a private conversation. But when he whispered against her skin in that rough voice, she was done in. Add in the erotic way his thumb stroked the inside of her thigh, the continual pass of his warm lips beneath her ear . . . Amery wanted to grab him by his fancy tie, drag him into the coat check room, and fuck him stupid.

"I like that purring sound you just made," he murmured against her throat. "Remember earlier when you said you'd give me anything I wanted?"

"No."

"That's okay because I do. But I'll warn you, baby, I will push your boundaries tonight."

Amery managed to stop the spinning in her head long enough to place her hand on his cheek, forcing him to meet her gaze. "Should I be scared?"

Ronin just bestowed that "Hallelujah Chorus" grin. "Probably. But I promise I won't do a thing you don't like."

The table jiggled and they both looked up.

Amery couldn't help her shock. Tyler and Chantal were seated at their table. Out of nine hundred and ninety-eight other possibilities for dinner companions, they ended up with these two?

Tyler offered a smarmy grin. "Well, isn't this a coincidence?"

Chantal didn't seem any happier than Amery about the seating arrangements. But she managed a cool "Hello."

Three other couples joined them. The foursome barely acknowledged anyone outside their group. The other couple, an elegant pair in their early sixties, were sniping at each other and then fell into glaring silence as they knocked back glass after glass of champagne.

"Good thing we like each other's company," Ronin said.

"No kidding."

The waiters kept the bubbly flowing in addition to bringing bottles of wine to the table.

Amery picked up the linen card—embossed in the exact same color of the tablecloth—that announced the evening's five-course menu:

Butternut squash soup with chive oil and radish seedlings

Pan-fried trout croquettes, breaded with blue corn flour and topped with tomatillo relish

Roasted beet carpaccio with seared goat cheese and mâche greens

Grilled filet of beef with caramelized shallot/red wine reduction, truffle-infused potato rösti, white asparagus, and morel mushrooms

Golden Colorado dessert, ripe Colorado peaches soaked in Colorado's gold-medal-winning red wine, topped with yogurt sweetened with honey

This menu was a little different than Applebee's.

Ronin leaned closer. "Problem?"

"Not exactly sure what some of the ingredients are in these dishes."

"Me either. I'm just glad one of the courses isn't sushi."

After the soup course was delivered to everyone in the room, a man stepped up to the raised dais and began to speak.

She tuned him out and talked to Ronin. "So, the guy earlier that monopolized your time? What did he want?"

"To convince me to teach a private kickboxing class for new Bronco recruits."

"What'd you say?"

Ronin looked affronted. "No."

"Why not?"

"I am not a kickboxing instructor."

"Saying no should've taken, like, two seconds. Why'd he keep you so long?"

"He mistakenly assumed everyone has a price and all he needed to do was charm me, or throw more money at me. Or threaten me and I'd fall in line."

Her eyes widened. "He threatened you? Was he just an idiot or did he have a death wish? Did you demonstrate jujitsu pressure points so he understands why ninjas like you don't teach kickboxing?"

"I said something like that, but more diplomatically."

"Darn. I'd like to see you in ass-kicking mode." Amery turned her head. Their mouths were only a breath apart.

The moment lingered and became even more perfect when Ronin murmured, "I am so crazy about you."

As the second course was delivered, Amery glanced up to see Tyler studying her. His gaze flicked to Ronin and then back to her.

That's right. This hot, successful man is crazy about me. So suck it.

More boring speeches were given by more people she didn't know while the third course arrived.

During a lull in the festivities, Tyler addressed Ronin. "Has the Platte Valley restoration project affected your business at all? That's where you're located, right?"

"We've been there ten years, so urban renewal is finally catching up to us. It's always good to have other businesses—regardless if they're retail or service or entertainment industries—in any area. But I haven't seen a direct impact positive or negative on my business."

"There is one negative thing about people flocking to the area," Amery said, shoving aside her salad plate only to have it immediately whisked away by a server.

"And what's that?" Tyler asked.

"Parking. It is impossible to find a decent parking place around the dojo. Wednesday night I swear I had to park six blocks away."

Ronin kissed the back of her hand. "I'm glad limited parking choices aren't keeping you away from me."

So what if Ronin poured it on a little thick in front of her ex? She'd do the same thing if she crossed paths with Naomi.

"How did you two meet?" Chantal asked with an air of boredom.

"We had to exchange names after he threw me on my ass."

Silence at the table. Even the cliquey foursome stopped whispering and stared at them.

"That isn't even funny," Chantal snapped.

Amery flashed her teeth. "But it's true. Sensei Black took me to the mat in a self-defense class I signed up for at his dojo."

"It's more accurate to say Amery knocked me to my knees the first time I saw her." Ronin kissed her hand. "I literally tried to sweep her off her feet to even things up a bit."

The foursome laughed, as did the other couple.

Tyler wasn't amused. Chantal alternated between shooting jealous daggers at Amery and Ronin and glaring at Tyler.

Amery probably shouldn't have signaled for more champagne as they waited on the main course.

Ronin kept watching her, an odd look on his face.

"What?"

"I want to act on my every dirty impulse right now. It's making me reckless—and I'm never reckless in public."

A feeling of power rolled through her. "Is it making you hard?"

He leaned in to whisper in her ear. "Put your hand on my groin and find out for yourself."

Her first thought was *no way*. She'd reach over and everyone at the table would know what was going on.

Her second thought was she'd never been the type who'd do something like that in public.

So that's precisely why she decided to do it.

Amery dropped her napkin and reached down to pick it up. When she returned upright, she set her hand on Ronin's knee, allowing her hand to inch up his thigh.

He'd left his napkin covering his lap so she could slip her hand beneath it. When she had to move slightly to reach him, she leaned in. "Who is sponsoring these awards tonight?"

"Colorado Athlete's Foundation in conjunction with Rocky Mountain Sports Coalition."

Her fingers reached the crease of his thigh. "Have you ever been nominated for one of these awards?"

"No."

"Why not?"

"I'm not a team player. I prefer to play one-on-one. It's more . . . intimate."

She felt his gaze burning into her. She met it head-on as her hand reached the promised land, scraping her fingernails up and down his rigid shaft. "Is it hard to get nominated?"

The only change in Ronin's face was the ripple of his jaw muscle— but even that was there and gone. "Very hard."

"Yes, it is." Amery squeezed his cock one last time and leisurely slid her hand back down his leg.

They exchanged private, provocative looks as the remaining courses were served. None of their tablemates engaged them in conversation.

After the dessert and coffee course arrived, Ronin pulled Amery closer. "Leave your napkin on your lap and pull your dress up."

Her head whipped around. "Excuse me?"

"You heard me. Slide your dress up so I can rub your clit until you come on my hand."

Amery's face flamed. "Ronin. There are over a thousand people here."

He bent forward until his lips connected with the skin in front of her ear. "No, baby, it's just you and me." He nuzzled her cheek. "Spread your legs for me."

The thought of baring herself as Ronin's rough-tipped finger abraded her clit . . . made her absolutely dripping wet.

She rested her head against his shoulder, shifting to get comfortable as she slid her dress up.

Ronin nonchalantly dropped his hand between her thighs.

She squeezed his hand, stopping his forward motion. "Since you're testing my control, it's only fair I get to test yours too."

"Now?"

"No. Later."

"Fine. But right now it's about you."

Emboldened, she bit down on the outside of his ear. "You sure? I think this fingering-me-until-I-tremble plan is about you and your need for control."

"Amery," he half growled.

Definitely about his control. She discreetly widened her knees.

She only allowed a tiny surprised flinch when his finger wiggled beneath the edge of her thong and slipped down her slit. And back up. And down. Featherlight but insistent.

Then Ronin drew circles around her clit as if he intended to torture her. Her quads tightened in response.

"Look at me."

Amery raised her head. His eyes were a shade darker than normal, but so compelling she couldn't look away.

He stroked, swirled, and flicked his finger across that swollen nub, increasing the pace.

Somehow she kept still when a hot wave started in her tailbone and radiated upward into soft, dizzying pulses.

"How sexy you are right now. Cheeks flushed, eyes unfocused, teeth digging into your bottom lip as you come for me. And no one knows but me."

Ronin's deep, quietly commanding voice rolled over her with as much power as the orgasm pulsating through her.

When the storm ended, he brushed his mouth over her temple. "You okay?"

"Better than okay." Then reality encroached. "Do you think anyone—"

"No. We appear to be exactly what we are: lovers enjoying a quiet moment together." Ronin discreetly removed his hand and tugged her dress down.

Amery didn't dare look around the table. "Now what?"

"Let's wander through the crowd and see if we can find trouble."

"Very reckless tonight, Master Black."

"You don't have any idea. And the night is young."

They exited the dining room and Ronin was waylaid several times. He remained polite but slightly aloof, which baffled most people. Including her.

So maybe seeing the many faces of Ronin Black bothered her. In the times they'd been together, had he really shown her the man beneath the mask? Or was that side of him a mask too?

They'd almost made it out of the ballroom when a barrel-chested man with thinning gray hair and an unlit cigar clamped between his teeth approached with what looked like a posse.

"I wondered what it'd take to get you out of that dojo on the wrong side of the tracks."

Ronin offered the man a slight bow. "Always a pleasure to see you again, Mr. Pettigrew."

Pettigrew. Even Amery recognized that name. Thaddeus Pettigrew of Pettigrew Petroleum, Pettigrew Properties, Pettigrew Mining, and the restaurant chain Pettigrew's. He was rumored to be the richest man in Colorado.

"Cut the bullshit, Ronin. I got a dozen people fawning over me every damn day calling me Mr. Pettigrew. You've more than earned the right to call me TP in public too. Anyway, glad to see you here. I wanted to bend your ear and it saved me a trip to the seedy side of town."

"Of which you currently own what? Twenty percent?"

Pettigrew grinned. "Closer to thirty now."

"Any pies you don't have your finger in, TP?"

"I steer clear of political soup. Since the bastards won't let me smoke in here no matter how much green I dump in the coffers, I was headed outside. Walk with me. We can discuss that family business issue you called me about."

Family business?

"I'd be happy to." Ronin nudged Amery forward. "I'll introduce my date before I leave her to her own devices. Amery Hardwick, Thaddeus Pettigrew."

Amery offered her hand. "A pleasure, Mr. Pettigrew."

"It certainly is." Pettigrew winked at her. "I won't keep your man long."

Ronin matched his pace to the lumbering Pettigrew and they exited out a side door.

Amery marched to the bar and ordered a drink. Twenty minutes passed with no sign of Ronin.

Someone moved in behind her and she turned, hoping to see her date, but Tyler invaded her space.

"Dance with me."

She looked at him as if he'd lost his mind. "Where's Chantal?"

"Who knows? You've been standing here by yourself for too long and so have I. The music is playing. Let's dance."

Amery's gaze darted around the room. No sign of Ronin. And to be honest . . . it annoyed her she'd been cooling her heels so long. "Fine. One song."

A rock power ballad came on. Tyler settled his hands above her ass. "Huh-uh," she said. "No junior high slow-dancing." She held up her hand in waltz formation.

He clasped her palm in his. "Did we ever dance like this when we were together?"

"I don't remember. Why?"

"It's nice. Better than the mosh pit at Theta Tau."

"I wouldn't know. I avoided that mass of writhing bodies back then."

"But now? If you had the chance to do it again?

"I'd try it."

"You've become the girl who'll try anything once, huh?"

Amery shrugged.

"Still a little coy, but I don't buy it because I can see how much you've changed." He twirled them backward. "So, out of curiosity . . . why did you bail from the apartment complex after things ended between us? You just vanished and I didn't know how to get in touch with you. I wondered if you were okay."

Bullshit. She'd just changed apartments, not jobs. "I left after having enough of living in Tyler Pessac's love hotel." She cocked her head and studied him. "Did Chantal ever find out about Brittney? Did either of them know about Lorena? Or was the fact that their apartments were on different floors enough to keep them from seeing you sneak out of the others' places?"

Tyler smirked. "See, that's where everything gets blown out of proportion. Lorena was just one of those things. Brittney was a flash in the pan. I'm really sorry that I didn't come clean with you about Chantal. There were better ways for you to find out—"

"Than letting myself into your apartment and witnessing Chantal bent over your couch as you fucked her? Yeah, you're probably right. An e-card or a text would've worked better as a breakup instead of the live sex show."

That took him aback. "You never used to talk like that."

"Wrong. I think you had some image in your head of me that's patently untrue. You never really saw me."

"I was young and cocky. Self-absorbed. People change."

It was on the tip of her tongue to point out that little had changed with him.

"Anyway, it's nice to see you've gotten out of the shell I could never crack."

That's because ham-handed you didn't have the right tool.

"Although I'll admit I didn't expect to see you at a ten-thousand-dollar-a-plate dinner."

Her head snapped up. "The pair of tickets for tonight's dinner was twenty thousand dollars?"

"You didn't know that? Black didn't brag how much money he was dropping on this?"

"Ronin doesn't brag." *He doesn't have to* went unsaid.

"Right. He's pure of thought, deed, and motive." Tyler spun them deeper into the dancers. "He'd like everyone to believe that. But the truth is he's a dangerous, violent man."

She shrugged. "Comes with the territory of living in the world of martial arts."

Tyler's eyes searched hers. "That's not what I was talking about. He's not what he appears to be, Amery."

"Don't pretend you know him. You don't."

"And you do?"

Sometimes. Other times he was as much a stranger as when they'd first met. But she wouldn't give Tyler the satisfaction of admitting that. "Yes, I do."

"Knowing him and him knowing you are two different things. Trust me. Break it off while you can."

"Come on, Tyler. That's a little vague. If you've got the low-down dirty on him, tell me." Of course Tyler didn't recognize her sarcasm.

"There've been rumors that he's not who he says he is. Rumors that he hasn't completely distanced himself from his violent past that financed his lifestyle and his dojo."

Ronin had told her his fighting skills earned the money needed to buy the building he owned, but she wasn't sure if that was common knowledge. "Where'd you hear that?"

"Denver is a small community in the realm of sports. Ronin is well respected, but he's feared too. Don't you wonder why? Don't you wonder how he's able to afford to run with major players like Thaddeus Pettigrew and Max Stanislovsky? His dojo is successful, but not to that extent."

"I wonder why you're so concerned about what kind of man Ronin is, and questioning his financial background, and listing who his friends are. Are you jealous?"

"No. I'm just worried about you. You're in over your head with him. You didn't see the self-satisfied looks he shot everyone who looked at you, but I did. He gets his kicks forcing you to do what he wants, when he wants, where he wants."

Amery looked Tyler square in the eye, despite her suspicion that he knew what'd gone on beneath the table during dessert. "No one forces me to do anything anymore."

Tyler stopped dancing. "Your blasé attitude is freaking me out. This is not you, Amery. What happened to the sweet, fun, shy girl from North Dakota that I loved?"

Her back snapped straight. "She grew up and shed that skin after the man she thought *she* loved made fun of her for retaining those embarrassing small-town traits. Now you're claiming I should still be naive and clingy because that's the version of me you loved? Bullshit. Need I point out that you couldn't wait to get the hell away from me when I was the sweet, fun, and shy gal? You don't need to worry for her, because she no longer exists. I know what I want and I ask for it because I deserve it. So back off. You don't know me now, Tyler. You never really did."

"Fine, I'll drop it. But I have to ask, what do your folks think of these changes in you? Do they approve of you being involved with a guy like Ronin?"

"I don't care. They're not in my life. It only matters that I'm happy with the changes."

"But are you making all these changes for him?"

"That's an insulting insinuation."

He grabbed her biceps and hauled her closer. "Listen to me. You may think you're tough because you live in a city now rather than a small town, but you don't have the experience to deal with a man like Ronin Black. Very few people do. He'll chew you up and spit you out."

Slightly alarmed by his vehemence, she said, "Tyler—"

"Let. Her. Go." A pause. *"Now."*

Ronin.

Tyler immediately retreated.

"Never put your hands on her like that again. It would end very badly for you. Am I clear?"

If Ronin's tone were a weapon, Tyler would be lying in bloody chunks on the floor.

Tyler raised his hands in mock surrender. "Sorry. We have a history and it was easy to slip into those old roles." He shot Amery a quick smile. "Great to see you, Amery. If you ever need to talk . . . now you know where to reach me." He spun on his heel and left the dance floor.

Then Amery was wrapped in Ronin's arms. She clutched his back and held on tight.

"Are you okay?"

"Yes. He's just a blowhard who hasn't changed, except he's become even more of an asshole."

"Why did you dance with him?"

"He asked me to."

His body stiffened. "That's it? That's the only reason?"

"Do you have any idea how long you were gone? I was just supposed to cool my heels until you returned? I've already done that once tonight, Ronin. I was bored and he was here."

He made that displeased noise.

"Besides, I was involved with Tyler for a few years. It's not like he was a strange guy hitting on me."

"I would've preferred a stranger hitting on you to him."

Amery tried to look at Ronin, but he kept the side of his face pressed into hers, holding her in place. "Why?"

"A stranger hasn't seen you naked. Hasn't touched you. Hasn't fucked you. Tyler has. Goddammit, he had you for three years. The realization that he'd screwed up by letting you go was written all over his face tonight."

Ronin had read that wrong. Tyler didn't want to be with her; he just didn't want her to be with anyone else. "It doesn't matter because I'm not with him. I'm with you."

His thumb swept over the pulse point in her throat. He repeated the motion and it felt as erotic as when he'd touched her clit. His scent, his touch, his uneven breathing stirred her hair and her desire. "But are you really with me?"

"I'm confused. With you how?"

"In every way I need you to be."

"Still confused."

"Come home with me and I'll show you what I mean. What I need. You said anytime, any way. I want you to prove it to me tonight."

She shivered. "Let's go."

They left the dance floor in the middle of the song.

CHAPTER FOURTEEN

RONIN held her hand as they waited at the valet stand.

Amery's entire body tingled just from Ronin lightly stroking the inside of her wrist with his callused thumb. How would it be between them when they were alone? Mind-blowing.

Maybe it did scare her how addicted she'd gotten to his touch. She shivered.

He swept her hair over her shoulder. "You're shaking. Are you cold?"

"A little."

"Here." He unbuttoned his jacket and shrugged it off. Then he draped it around her shoulders. "Better?"

This was worse actually. The body-heated fabric that carried his scent completely surrounded her. "Yes. Thank you."

He curled his hands around her face. "Baby, what's wrong?"

"I can't think of anything else but you."

"Why is that making you frown?"

"Because you overwhelm me. Maybe I'm saying this because of my run-in with Tyler, and realizing he never knew me, not in the three years we were together. You've been in my life less than three weeks and you already know aspects of me better than I know myself. You don't have any problems pushing my boundaries."

"Are you afraid I might push you too hard?" he asked softly.

"No. I'm afraid that I'll find out that I don't have any boundaries at all when it comes to you."

Ronin rested his forehead to hers. "You have no idea what you do to me when you say that."

The valet broke the moment. "Your car, Mr. Black."

Ronin released her and opened her car door. Then he skirted the front end and slipped into the driver's side.

As soon as they were on the road, he said, "You are spending the night with me."

Not a request. "We'll have to swing by my place so I can get some clothes."

"I still have your jeans. I'd like to see you in one of my shirts."

"Then I guess we'll go straight to your place." Feeling buoyed by her confession, Amery unbuckled her seatbelt. She leaned across the console and worked the knot in his tie. "Don't think I've forgotten about the equal time."

"My tie isn't connected to my zipper."

"Want me to go straight for the good stuff?"

Ronin gave her a look so hot it scorched the breath from her lungs. "Yes."

"Eyes on the road." Amery found the buckle on his belt and unhooked it. She unzipped his pants, and his shaft jumped against her hand. "Spread your legs wider."

He hissed in a breath when her fingertips brushed the crown of his cock.

With the angle of the seat, she couldn't de-pants him and she couldn't play with his balls, so she pulled his cock through the opening in his boxer briefs. She glanced at his hands, gripping the steering wheel much more tightly than before. She lowered her head and swallowed as much of him as she could.

"Sweet Jesus."

Amery let his shaft slide back out of her mouth. She did that a few more times and his legs went rigid. "Do you wish you had my hair in your hands so you could force me to keep this cock in my mouth?"

"Yes."

"Pay attention to the road, Sensei. I know how you prefer to look at me while I'm blowing you, but I don't want to die choking on your dick after you wreck your fancy car." Amery let her mouth slowly engulf his cock. When she started bobbing her head, the hard shaft bumped the back of her throat on every pass. She hollowed her cheeks and sucked, loving the musky tang of him and the feel of his velvety-soft, steel-hard shaft gliding over her tongue. Flicking the very tip and the thick ridge beneath the cock head before taking him deep. She circled the root and stroked up as her mouth slid down.

"Don't use your hands. Just your mouth."

Bossy man preferred her hands on his thighs or his abdomen, or gripping his butt cheeks when she was on her knees before him. Pleasing him gave her such a heady sense of power. But this time she controlled him. She pushed him to the edge at full throttle. No reason to drag this out. She wanted—no, she'd *earned* the right to make him soar and swallow him down.

"Amery. Fuck. Stop."

She pulled her mouth away long enough to say, "No, give it to me. All of it," before she took him back in.

Ronin swore under his breath.

His body went rigid. She heard his grip increase on the steering wheel. He bumped his hips up and she felt that moment when he let go. His cock hardened further for a split second and then hot, wet spurts hit her soft palate. She firmed her lips as she swallowed.

As soon as his orgasm ended, she licked the shaft and lightly tongued the tip. He'd never given her the opportunity to nuzzle and kiss his softening flesh.

He tugged on her hair. "Baby, you have to stop. I'm about to wreck the car."

Amery kissed the head of his penis before pushing upright. "Why were you going to wreck the car?" she asked innocently.

"Because instead of throwing my head back and closing my eyes like I do whenever your hot mouth works me, I focused on the road. But my foot stepped on the gas and I don't need a ticket for a hundred and seventy miles an hour."

"We were going that fast?"

"Almost before I blinked."

She zipped his pants, then refastened his belt. "There. You don't look so disheveled."

"I like that look." He snatched her hand and kissed the center of her palm. "On you. And by the time I finish with you tonight? You will be thoroughly disheveled."

Silence settled between them, only broken by the hum of the engine.

Amery angled her head in the confines of the car and stared at the Denver skyline as it came into view. How many of the people at the party tonight lived in the expensive high-rises with the gorgeous view of the mountains? Probably their places made Ronin's penthouse look like a dive. But how many of them were poseurs like her? Only there rubbing elbows with Denver's elite because of a benefactor who invited them to the fancy shindig?

"What're you thinking about?"

"The ratio of people at tonight's party who were filthy rich and how many of them were pretending to be. Tyler told me the event tickets were ten grand a pop."

"They are. But for all the glamour and glitz, it is a worthwhile cause. The bulk of the money goes to the organizations, not to fund a party, which is why I'm still donating to them."

Twenty grand. Poof. All that hard-earned cash just passed over and tucked in someone else's pocket. Amery didn't know if she could ever be that cavalier about money. Ronin must be doing better in his dojo than she assumed if dropping that many Benjamins didn't put a dent in his checkbook.

She hated that Tyler's questions about Ronin's finances jumped into her head.

"Don't fret about the money, Amery."

"I can't help it. I feel like I owe you."

"You owed me nothing but the pleasure of your company tonight, and you provided that beautifully."

Amery noticed they were close to his building and he turned into a parking garage. "Did the blow job fluster you so much you forgot where you live?"

"No. It's the closest place to keep my car. This one doesn't get parked on the street." He pulled into a spot resembling a concrete bunker. After they climbed out of the car, he clamped a tire lock on the front tire. He brushed his hands and sent her a sheepish look. "I make this car as hard as possible to steal." Then he wrapped his arm around her shoulder. "Is the jacket keeping you warm?"

"Yes. Thank you." She glanced at his thin dress shirt. "Aren't you cold?"

"Rarely. I'm pretty hot-blooded."

"I'll say."

Ronin brushed a kiss on the top of her head. "And you ain't seen nothing yet."

They walked at a decent clip to his building and her feet were starting to get sore. Ronin opened the front door instead of entering through the alley. By the time they'd reached his penthouse, Ronin took it upon himself to ignite the fire that simmered between them with an urgent kiss.

His jacket hit the floor first. She wrapped her hands in the loose ends of his tie and pulled him closer to kiss him harder. Then she started in on his buttons.

He didn't attempt to undress her; he just controlled her mouth as he controlled the direction they headed.

Once Amery had his shirt undone, her hands roamed over his torso, from his pectorals, to his rib cage, to his six-pack abs. Her thumbs traced the deep cut of his hip muscle until it disappeared into his pants.

His intense kiss didn't falter.

She knew the instant they were in his bedroom. Not only did the flooring change, but Ronin changed. He ended the soul-deep kiss, but his mouth kept teasing hers with licks and nibbles and a teasing glide.

"I want you, Amery. But I want you my way."

"Which way is that?"

"My way," he repeated. "And you'll have to trust me. Can you trust that I'll make you feel beautiful and bold?" He tilted her head to kiss below her jawline. "Trust me to worship your body the way it's meant to be?"

"Didn't I already say yes?"

"You did." His teeth followed the tendons in her neck. She shuddered in his arms and she felt his smile against her skin. "But I want to blindfold you so you can focus on how you feel, not on what I'm doing."

"What will you be doing to me?"

A kiss below her ear. "Teasing you." A soft kiss in front of her ear. "Pushing your boundaries." He gently blew in her ear. "Boundaries that you claimed earlier might not be boundaries at all."

She wanted this sexy, intense man to make her so mindless with lust, to get her so drunk on him that she couldn't think. She nuzzled the base of his throat. "No boundaries, Ronin."

He kissed her with zeal. With finesse.

And she lost herself in him.

"First I want to get you out of this dress." Ronin turned her around and undid the zipper. Slowly. He dragged his fingertips up and down her spine in a featherlight touch that brought all of those nerve endings alive. He slipped his fingers across her shoulders and loosened her dress.

Amery felt the beaded material slipping down her chest and she stopped it just before it cleared her nipples.

Then Ronin stood in front of her. He traced the edge of her jaw. "Do you have any idea how appealing you look right now? With your hair tangled from my fingers. With your mouth so full and ripe from kissing me." His rough thumb followed the upper and lower bow of her lips. "With your sexy little dress clutched over your breasts, attempting to conceal what's mine tonight."

The man had a way with words that made her tremble.

"Drop the dress, Amery."

She let go and it landed on the floor in a soft whoosh.

"Bend over and place your hands on the bed."

Amery put an extra swing in her hips as she rolled herself down until her palms were flat on the mattress. Ronin stared at her ass so intently she swore his heated gaze singed her skin.

"Head up." Ronin nestled his groin against her ass.

A spike of desire nearly shot her through the roof.

Then something soft and silky covered her eyes and everything went dark. "Is that your tie?"

"Yes." His fingers hooked inside her thong and he slowly dragged it down her legs. Once it reached her ankles, Ronin dropped to his knees. He tapped the inside of her right calf and she lifted her foot, expecting he'd take her thong off. "No. Widen your stance with the thong where it is."

His commanding presence filled the room, permeating the air. His will seeped through her skin and settled into her bones. And it was like this every time they were together. Would it flame out because it burned so hot?

"Hey, baby. Where'd you go?"

That quietly controlled voice caused her to jump. "What?"

"You were relaxed in a happy place and then you weren't. What changed?"

"I had the fleeting fear this would burn out."

"Don't think." He pressed openmouthed kisses across the backs of her knees. "Stay steady. Even when I do this." He licked the crease of her knee, a soft tickle of his tongue while trailing his fingers on the outsides of her thighs.

Amery was half tempted to fall face-first into the puffy mattress; her legs and arms were absolutely quaking from his wickedly talented mouth. When he swept butterfly kisses across the curve of her ass cheeks, she made a low moan of need.

Even that didn't hurry the man up. If her groin was closer to the bed, she'd be grinding her clit against it, trying to come. She sighed when Ronin gently urged her passion-flushed face to press against the mattress.

"Put your hands behind your back, palms facing out."

Thank God for yoga. What would he do if she couldn't hold the position he demanded? Spank her?

That's where she'd draw the line. She'd been spanked as a child, by her father's hand, a ruler, a hairbrush, a plastic pipe.

"Amery. Stop thinking." He twined something soft around her wrists. As soon as he finished, he caressed the skin above where he'd secured her hands. Then he rested the side of his face against hers, his chest to her spine.

Having her vision blocked heightened her anticipation. She wanted the intimacy of skin on skin so much she squirmed.

"Stay still."

"I can't. I want—"

"I know what you want. Are you wet enough for it?"

"Yes."

His hand slid around her waist and through the thin strip of hair covering her mound. That long, deadly accurate middle finger slipped inside her. "You are wet." He plunged in and out a few more times, stroking and teasing the swollen flesh. "Wouldn't take much for you to come."

"You touch me and I can't help it."

"But you won't come until I say."

"Are you punishing me for something?"

"No, baby, I'm giving you this. So relax and let me." Ronin began drawing tight circles on her clit. Immediately she started to tremble—inside, outside. He held her down and steadily increased the pace of his finger until her body tensed. When he whispered, "Now," she went off like a bottle rocket.

Every molecule in her body went taut, leaving her breathless and dizzy.

Then Ronin was slamming into her as the last pulse lingered, setting off another wave of contractions in short, sweet bursts.

His hands bracketed her hips as he powered into her with forceful thrusts. There was a frantic edge to the way he fucked her. Animalistic. Fast. He had no intention of making this last.

As she felt the third orgasm of the night gathering steam, she didn't care if he fucked her fast or slow or even upside down. This man knew what she needed and gave it to her without question.

Ronin came in silence, as he often did. His pelvis slowed in rhythmic increments. The evidence of his release came in a hot wash against her pussy walls.

When he stopped moving and returned to himself, that's when he made the noise—a deep-throated hum of satisfaction.

She smiled.

He murmured, "Your skin is glowing. It's breathtaking."

"Ronin."

"Stay like this. I'll be right back."

She stayed, content, sated, and yet revved up.

Amery didn't hear him rustling around in the room. She heard a whisper of cloth and then Ronin's fingers were undoing the ties around her wrists.

Then he flipped her over, teased her lips until she opened for him, letting his tongue dart inside. Their mouths clashed, tongues tangled, and he stoked the fire of passion again before the first embers had even waned.

From the energy pulsing off him, she understood this would be a long night; they'd only finished the second course of a five-course meal.

"Will you let me show you in my way how beautiful you are to me?"

"You do that every time you look at me," she said softly.

"You're blindfolded. How can you tell?"

"I can feel it."

"You undo me." Ronin kissed her forehead. "Hold on." He lifted her into his arms and spun her around.

She shrieked, "Stop, you'll make me dizzy."

"There goes my plan to play pin the tail on the donkey."

"But I'm sure you have other games in mind." She bounced in his arms as he continued to move around.

"I could show you."

Amery turned her face toward his neck and placed a kiss on the pulse bounding in his throat. "I'm game."

"Good answer." He set her on her feet.

"Can I take the blindfold off?"

"Not yet." His palms skated up her arms and he draped them over his shoulders. "Come here. I can't get enough of your mouth."

Lips as soft as silk brushed against hers. Once. Twice. Three times. Ronin mixed it up every time he kissed her. Which always left her craving more.

"On second thought, why don't you sit?" He gently pushed on her shoulders until her butt met a padded bench.

Ronin must've brought her into the living room.

"Sit forward and hold your arms out slightly. Knees together."

As much as she wanted to ask questions, a different vibe surrounded Ronin that kept her quiet and still.

Fingers brushed the outside of her calves, and then her ankles were pressed together and wrapped in . . . what?

Before she could ask, something circled her wrist and then it was pulled taut. Same thing on her left wrist and then both arms were pressed together behind her. Tightly behind her. She could feel his movements but couldn't see what he was doing. But whatever it was pulled her forearms together and weighted her hands down. She couldn't raise her arms at all.

"Ronin?"

No soft assurances from him, just silence.

This isn't right.

But she trusted him.

Didn't she?

You told him you were into anything he wanted. This is what he wanted. Just keep your mouth shut and go with it.

That spiked her unease. Hadn't she stopped being that eager-to-please girl years ago? The girl who wouldn't make waves or speak up even when she needed to?

Yes.

So why was she reverting when something felt off about this situation? Like really, really off?

"Ronin. What's going on?"

No response.

Why wasn't Ronin answering her?

Had he left her alone?

Panicked, she wiggled side to side to try and free herself, and the blindfold slipped. She squinted at the unfamiliar space.

Where was she? She'd been in every room in his penthouse except for the locked storage room down the hall from his bedroom. Why had he brought her here?

In the dim lighting Amery couldn't see much beyond the wall directly in front of her. But what she saw on that wall froze her blood.

Coils of rope. Dozens of different kinds. Some colored, some plain, a variety of thicknesses and lengths. Why would he need so many ropes?

Her mouth dried when she saw the wall of swords. He'd flat-out told her he was an expert with knives. With his martial arts background, he could kill with his hands.

Fear hit her so hard she couldn't breathe. Ever since the first time they were together, he'd used something to tie her up. He'd made it sexy and exciting and he'd never hurt her, so she hadn't examined it too closely. But now, being in this room, a room he'd had to keep locked because it appeared to contain instruments of torture, she wanted to scream. Except that no one would hear her.

She'd really fucked up this time.

Between the voices from the past, and her fear that she wouldn't have a future, she thrashed so hard the bench started to move.

"Amery. Take a deep breath."

She had a momentary sense of calm before she realized the soothing tone was part of his mind tricks to get her to relax her guard. "Why do you have me all tied up? What is this place? A secret torture room?" Amery felt the immediate change in his demeanor. Although it wouldn't do any good to beg, she couldn't stop the "Please don't kill me."

Ronin yanked off the blindfold completely. "Kill you? What are you talking about?"

But Amery was too busy craning her neck around to gawk at the room to answer.

Next to the wall of ropes was a wall of silk scarves. When she tilted her head back, she noticed eye hooks and pulley systems permanently embedded in the ceiling. Had he faced her this way so she couldn't see what was on the wall behind her? Oh God. Was it really that bad? She craned her neck around and saw what looked like an altar. For sacrifices?

"Amery," he said sharply. "Look at me."

She shook her head.

"Why would you think I planned to kill you?"

"Because you blindfolded me. You've tied me up with actual ropes. You're strong and you know I can't fight you off. All those other times led up to this, didn't they? You got me to trust you and—"

"Stop babbling."

"You'd like that, wouldn't you?" She twisted her body against the bindings, trying to get away from him.

"Don't. You'll hurt yourself."

"Why do you care? You're going to hurt me anyway, aren't you?"

He grabbed her chin, forcing her face up. But he couldn't make her look at him. "I won't hurt you. Ever."

Tears leaked out the corners of her eyes because even now, when she was scared spitless, she wanted to believe him. "Let me go."

"Talk to me."

"Untie me."

"If I untie you will you talk to me?"

No fucking way. I'll run. But she didn't voice her plan to flee, just nodded at him.

Ronin reached down and tugged, releasing the binding from her ankles. He undid the ties around her arms so quickly she almost fell forward off the bench.

As soon as she was free, she left the chamber of horrors, heading toward his bedroom. She opted not to make a break for the elevator, first because she was naked, second because Ronin might tackle her to keep her from leaving.

Don't be ridiculous. If he wanted to kill you he wouldn't have let you go.

Amery sensed him leaning in the doorway to his bedroom, watching her as she slipped on her thong and bra. After she got the dress on, her hands were shaking so hard she couldn't get it zipped.

"Will you let me help you?"

"No!" she practically shouted. "Don't touch me."

But as usual, Ronin did as he liked. He clamped his hand around her hip and tersely said, "Hold. Still."

Her traitorous skin broke out in goose bumps when his rough-tipped fingers connected with her flesh as he zipped her up.

"Now will you talk to me?" he asked softly.

She shook her head.

"Baby. Please. What is going on with you?"

That's when she spun around and looked at him. "How did you expect me to react when you trussed me up and left me in a secret room full of ropes and God knows what else? What did you plan to do to me?" The fear returned and she started to cry.

"You said you trusted me."

"How can I trust you when it's obvious I don't even know you!"

Ronin's face showed no emotion.

"I want to leave."

"It's one o'clock in the goddamn morning."

"I want to leave," she repeated stubbornly.

"And you're planning to do what? Walk home?" His gaze swept over her. "Dressed like that? I don't think so."

"I'll call a cab. Just . . . let me go."

"Jesus, Amery, don't be ridiculous. I'll take you home."

Shaking her head, she slipped on her shoes and walked to the elevator. On her phone, she scrolled through the information for taxis and called the first one on the list. After rattling off the address, she learned it'd be a ten-minute wait.

After she hung up, Ronin said, "You'd rather get in a car with a stranger than trust me to take you home?"

Amery looked away.

"I'm not a killer. And it wounds me in ways you can't even begin to imagine that you'd think that of me."

You know he's right.

"I thought you'd be okay with the binding, since I've used scarves and belts and ties on you before."

"But not ropes."

"Is it really the ropes that set you off?"

"Yes. And the swords. And . . . everything."

"I'm sorry that scared you. I . . ." His jaw muscle flexed. "I should've told you."

"About the secret locked room?" Even saying that sounded scary and surreal.

"That and other things. The ropes are for . . ." His face hardened. "Don't look at me like that. The ropes aren't for torture. I use them in kinbaku and shibari bondage."

Amery wrapped her hands around her upper arms and shivered. "What the hell is that? A jujitsu thing?"

"No, but that's where shibari and kinbaku came from," he said evenly. "Please come back upstairs with me and I'll explain everything."

Did she even want to know?

Yes, she did. But her emotions were too raw, too unstable to process anything right now. She managed to choke out, "You should've told me."

"I know. So will you please come back upstairs?"

She shook her head. "I can't. Not now."

"If I give you a few days, then will you talk to me?"

"I don't know."

"This is killing me," he said softly. "Absolutely fucking killing me to see you so miserable and scared and looking at me like I want to cause you harm. When all I wanted . . ."

Amery wiped her fingers under her eyes, completely unaware she'd been crying. "When all you wanted was what?"

"For you to understand who I am. To show you this part of me."

That caused her to cry harder.

The tense silence between them stretched until Amery felt a black hole had opened up, threatening to swallow them both.

The cab pulled up out front.

Before Ronin unlocked the door, he stood behind her and spoke into her ear. "This isn't over between us. I'll give you time to come to terms or process or whatever you need. But you owe me the courtesy of a conversation. You need to listen to me with an open mind. And sooner, rather than later, would be better for both of us."

This was the Ronin she knew—the one she wanted. Reasonable, but determined. Amery wanted to throw herself into his arms, bury her face in his neck, and just breathe in the scent of him. Pretend nothing had happened.

When his words *for you to understand who I am* echoed back to her, she realized this secret would've come out eventually.

The cab honked.

"I've got to go."

"One week," he said hoarsely. "You call me or come to me within a week or I'm coming to you."

CHAPTER FIFTEEN

SHE didn't sleep well. Tired of tossing and turning, she rolled out of bed at nine and cleaned her loft from top to bottom. Pathetic that she'd fallen into that old habit of scrubbing the shit out of everything when she was upset. Next would she start wearing the finger-to-elbow rubber gloves her mother favored?

No. You are not your mother.

Marion Hardwick would never put herself in a situation like the one with Ronin in the first place. But if she had made a judgment error, she'd walk away and never look back. She'd never give him a chance to explain. She'd never satisfy her curiosity about what made a man like him tick.

So, if she wasn't like her mother . . . then why was she acting exactly like her? Cutting Ronin off at the knees and refusing to hear him out? She hadn't already judged him . . . had she?

God. This was so fucked up.

Since she'd had such a good go of numbing her mind with cleaning, she tackled her office. By the time she'd showered off the grime, the clock read five. All she wanted to do was hole up and eat pizza and a pint of Oreo mint ice cream. Lose herself in bad TV. Watching back-to-back-to-back episodes of *Storage Wars* was better than fretting about the fact that she'd called Ronin a killer.

A *killer*, for god's sake.

Talk about a knee-jerk reaction out of fear.

Talk about stupidity.

She'd immediately judged something she didn't understand as . . . bad? Wrong? Scary? Freaky? When she'd been fine with it before when Ronin used scarves instead of ropes? When she didn't know what it was besides that it turned her on?

She didn't know enough about bondage or whatever the fuck it was to form a subjective opinion. Since education was the only way to dispel fear, Amery cracked open her laptop and punched *shibari* in the search engine.

Holy shit. Over eighty thousand hits showed up.

Okay, maybe she was living under a rock; obviously it wasn't as obscure a practice as she'd initially believed.

The first thing she looked up was the definition.

> *Shibari/kinbaku is the technique of using ropes to create sensual, dramatic, and erotic bondage that has roots in 16th-century Japanese martial arts, 18th-century historical Japanese judicial punishments, and 19th-century Japanese theatrical productions.*

She read further and learned that the practices were originally based on the jujitsu bondage punishment called hojojutsu. No wonder Ronin had an interest in it, since the practice had been borne out of the martial arts discipline he'd trained in his entire life. As far as she could tell, hojojutsu had been around since the time of the samurais. When samurais transported prisoners, they'd used ropes to bind and control them after capture. Some samurais became well known for their rope handiwork, which had to be functional and yet humane. Competitions arose between the samurais—the more

intricate and distinct designs, the more respect the rope master garnered.

Amery also learned the terms were slightly different branches of
the same bondage discipline. Shibari was more artistic, focusing on
the beauty of the finished rope design on a human canvas, composed
of elaborate patterns and often demonstrated as performance art. Kinbaku, while employing many of the same knots and wraps as shibari,
was more sexual in nature. A bond between the rope master and the
one being bound focused on skin contact during the tying process,
oftentimes with knots strategically placed to heighten sexual response.

When Amery finally closed her laptop a few hours later, her
head was swimming. But the questions foremost in her mind remained. Where had Ronin learned how to do it? If kinbaku was as
much a part of him as he'd claimed, then he'd need to practice to
reach master status.

*Do you really think with the way he looks and his forceful persona he'd
be short on female volunteers to be stripped naked and tied up and then
fucked by him?*

No.

It wasn't anger that surged but jealousy. And that was just too
fucking weird because she had no right to it.

Did she?

Frustrated, she shut off her laptop and flipped on the TV.

MONDAY morning Chaz pressed her for details about the gala.
Amery regaled him with tales of who she'd seen, of what the ballroom looked like, and she dished on the food and the clothes. She
got the appropriate expression of outrage from Chaz that she'd been
subjected to spending time with Tyler. He was satisfied enough that
she didn't have to tell him what'd happened afterward. Because
chances were high she'd break down. But she couldn't tell the truth
because Ronin deserved privacy about his lifestyle choices.

Molly had hung back during the conversation. As soon as Chaz and Emmylou were off bickering in Emmylou's studio, she approached Amery.

"That isn't all of it."

"What do you mean?"

"I mean you did mention how fantastic Master Black looked a couple of times. But beyond that you didn't talk about him at all, and that is not normal for you . . . so what gives?"

Amery recalled that during her years spent as the bookworm in the corner, she'd honed her ability to read people since none of them talked to her. It shouldn't have surprised her that Molly was so intuitive—they were a lot alike. "Ronin and I had a big fight. I'll spare you the details, but we're in a cooling-off period for a week."

Molly rubbed her arm. "I'm sorry. I know you really like him."

Like. Not liked, past tense. That's when Amery realized she didn't want to think of Ronin in the past tense either. "Thank you."

"Is there anything I can do?"

"You're doing it."

"I imagine you're not coming to class with me this week?"

That was another wrinkle; he'd hired her and she hadn't completed the last phase of the project—she'd been dragging it out as another way to keep in touch with him. After their conversation about Brazilian jujitsu, she'd designed new graphics to promote the newest discipline offered at Black Arts, that is, if Ronin ever followed through with it and hired an instructor. She'd enjoyed the challenge, but the bottom line was she needed the work and she couldn't quit just because there were issues in their personal relationship. In the last year many of her clients had started bringing design work in-house. If business didn't pick up soon . . . She didn't even want to think about having to let Molly go. She worked more hours than she got paid. Plus, she excelled at creating Web sites, animated banners, and ads where as Amery preferred to work with text, images, and personalized photography—which was why they made such a good team.

"Amery?"

She glanced up. "Sorry. I guess we'll see. Can you help me today? I've got a bunch of shots to do for the Wicksburg Farm flyers."

"Sure. What props are they sending this time?"

A large portion of Amery's clients catered to organic food consumers, so she'd carved out a niche in the natural food market crafting unique ad campaigns. She had a different approach and it was the one aspect of her business that was easily recognizable in her design work. "They're sending a bunch of different kinds of mushrooms and they want them photographed in a natural environment, so . . . they're delivering dirt today."

"I'll get the vacuum. What else?"

"I just hope they're not bringing the beehives for the honeycomb photos."

Molly grinned. "Funny. But I have my EpiPen just in case."

Later, after she'd sent Molly home for the day and she'd sorted photos into folders, her e-mail dinged. An unfamiliar name on the subject line. Hopefully it was someone looking for graphic design work. She opened the e-mail.

Hardwick Designs,
I was browsing on your Web site and saw that you do custom photographic work. I love the perspectives on inanimate objects as well as how you're framing them. I'm an author and I'm looking for a unique—not stock photo!—image for my next book cover. Is that something you'd be interested in giving me a quote on?
Thanks for your time and hope to hear from you soon.
Cherry Starr~

She knew a few freelancers who'd jumped on the digital book bandwagon and offered design services from covers to formatting for authors trying their hand at publishing their own work.

While she was interested, she wasn't sure of the industry standard pricing structure for custom photography versus revamping stock photos to suit the client's needs.

She headed to Cherry Starr's Web site to see what types of books she wrote. Oh, wow. She wrote naughty books. The stuff Amery's mother would've called filthy porn. Then again, her mother hadn't balked at all when it came to sneaking *True Confessions* magazine.

The world was full of judgmental hypocrites.

The title *His Whip-smart Mistress* had an intriguing cover. A half-naked woman in knee-high leather boots, a miniskirt, and a bustier, wielding a whip over a man on his knees, his arms tied behind his back with rope, his head bowed.

That's when the first warning bell chimed.

Amery clicked on the next title *Hog-tied and Whip-kissed*. That cover featured a bare-chested man holding the end of a whip to the woman's bright red lips. Her torso was completely wrapped in rope and she was bent at such an angle that part of her butt cheek showed—a butt cheek that the guy had his hand on.

So today, of all days, she would get contacted by an author who writes books about . . . the type of tying-up things that Amery was dealing with understanding about Ronin?

Bullshit. She did not believe in coincidences. Ronin had to have given this woman her contact information. Projects of this nature did not just fall in her lap. Amery hit REPLY.

Cherry Starr,
Before we get into the quote stage, may I ask how you got my name?

> *Best,*
> *Amery Hardwick ~*
> *Hardwick Designs*

Rather than fuming about Ronin's stealthy approach—throwing her a new business bone in the hopes it'd spur her to contact him sooner—she closed up shop for the day.

Needing fresh air, she strolled down to the Sixteenth Street mall. The Greek place still ran a four-dollar gyro special on Mondays, so she took her sandwich and salad outside beneath the umbrella and people-watched, hoping it'd clear her mind.

Fat lot of good that did. She saw scarves hanging in the windows and thought of Ronin. She saw candles in the window and thought of Ronin. She saw a display of men's ties and thought of Ronin. The Japanese takeout place reminded her of Ronin.

That's because this issue isn't going away. You can't ignore it. And your biggest problem is that part of Ronin intrigues and excites you as much as it scares you.

That stopped her in the middle of the sidewalk.

She had liked it when Ronin used scarves or even her own clothing to tie her up during foreplay and sex. She'd found an odd kind of freedom in knowing it pleased him.

Didn't that make her subservient? Putting his needs above her own?

But Amery couldn't come up with a single instance where Ronin hadn't seen to her needs first. Every. Single. Time.

Plus, Ronin never made her feel subservient. She wasn't there strictly for his pleasure. If anything, the opposite was true. He went above and beyond giving her pleasure . . . and always first.

Now that she'd sorted that out, what did she do next?

By the time Amery had returned to her loft she hadn't come up with an answer.

Out of habit she turned on her laptop and checked her e-mail. Well, well, another e-mail from Cherry Starr.

Amery,

I know your work because you've done some brochures and flyers for my family's campground. And sorry for coming off mysterious, but Cherry Starr is my pen name and no one in my family knows I write erotica—and I'd like to keep it that way.

Before we go any further, is there such a thing as client confidentiality?

Cherry~

Amery had done several brochures over the years for different campgrounds. Some camps were church based; some were family focused and wouldn't allow singles or couples without children to camp there. She understood Cherry's reluctance to reveal her identity without some guarantee Amery wouldn't blab. She typed back:

Cherry,

Yes, I can promise you client confidentiality. I'm not trying to be rude, but I see that you write books about bondage, and I'm wondering if you'd be willing to tell me about the BDSM lifestyle. What does this have to do with your cover design? Not a damn thing. So my questions really are more on a personal side.

A~

Two hours later, a response popped up in Amery's in-box.

Amery,

I actually don't mind answering questions—knowledge is power, and I'm happy to use my experience—limited as it is—to clear up misconceptions.

No, I'm not in the life. I've dabbled and done a few "drive-bys," but I haven't found a situation or a man who . . . fit me. That said, there is a difference between BDSM and bondage.

In the BDSM lifestyle one person is the Dominant and the other submissive—even if they're "playing" for only one night. The relationship between the Dom and the sub is sexual—more often than not.

Things are . . . a little trickier when it comes to explaining bondage. It's a release for some people to be tied up to the point they can't move, they can't think, they exist solely as a vessel. Some rope enthusiasts want to be bound by someone they have no other intimate relations with, so the binding process is not always sexual. Sometimes it's strictly psychological. Then there are the artistic bondage disciplines, where the beauty of the ties and configuration of knots is more about showcasing the rope master's artistry than emphasizing the sexual aspect of the scene.

Amery pushed away from the computer screen and rubbed her eyes. Every time Ronin had immobilized her, he'd made it sensual. He couldn't touch her enough. Being bound had allowed him to explore her body and her reactions without restriction.

And the truth was, she'd liked it, even when she hadn't known what he was doing to her had an actual official name.

Maybe she was naive, but she'd had no idea relationships like those—BDSM, Dominants, submissives—existed. She considered herself open-minded, but it'd never work for her. If it worked for other people, great.

She sipped her coffee and grimaced that it'd gone cold before she continued reading Cherry's response.

Still interested in working with me? I obviously have no opinions on this—LOL.

Cherry~

After rereading the e-mail, she pulled up her history from last night and spent another hour reading about shibari and kinbaku, determined that when she and Ronin finally had an honest conversation about it, she wouldn't be completely clueless.

"A dozen? Sure, that'll work." Amery kept her head tilted toward her shoulder to hold the phone receiver in place as she typed the information into her weekly calendar. "No, thank you. I appreciate the business and I'm always excited to work on new projects." She laughed. "Take care. See you Thursday."

She dropped the receiver in the cradle and moved her neck in a circle to get the kinks out.

"You really need to invest in a wireless headset," Molly said from the doorway.

Amery looked up. "I know. But the number of choices overwhelms me and I always end up walking out of the store without buying anything."

"Do me a favor. Next time, let me come with you."

"Deal. Did you need something?"

Molly glanced over her shoulder. "There's someone here to see you."

Ronin.

Her face heated. Since their "break" she'd kept herself occupied from the moment she woke up until her head hit the pillow in an attempt to stop thinking about him. It hadn't worked, which annoyed her to no appreciable end. They'd been involved for three weeks. *Three weeks.* She shouldn't have such a . . . bond with him. She'd certainly never missed Tyler the way she missed the sexy sensei. But she honestly didn't know what she'd say to Ronin when she saw him, or why the prospect of seeing him made her heart race.

"Will you be disappointed that your visitor isn't Ronin?"

The way her stomach plummeted, the answer to that would be a resounding yes. "Then who is it?"

"Shihan Knox from the dojo. Do you want me to tell him you're on a client call?"

"No. Send him back." Amery barely had time to clear off a place for him to sit before all six feet four inches sauntered into the room.

He smiled at her before he closed the door.

"I usually leave my door open."

"I figured you'd want it closed for this conversation." He plopped in the chair and cocked his head. "Unless you already told your office mates what happened between you and Ronin Saturday night?"

"It'd be hard to tell them when I'm not exactly sure what happened myself."

"I can guess exactly what happened."

She frowned. "Ronin didn't tell you?"

"Nope. In fact, he doesn't know I'm here."

That startled her.

"I'm betting you freaked out after Master Black broke out the ropes."

Amery blushed.

"Did he show you his practice room?"

"That's what he calls it?"

"What else would he call it?" Knox's eyes narrowed. "Maybe the question is, what did *you* call it?"

She blushed harder, if possible when she admitted, "Nothing I care to repeat because I said it out of shock and fear."

"Understood." Knox leaned forward, resting his forearms on his knees. "Look, Amery, I don't know you, but I'd like this to be an honest conversation, okay? Whatever you tell me won't get back to Ronin. But I need to know where you're at right now."

"You think I should tell you before I tell the man himself?"

"Yes."

"Why? So you can break it to him gently that I'm walking away?

Bullshit. Ronin Black doesn't sugarcoat anything, so I doubt he'd expect that in return from me or you."

Knox grinned. "You're right. Which is why I'm here." His smile faded. "You really walking away from him?"

"If you had asked me Saturday night, I'd have said more like I was running away." Amery twisted a section of hair. "But now? After I've calmed down and gotten some perspective from doing research, I don't know."

"At least that's not a flat-out no."

"If it was no, would you still try to sway me?"

He shook his head. "I have a proposition for you. Master Black is highly regarded for his rope skills. He's considered a shibari and kinbaku rope master. He gives demonstrations at a local club, and I think it'd be beneficial for you—for both of you actually—to see him showcasing his rope-tying expertise."

"What kind of club?"

"A private club. Some call it a sex club, but that's a simplistic description."

Her jaw dropped. "There's a sex club in Denver?"

"Lady, there are a dozen different underground private sex clubs in Denver."

"Oh. You can tell I don't get out much."

"It's not like they're advertised."

The conversation she'd overheard between Ronin and Knox at the dojo, where Knox asked if Amery was the reason Ronin hadn't shown up at the club, made more sense. "So you're offering to take me to this sex club?"

"Yes."

"Will you tell Ronin if I decide to go?"

"Not sure. I'd hate to tell him you'll be there and then you get cold feet and pull a no-show."

Amery started to protest that she wouldn't do that, but she couldn't guarantee it. There was a huge chance she *would* chicken out.

"Ronin hasn't said anything about what went down between you two. Not that I'm surprised; he's the most private man I've ever met. I've worked for him for years and still only know parts of him."

"That drives me crazy."

He shrugged. "It is what it is and that's the way he prefers it. What I do know of him I respect the hell out of, so it makes it easier to accept the walls he's built around himself to maintain that privacy."

No doubt Knox had Ronin's number.

"The other reason I know something unpleasant happened is that Sensei has been a fucking taskmaster the past three days. His training regimen for advanced students is difficult, but he's kicked it up a notch to brutal. And that's with all his classes, not just the higher-ranking belts and the MMA trainees. He's been equally brutal on himself—driving harder than usual during his workouts."

She had a moment of relief that Ronin wasn't unaffected by what'd happened between them.

Knox stood. "So think about it." He handed her a business card. "Call me either way."

"I will."

"I'm really hoping you'll say yes."

AFTER two restless days and two sleepless nights, Amery called Knox on Friday morning and agreed to go to the club. And she told him to make sure Ronin knew she'd be in attendance.

That decision made, she tackled the next one on her list.

She'd been vacillating about agreeing to work on Cherry Starr's project, given the erotic subject matter. She didn't want to alienate her existing clients, some of whom were religious organizations.

On the other hand, broadening her job opportunities made good financial sense, especially in this economy. Besides, she could call that branch of her design company something else. Like Hard-time

Designs. Or Hard-up Designs. Or Hard-on Designs. She snickered at
the last one, opened her e-mail, and started to type.

> *Cherry,*
> *Again, thanks for your honest and informative response. I'm very*
> *interested in helping create a sexy cover for your book. If you want*
> *to send me the parameters for the image as well as what you*
> *envision for art and an approximate deadline, I'll get started on it*
> *as soon as possible.*
>
>   *Thanks,*
>   *A~*

CHAPTER SIXTEEN

"WHAT does one wear to a bondage sex club?"

Knox looked up at Amery sharply. "Ronin didn't instruct you on what to wear?"

"I haven't heard from him. So I was surprised he told you to bring me to the penthouse first." She paused. "Is that part of the scene? The rope master or whatever he's called specifies clothing?"

He nodded. "Especially if you're being displayed."

Displayed. That word twisted the knots in her stomach tighter. Amery almost bailed on this adventure right then.

But she knew she had to go.

She wandered to the window. Twilight sent a pinkish orange glow across the Denver skyline. "What time are we supposed to be there?"

"In an hour."

"Doesn't exactly give me any time to shop." Wasn't as though Amery could call up Emmylou and ask to borrow fetish wear. Or Chaz either, for that matter, but if she had to lay odds on who owned leather and rubber clothing, she'd pick Chaz.

"I have a suggestion," Knox said.

"Me going naked is not an option."

Knox let loose a big booming laugh. "Ronin would have the head of anyone who saw you naked without his permission—including mine."

Again she fought the urge to bristle at the word *permission*.

"I think the reason he wanted you here is that there are women's club clothes in storage on the fifth floor."

Amery asked, "Whose clothes?" even when she knew the answer.

"They belong to Ronin," Knox said diplomatically. His gaze moved over her clinically. "You're the right size."

"So Ronin has a type?" she snapped. "Average-height strawberry blondes of Nordic descent with small breasts and pasty white skin?" *And no backbone.* "Is that what Naomi looks like?"

Knox stared at her as if she'd crossed a line.

"What?"

"You're wrong. Naomi is nothing like you."

"What do you mean?"

"Well, first off, she's Japanese."

Why hadn't Ronin told her that?

Because Ronin doesn't tell you much.

"Do you want to wear the clothes or not?" he asked.

"It's not like I have a choice." She headed to the elevator. "Let's go."

Knox curled his hand around her biceps, stopping her. "The storage room is off-limits. I'll grab a few things and bring them to you."

She bit back her sarcastic comment about actually being allowed to choose her own clothing and returned to pacing in front of the window.

What should she expect at this club? Would she see members getting whipped and spanked? Would there be lewd sex acts? What qualified as lewd in a sex club anyway?

And where did bondage master Ronin fit in? If she was disgusted or scared by what she witnessed, would she ever speak to him again?

Or maybe you're more worried it won't disgust you at all.

But what woman wouldn't freak the fuck out if her lover brought out a coil of rope and demanded, "On your knees, hands behind you"?

Amery rested her head against the glass. She was so confused about all of this. Would tonight clear it up or further muddy the waters?

The elevator doors opened. Knox approached her, holding out half a dozen hangers enshrined in plastic dry cleaners bags.

"I brought a variety. You are a guest tonight, so that will create some interest. But I'd suggest understated clothing if you don't want to stand out." He offered her that same slight bow she was used to from Ronin and left the room.

Amery stripped to her bra and panties in Ronin's bedroom. She snagged the black leather miniskirt from the first bag. She hated that it fit her like a dream. Had Ronin seen Naomi in this skirt? Had he slid his hands beneath the hem and cupped Naomi's ass?

Stop it.

But the image wouldn't go away, now that she had a better idea what Naomi looked like—probably exotic in that Japanese geisha way—so she nixed the skirt.

The second dress was one piece; not leather, not rubber, but somewhere in between. Composed of funky cutouts that left her midriff exposed and a sweetheart neckline, it might've been okay except for the rings on either side of the neck that were probably meant for a leash.

Definitely the *no* pile for that one.

The next number was hot pink rubber. Amery couldn't figure out how the hell to get it on, so it hit the discard pile.

The last item was a pair of leather pants. She worried she'd have to grease her legs to squeeze her thighs into them, but they molded to her contours as if they were made for her. Glancing at her ass in the mirror, she grinned. Her butt looked fantastic.

The shirt selection left a lot to be desired—either see-through or midriff. She eyed her lacy black bra. Although it wasn't any more revealing than a swimsuit top, she couldn't waltz into this club wearing leather pants and her bra.

On a whim she opened Ronin's closet. She flipped through the dozen white dress shirts until she found one in the back that looked smaller than the rest. She slipped it on and Ronin's scent washed over her. She closed her eyes against the pang of longing. How could she miss him so deeply when at the same time she felt she didn't know him?

She stepped in front of the full-length mirror. The shirt was too big. Grabbing the ends, she tied a knot at her waist. Her black bra peeking through was a little trashy, but a better choice than a rubber dress with her ass cheeks hanging out.

Amery wandered out of Ronin's room and Knox looked up from his cell phone. "That'll work."

"Good. So we what . . . just go? You're driving us?"

Knox shook his head. "Ronin is sending a car. It'll be about fifteen minutes."

"Oh. Okay." She headed for the bar and made herself a dirty girl lemonade—vanilla vodka, Chambord, triple sec, sour mix, and Diet Sprite. She looked at Knox when he perched on a barstool. "Can I get you something?"

"No. I don't drink on club nights. I'd take ice for my water, though."

Amery dropped cubes in a glass and slid it in front of him. "Maybe you'd better fill me in on sex club etiquette."

"You're a guest, so rule one is observation only. In scenes where there are whips or paddles and you hear the submissive saying no, understand that's part of the game. There are members who like getting pain and others who like giving it. Do not intervene."

She sipped her drink. "Is Ronin one of the types who like to give pain?"

"Not directly. He has several bondage suspensions that end up being painful enough to be called punishment."

"Bondage suspensions," she repeated. "As in hanging a person from the ceiling by a rope?"

"By a series of ropes."

"You'll tell me to direct my questions to Ronin, but what is he like in his public persona as rope master Ronin when people are watching his every move? Especially since he has the strict 'no observation' rule in the dojo?"

Knox looked uncomfortable. "Ronin is a fucking master with ropes. He's artistic and sensual, unlike some other so-called rope experts, who've turned shibari and kinbaku into weird performance art. He's in high demand as a teacher. So the nights he schedules a demo at the club, it's usually packed."

She wanted to ask if Ronin had sex with his models, or if he had sex with certain people at the club because . . . *hello*, it was a kinky sex club. Why would he be a member if he didn't want the free sex benefits? "Are you a master with ropes too?"

"I'm better than average because Ronin has mentored me. I don't teach but I do practice. My area of expertise in the club is different than his."

"What is your area of expertise?"

Hard blue eyes hooked hers. "Pain. Some members want it and they come to me to dish it out."

Yikes.

"Ronin asked me to ask you if you'll make time for him after the demonstration ends."

"Make time where? At the club?" In front of everyone?

"Either at the club or here, since you're leaving your things here."

"Can we see how it goes first?"

Knox frowned.

"I'm afraid to say yes because . . . what if I can't handle what I see? Not only Ronin's part, but the rest of the club stuff?"

He studied her for a few moments. "Think of it this way. These members' choices are not your choices. What you see them doing is no reflection on you, or the type of sex you're comfortable with. As you're walking through, realize it is an exclusive club. You may never get to see anything like it again. And more likely than not, you'll end up aroused by what you see. That's the hardest part for most people to handle." He looked at his phone. "We need to get downstairs."

Amery upended her drink. "Do I need to bring a purse or money or my certificate of clean health or anything?"

Knox grinned. "Nope. Just an open mind."

THE driver parked in an underground garage and accompanied them into the building. He and Knox exchanged pleasantries about the packed house for the night, but it meant nothing to her.

The elevator stopped on an unmarked floor. She squinted at the panel. None of the buttons had numbers. The elevator doors opened to a small reception area. The guy behind the desk looked like a Broncos defensive lineman—an armed lineman.

He nodded at Knox and handed Amery a clipboard. "Privacy form. Read it. Sign it. Believe it. Understand if the privacy rules are violated, we will prosecute to the fullest extent of the law. And yes, we have ways of knowing exactly who violates the contract and when. And yes, our legal team has dealt with such matters expediently and with the harshest penalties the legal system allows. Do I make myself clear, Ms. Hardwick?"

"Yes." Amery took the clipboard and sat on the lone chair in the room to read it. Nowhere on the form did it indicate who owned the business, but she did find the DBA listed as Twisted, so she knew the club had a name. The agreement prevented the signee from discussing the club, its location, its purpose with any persons who weren't members or on an active guest list status. No exceptions. Members of the club adhered to strict anonymity outside the club—members violating that stipulation would be removed from club membership rolls and prosecuted for breach of contract. No exceptions.

As much as the legal side of this scared her, she signed her name anyway. This would be her only visit to the club and she intended to leave as soon as Ronin finished his demonstration. She passed the clipboard back. Then to her surprise their chauffeur notarized it. Handy.

Then the supersized desk clerk addressed Knox. "You or Master Black can ensure that she will not be unattended at any time?"

Knox said, "I'm here strictly in escort capacity tonight, and as Ronin's fill-in."

Fill-in? What was that?

The clerk handed Amery a lanyard with a plastic card affixed to the clip. It read GUEST. He tied a black ribbon around Knox's biceps. Then he punched a code into a keypad and the chauffeur/notary guy/elevator operator opened the door for them.

Amery tried to act cool, but her heart raced as they stepped through the doorway.

Knox didn't take her arm. In fact, he hung back to see which direction she'd go. She opted to go right.

The open area looked like a dance floor at any club downtown. High ceilings. No windows. Conversation areas on the outskirts of the floor. She tried not to gawk at the people dancing naked. Or the people with collars on with leashes attached. No one paid attention to her, although a few nodded at Knox.

Once they'd crossed the room, she asked, "Is Ronin already here?"

"Yes."

"How long until the demonstration starts?"

"Half an hour. Is there something specific you'd like to see?"

"I don't know what my options are."

"I'll give you an overview."

She pointed at his armband. "What's that for?"

"To let members know I'm not available tonight."

"Oh." She paused. "Is that unusual for you?"

"Very. Come on."

Knox told her about the club, three levels with a fourth level reserved for private events. Amery didn't ask what constituted an event.

People roamed the halls. Normal-looking people. Some wore fetish wear, but it didn't seem as odd as she'd imagined.

Until they reached the next floor. Holy. Fuck. This area was set up like a big barn with stalls. The first four had stationary X's, which Knox explained were St. Andrew's crosses. In the first stall a naked woman was secured face-first to the cross. A man, cracking a whip, decorated her skin with welts across her backside from her calves to her shoulders.

Every time she cried out, Amery winced. In the far corner a woman on her knees, arms handcuffed behind her back, gave a blow job. A rough blow job since the guy was slamming his hips and fucking her face, while another guy stood behind them, his dick in his hand as he jacked off.

They continued down the hallway. Before they reached the next stall, she asked Knox, "The rules here are anyone can participate? Is there a hierarchy? Are the members singles or couples?"

"There are single submissives and single Dominants. A single submissive not paired with a Dominant is fair game, which is what submissives want. They negotiate what happens between them. It's all consensual. Some members come here to swap partners. Some couples join to use the equipment and indulge in themed rooms. Others join because they're exhibitionists or voyeurs. There are as many different reasons for belonging to the club as there are types of people who belong."

Amery nodded. She couldn't imagine dropping to her knees and giving her lover a blow job in public because he demanded it. In private? When Ronin commanded her to do something, it was sexy and thrilling because she knew she'd affected him deeply enough to earn that demand. Made it sweeter and hotter because it was just between them.

The next stall had chains dangling from the ceiling and O-rings embedded into the floor. She thought it was odd that it was unused until she saw the RESERVED sign.

When Knox said, "Are you ready to go upstairs?" in her ear, she jumped.

"Uh. Sure. I don't suppose there's a real bar around here?"

"'Fraid not. No alcohol on the premises."

So all these people acting this obscene way were completely sober.

Don't do that. Don't judge them. Not your life, not your business.

But part of her worried about what Ronin might expect from her. Maybe the reason such a hot, sexy, intense guy like Ronin was still single at thirty-eight was that he had kinky tastes that most women couldn't handle.

Very scary thought.

They stopped by the elevator and Knox stepped in front of her, blocking her from view.

She looked up at him. "What?"

"You need to lose the scowl."

"I'm scowling?"

"And looking disgusted, which doesn't go over well here as you can imagine."

Amery inhaled a deep breath and let it out. "I don't think I can do this, Knox."

"Can't do what?"

"Any of this stuff. Maybe I am a prude. But I don't ever see myself getting fucked on a pool table in front of a bunch of strangers. I'd be crying for real if I was tied up and being whipped. I'm not saying it's dirty or bad or wrong, it just isn't me."

Knox looked confused. "Why did you think it had to be?"

"Ronin is a member. And doesn't that mean . . . ?"

"You're here to learn, Amery. Ronin has asked that you watch the demo and then talk to him about it. That's the only thing you need to concern yourself with tonight."

So Knox hadn't denied Ronin participated in scenes like those—but he hadn't confirmed it either.

"Come on," Knox said. "The room has probably started filling up."

The cavernous room had a stage on one end, complete with billowing curtains. A lone chair sat close to the stage, with other chairs in a semicircle behind it. People were spread out against the back wall for the best vantage point. Conversation was hushed. The vibe was different in here than the other scenes. No props decorated the stage.

Knox pointed to the chair. "You'll be front and center."

"But I don't want to sit in the front. I'd rather be in the back so I'm not a distraction." She paused. "Not that he'd be distracted by me, but why take the chance?"

"Because that's how Ronin set it up and where he expects you to be."

Feeling conspicuous, Amery sank into the chair. Knox stood beside her and scanned the crowd. When the lights dimmed he squeezed her shoulder and disappeared.

She awaited the dramatic flair that would announce Ronin's entrance: smoke machines, swirling colored lights, epic music. Everything went dark except for the stage.

Here we go.

A woman wearing a white robe entered stage right. She didn't drop to her knees. She stopped and kept her head bowed as she waited.

When Ronin moved across the stage, Amery could feel the energy crackling from him. He wore white gi pants and a white tunic that set off his coloring to perfection. Were his eyes warm like topaz? Or that molten color of blackstrap molasses that indicated his arousal?

Ronin dropped coils of rope at the woman's feet. Then he swept her long brown hair aside and murmured in her ear.

Goose bumps cascaded down Amery's skin. She knew exactly how it felt to have Ronin's warm lips in that spot. How his deep voice seemed to burrow beneath her skin.

Then Ronin pulled the silk sash from the robe and folded it in half, using it to secure the woman's hair. She kept her head bowed. Ronin slipped his fingers beneath the collar of the robe, pushing it off her shoulders. The satin material caught in the bends of her elbows before he straightened her arms and the robe pooled on the floor.

The woman was naked. Her thighs were a bit heavy, her arms thin. Her belly pouched out. She had several tattoos on her arms and a flower above her pendulous breasts. An enormous bright blue bird of some kind decorated the outside of her right thigh from her outer knee to her hip. Everything else about her was ordinary.

Why did Amery feel the need to scrutinize this woman's body?

Because Ronin's hands would be all over it. She had to convince herself this woman was nothing special. Just a random model plucked out of this club specifically for this purpose.

So why did the woman's head fall back when Ronin spoke to her? That's when Amery suspected this woman was no stranger to Ronin's touch. She knew exactly what was coming.

A jealousy that she'd never experienced rocketed through her.

Then her lover was running his hands down the woman's chest. Cupping the weight of her breasts in his palms and moving south to map the curves of her hips. He reached for the coil of rope and retreated to stand behind her.

The rope Ronin used was vivid blue. First he turned her so her back was to the audience, allowing everyone to see how expertly he immobilized her wrists after pinning her forearms together. Then he faced her forward.

Amery watched Ronin winding the rope, his fingers connecting with the woman's skin on every pass. She felt the gentle scrape of his calluses. When he circled the next section of rope around the women's midsection, Amery's abdomen contracted as he wound it tighter. Then he crossed the ropes over the model's breasts, compressing the flesh, and Amery felt the air leaving her lungs as he pulled the ropes almost to the point of pain.

All eyes were focused on the woman. Her body decorated with crisscrossing ropes and knots, her rapid breathing, sweat shining across her chest.

Just for an instant it wasn't some nameless woman onstage. When she lifted her head, Amery saw her own face.

CHAPTER SEVENTEEN

THEN Ronin spoke to the audience. "Feel free to take a closer look at this shibari technique called 'zigzag.' The model has consented to be touched as you examine the tying techniques."

Holy shit. The woman had agreed to let strangers touch her without restriction?

"No questions directed to me, please. Admire the beauty of the canvas and not the painter." Then he disappeared into the shadows.

The crowd swarmed the woman. The last thing Amery saw was an expression of bliss on the woman's face as she gave herself over to the touch of hands.

Knox crouched in front of Amery. "Don't you want to look?"

She shook her head.

"Why not?"

Don't tell him. She let her hair fall over her face, hoping it hid her blush.

"Amery. This is an important part of who Ronin is. That's why you're here. Don't you want to witness his mastery?"

She lifted her head and wished she was confessing this to Ronin. "No. I don't want to see Ronin's mastery with erotic bondage on her body. I want to see it on mine."

Knox's eyes searched hers. "Tell him that. There's an unmarked dressing room at the end of the hall. He'll be in there after this."

The crowd returned to their seats instead of exiting the room. Wasn't this over?

Ronin returned to the stage.

Apparently not.

Amery watched Ronin untie the woman's hands. Speaking to her in a low tone. Caressing her. How she hated to see Ronin's hands on that woman because she knew exactly how wonderful it felt to have his hands on her.

He removed the ropes.

Someone behind Amery said, "What's going on?"

Another voice answered, "He's dragging this out as he unties her and reties her differently. Then he'll fuck her."

Was this what Ronin had been doing the Saturday nights he'd been unavailable to her? Demonstrating his rope skills on women and then his skills as a dominant lover?

Her entire body seized up with shame. She'd trusted him. She'd had sex with him without a condom, for God's sake.

Then Amery shut out the judgmental voice that'd been with her since childhood, reminding herself not to jump to conclusions.

She refocused on the stage as Ronin created a new rope configuration on the woman's lower half. Smoothing his fingertips along the rope lining her belly and hips. He crafted knots that ran in a straight line down her abdomen, across her hips, over her mound, and between her legs.

But Ronin's hand didn't drop over the woman's pussy. He tugged on the remaining rope as he instructed her. She turned around and spread her legs, showing everyone the rope work that framed her pussy and her anus, but left her completely accessible.

And Amery felt an entirely different type of jealousy. What would it be like to be that free and accepting of your own sexuality and your body? Not only in private, but in public as well?

"This kinbaku technique is called 'exposing the cherry.'" Ronin affectionately ran his hand down the woman's spine. He bowed to her and then to the audience. He nodded to Knox, who quickly joined him onstage.

Knox returned the bow and then lightly slapped the woman's ass cheeks. She gasped in surprise.

The anticipation in the room increased. Especially when Knox hauled her upright and began kissing her nipples and fondling her breasts while his free hand pulled on the crotch harness, dragging the knot across her clitoris.

Amery tried to wrap her head around what she was seeing. When Knox directed the woman to unzip his fly and pushed her to her knees, she fled.

People had started to exit the demonstration room by the time Amery realized she'd zoned out in the middle of the hallway—afraid to go forward or back.

Then she spied the unmarked door at the end of the hallway. After she reached it, she paused, unsure if she should knock or just go in.

Quit being a chickenshit. He's expecting you.

She turned the handle and stepped inside the room.

Ronin's broad back was to her. He'd taken a shower since the familiar scent of his soap hung in the humid air and he'd changed clothes. He was so lost in thought he didn't turn around until she clicked the door shut.

"Amery."

Her name sounded beautiful coming from his sinful lips—almost like a benediction. Should she go to him? Her feet wanted to move but her brain screamed at her to be cool, to make him come to her. She'd already taken the first step by showing up at Twisted tonight.

Ronin combed his fingers through his damp hair. "I'm glad you came."

"Me too."

"Are you okay?"

"No. I'm so not okay right now, Ronin. Not at all." Despite her efforts to stay calm, she began to shake.

He crossed the room and crushed her to his chest. "Baby. Stop. Just breathe. You're here now. That's all that matters."

She closed her eyes and clung to him. "Is it really?"

"Yes." He whispered, "I've missed you," into her hair.

"I missed you too." Amery dug her fingers into the hard muscles of his back and burrowed deeper into the spot between his chest and chin that her head fit into perfectly.

After several glorious minutes of being in his arms, Ronin tipped her head back. "I know we need to talk. But first I need this." His mouth came down on hers. Kissing her as if he might never get another chance.

Amery basked in the passion that ignited between them. Every kiss, every touch was filled with heat and promise.

"Come home with me," he murmured. "We'll talk all night and all day tomorrow if you want." He pressed soft kisses down the side of her neck. "Please. I'm dying for you."

"Yes."

Ronin slowly released her. "Let's get out of here."

Amery scarcely remembered leaving the club. She wasn't sure they spoke at all during the drive to his place.

Upon reaching his penthouse, she kicked off her shoes and Ronin reached for her. He traced the edge of the cotton material to the V of her cleavage. "I like you in my shirt."

"I'm a little low on sex club wear. And I should change."

"Don't. You look great." He took her hand and led her into the living room.

Amery sat on one end of the couch, facing the opposite end, with her feet in the middle cushion, putting some distance between them.

Ronin mimicked her position, but he immediately grabbed her

foot and set it on the inside of his thigh. His fingers swept over her ankle bone and the back of her calf in a continual arc.

The man's face gave nothing away, so the fact that he needed to touch her to establish a physical connection allowed her to relax. "I'm so sorry for the shitty things I said to you last Saturday."

"I know you are."

"Can you forgive me or will my knee-jerk reaction always be a sticking point between us?" When he didn't immediately respond, another thing occurred to her. "I'm not the first woman to react that way, am I?"

"No. You'd think I would've learned my lesson. Or at least learned to have better timing."

"Why did you pick Saturday night?"

Ronin's dark eyes bored into hers. "Because you told me no boundaries and I ran with it."

She had tossed that out. Why had she been so shocked he'd taken her bold words at face value?

Because you're never reckless and you expected civility from a man who deals in violence.

"In retrospect . . ." He shook his head. "Just ask me the questions I see in your eyes."

Unsure on how to phrase her question or issue or whatever the hell it was, Amery focused on her ragged cuticles.

But Ronin didn't allow it. He moved closer. His warm fingers slid below her chin and he tilted her face up. "Don't be shy with me, Amery."

"Why didn't you tell me about the rope stuff from the start? If it isn't a hobby and it's part of who you are?"

"I've hidden a lot from you. I don't blame you for wanting to get away from me."

Amery watched as his features softened. And dammit, the vulnerable side of him softened something inside her.

"I've been training in martial arts every day for as long as I can remember. And by training, I don't only mean the physical side, but the psychological aspect, the spiritual aspect, and the long-held traditions that are part of the discipline. Living the philosophy really kicked in when I sequestered myself at the monastery."

"On a spiritual level?" she asked.

"To some extent. I immersed myself in training. Over the years I'd worked with swords, knives, sticks, every weapon at my disposal. To be honest, I wasn't particularly skilled at any of them. I excelled at the hand-to-hand drills and utilizing pressure points to disable an opponent. So the idea of learning the ropes, so to speak, didn't excite me." He paused. "It surprised me when a rope in my hand felt natural and I picked up everything quickly.

"By the end of my second year of training, at age nineteen, I equaled my teacher in skill. He enlisted help from another rope master. His specialty was . . ." Ronin's eyes met hers. "Shibari."

"Did he demonstrate on you?"

Ronin shook his head. "He had three female companions he 'lent' to me. They were knowledgeable and vocal about what did and didn't work in my tying techniques."

That crazy punch of jealousy hit her again. "These women had no issue being *lent out* to you by their master like some kind of fuck toys?"

"I didn't fuck them, Amery. I bound them."

"Oh." But she couldn't let it go. "Were those his rules? Or their choice?"

"Are you asking me if I would've fucked them if they'd wanted it?"

Amery raised her chin. "Yes."

He twisted a hank of hair around his fingers and tugged her closer for a quick kiss. "No. They were strong with supple bodies and completely unashamed of their nakedness. During that time— I didn't treat them like women, but as objects I could bend to my will. To my vision. That's when I understood I needed the beauty and artistry of shibari and kinbaku in my life as more than just tying a woman up like a package. I wanted the intimate connection."

This was a much deeper look into him than she'd expected to get from him tonight. Amery reached for his hand. It was the first time she noticed his knuckles were raw, red, and scraped up more than usual. "What happened?"

"I worked out harder this week than what I normally do."

Knox had mentioned that to her. "Why?"

Ronin twisted his hand and brought her knuckles to his mouth for a soft kiss. "I was on edge and needed a way to channel my frustration besides taking it all out on my students."

"So you . . . ?" she prompted.

"Hit the heavy bag. A lot."

"Ronin. Why didn't you wear hand protection?"

"I did."

She closed her eyes. Images of him methodically beating the shit out of a heavy bag, his face placid as pain exploded from his hands, twisted her stomach in knots. "Does it hurt?"

"What? My knuckles?"

"Yes."

"I've had worse." He paused. "Do the marks and scabs bother you? Would you rather I didn't touch you until they're healed?"

Amery opened her eyes. "It bothers me that you've been hurting."

"Being in pain is the story of my life. These hands have been broken, bruised, bloodied, scabbed, and scarred. I've hurt people with these hands." Ronin dropped his head and stared at his hands, turning them over to look at the palms. He curled his fingers in and then stretched them out. "When I realized I had a knack for ropes, I wanted to find balance between using my hands for pain as well as beauty. I wanted to create something beautiful, even if it was as fleeting as pain. I'll never be an artist in traditional mediums, but with a rope in my hands and a vision in my head, I become an artist."

Amery let his words flow through her and it set something inside her free.

This man was beauty.

She dropped to her knees in front of him.

Ronin's surprised eyes hooked hers.

She took his right hand in her left, threading their fingers together until their palms met. Then she brought his left hand to her mouth, letting her lips drift across his ravaged knuckles. She pressed kisses on the back of his hand, the joint of his thumb, and the tips of his fingers. Then she pressed his hand to the side of her face. "I think your scarred hands are beautiful. Will you use them to create that rope artistry on me?"

"You really want that?"

"I really do, now that I understand it. Now that I understand you."

"You undo me, Amery." He stroked her cheek with the ragged pad of his thumb. "I should be on my knees before you."

She melted.

Ronin stared at her, his face again devoid of expression and it scared her.

"What?"

"Do you know why I took an interest in you that first night you showed up at my dojo?"

Hoping to lighten things up, she tossed off, "There's another reason besides you recognizing my natural untapped abilities in martial arts?"

Ronin smiled. "Besides that. Although you missed class this week and you will be required to make up the session."

"In private? With you?"

He shook his head.

"Shoot. Anyway, tell me why you took an interest in me."

"Because of this." He tugged the shirt down, below the ball of her right shoulder and traced the raised flesh of her scar. "How did you get this?"

She glanced at the white lines an inch apart that ran parallel for two inches up her biceps and the thick line at the top that connected the two lines. "The summer I turned eight my parents sent me to stay at my grandparents' farm. After living under my parents' iron rule . . . I went a little wild. Got a little reckless."

"Your first experience with no boundaries?" he said wryly.

"Something like that. Anyway, somehow I ended up in the bull pasture and those mean motherfuckers chased me. When I reached the fence, I dove through it, scared to death of being gored by a bull. In my haste to escape, I got caught up in the barbed wire. I twisted and jerked until I freed myself. I didn't realize how deeply the barbed wire had gouged me until I felt blood running down my arm.

"At that age I was more worried that my grandma would be mad I'd ripped my shirt than that I'd injured myself. Long story short—I covered the wound with duct tape and that stopped the bleeding. But I hadn't gotten it clean, which made it itch, so I picked at the scabs and ended up with a scar." She looked at him. "Why? Are you into scars?"

"Never before now. But this one"—his finger followed the white lines—"threw me off."

"Why?"

"Because it's nearly identical to the Japanese symbol for a rogue samurai warrior."

"Seriously?" Amery glanced down at it. "I'd think it was weird that you knew that, but given your background . . ."

Ronin placed his fingers beneath her chin, forcing her to meet his gaze. "Do you know what word is the English translation for a rogue samurai warrior? A samurai without a master?"

The intensity in his eyes caused her heart to skip a beat. "No. What?"

He paused and said, "Ronin." Then he angled his head to place his lips on the scar. "You have my name etched on your skin, Amery. I considered that a sign." His eyes met hers again. "Wouldn't you?"

The room spun. She didn't trust herself to open her mouth, so she rested her head on his leg.

He silently stroked her hair.

Finally she said, "I know we need to talk some more, but I'd really like to wrap myself around you for a little while."

"Here on the couch or up on the roof?"

Amery lifted her face and looked at him. "What about your bedroom?"

Those golden eyes gleamed. "I have willpower, but not that much after a week without you. I can't promise to keep my hands to myself."

"I'm not asking you to."

Without a word Ronin scooped her into his arms and carried her into his bedroom.

CHAPTER EIGHTEEN

THEY stripped down to their underwear and crawled beneath the cool sheets. Entwined together with Ronin in the dark, Amery suspected nature would take its course. And it did, just not in the way she imagined. They fell asleep.

She woke up disoriented and peeked over Ronin's shoulder to check the time on the alarm clock. Seven a.m. Wow. Neither of them had stirred all night.

Ronin murmured, "Where you going?"

"Nowhere." She snuggled back into him and closed her eyes.

But now that she'd awakened him, he trailed his fingers up and down her spine. "Guess we both needed rest." He kissed the top of her head. "I didn't sleep worth a damn last week."

"Because you missed me?"

"Could be. Or could be the extra hours working out. Or a combination. How about you?"

"I slept like a baby."

He made a displeased noise and quickly pinned her arms to her sides. "Is that so?"

"Yes, because babies wake up several times in the night and

need comforting. Or food. Since I didn't have anyone around to comfort me, I cracked a pint of Häagen-Dazs at two a.m."

"You wallowed in sugar; I wallowed in pain. Why exactly was it we weren't wallowing together?"

"Oh, a little thing about you neglecting to show me your ropes before you tied me up in them."

His arms tightened around her. "What now? I've got you locked down. Without ropes."

"Well, I have a weird question we didn't talk about last night."

"Which is?"

"Does it always have to be kinky between us?"

Ronin rolled her to face him. "What do you mean?"

She tried not to fidget under his sharp stare. "Will you need to tie me up every time in order to get off?"

His eyes narrowed.

"Oh, don't try and scare me with that sensei glare."

"I haven't even begun to scare you."

"I'm serious, Ronin."

"So am I."

Somehow Amery got the drop on him and was striding into the living room before he could grab her.

He spun her around. "What the hell? You just walk away in the middle of a conversation?"

"I asked you a question and you hedged. Normally that's not a big deal because you do it all the freakin' time. Last night I listened to you and I have a better grasp on this part of you. So I deserve a straight answer on whether we can ever have sex without the bondage stuff."

Ronin stared at her so long she geared herself up for another non-answer. But he curled his hand around her face. "It doesn't always have to be that way. And you must be aware of that, since it hasn't always been that way between us."

"Bondage of some sort has played a role in most of our sexual encounters."

"I suppose maybe it has." This being Ronin, he didn't offer an explanation or an excuse for it. He jerked her body against his. "Understand one thing. I don't always need ropes or ties, but I am always in charge. That's one thing that won't ever change. And I intend to prove it every chance I get."

That declaration in his sleep-roughened voice made her tingle everywhere.

"You got that?" he asked.

"Yes, sir."

"Good." He stepped back and crossed his arms over his chest. "Lose the bra."

Amery unhooked it and tossed it aside.

"And the panties."

She shimmied the black silk down her legs. Completely bared to him, she wondered what sexual treat he had planned first thing.

"Now let's have some breakfast."

"But I'm naked!"

"So you are. Looks like I'll be frying the bacon."

"Ronin." She placed her hands on her hips and tapped her foot. "Aren't you supposed to be proving that you don't need kink all the time?"

"That only applies to the sexual side of our relationship. Besides, eating breakfast in the buff isn't kinky."

"It is for me!"

"You'll get used to it." Then he sauntered into the kitchen.

TWO hours later they were lounging by the pool.

Ronin said, "What would you like to do today?"

Amery cracked a lid open. "Besides this? Nothing."

"Nothing? Not one thing?"

"We could roll around in your big bed. Get ourselves hot, sweaty, and sticky and then jump back into the pool."

"You have a thing for my pool."

"No, I have a thing for *you*. The pool is just a bonus." She looked at him over the top of her sunglasses. "You up for a tumble?"

"Actually I wanted to talk to you about that." Ronin reached for her hand. "Since you've agreed to let me bind you, I'd like the first time to be a little more formal."

Her belly made a slow roll. "Can you explain that?"

"I want you in the right headspace from the start. And knowing that you're in my practice room, waiting for me, will put me in the right frame of mind too."

"Okay. But what does that have to do with us taking a tumble right now?" She paused. "Oh. Do you want to tie me up right now?"

"No. But as much as I want to build the anticipation of the binding, I'd like to build the anticipation of the sex after the binding, by abstaining from it."

"You're serious."

He kissed her knuckles. "Completely. It isn't like I expect to hold off for a week, just until tomorrow night. Can you be here at nine?"

Amery smiled. "Looking forward to it."

"Perfect. I'll leave instructions for you in the room."

Instructions. That did sound formal.

"Would you like a peek in the practice room?"

She'd wondered if he'd offer. "No. I'd rather it retain some mystery."

"Good point."

"Besides, the room is for you, not for me."

"Another good point. But I promise we'll both enjoy it."

She didn't doubt that for a second. "So now that I know sex is off the table for today . . ." She stood and whipped off her bikini top, then ditched her bottoms. She threw a grin at him from the edge of the pool. "Let's swim naked."

"You are getting bolder." He shed his swim trunks and moved in behind her.

"Yes, I am. And I'm blaming it on you." Then she wrapped herself around him and tipped them both into the deep end.

THE following evening Knox let her into the penthouse. If he noticed she was nervous, he didn't mention it.

Amery's steady heart rate skyrocketed when she opened the door to Ronin's secret room.

Spread out across the bench was a satin kimono the color of cherry blossoms—pale pink that gradually morphed into a deep rose at the bottom hem. She picked it up and rubbed the silky fabric against her skin, half expecting the sweet aroma of cherry blossoms to surround her. But Ronin's scent teased her nose and she breathed it in.

A piece of paper fluttered to the floor. Amery picked it up, realizing it was a list for her. Ronin's precise penmanship stood out in black, a sharp contrast against the thick white paper. She read:

INSTRUCTIONS
Strip and wear nothing beneath the robe.
Leave your hair down.
Kneel on the pillow in the center of the room.
Close your eyes and allow your mind to drift.

No wasted words. No surprise there.

As Amery ditched her clothing, the balls of nerves knotted in her chest, her belly, and the back of her neck began to loosen. She slowed her breathing and focused on her senses.

The cool robe slithered against her naked, heated skin. The velvet pillow provided cushioning for her knees as she rested back on her haunches. The only scents she could distinguish were Ronin's and the slightly bitter tang of her own sweat. Her mouth remained dry, but she could taste the remnants of her breath mint. Placing her hands palms up on her thighs, she searched for the quiet place inside her where unease didn't have a foothold.

Her happy sense of calm wavered when the door snicked shut. *Breathe.*

Then Ronin's hands were on her scalp. Petting her, following the length of her unbound hair to the ends in the middle of her back. His mouth brushed her ear. "Nervous?"

"Yes."

"Good."

Not the response she expected, which caused her to bristle and ask, "Are you nervous?"

His softly whispered "Yes" was there and gone.

She permitted herself a small smile.

He said, "Stand," and helped her to her feet. From behind he untied the robe's sash at her waist. He slid his palms up the length of her arms. He peeled back the fabric from her shoulders, and the satin fell to the floor.

Amery had been naked in front of him before, but this seemed . . . new.

Then his lips were on her skin, trailing down the side of her neck in a silent command to arch to the opposite side. Her hair swished against her back in an erotic arc as she complied.

"So lovely," he murmured, while pulling her arms behind her back. "Is it comfortable for you to grab your elbows?"

She maneuvered her arms into a better position.

"Perfect. I'm going to start tying you now."

Her stomach lurched in a combination of fear and excitement. She blurted out, "Am I supposed to keep my eyes closed?"

"Up to you."

"Me watching you won't bother you?"

Ronin stepped in front of her. "No. The only thing that will bother me is if you're not honest about how you're feeling. Blocking your sight will strip away another layer of your control. I can blind-fold you if you'd prefer."

"Oh." Part of her wanted to be blindfolded to get the edgier experience, but a larger part wanted the option of watching him as he bound her.

"So what'll it be?"

"I'll wing it."

He pressed a kiss on her lips. "Stay still. I'll be right back."

Amery watched as he selected three plain white rope bundles from the far wall. And she managed a clinical detachment about what he intended to do with the rope until he loosened the first bundle. She squeezed her eyes shut.

"I'll start with a chest harness that will also immobilize your hands."

"Okay."

That's all Ronin needed. The first wrap circled her chest below her armpits. As did the second and the third. Then he crossed the center of her chest, and that pulled the bindings tighter as well as squeezed her breasts.

She contemplated looking down to watch him at work, but she focused on his rough fingertips gliding across her skin as he checked the tightness of the bindings. And yeah, they were plenty tight.

"Are you holding your breath?" he asked in that low, com-manding tone.

"Maybe a little."

"Inhale and exhale slowly. Even more exaggerated breathing than you use in yoga."

She nodded and filled her lungs.

Ronin didn't miss a beat and kept wrapping.

When he tugged the rope across her nipple, she sucked in a surprised breath.

"One more like that."

The second wrap compressed her nipples between the two ropes, creating a pinching sensation, and her eyes flew open. She glanced down and saw her nipples elongated from the pressure and jutting out from the ropes.

His thumb swept over the left one as his right hand held the coil of rope. "Does it hurt?"

"Not when you touch it like that."

Ronin kept stroking it, staring into her eyes. "This tie is called 'string of pearls.' See how the binding makes the tips of your nipples round?"

"Yes. Just as long as it doesn't cut off my circulation entirely and turn them white."

"I know how sensitive your nipples are. Plus, my mouth will help restore blood flow when the time is right."

That brought forth a flash of heat between her thighs. She closed her eyes.

He said, "Breathe, baby," and wound the rope around her rib cage.

There didn't seem to be a point when his hands weren't on her. Or when she couldn't feel the heat of his body against hers. Or feel his lustful gaze studying her reactions. It was heaven, being on the receiving end of his total attention.

Another shiver broke free when his fingers followed the contour of her belly down to the rise of her mound.

Ronin pressed against her clit and dragged the pad of his thumb down the seam of her sex and back up. He pushed against that bundle of nerves again. But the pressure was different. She sucked in a quick breath when she felt the rope sliding along the split in her sex, one on either side of her labia. Then he pulled it between her legs and up the crack of her ass.

His mouth grazed her ear. "Do you know how beautiful you look?"

"No."

"Or how fucking hot it is that I can make you come whenever I want just by doing this." He tugged on the ropes, sending a shooting sensation from her nipples to her clit, then down her pussy, across her anus.

She gasped, shocked that the sharp bite of pain morphed so quickly into pleasure.

He snatched the two rope ends tickling her back and attached them to the rope threaded between her thighs, tying them to her bound arms.

Amery's breaths had become labored—from the tight bindings or her lack of control or a combination of both.

"Slow and steady, remember," he said in that deliciously deep, calming tone.

But it didn't soothe her this time. She thrashed around in an attempt to get free. "I can't get enough air."

"Amery."

"I can't fucking breathe."

"Stop. Think. You're safe."

"No! Let me go."

Ronin abruptly stepped away, leaving her alone.

That kicked her sense of panic higher. The rope sliced into her every time she moved, burning tender flesh. She twisted her shoulders, trying to shake loose. A scream of frustration got stuck in her throat and the only sound she could make was a pitiful whimper. All she heard was the rush of blood in her ears.

Then firm, warm flesh pressed against her back.

Ronin.

He pulled her lower body against his with his right forearm, which also stopped the rope from moving and abrading her skin. Ronin curled his left hand around her throat and jaw, holding her in place.

His complete immobilization of her didn't create additional alarm. It somehow . . . settled her. He didn't say a word; he just held her. He made her feel safe.

Keeping her eyes closed helped her focus.

"Better?"

"Yes."

"I'm going to let you go. Are you ready for me to finish binding you?"

"Okay."

Whatever configuration he used connecting her arms to the chest harness took longer than she'd expected. So by the time he finished, she'd drifted into that floaty headspace she'd experienced when he tied her to the chaise. She was attuned to every nuance in her body. The tug in her sex. The constriction around her chest. The position of her arms and hands that rendered them useless.

Ronin's warm breath drifted over her damp skin as he made adjustments. Intensity radiated from him.

His fingertips followed the bindings from her chest to her belly, over her slick pussy, up the crack in her ass, and then from her shoulders down her arms to her wrists. He didn't say a word, but Amery knew she'd pleased him.

A gentle push indicated she needed to return to her knees. Her head tilted forward and the ends of her hair brushed the tops of her thighs.

She wasn't sure how much time passed before she felt Ronin behind her. His hand went to her hair, pulling to get her attention as that hot, wicked mouth of his assaulted her neck. Biting, sucking, sending tremors of need through her and yet she knew she remained under his control. She couldn't touch him. Or herself. She couldn't do anything but surrender.

And what a sweet, sweet surrender it was.

Ronin lightly tugged on the rope with the knot teasing her clit. His other hand toyed with her nipples. Sometimes pulling. Sometimes pinching. Sometimes just giving her a featherlight stroke over the aching tip. He held her head in place with his hand and nuzzled the skin beneath her ear. "Amery."

"Mmm."

"Are you close to coming?"

"No."

He increased the speed and pressure of the rope on her clit and she sucked in a sharp breath. "Better?"

"Some, but I don't think I can . . . without direct contact."

Then Ronin slid in front of her and let his tongue flick across her nipple. He bent his head to her other breast and scored the tip with his teeth.

Her head fell back.

He moved the small knot in the rope away from her clitoris and stroked with his thumb. Side to side at first, bringing blood to the nub.

Amery clenched her thighs in anticipation. Every rapid stroke on her engorged clit pushed her closer to the edge. The binding around her chest forced only reedy breaths, increasing the dizzy sensation.

Then Ronin's mouth was sucking in that spot below her ear— the spot that shot an electric charge to her nipples and ricocheted to her pussy. She had about a five-second warning before she came undone. And right after that first hard pulse rocked her, Ronin snapped the knotted rope into place over her clit.

The spark of pain lasted a split second before the pleasure hit and her cunt spasmed. Every pulse felt like another hard snap of that rope.

She arched back but didn't have anywhere to go with her hands tied. Ronin's mouth suctioned to her neck as his fingers twisted her nipple to the pulsing rhythm coursing through her.

By the time she floated back down, Ronin's touches were aggressive.

He shifted her into the position he wanted—on her knees on a training mat, her chest against the cool vinyl, her ass in the air. Those skilled hands skimmed her naked back from the start of her spine to where her bound hands rested above her ass. Her name tumbled from his lips as soft as a sigh, but with as much reverence as the way he touched her. His potent mix of affection and need flowed through her when he clamped his hands on her hips and anchored his body behind hers.

The thick head of his cock circled the opening once before he plunged into her pussy to the hilt.

Although she was wet and she'd already come once, the ferocity of his thrusts made her breath catch. Good thing he'd switched his grip from her hips to the ropes binding her arms or she would've gone skittering across the mat.

But it felt good. Empowering. She'd driven Ronin Black to the tipping point. And he was proving his mastery with every hard, driving thrust. He didn't speak. The only indication he'd finally reached the end of the climb was when his fingers dug into her hips and he released a soft grunt as his heat filled her.

Afterward Ronin retreated and pulled her to her feet. He immediately picked her up, cradling her in his arms as he carried her to his bedroom. The man wasn't even breathing hard when he laid her on his big bed.

He kissed her with hunger and delicacy. First her mouth, then his lips meandered down her torso, stopping at her swollen clit. He was ruthless in bringing her to climax again with his tongue and soft, sucking kisses.

Amery sighed, surprised she had breath enough in her lungs to make any noise at all.

He traced the skin above the first rope wrap as he untied it. "You are beautiful bound. Beautiful in your surrender to me."

"Even when you had to talk me down?"

Those ever-changing brown eyes hooked hers. "Especially then."

"Ronin—"

"Hold on for a second." He helped her into a sitting position and wedged himself between her knees. One quick tug and one of the knots on the chest harness loosened the binding above her breasts. Blood rushed in and the painful pins-and-needles sensation would've brought tears to her eyes if not for Ronin's mouth being right there to alleviate the sting.

"Oh my God."

"You like that?" he murmured, moving to her other breast.

"It hurts. Then it doesn't. Is it weird I miss the hurting sensation, but at the same time I don't?"

"No, baby, it's not. That's why it's called the edge between pleasure and pain."

"It's easier to understand when I'm actually dancing on that razor's edge." She let her head fall back as Ronin kissed and nuzzled every section of her chest where the ropes had been.

Then he was in her face wearing a look of satisfaction. "You took to bondage amazingly well." He kissed her forehead. "Is that something you'd like to continue to explore with me?"

Amery blinked at him. "Why would you think I wouldn't be interested?"

"I never assume." Ronin brushed his cheek over hers. "You agreed to try it. That's it."

"And I liked it," she blurted. "A lot."

"Good to hear. I have plenty more ideas on how I'd like to bind you."

She shifted her head and saw the red marks on her skin. All over her skin. Would the marks still be visible in the morning? Would her friends and clients recognize rope burns on her wrists?

He tipped her chin up. "Hey. Where'd you go?"

"Just worried about"—*what other people will think?* jumped into her head before she blocked it out. "How long will the rope marks show?"

"They'll be gone in a few hours. But you've got to expect to have marks every time I bind you. It's physics. Something coarse rubs against a soft surface and it'll result in a mark." Ronin dragged a fingertip across the red line above her left breast. "Some who are tied want the marks. In fact, the more marks the better. It's a badge of honor for them."

"But they don't have mainstream jobs where they have to face, say, the church camp counselor, who's picking up promotional materials and she sees the graphic artist with rope burns on her arms, wrists, and ankles."

"Amery, I'd never put your livelihood in jeopardy. But there will be times when the marks won't fade as fast as tonight. It depends on the size and type of rope, what pattern I'm attempting, where I tie you, if I use suspension, and even if I fuck you when you're bound."

"So maybe the question is, how often do you want to bind me? Every time we're together? Will you demand it? Do you need it?" Sitting on the bed, naked, talking about bondage specifics should've made her feel sexually free, but mostly she felt confused and exposed.

Ronin gathered her into his arms.

Almost immediately, she relaxed.

"One thing at a time, okay?"

She nodded.

"There's no need to set a schedule, like I'll bind you on Tuesdays and Saturdays, and Wednesdays and Mondays are no-tie days. Kinbaku can be spontaneous. But I can also plan to practice a specific binding on you several days in advance. So I'd let you know, like tonight, that we'll be in a more formal situation. Does that work for you?"

"Yes."

He kissed her temple. "You can ask me to tie you. If you ever want to look at pictures of possible poses you'd like to try, let me know. Will I demand that your body becomes mine to play with? Sometimes. But you can always say no."

"I heard about safe words and—"

"We won't need one because if you aren't in the mood, all you have to say is no. If you have a panic moment while you're bound and you want me to untie you, I'll probably first determine why you want to be released, and if it's not a health or safety concern, chances are good I can just talk to you to figure out the issue, okay?"

"Okay."

"As far as me needing to bind you . . . that's a trickier answer. Obviously I like the way you look when you're bound. Working with ropes centers me in a way nothing else does. And like with any other skill, if kinbaku and shibari aren't practiced regularly it fades. So it falls somewhere between a compulsion and a skill for me."

She said, "Oh, I get it," even when she didn't, but she was trying. "If I decided I'm not into the kinbaku aspect of our relationship anymore?" Amery felt him smile, as if he didn't believe that'd happen.

"Then we'd have to revisit a few things in our relationship."

"Such as?"

"Such as you understanding that I would be binding other women. Which leads to my next question." He shifted to look at her face. "I'm a teacher. I give demonstrations. Would you be willing to be bound in public?"

Amery shook her head. Vehemently. "No way."

"Which is fine, just as long as you're aware that I will use other models in public venues and possibly in private when I need to practice."

Jealousy stabbed her in the gut.

"I won't fuck them, but I will touch them in a sexual manner."

She noticed he didn't ask her permission. The thought of him touching another woman . . . made her want to try out a few of the choke holds he'd taught in her self-defense class on said women. She had to act mature—even if she didn't feel it. "I wish I had the guts to bare myself like that, but I don't. It's been enough of a challenge baring myself to you. I won't give you false hope that I'll ever 'get over' it either."

"I'm not asking you to." Ronin softly pressed his lips to hers.

"As long as we're discussing expectations, there's something I'd like to talk about."

"Shoot."

Amery rolled to face him, placing her palms on his smooth pectorals, secretly marveling at the perfection of his chest. "You're at the dojo late most nights, which doesn't allow us much time together during the week. So I'm fine with hanging out here or at my place in the evenings. But on the weekends, I want us to go out and enjoy the Denver area. That's the only aspect of being part of a couple that I missed."

"Doing couple things?"

"Yes. It isn't like I've been sitting at home, letting life pass me by while I wait for that couplehood. It's just some activities are more fun when you're sharing them with another person."

Ronin smiled. "I couldn't agree more. So do you have things planned for us?"

She exhaled a quiet relieved breath. She hadn't been sure how he'd take her suggestion. "Hiking in Rocky Mountain National Park?"

"Cool. I haven't been up there in a while. What else?"

"I've never been to the Coors Brewery Tour in Golden."

"I'm always down with drinking beer right after it's been tapped." At the word *tapped*, he patted her ass. "These are great ideas. Keep going."

Encouraged, Amery rattled off her next set of ideas, which included a visit to Tiny Town, Colorado, and attending an ice-skating extravaganza at the Pepsi Center. "I don't want to overly plan so we have time for spontaneity."

"Good. As a matter of fact, I'm feeling spontaneous right now."

She squealed when he lifted her up, straddling her across his groin. "But you'll be doing the work this time."

"Yes, sir."

CHAPTER NINETEEN

THE sidewalk was wet when they exited the theater out the side door to avoid the crowd. The rain had left a chill in the night air. Amery snuggled into Ronin and he wrapped his arm more securely around her shoulder.

"So? What did you think?"

"Interesting. Never heard a Christian death metal band before." She laughed. "Most people haven't."

"How did you hear about them? And more important, how does this correlate to your upbringing? Because I took you to kabuki theater last weekend and you took me to a rock concert."

They'd spent the last two weekends doing couple things. But it hadn't cut into Ronin's plans for her—just seemed to reinforce his constant desire for her. He'd bound her standing up, similar to the tree pose in yoga: her heel pressed into her thigh, her arms above her head, hooked to the ceiling. He'd made her come three times before he fucked her like that.

"See? You're quiet because you can't justify it."

"I took you to a *Christian* rock concert," she corrected. "And it correlates because the lead singer and I are from the same area in North Dakota. We attended some of the same church camps. He always wanted to kick up the youth worship services with contemporary music to make it more relatable. You can imagine how well that went over. Rick left town, moved to Minneapolis, and started this band. I'd lost track of him over the years, so when I saw how popular they've gotten in the Christian music scene and were playing in Denver, I thought it'd be fun to check it out."

"I was surprised to see so many people there. Who knew the devil's music wrapped in angel's wings had such a strong following?"

Amery elbowed him. "Not funny."

"Although I wasn't sure if I was disappointed or relieved there weren't any animal sacrifices onstage."

"Says the Buddhist with an altar in his practice room."

"It's not a Buddhist altar; it's a Shinto shrine. And if you noticed, I didn't buy a CD, but I was in the minority, so they are doing well, at least on the merchandising side."

"I'm happy he's successful doing what he loves. Not everyone is so lucky in their working lives."

He kissed her temple. "We are."

"For as long as it lasts for me."

"Meaning what?" They cut across the street and walked past abandoned buildings that lined both sides of the block. Showing up late to the event meant all the prime parking spots close to the venue had been snapped up, so they'd parked several blocks away.

"Meaning I've been scrambling to find new business. With so many places taking their graphic needs in-house, not only have I lost clients, but it's harder picking up new ones. I've tightened my belt as much as I can, but unless things pick up soon, I'll have to let Molly go."

Ronin stopped and faced her. "Amery. Why haven't you told me this?"

"Because it's hard to admit, especially to someone who's running a successful business. I doubt you've got downward trends like in the line of work I'm in."

"I've had some pretty lean years and done what I had to, to make ends meet." He brushed a stray hair from her cheek. "Is there anything I can do?"

"Besides line me up a million-dollar client?" she joked. Then she kissed the frown on his mouth. "Kidding. One good thing is even if I have to close up shop and go to work for another company, I won't lose my apartment because of the storefront rental income from Emmylou and Chaz. It's just I feel guilty about Molly."

A metal *clank* echoed and she spun around to see where the noise had come from. But there weren't any streetlights and the area was completely deserted.

How could that be? For as many people who'd attended the show, there should be more people heading back to their cars. But the sidewalk was empty and no cars zipped by. She got a little creeped out in the eerie silence. "Are we going the right way?"

Ronin looked around. Frowned at the darkness. "This doesn't look right. We must've gotten turned around and exited on the wrong side. My car is the other direction."

They reversed course. Right after they crossed the street, two guys stepped out of the shadows.

Amery almost screamed, they'd slunk out of nowhere so fast.

"I see we got us some tourists in our neighborhood," one guy said to the other.

"Know what we do to tourists who find themselves 'lost' in our neighborhood, bro?" the other guy said.

"We charge them a finder's fee."

"So pay up, motherfuckers."

Fear slammed into her.

The two guys moved in uncomfortably close. She heard a noise and looked over her shoulder to see two more guys spread out behind them.

They were fucked.

Then Ronin put his mouth on her ear. "Stay behind me and out of the way."

"I don't like you whispering to your bitch, so knock that shit off and pay the fuck up."

Ronin said nothing. But she noticed he'd maneuvered them so she was behind him and his back was to the wall.

The Hispanic guy taunted, "Don't got nothin' to say, *ése*? We're insulting your woman and you're gonna stand there and take it?" Then he leered at Amery. "Got a mind to prove to you what it's like to be with a real man, *puta*. Make him watch how I can make you scream."

Laughter echoed around them.

"None of that yet, bro." The other guy gestured with his chin to Ronin and crossed his arms over his chest. "Hand over your wallet, watch, and everything in your pockets. Do it fast."

Ronin didn't budge.

Which pissed off the black guy. "You deaf? Or you need an incentive to do what the fuck we tell you?"

"I'm not deaf. I'm also not handing over my wallet. Here's your warning to back off."

"Back off? Or what? You're outnumbered, dumb fuck."

"Got ourselves a real hero here," the other guy drawled. "Let's see how tough you are."

Please no. What if the guy had a gun? Or a knife?

The Hispanic kid moved in on Ronin's right side as the black guy came at him from the left. She wasn't sure where the two other guys were. She just knew that four against one were shitty odds and she couldn't get to her phone to call 911.

Everything happened in slow motion—but also lightning fast.

Ronin stepped forward as the Hispanic attacker came at him. He delivered an open-handed strike to the guy's nose and swept his feet out from beneath him. The guy hit the ground hard and howled in agony, clutching his broken nose.

The black guy didn't spare his buddy a glance; all his rage was focused on Ronin. He held his arms up and in front of his face and performed a couple of shadowboxing moves. But as soon as he led with his right hand, Ronin grabbed it, twisted the dude's arm entirely behind his back until something popped. The guy yelled—as much from pain as the fact that he also found himself on the ground eating dirt.

In that moment Amery couldn't look away from Ronin's effortless control of the situation. He'd barely moved; he hadn't even broken a sweat.

When the other two thugs—both white punks—approached him, Ronin said, "Walk away."

"Fuck you," one of the guys retorted. He jumped into the fray only to find himself facedown on the filthy wet pavement clutching the knee Ronin had kicked.

The other one turned tail and ran.

Amery thought they'd get out of there pronto, but Ronin was patting down each guy. When he found two guns, she had another resurgence of fear.

What if the guy had just pulled out a gun and shot them both?

Breathe. Come on, Ronin. We're supposed to run. Remember what you taught me?

She watched in horrified fascination as Ronin ejected the clips from the guns, pulled back on the thumb release, and dumped the bullets on the ground. He wiped down the metal before he whipped the empty clips into the street drain. Then he jammed one gun beneath the waistband in the small of his back and let the other gun dangle in his hand.

Ronin backed away and said, "Let's go," to her.

They remained silent on their brisk walk back to his vehicle. They only stopped once at a Dumpster to ditch the guns. He opened the passenger door to the SUV, hoisted her in, and didn't speak until they were out of the sketchy part of town.

"Are you okay?"

She shook her head.

He picked up her hand and kissed it. "What can I do?"

"I don't know."

Even after they parked his car and took the elevator to his place, Ronin gave her a wide berth. Maybe fighting and ditching firearms were just par for the course with him, but they weren't for her. Not at all. Her body hadn't settled down from the adrenaline rush. She shook so hard she thought she might be sick. As soon as the elevator doors opened to his penthouse, she made a beeline for the bathroom.

He didn't try and barge in.

She splashed cold water on her face and gulped several mouthfuls of water before exiting the bathroom.

Ronin waited outside the door. "Can I get you anything?"

She shook her head and wrapped her arms around herself.

"Amery. Talk to me."

"I don't know what to say. I just don't understand."

"What do you mean?"

"Why did you take their guns? Why didn't we just leave once you had them on the ground?"

"You think I wanted to take a chance they'd shoot one or both of us in the back? Not happening. I disarmed them, broke their guns down, and scattered the pieces."

"Why not turn the guns in to the cops and tell them we were attacked?"

"Chances are slim the guns were registered. Those thugs won't report them as missing. If I file a report and the cops go looking for those guys, and the guns I ditched, I could end up in a lawsuit and I sure as fuck don't want those guys knowing who I am and where I live."

Amery hadn't thought of it that way.

"Plus, given my background in martial arts, lots of people, including cops, believe I go looking for fights. I don't. But there is that perception and I'll be goddamned if I'll defend myself to anyone— including law enforcement—for my right to defend myself when under attack." He breathed deeply. "You were there. You'd rather I would've done the PC thing, given them what they wanted? Because I can guarantee you neither of us would've walked away unscathed. And because I reacted the way I did, the way I've been trained to react, we're both here, in one piece. I won't apologize to you for that either."

When Ronin turned his back to her, she noticed he was vibrating with anger.

Maybe she'd been freaking out about the details and had missed the big truth. Ronin's quick thinking and years of training had gotten them out of a potentially deadly situation. She oughta be thanking him, not questioning him.

Amery moved in behind him. "Thank you for saving me tonight, Ronin." She took a chance and circled her arms around his waist. "Sorry if I seemed ungrateful. I'm not."

"Amery—"

"Let me finish. I've never seen you like that. In ass-kicking Master Black mode, showcasing your eighth-degree black belt skills in the real world."

"You weren't put off by seeing that violent side of me?"

"Shocked at first. But now? I'm more than a little turned on, if you want to know the truth. You moved so fast." She stood on her toes and kissed the back of his neck. "It reminded me you don't play at self-defense. Your body responds instinctively because that's how you've trained it to respond. It's sexy as hell." She kissed the slope of his shoulder. "Makes me want you. Right now."

Ronin whirled around. His mouth was on hers, his hands were on her, and nothing else mattered.

Her fingers automatically went to the buttons on his shirt, while

Ronin's hands made quick work of the zipper on her jeans. They managed to get undressed. He lifted his mouth from her throat long enough to say, "Bedroom is too far away. I want to fuck you here." He pushed her up against the wall.

She groaned when his teeth scraped down her throat. "No. On the floor. Like a takedown."

Next thing she knew, they were on the hardwood with her knees clamped against Ronin's ribs as he slammed his cock inside her.

"Yes. God, yes, do that again."

He withdrew and rammed into her with long, deep strokes, his mouth at her ear. "I want to feel your nails digging into my back and my ass. I want to feel your teeth on my skin. I want to wear your marks."

She just about came right then.

As he pounded into her with enough force they slid across the floor, Amery sucked a love bruise on his pectoral. She dragged her nails down his back when his tongue flicked across the sweet spot in the curve of her shoulder. She arched and ground against him, giving herself over to this primal mating. This physical testament that they were alive.

Ronin's hands pushed her knees until the outside of her thighs pressed into the floor. That change forced his pubic bone to keep continual contact with her clit and she gasped.

"Hands on me," he demanded.

With his mouth sucking on her nipple, it only took six short strokes and she came so hard white spots obscured her vision. Ronin's orgasm started on the tail end of hers and she dug her nails into the back of his neck, his long moan sweet to her ears since the man usually came in near silence.

They stayed slumped together in a sweaty pile, breathing hard, until the chill from the floor caused her to shiver.

Ronin pushed up and looked into her face. "You blow my mind every fucking time."

"And just think . . . you didn't even have to break out the ropes for it to be that hot between us."

"Smart." Kiss. "Ass." Kiss.

She reached up and touched his face. Sometimes she couldn't believe this gorgeous, complicated, kinky man was in her life.

"Why are you looking at me like that?" he asked softly.

Rather than tell him again how hot, sexy, and amazing he was, she said, "Thank you for your quick thinking and getting us out of a bad situation tonight."

"My pleasure." He kissed her with such sweetness tears stung her eyes. "Let's get cleaned up and ready for bed."

"That means I'm staying over?"

"Be a little hard for you to leave after I tie you to my head-board."

She laughed, but come to find out . . . he hadn't been joking.

AMERY showed up for work thirty minutes late on Wednesday morning. She hadn't tried to sneak in, but after seeing her friends circled around Molly's desk, loaded for bear, she wondered if she should've made her appearance after lunch and claimed a new client meeting had kept her away from the office.

"Well, well, look what the cat dragged in," Chaz said with no hint of a smile.

She wasn't exactly surprised by the ambush since things had been tense for the past couple of weeks. Chaz defined surly, even in casual conversation. And after Emmylou returned from her on-site jobs, she grumbled and slammed her office door. Amery had tried talking to each of them, in person and via text, but neither had responded, so she figured the issue was between them and they hadn't wanted to drag her into it.

But it appeared the issue was about her—and they'd joined forces.

"What's going on? Did I miss a memo for an interoffice meeting?"

"Call it what you want, but we need to talk to you."

"Who's we?" Amery asked.

A blushing Molly put her hands up in defense. "I want no part of this."

"Why don't you take a thirty-minute break at Lisabet's Patisserie?"

"Sure. Would you like me to bring you anything?"

She shook her head. No one spoke until Molly had left and Amery had settled in with a cup of coffee. "So, besties, why does this feel like an intervention?"

Chaz lifted an eyebrow. "Is there something bad and wrong you've been doing that requires one?"

"Besides Ronin Black?" Emmylou added snarkily.

What the hell? "Whoa. This is about Ronin?"

"Of course it is, because you're all about him lately, aren't you?"

She bristled. "What about him?"

Emmylou and Chaz stared at her in silence.

"So you decided to jump me about the man I'm involved with but you aren't telling me why?"

"You know why."

Amery shoved down the worry that her supposed friends had figured out what she and Ronin had been up to behind closed doors. He was always so careful not to leave excessive marks when he bound her. The rarely seen devil on her shoulder reminded her that what she and Ronin did in the bedroom was no one's business. "No, I really don't."

"Don't you see that you've immersed yourself so much in this relationship with him that you're losing yourself? We rarely see you anymore after work hours because Ronin monopolizes all your time and you let him," Chaz said.

She blew across her coffee before taking a sip. "Monopolizes," she repeated. "Really? If I recall correctly I asked you to lunch last week, which you declined. I also asked if you wanted to have a drink with me, which you also declined. And the reason you declined is that hot little Latin piece of ass you're hiding from Andre, remember? The week before that you couldn't be bothered to answer a single text from me. That is somehow my fault? Bull. Shit."

"See? This is why we're worried about you. You snap at the drop of a hat and if anyone raises any questions about Ronin, you get defensive. And I'll be frank—I'm worried that the only reason he's teaching you how to fight is so you can be even more like him."

Her angry gaze zoomed to Emmylou. "You've got to be kidding me."

"Look at this from our point of view. Ronin's job is all about violence. Are you telling me that you don't see anything wrong with how he's isolated you from your friends?"

"You think he's isolated me? How the hell would you know that?" she demanded of Emmylou. "You were out of town all last week. The week before that the only time you approached me was the night of the self-defense class I've been taking for weeks, which, again, just indicates how little you care about the important things going on in my life."

"And you've deemed Ronin the most important thing in your life after only a few weeks? You don't see anything wrong with that?" Chaz asked. "Right after you started seeing him you refused to go to the bars you've always gone to with us. Is that something Black demanded from you? Telling you that you couldn't hang out with us anymore?"

"I cannot fucking believe we are even having this conversation. And excuse me for being a total selfish bitch, but after years I'm done going to strictly gay hangouts. Why is that? Not because Ronin decreed it, but because I can't count the number of times you—both of you—have ditched me during happy hour and I ended up going home by myself anyway. So the way I see it? You're pissy that I'm not at your beck and call anymore to fill the void when you get bored and don't have anyone else to go out with.

But guess what? I don't give a shit what you think about Ronin. I am perfectly capable of making my own decisions about things, including who I choose to spend my free time with, so suck it up. Both of you."

Chaz and Emmylou stared at her in total shock.

"So, is there anything else? Or are you still going to try and convince me the time I spend with Ronin is the real issue here?"

Silence.

"Good. Now if you'll excuse me, I do have actual work to finish." Amery spun on her heel and headed to her office.

She let out a little scream when she was abruptly jerked back. Then both Chaz and Emmylou were right in her face.

"Looks like North Dakota has grown some big, sharp teeth. Brava, darlin', but that's not what this is about."

Amery snapped her teeth, which caused both Chaz and Emmylou to take a step back. It just further annoyed her when Chaz and Emmylou exchanged a pointed look. "For Christ's sake. Tell me."

"You want to play hardball? We're game. We've heard things about Ronin from people who've dealt with him," Emmylou said.

"He's a scary man, *chère*," Chaz said. "And the cautionary tales we've heard don't make him fairy-tale prince material like he's led you to believe."

"He's an eighth-degree black belt and a martial arts master; of course he's scary." Amery's eyes narrowed. "And who exactly did you hear these *cautionary tales* from? Because I know Ronin's confidantes, and they wouldn't tell tales out of school. Literally. So that makes me question your source."

Chaz looked cowed, but Emmylou remained defiant. "All I can say is it came from a reliable source. Someone who's in the Denver sports world."

Where would Emmylou have picked up something like that? Then she remembered Emmylou had done on-site work with the Rockies last week. And the one person in the Rockies organization who might have any interest in her relationship with Ronin was . . . Tyler.

No. A sick feeling took hold of her. Surely Emmylou wouldn't listen to Tyler. "Tell me the name of your reliable source."

When Emmylou dropped her gaze, Amery knew.

"Tyler Pessac, my self-absorbed asshole ex who annihilated my confidence and was the direct cause of me licking my emotional wounds for over a year, is your reliable source?"

Fury boiled up. Amery inhaled two deep calming breaths before she spoke again. "Did you even consider, for one fucking minute, that Tyler approaching you with information about the dangerous Ronin Black might be born out of jealousy? Tyler saw me with Ronin at the Colorado Sports Banquet. He saw how happy I was. He knows Ronin is a better athlete, better looking, better connected, and a better man in all the ways that really count. He also saw that Ronin is crazy about me. And that made Tyler a little crazy because the only time I *ever* appealed to him after he started cheating on me? Was when another man was attracted to me. That's the only thing that ever validated my worth in his eyes.

"You know how long it took me to dig out of that pit after Tyler dumped me. Or at least I thought you did because you were there supposedly supporting me. So I can't believe . . ." The word came out choked and she took a second to breathe. "I can't believe you'd take that lying sack of shit's side and even bring this up with me. Especially when I'm truly happy with a man for the first time in my life."

Chaz turned on Emmylou. "Tyler was your source? Are you fucking kidding me?" Then he faced Amery, his eyes filled with remorse. "I swear to god I had no idea or I wouldn't have—"

"Back off. Both of you. Leave her alone," Molly said hotly. She walked over and inserted herself between Amery and Chaz and Emmylou. "I came back to get my purse, so I overheard Amery having to defend herself to you two. Friends don't do that shit and you both know it. Now get out of this office and don't show your faces again until you can apologize. I mean it."

Chaz and Emmylou both slunk out.

Immediately Molly gave Amery a hug. "I'm sorry you had to deal with that. I overheard them bitching about you spending all your time with Ronin and I thought that's all they were going to talk about with you. If I'd known what they really had planned . . ."

"Molly. It's okay. Thank you for jumping in."

"No, thank you for teaching by example. I've learned so much from you—it's important to stand up for myself and be there for my friends."

"You are a good friend." Amery squeezed her one last time and closed herself in her office.

The shitty start to her morning continued throughout the day. She lost another existing client to the company's in-house restructuring, and a potential client went to another agency. She spent more time on the phone than working, but at the end of the day, she couldn't remain in her office a minute longer. After changing into workout clothes, she climbed into her car and headed toward Black Arts.

Maybe beating the shit out of a punching bag would cleanse her mind, body, and spirit.

CHAPTER TWENTY

YONDAN Deacon McCloud was a mean son of a bitch.

Amery fantasized about throwing him on his ass. Kicking him in the shins. Slamming her hands into his ears with her newly learned thunderclap technique. Sinking her teeth into his tattooed biceps.

The man claimed that missing a self-defense class meant he needed to push her harder. He showed her new moves and drilled her over and over until she was gasping for breath. Then he'd start in again.

He made Sensei Black look like a kindergarten teacher.

Not that she'd share that insight with the dojo's Grand Pooh-Bah. She used a hand towel to mop her face.

"Come on, flavor of the month. Quit stalling. We're not done."

"You're killing me."

He grinned.

Holy shit. That was the first time she'd ever seen Deacon smile. It kicked his attractiveness up a notch or ten, but it also made him look ten times scarier. Bald, tattooed, excessively muscled, and overly intense men hadn't appealed to her before, mostly because she'd never been around any. She definitely saw the appeal now.

"So, you gearing up to kiss me or what? 'Cause that sure ain't a defensive fighting stance, cream puff."

"Cream puff? I'll show you cream puff." Sick of Deacon's smarmy comments about being Ronin's flavor of the month and her lack of defensive know-how, Amery twisted the towel, intending to snap him with it. But he snagged the end and did some fast maneuver that wrapped the towel around her own wrist. Then he twisted it until her arm was behind her back and she dropped to her knees. She gasped, "Uncle."

He laughed—a little maniacally. "Sucks when your own weapon is used against you, doesn't it?"

"Yes."

Deacon released her. "Get up and let's go again."

Amery muttered, "Sadistic bastard," as she rolled to her feet.

"I'm not a bastard—my parents were married when my ma birthed me. But sadistic? Yeah, I'll cop to that one." He switched his stance. "Block me."

Before Amery gathered her wits, Deacon was in her face, sweeping her legs out from under her. She hit the mat butt first. Rather than lie there humiliated, she latched on to his pant leg and tugged.

Deacon turned his upper body, which allowed her to kick him in the back of the knee. He immediately went down to one knee. He raised a surprised brow. "Good work. Self-defense is eighty percent improvisation in the moment."

"What's the other twenty percent?"

"Ten percent is using learned skills and the last piece of that pie chart is utilizing fear. Without fear we'd have no need for self-defense."

"Gee, Yondan, you almost sounded like Sensei with that bit of philosophy," she teased.

"I can only hope his influence is rubbing off on me. Now show me strikes."

"Which ones?"

"All of them."

By the time she finished, the class had run thirty minutes over and she dripped sweat.

Yondan looked as fresh as a daisy. "I'll let Sandan Zach know you're caught up with your class."

"Thank you."

"You can find your way out of the maze?"

Amery nodded.

He offered her a slight bow and exited the room.

She'd intended to go straight to the locker room and change, but she took a wrong turn and ended up in an area she'd never been in before. She stopped in front of a five-foot-wide window that looked into a training room. Given the dark tint of the glass, she doubted the people inside the room could see out.

Her gaze was immediately drawn to Ronin at the front of the classroom.

With his hair pulled back, his shrewd eyes assessing his students, his don't-fuck-with-me posture—he was a magnificent sight to behold.

He wore black gi pants and a red gi top. Knotted at his waist was his black belt with eight red stripes embroidered across the width and his master level in Japanese below it to the tip of his belt. The upper patch on the left side of his chest read SENSEI BLACK. Below that was the American flag patch, a smaller Japanese flag below that, and four small patches she couldn't read. He had more patches on the sleeves of his gi top—on both sides—and on the right side of his chest was the new Black Arts logo she'd designed.

She grinned. Hadn't taken much time for the design to be integrated.

Since Amery didn't have anything better to do, and she figured he couldn't see her anyway, she decided to observe him in teaching mode with what looked like advanced black belt students.

After the sixteen students rose to their feet, he paired them off. Even when they were performing warm-up exercises, Ronin corrected strikes and postures. And more than a few students tensed up when he assisted them. Sensei Black definitely ruled with an iron fist.

As she watched him interact, she didn't see a glimmer of the Ronin she knew. No smile. No banter. His posture was as rigid as the set of his jaw.

The disjointed feeling should've made it easier to slink away from this man she didn't recognize. But it locked her in place, keeping her hopeful she'd catch a glimpse of her lover.

When the grappling started, she expected he'd sit on the sidelines, but he surprised her again and forced each student to demonstrate the technique on him.

Or maybe a more apt description was they all *tried* to demonstrate the technique and their teacher summarily dumped them on their face into the mat.

It wasn't Ronin's facial expression or body language that telegraphed his displeasure that not a single student had properly demonstrated the technique. He barked out an order and even Amery jumped.

A student left and returned within a few minutes with Knox.

Shihan Knox practiced the technique and immediately employed it perfectly. Amery suspected Ronin had sandbagged his response. Then the sensei challenged Shihan once again, after he'd given a slow-motion demo on the basics of the technique.

That time Shihan ended up in a submission hold.

As he did the next time.

That's when Amery realized neither man had held back.

And still, even with Shihan Knox in the room, there wasn't any sign of the Ronin she knew. She really didn't recognize him when the kicking sequence began. Sensei's kicks were hard and lightning fast against the practice bag.

How much have you ever really known of this man?

After she'd calmed down, she'd been grateful when he disabled the attackers that night. But now seeing how quickly he could explode into violence and how impassive he remained through it, she knew he'd kept a large part of who he was hidden from her. Right now his ability with ropes didn't frighten her nearly as much as his easy segue into calculated violence.

She fought a shiver and stepped back.

At that moment Ronin looked up and she swore he knew she was there, breaking the rules.

Amery ducked down and managed to sneak out before anyone caught her.

Or so she thought.

An hour later when Ronin showed up at her place, he was in a mood. Usually after he'd washed away the sweat and violence that clung to him after hours in the dojo, he reconnected with that Zen vibe and he rarely let her see his agitation.

Not tonight.

She knew if she asked what'd wound him so tight, he'd refuse to confide in her, but she guessed his students' lack of progress played a big part in his edginess—not that she could mention she'd watched him with a class, since that was a total breach of the "no observation" rule.

Hoping to improve his mood, Amery offered to use her personal massager on him, joking that it'd finally be used as the manufacturer had intended. Instead of what she'd planned, rather naively, it turned out—to rub every inch of the vibrating head over his muscular body to try and soothe him—Ronin had set his own plans into motion.

Only after he'd caressed her, aroused her, and divested her of every stitch of her clothing did she notice he'd cleared off her coffee table.

"Ronin? What are you—"

"You know what I want," he murmured against the curve of her neck as he knotted her hair on top of her head with a pen. "If you don't want this, tell me no."

Her mouth remained closed.

"Good." Then he brought out camouflage rope.

She shivered when his fingertips traced the outsides of her arms to her wrists.

"Arms behind your back. Make sure you've got good circulation because this might take a while." He brushed a tender kiss across her shoulder. "I'm practicing tethered turtle on you."

While his touches were gentle, she sensed him hanging on to his control by a thread. Since he'd demanded honesty from her, she deserved the same courtesy. "You seem on edge."

"I am." Ronin's voice burned her ear. "Why do you think I enforce the 'no observation' rule in my dojo, Amery?"

Shit, shit, shit. Master Black *had* seen her through the two-way glass or else his super-ninja instincts had sensed her.

Or maybe . . . Yondan Deacon told him you were skulking around after your lesson.

Dammit. Maybe letting her roam free had been some kind of test to see if she'd follow the rules even when there didn't appear to be anyone around to enforce them.

Well, she'd flunked that test big-time.

"I asked you a question," he said in that pseudo-reasonable tone.

"No, sir, I don't know why you have that rule."

"I set that rule to allow my students to fail in private because failure is the best way to learn, adapt, and change."

"Are you going to punish me for my failure since I broke that rule?"

"No. You were under Yondan's supervision tonight; it's his call on how to deal with it."

That wasn't reassuring. "So this turtle pose or whatever it's called isn't a punishment pose?"

Ronin's lips swept across the shell of her ear. "You sound disappointed."

"No! I'm not."

"If I wanted to punish you, I'd use a hojojutsu binding." His arm snaked under hers and he wrapped his fingers around her throat. "Those ties include neck restraints."

She swallowed hard.

"The challenge isn't in the binding but in the chase and capture beforehand."

Holy crap. A chase? Then a capture? That sounded a little scary.

"I feel your heart racing, Amery. Relax. Tethered turtle pose celebrates the duality of the creature—the beauty of a hard exterior that protects the inner softness."

"Oh."

"You ready to begin?"

"Yes."

"Climb onto the coffee table and I'll arrange you."

Once he'd positioned her, she rested her cheek against the cool wood, breathing in the scent of lemon furniture polish. Her knees were spread wide, but the rest of her body was curled in—a turtle in its shell.

"Beautiful." He scraped his fingers down her naked back from her shoulders to the curve of her ass. "Breathe, baby, because it's going to get tight."

Those words, uttered in his velvety rasp, jolted through her like a shot of pure adrenaline. Anticipation was her new drug of choice administered by the man with magic hands. She craved that sense of helplessness as he bound her . . . and then the calm he bestowed on her that followed after the binding.

Out of the corner of her eye, she saw his black T-shirt hit the floor. He stood close enough that she saw his toes peeking out from beneath the frayed hem of his worn jeans.

Lust slid in and piggybacked on Amery's anticipation. She

knew exactly what he looked like looming above her—the strong, sexy, determined rope master. His muscles flexing. His dark hair untamed around his chiseled face. His eyes would flicker from amber brown to inky black, gauging her every reaction as he knotted the ropes and stretched them against her pale skin. His full lips would be pursed with concentration. His jaw set. His breathing faster than normal because her submission excited him.

It excited her too, more than she'd ever imagined. But along with the excitement was fear. And a little shame, which she understood was part of the appeal for her because it was shame she could control.

Ronin placed a kiss on her skin, as he always did. "I'm going to start tying you now."

And as always, her pulse leaped when she heard the whisper of friction as he uncoiled the rope.

Relax. Breathe.

He knotted and twisted the ropes, starting at her ankles and working his way forward, until her entire body was covered. She felt as if he'd spun a spider's web around her. Although it'd taken him a while to bind her, she hadn't drifted into the floaty headspace yet.

Ronin had left her head and neck free from restraint. She understood he expected her to stay in position just by his will alone. His fingers tightened and tested the configuration. When the ropes abraded her flesh, his caresses eased some of the sting.

Some, not all.

If there wasn't any pain and fear with this bondage, would she still participate?

The word *no* sprang into her head, unbidden.

Sweet baby Jesus. What kind of woman liked—no, *craved*—the way this man trussed her up every chance he got?

Then Ronin's clipped voice burrowed into her ear. "Will gagging you keep you from giving voice to those negative thoughts in your head?"

He'd immediately sensed her internal war with herself. His intuitiveness would freak her out if she wasn't so grateful for it and the verbal reminder on why she trusted him. "Please don't gag me."

"Who is holding you prisoner right now? Your thoughts?"

"No."

"Then who?"

"You are."

"By choice?"

"Yes, by choice," she repeated, once out loud and then again to herself, almost as self-affirmation.

He added more pressure to the binding across her shoulders. "That's right. Every thought, every breath, every heartbeat, every pulse of blood, every whisper, every sigh, every gasp of pain, every moment belongs to me. I'm pushing you to the place where negative thoughts don't have any hold on you and you are exactly as you were meant to be. So you will let me do this. To you. For you." He paused. "And for me."

"Yes, sir."

"Lose yourself in what I give you." His warm, soft lips brushed the sensitive skin beneath her ear. "Remind yourself what your surrender means to me."

Everything.

Tears stung her eyes. "Thank you."

He murmured in Japanese and retreated.

She half expected his touches to become reverent, but if anything, his hands became harsher. The web of constriction more pronounced. He crafted a shell around her, even as she became the shell. Curled up and bound, she felt safe. Protected. Tethered to the table and to him.

His pleasure in her submission sent her soaring.

Amery knew the moment when he stood back and admired his handiwork. The glow of his pride flowed over her as he studied the beauty of her body reformed by his ropes. His scrutiny lasted anywhere from a minute to what seemed like forever. Then he'd untie her. Check for rope burns and thoroughly inspect her reddened flesh for other marks. He'd deal with any abrasions with tender touches, whisper-soft kisses, and on rare occasions, first aid ointment. After that he'd wrap himself around her until she settled back into normalcy from the bondage high.

But that wasn't the game plan that night.

She was still floating in that happy place when a familiar buzz yanked her out of subspace.

"Very sweet and thoughtful of you to offer up your toy for my use. But the better choice is for me to use it on you."

What? No. What the hell was he thinking?

Before she opened her mouth to protest, he placed the buzzing head of her massager directly on her clit.

Amery gasped, trying to shift her hips away, but he'd locked her down completely.

"How fast does this get you off?"

Now she wished he *had* gagged her so she wouldn't have to answer.

"I'm waiting."

Shit. "Two minutes." Tops. Sometimes it took under a minute. Not that she'd admit it to him. Ever.

"Where's the fun in that? Or the challenge? I like taking my time. As you well know. Slow and steady wins the race."

"Are you seriously spouting lines from the freakin' 'Tortoise and the Hare' at me?"

"I thought it appropriate, given the circumstances. Given the fact that you also have a rabbit vibrator in your collection of toys. Would you prefer me to use it instead?"

"Don't you dare torture me with my own vibrators, Ronin Black."

"Or what?" When he nestled the buzzing vibrator head at the top of her cleft, her soft tissues got all tingly. "You're short on options.

The way I see it, you've got two choices. You can stay here and take it." He dragged his mouth across her skin, employing those open-mouthed kisses that made her buck and moan. "Or you can stay here and take it."

Cocky bastard.

"So what'll it be?"

"I can take it."

Ronin began drawing buzzing circles around her clit. "You sure?"

"If you'd hold it there longer than three seconds, I guess you'd find out."

His chuckle tickled her ear. "Acting a bit bossy for a woman wearing my ropes."

"You're acting a bit threatened by a vibrating piece of silicone and plastic."

While he held her vibrator directly over her clitoris, his mouth found all the hot spots down her neck and across her shoulders that made her writhe and moan. Then he sucked and tongued them unremittingly.

"Ronin."

"Stop thinking. Let go. Give it to me."

Give it to me. Bound by him, he reminded her that her pleasure belonged to him.

Then the man bombarded her senses until *bam!* she was slammed into that white void. Mouth gasping, pussy throbbing. Coming so hard she felt it in her teeth, her toenails—even her earlobes prickled.

She'd stretch out and purr like a contented cat . . . if she could move. It wasn't lost on her that if Ronin could reach her clit with the vibrator, then he'd tied her up so he could fuck her. He didn't always bind her with sex in mind. But whenever he did, she relearned the meaning of the word *unravel.*

"I timed you," he said. "Three minutes. Next time I make you come it will take longer. But there's a catch." His deep voice sent a hot curl of want straight to her core. "Come out of that shell and beg me to fuck you, turtle girl."

Yes. Please, please, please.

No. Show some restraint. He'll reduce you to a whore.

Amery gritted her teeth against the judgmental voices that had ruled her since childhood.

No. He's not reducing me to anything. He's empowering me to ask for what I want.

"I don't hear you begging. Do you want me to leave the room and give you some time to think about it?"

"Ronin. Please."

"You want it." His tongue traced the shell of her ear. "Ask me. Beg me. Plead with me. Prove to me you can. Just say the words I need to hear, Amery."

The seductive tone, the fleeting touch of his lips on her skin, that overwhelming want . . . finally it all came together to drop-kick those annoying voices right out of her head. She blurted, "Fuck me. Right now. Fuck me into an orgasmic stupor. Fuck me until I can't walk." But the part of her that liked to taunt him added, "If you think you're up for it. Or are you waiting because you fear a . . . jackrabbit finish?"

A growling noise reverberated against her neck one second, and the next Ronin was braced above her, shoving his cock into her so forcefully he rocked the coffee table.

Between his hard-driving thrusts into her primed body, neither one of them hit the three-minute mark before they both exploded.

As soon as Ronin caught his breath, he said, "You still with me?"

"Barely."

After he climbed off, he crouched in front of her and ran his knuckle across her cheek. "Ropes off?"

"Yes, please."

It amazed her how quickly he released the bindings, since he hadn't rushed getting them in place.

Ronin picked her up, arms still bound, and carried her to bed.

After his full-body inspection, he held her face in his hands and took her mouth in one of those heart-melting, knee-knocking, sigh-worthy kisses that she never wanted to end. She snuggled against his body after he released her. "So that configuration was called the tortured tortoise?"

"Tethered turtle," he corrected.

"Same thing," she retorted. "I take it you've done that pattern before?"

"Never on you." Ronin kissed the pink marks on her wrists. "You were amazing. You looked gorgeous. I wish you'd let me . . ."

Amery shook her head. They'd gone round and round about him taking photos of her bound, to show her how beautiful she supposedly looked. But she wasn't ready for that. She didn't know if she ever would be.

"Anyway, thank you."

"I enjoyed it." She drew circles on his chest. "Are you staying tonight?"

"Yes. Now wrap yourself around me like you're prone to and go to sleep."

She smiled because she knew how much he liked having her wrapped around his body—even when he wouldn't admit it.

CHAPTER TWENTY-ONE

THE following week, after one of the worst days of her career, Amery dragged her ass to a hole-in-the-wall bar that served strong, cheap drinks. It was the type of joint where people went to drown their sorrows alone. No guys trolling for a hookup. No bar floozies scamming on guys to pay their tab. No crazy sports fanatics with the TV cranked to ten thousand decibels. No annoying blowhard carrying on a never-ending cell phone conversation. No perky wait staff in skimpy clothing. Just an old bartender with a limited mixed drink repertoire and plenty of isolated booths and tables for one.

She ordered two gin and tonics at happy hour prices and drained the first one in two gulps. After the booze took the edge off, she leaned her head back and closed her eyes.

In addition to business problems today, her mother had called to nag her about her father's clergy anniversary party. Being in a lousy mood gave her the balls, guts, whatever to tell her mother that she wouldn't be attending the party.

Shocking that a minister's wife knew so much profanity and had no issue using it on her daughter. Pissed off and pushed into a corner, Amery had hung up on her, which carried the unhappy consequence of receiving a phone call from her father. She shouldn't have answered, but being in a foul mood had allowed her to unload on him and he'd hung up on her too. After that, she'd half expected a stranger to walk in and stage a religious intervention on her parents' behalf—or possibly they'd just hire an exorcist—because obviously she was possessed by the devil if she dared to speak to her parents in that manner.

She snickered.

No one in the bar looked at her as if she were crazy for laughing alone in a dark booth while knocking back two-for-one mixed drinks.

Maybe she'd had a fight with her parents, and her friends, and she might be cracking the want ads for a new job, but at least she had a decent relationship for once in her life.

Although maybe indecent was a better term for what was going on with Ronin. The man could fuck like a dream. He made her feel like the most beautiful woman on earth every time he touched her. He demanded and yet he gave back. Sexually everything was going great. She trusted him with her body, knowing they could give each other exactly what they needed. .

But on a personal level? When she wasn't basking in the afterglow of astounding sex, or when he wasn't literally tying her up in knots, and she considered what she knew of him beyond the surface stuff . . . she realized it was only surface stuff.

He focuses on you so completely that he reveals little of himself.

What he'd told her of his life and training wasn't an intimate peek into him, but information she could've found on his Web site. And since the night she'd gone to the club and afterward they'd had that shockingly intimate conversation . . . he hadn't revealed anything personal about himself. So that, coupled with Deacon's comments about her being in Sensei's flavor-of-the-month club, brought her doubts about the seriousness of their relationship to the surface.

Speak of the devil. Her phone dinged with a text message from him.

RB: Where are you?

Drinking. Where are you?

RB: On my way to get you. Tell me
where you are.

I'm lousy company. I'll call you later, k?

RB: Not okay. Where are you?

I don't need a babysitter. I'm fine.

RB: I won't baby you at all if you
just tell me where you are.

Why?

RB: I want to see for myself that you're
fine.

See? Now, that was boyfriend-ly concern, wasn't it?
No—he wanted control.
Bullshit. He cared about her.
Didn't he?
Screw it. Even if he didn't and this was a fling, she wanted to
see him tonight.
She typed I'm at the Rialto Lounge.

RB: On my way, hang tight.

Too late, I'm already loose.

Then she shoved her phone in her purse and bought herself
round number three.

So her vision was a tiny bit blurry when he walked toward her, but Amery would recognize that distinctive gait even four sheets to the wind. "Hey, sexy man. Lemme buy you a drink."

"No, thanks. I'm your DD since it appears you could use one." Ronin looked around. "Interesting place. Come here often?"

"When I need to."

"What happened that sent you scurrying into this lounge lizard's paradise?"

She wasn't drunk, but she had a buzz, and that conversation would be a buzzkill. "Bad day and no, I don't want to talk about it."

Ronin grabbed her chin and peered into her eyes. "Too bad, beautiful. Why are you drinking alone?"

"You're here now, so technically I'm *not* drinking alone. Just buy me another drink and quit judging me."

He headed to the bar and returned with a tall glass.

"What's this?"

"Coke. I'm not down with your plan to keep drinking until you pass out. I snagged you some pretzels too."

"Gross. These have been gathering dust for twenty years." She shoved the bowl aside and eyed the soda.

"Amery." He plucked up her hand and kissed her fingertips. "Baby, please talk to me about what's going on with you."

Instead of immediately relating her job woes, she took the opportunity to address something else that she hadn't brought up. "It bothered me more than I let on, watching you training with your black belts last week." When he stayed silent and watchful, she continued. "Everything happened so fast the night we were attacked that I didn't appreciate the nuances of your martial arts skills. Maybe it makes me naive, but I've focused on the graceful way you move, not *why* you can move with such stealth and precision. So when I witnessed your physical power and understood you are a force beyond anything I've ever seen? Seeing that side of you scared me."

"You know I'd never hurt you."

"You're missing the point I'm trying to make. It's like I was seeing you for the first time. What you do as a martial artist is so much a part of who you are. And since I don't know that side of your life, you can understand why I'd feel like you're a stranger sometimes. Why it feels like the only time we're intimate is when we're naked. You expect me to tell all and you don't reciprocate."

Ronin's gaze roamed her face. "I've shared more with you than anyone."

"You mean the kinbaku and shibari?"

"Not just that and you damn well know it."

"That's the thing, Ronin. I *don't*. There's so much you're holding back from me. And what's hidden beneath the surface might be some scary shit."

"Amery—"

"So I'll show you how this sharing thing works. Today, one of my biggest clients informed me they'll be taking their graphic design work in-house rather than outsourcing starting the end of the month. And yes, I understand it's just business, but it's killing my business. I've lost accounts over the past few months for the same reason. I picked up a couple new projects, but this is my bread-and-butter client. I always worried about having a client like that, because I feared this very thing would happen. Now it has."

"I'm sorry." He kissed the back of her hand.

"I could look on the bright side and be glad they aren't giving me the old heave-ho because the quality of the work has gone downhill or I'm slow in responding to their needs." She swigged the Coke. "But I can't think of anything besides that I'll have to let Molly go."

"It doesn't help to conjure up worst-case scenarios."

"I don't need to conjure them, Ronin, because they're already here. This is the reality of the situation. I set out to drown my sorrows so I wouldn't have to think about it for the rest of the night, and I don't appreciate you showing up here and forcing me to think about it."

"Why aren't your friends here supporting you?"

Amery sighed. "They ditched me to go to their gay bar hangouts."

"They left you alone after you'd been drinking?" he asked sharply.

"No. I meant I didn't invite them to my pity party because we had words and we still aren't speaking. The words I'm waiting to hear from them haven't made it back to me yet." She wouldn't tell Ronin he was the source of discord between them. "But in my defense of drinking alone, I wouldn't have attempted to walk home alone. I would've waited until I sobered up and called a cab." She poked his chest. "Self-defense rule number one I learned at Black Arts. Avoid dangerous situations. See? I paid attention in class."

"Do you have plans for the rest of the night?"

"Wallow. Then wallow some more."

Ronin framed her face in his hands. "Come wallow with me in the pool. Or in the garden. But if you'd rather we can go to your place."

Amery looked into his eyes, entranced by how they changed color. Right now they were a warm, soft brown and filled with concern. Then she felt guilty for saying she didn't know him when very few people got to see this caring side of Master Black and he showed it to her—even if only limitedly. "Your place has more toys." When Ronin raised his eyebrows she amended, "Not what I meant."

"I'm calling that a Freudian slip anyway."

"Whatever. No weird sex toys," she warned.

"I promise only to use the usual sex toys." He smooched her mouth.

"Meaning ropes?"

"Among other things. Let's go."

Amery perked up at seeing Ronin's motorcycle parked by the curb. "Did you bring me a helmet?"

"Of course."

It seemed as if Ronin took the long way back to his place, but Amery didn't mind. There were worse places to be than twined around his strong body.

They held hands during the elevator ride.

Ronin asked, "Are you hungry?"

"No. I'd rather swim."

"Are you changing in my room?"

"I left my swimsuit in the guest room."

He kissed her forehead. "I'll meet you at the pool after I shower."

She opened the drawer where she'd stashed the two new swimsuits Ronin had bought her. As soon as she ditched her workday clothes, she breathed easier. Which was ironic since she'd never been comfortable in swimwear. Spying Ronin's white dress shirt on the back of the door, she slipped it on as a cover-up.

The elevator spit her out on the roof and she practically skipped to her favorite chaise on the pool side. With half a buzz relaxing her, she closed her eyes and basked in the sun's fading rays.

The next time Amery opened her eyes, the sun had dropped in the horizon. She scrambled upright and looked over to see Ronin stretched out beside her. Watching her. "Crap. Did I fall asleep?"

"Only for an hour."

She ran a hand through her hair. "Sorry."

"Don't be. You must've needed it."

"So you've been up here listening to me snore the whole time?"

"Except for the call I had to take right after I got out of the shower."

Was this his way of sharing? "What was the call about?"

"Boring business stuff."

And . . . not so much with the sharing.

But he did reach for her hand. After a bit, Ronin said, "I've been thinking."

"About?"

"Your financial situation."

Hard not to get her back up. "And?"

"And I came up with a way to help you."

"Ronin. I already designed a new logo for Black Arts. As a matter of fact, I saw the new patch on your gi top."

"Looks great, doesn't it? But you piddling around with graphic stuff for my dojo wasn't what I had in mind."

"Then what?"

He stood and moved to sit on the bottom of her chaise. "Please hear me out before you jump in and say no."

That definitely got her back up. "I'm listening."

"You've got a good thing going with your business. Unique, yet mainstream enough you haven't locked yourself into a niche market. I suspect given the chance you could spin it into a bigger agency. Not now but a few years down the road. Which is why I want to invest in Hardwick Designs."

"Invest in?"

"I'd give you a year's worth of operating capital so you could keep Molly on."

"Give?" she repeated.

He squeezed her knee. "Loan, if you prefer. You wouldn't have to start repayments until your company was operating in the black again."

"What's the interest rate for this investment?"

"Standard business rate. The whole point of this is to keep your business afloat during these market fluctuations. It'll level out sooner rather than later. The signs are already there with the unemployment rate dropping, new construction rates slowly climbing again, and the upswing in the stock market."

Amery stared at him. Since when did Zen Master Black give a damn about the effects of the economy?

Just another sign that you don't know him beyond sexually.

"I would be a silent investor, so you needn't worry I'd take over your business. I'm already running the dojo and dealing with other family pressures. I wouldn't require much for financial reporting besides a basic idea where you are bi-monthly on the profit and loss."

As much as she wanted to snap, *No way in hell am I ever taking a penny from you,* and then list the reasons as dispassionately as he had done, she coolly asked, "Are you finished?"

His eyes narrowed. "Don't you have questions?"

"Just one." She cocked her head. "Will you take business advice from me?"

"Sure."

Maybe the buzz of anger gave her the push to address the grumblings she'd heard in his dojo. "Pull out whatever stick you've got up your ass about Brazilian jujitsu and consider adding that martial arts discipline to the Black Arts class schedule. You've already got self-defense classes, kickboxing classes, you're training mixed martial artists, and your staff offers personal protection training. I heard Ito talking to Knox about his judo background. He should also be teaching judo classes, which would be another addition to the lineup. Right now you have space to expand into on the third floor and a diversity of classes, including Muay Thai, would increase your income base."

If she expected a stunned reaction from him that she'd poked her nose into his business, or that her attempt at redirection would actually work, well, she was sorely mistaken. Ronin's expression didn't change. He merely said, "So noted. Any questions about the business solution I proposed to address *your* issue?"

"No, because I already have an answer."

"Which is?"

"Hell no." She pushed off the chaise.

"Where are you going?"

"For a swim. Alone." Amery dove into the deep end and popped up like a cork. The water temperature was perfectly refreshing and cooled off her hot head. She floated in the warm void, eyes closed.

Filling her lungs with air to keep herself afloat forced her to focus on her breathing.

But eventually her ears picked up weird sounds underwater, distorting them to the point she couldn't figure out what they were. She remained perfectly still.

One sound that she didn't need to decipher: a body diving into the pool. She righted herself after being tossed around by the waves and then Ronin was right there.

Amery backed up.

He followed her.

"What part of 'I want to swim alone' is confusing to you?"

"What part of 'this is my pool' is confusing to you?" he countered.

"Fine. I'll get out."

He blocked her exit. "Can we finish our conversation?"

"We did. Now move."

"No." Ronin latched on to her biceps, careful in the way he held her—firmly, but not too closely. "Talk to me."

"There's nothing to say."

"If you're so pissed off at me about this, why aren't you lashing out at me?"

"Oh, I'm supposed to be rude after turning down a business proposition from my lover? Sorry, I'm unfamiliar with protocol."

"Jesus, Amery."

Her eyes searched his. "You even offering me a loan has changed things between us."

"Bull."

"And I'm really sorry I told you about my financial issues, which forced you into a heroic attempt to save my business. So forget I brought it up and we'll keep this"—she gestured between them—"the way it's been."

Ronin moved in close—dangerously close. "And what way has that been?"

"Fun. No pressure to make it into something it's not."

"Like what?"

"Permanent."

"Permanent," he repeated.

"Yes. If you loaned me money, then we'd be tied together, for at least a year, making it awkward when one of us walks away."

Evidently that was the wrong thing to say.

Ronin's mouth crashed down on hers. The kiss was ferocious. Uncompromising. So blistering hot Amery was shocked the water around them wasn't boiling.

Hard hands on her body, in her hair. She couldn't catch her breath, his mouth was so demanding.

He ripped his lips free of hers, and his voice reverberated in her ear. "I'll show you tied together." Then he sank his teeth into the skin at her throat and pulled her head back. His eyes burned into hers. "I have you where I want you, how I want you, and you'll be mine until I release you."

She should've protested his tight hold on her or his warning. But she didn't. She wanted to experience every dirty, bad, harsh thing he wanted to do with her.

"Do you understand?"

Primal lust and the need to . . . master her shone in his eyes.

In that moment she realized he wasn't talking about binding her with ropes, but with this sexual obsession. He hadn't disputed her claim that there'd never be permanence between them. Any other time her brain would've taken over, dissecting every word. But her brain wasn't in charge right now; her body was. And it had already readied for him: heart racing, blood pumping, pussy wet, clit swollen, nipples tight. So she gave him the answer they both wanted—even when it frightened her how quick and visceral her response to this man had become.

"Yes, I understand."

Ronin took her to the ground and fucked her until his knees were raw and her back bore the cement scrape marks of his possession. After he'd turned her mindless, he fucked her again in the swimming pool. No words exchanged. The sounds of heaving breathing, soft grunts and sighs, and splashing water became the only conversation they needed.

There was no tenderness in the aftermath. And for the first time with him, Amery felt ashamed of what they were doing to each other—not sexually, but emotionally.

"Ronin."

"I know, baby."

But he didn't know. And worse, he didn't ask what she'd meant. He retreated from her again.

They remained like that, side by side on the pool deck, staring up at the sky, not speaking because neither knew what to say.

CHAPTER TWENTY-TWO

AMERY had just settled in behind her desk on Friday morning with a cup of coffee when her office door opened.

"Delivery for Amery Hardwick."

She glanced up. Chaz stood in the doorway holding an enormous bouquet of flowers.

He lowered them and met her eyes. "A peace offering for jumping to conclusions and jumping your shit. I'm sorry. It was a dick move and it'll never happen again."

"You sure about that?"

"Oh, I'll probably be a dick to you again, but it won't be for the same reason." He set the flowers on top of the filing cabinet and fiddled with them. "Friends support each other. I didn't support you, ergo, I'm a shitty friend. I've felt so freakin' guilty I couldn't even show my face around here."

"I missed your ugly mug, Chaz."

"Not even on my worst hair day am I ugly on the outside." He sobered. "But on the inside . . . different story."

Amery got up and gave him a hug. "We all have ugly days. I'm glad today isn't one of them."

"I am too, *ma chérie*. So am I forgiven?"

"Only if you buy me lunch."

"Done. Indian sound okay?"

"Sounds perfect." She gave him one last squeeze. "Thanks for the pretty posies."

"Guilt flowers are the best kind."

"HARDER."

"No."

"Yes. Move into it with your whole body. Perfect. You've got the rhythm. Now pull back slowly."

Amery panted and slumped against him. "You're wearing me out, Ronin."

"That's the point. Come on. Stay with me here. We're almost there."

"I can't."

He peered down at her, their faces so close she saw sweat beaded on his jawline. She licked her lips, wanting a taste of salt and Ronin.

"Stop with the bedroom eyes. Take a breath. Then we're going again."

She moved back and brought up her hands into position. Then she let fly, hitting the heavy bag with all she had.

"I knew you could hit harder."

"That's because I superimposed your face on my target area," she panted between punches.

"Whatever works. Fifty more. Make them count and this will be it."

Amery gritted her teeth and smacked the meaty part of her forearms into the bag. Left, right, left, right.

"Don't hunch your shoulders. Change the pattern. Three strikes with the right, then one with the left."

She kept that pattern for a dozen strikes and focused on a fast switch when he changed the rhythm again to two and two.

"Ten left. All left strikes."

Wham. Wham. Wham. So much sweat ran into her eyes she could hardly see. But she didn't let it deter her as she counted out the last seven blows.

"Strong finish. Excellent work. Grab a drink."

"I don't think I can move." Her words were muted since she'd face-planted into the heavy bag.

"Either let go and get a drink or I'll add another hundred drills."

She cracked one eye open and glared at him. "Bite me."

Outside class Ronin would've laughed at her. But being as they were in the dojo . . . he lifted one imperious eyebrow.

"Sorry, Sensei. Getting a drink now." She trudged to the bench and uncapped her water, taking four gulps. Maybe she wasn't supposed to sit on the bench, but she didn't care. Her legs were noodles.

"The extra training classes show marked improvement in your form and stamina."

"How did this go from being in a self-defense class to private instruction with boxing and takedown techniques?" She knocked back another mouthful of water. "You training me for women's MMA?"

"Not hardly."

"I'm getting special treatment because . . . ?"

"I deemed it so."

"Or because I'm fucking Sensei Black?"

Ronin smirked. "That too."

"I know I'm supposed to respect the teacher/student line when we're in the dojo."

"But?"

"But all I can think about is you tying my arms with that nylon resistance strap and fucking me against the wall."

"For that obvious insubordination, I'd give you ten lashes with that strap before I bind you and fuck you."

Amery hid her smile behind her water bottle. "I apologize for putting such raunchy thoughts in your head, Master Black."

"Class dismissed, Ms. Hardwick."

"Does that mean we can . . . ?"

He made that low growl. "Not here. But I'd better find you on your knees in my practice room in an hour to make the raunchy images you put in my head a reality."

Her pulse spiked.

"Am I clear?"

"Yes, sir."

He stopped in the doorway and turned to give her a slow once-over. "Don't bother showering. You'll need another one by the time I'm through with you tonight."

A shiver worked through her. She couldn't wait.

A few days after Chaz apologized, Emmylou had shown up at Amery's loft after hours, with a bottle of whipped cream vodka and two bags of Amery's favorite Lindt chocolates.

The conversation had started out surprisingly awkward. Emmylou had apologized for listening to Tyler and not recognizing his true motives. But then she'd admitted Tyler wasn't the only one who'd expressed concerns about Ronin and his business connections. One of Emmylou's clients had seen Ronin leaving Amery's business when she'd come in for a massage.

She'd assumed Ronin was Emmylou's massage client and proceeded to tell her about Ronin's connection to Thaddeus "TP" Pettigrew, the mogul who owned half of Denver. The source swore that several years ago Ronin had dealt with the vagrants, dealers, and squatters at several abandoned buildings in the Platte River Valley District. Once the commercial and residential buildings had been cleared of undesirables, including existing tenants who put their buildings up for sale, TP bought up a huge chunk of the area and applied for urban renewal funds.

Not exactly illegal, but it sounded suspicious given Ronin's hard stance on ethics in and out of the dojo.

Emmylou's source, a real estate broker, swore it was common knowledge but no one had shared details on exactly what Ronin had done to force people out. But rumors ran rampant.

So despite Emmylou's apology, Amery had a sense of disquiet about the information. Especially since she knew Ronin and TP were friends and they'd left the Colorado Sports Banquet for a private business discussion. She'd tracked down a few articles on TP, and the more she read, the more disparaging the pieces were on TP's questionable business practices and the organizations he supported. Being associated with TP often resulted in a tainted reputation—guilt by association. So why would Ronin subject himself to that?

Maybe he didn't have a choice.

Amery continued to worry that she wouldn't have a choice but to let Molly go. What sucked was she had no one to discuss her business issues with. Chaz couldn't keep a secret. She'd considered talking to Emmylou, but with Amery being her landlord, admitting her financial struggles might send Emmylou looking for a different place to set up shop, and Amery depended on her rental income.

Shaking herself out of her reverie and needing a break, she wandered into the massage studio and paused in the office doorway.

Emmylou glanced up from her laptop. "Heya, girlie. What's shakin'?"

"Not much. I'm making a Target run and wondered if you needed anything."

She set her zebra-striped reading glasses on her desk. "You need me to keep an eye on your side while you're gone?"

"Nah. Molly is here holding down the fort."

"Cool. I could stand to pick up a few things myself." She grabbed her purse and rounded her desk. "Mind if I tag along?"

"Not at all. But no teasing me about my love of sour green apple Icees."

Emmylou tapped a finger on Amery's lips. "Anything that turns your mouth bright green and makes you look like you just sucked off a Martian is always subject to ridicule."

Amery hip-checked her on the way out the front door. "I oughta make you ride in the back."

"You miss me yankin' your chain. So, what's up with this emergency run to Target? Is BOB out of batteries?"

"BOB is a cliché. My vibrator is named WON."

"WON?" Emmylou repeated, stopping in the middle of the sidewalk. "As in Don Juan?"

"Nope. It's short for Want Orgasm Now. WON." She grinned. "I put an accent on it to make him sound more sophisticated."

"Bet poor WON has been gathering dust. I doubt you use him when you've got your sexy stud around."

"Except for when Ronin uses WON on me," she muttered. She glanced across the roof of the car to see if Emmylou had heard that, but she'd checked her ringing phone and gestured that she needed to take the call.

Amery slid into the driver's seat and started the car, welcoming the cool air blowing on her heated face. The memory from last night with WON once again under Ronin's control rolled through her like a violent summer storm filled with lightning, thunder, tornadoes, and hail.

The car jiggled as Emmylou climbed in. "Sorry about that. Two injured Rockies players need immediate massage therapy sessions, so I had to shift my schedule for tomorrow."

"Doesn't immediate mean . . . now? Today?"

"It would if they were in town, but they're on the road, so luckily it means tomorrow." Emmylou's eyes narrowed. "Why are you all flushed?"

Wet daydreams courtesy of Ronin Black. "Because I've been sitting in a hot car waiting for you."

"Then let's hit it, sista."

Horrible traffic meant it took twice as long to reach the Super Target in suburbia.

They each grabbed a cart and separated. Amery stocked up on fruit, produce, Noosa yogurt, deli fixings, and frozen entrées for one. Then she tracked down the remaining household items on her list before heading into the health and beauty section. Face wash, hair products, mascara, and lip gloss added to her cart, she cut down the feminine products aisle.

She stopped in front of the depilatory creams, waxes, and concoctions devoted to aiding in the removal of unwanted hair. As she debated choices on what would work best around her bikini line, Emmylou barreled around the corner.

"There you are. I worried I might find you cooing over baby clothes again."

"I did that one time and it was a fluke." She'd hoped for privacy in making this personal grooming choice, but Emmylou gave her none.

"What're you doin' down this aisle anyway? This stuff is crap. You want to skin the beaver you go to a professional."

Amery blushed. "Jesus, Emmylou. You didn't have to shout that."

"I didn't. Why are you embarrassed?" Emmylou pushed her cart closer and peered into Amery's face. "You've never been professionally waxed, plucked, or creamed, have you?"

"No. I can't imagine spreading my legs and showing my naked feminine bits to a total stranger. I'd die from that much exposure."

"Sweetie. It's clinical. No different than goin' to the doctor."

"Wrong. I know it seems old-fashioned and ridiculous, but I don't ever see myself waltzing into a salon and asking some stranger to pour hot wax on my crotch."

But you had no issue with Ronin pouring hot wax all over your breasts.

Not the same thing.

Emmylou kissed her forehead. "Darlin' girl, I'll never make fun of you for that. But if you really want to try waxing the lady taco, I'll do it for you at the studio. Takes, like, ten minutes to heat up the wax tank."

"Since when do you give wax jobs?"

"Since always. Some of the guys who come to me for a massage are apelike hairy. The fur on their backs grosses me out and reminds me why I prefer to eat the banana split rather than the banana."

"Emmylou!"

She laughed. "I love shockin' you, sugar. Anyway, it's easier if I have to do a deep-tissue massage to remove the man pelts before-hand. Word spread among my clients that I'll wax backs, chests, eyebrows, ears, bellies, and the old twig and berries for an extra fee. I don't broadcast those services, but I figure I'm doin' hetero women a favor by secretly providing manscaping for these macho athletes who'd never set foot in a man salon."

Amery frowned. "But you have waxed women before?"

"I wax myself. I waxed Helena. In fact, I still wax her."

"Your ex?"

"She hasn't found anyone who'll wax her better." She waggled her eyebrows. "And you don't need to worry I'll be scheming ways to take a bite of your naked peach. While I'm sure it's a pretty pussy . . . kitty-cat, you're just too vanilla for me."

I'm not as vanilla as you think and I've got the rope marks to prove it.

Amery just smiled and said, "Probably."

WAXING hurt.

Like really fucking hurt.

Even after Amery followed all of Emmylou's aftercare instructions, she felt too sensitized to spend the night with Ronin. Seeing him wasn't in the cards because seeing Ronin meant fucking Ronin.

In true Ronin form, he hadn't demanded an explanation on why she'd canceled. He hadn't been happy she'd backed out of their dinner plans, but he'd retreated to unflappable Master Black and ended the conversation.

That caused a pang of . . . not sadness, but something she couldn't put her finger on. Almost as if he didn't care what she did when he wasn't fucking her or binding her.

Her acceptance of his kink and the shocking self-discovery that she liked it had intensified their connection when they were alone. Their foray into doing couple things had lasted barely a month. They rarely went out together in public.

Although that wasn't entirely his fault. Amery had been content to hang out with him in his penthouse. Whenever he showed up at her loft, they were all over each other and fell asleep afterward.

How long had it been since she'd gone out for a drink just because she could? She'd also gotten out of the habit of trying a new restaurant every week.

That's when she realized she'd thrown herself into this affair with Ronin just as she'd done with Tyler. She'd adjusted her schedule to fit Ronin's and he'd kept odd hours recently, but when pressed on his nocturnal activities, he'd said, "Business," and ended the conversation.

She reminded herself of how hard she'd worked to be independent. It'd been a point of pride the past few years that she'd learned to enjoy doing social things alone.

So there was no reason to stay home and mope because she couldn't see him. She'd dress up and head down to the Bistro. Listen to some light jazz, knock back a Moscow mule, nibble on a plate of bruschetta, partake of Denver's nightlife for a few hours.

Just as she stepped into the alley, she heard the whirring whine of Ronin's motorcycle.

He killed the engine and removed his helmet before dismounting from the bike. He dropped his gaze to the toes of her high-heeled boots; then his eyes wandered up her skinny jeans, over her dusty rose lace blouse, and stopped on her face. "Going somewhere?" he asked coolly.

"Ronin—"

"Who are you meeting?"

"No one."

"Bullshit. You're dressed to go out. Did you cancel our plans tonight because you received a better offer?"

Amery stomped over to him. "No. And fuck you for thinking so highly of me. I was headed to the Bistro, by myself, to grab some food, a drink, and take an hour to unwind."

"By yourself," he repeated.

"Yes. I used to do a lot of things by myself. I realized tonight since I've hooked up with you I stopped doing some of the things I used to enjoy."

"That's why you didn't come over? Because you need to prove you'll be fine going it alone after we're done hooking up?"

He added a sneering tone to the words *hooking up* that set her on edge. "You're taking this completely out of context."

"Then explain it to me."

"I don't owe you an explanation. Good night, Ronin." Amery slammed the back door and locked it.

Then she found herself pushed up against the cold steel. Calm, cool, and collected Ronin? Gone.

It boosted her confidence that she could rattle him outside the bedroom. "What?"

"What is going on with you? You never play these games."

"Not a game. Tonight I wanted to go out. That's it."

Ronin studied her in that unnerving manner of his. But she caught a rare flash of vulnerability, and her heart caught.

She tried a less combative tactic. She curled her hands around his face. "Come with me to the Bistro. We'll split an appetizer, have a drink, soak in the weeknight crowd in a Denver hipster bar. It'll be fun."

His rigid stance relaxed. He rested his forehead to hers. "I'd like that."

"Let's go." She pecked him on the mouth and he stepped back. "It's two blocks down."

Ronin took her hand and led her to his motorcycle. "I'll drive slow since I didn't bring your helmet."

Amery shook her head. "It's a short walk."

"I like you on my bike. And that wild girl wants to feel the wind in her hair even if it's only for two short blocks." He traced the edge of her jaw. "Or are you saying no because it's not cool to show up at a hipster bar on a Jap bike? We'd fit in better if we pulled up on a Vespa?"

She laughed. "Fine. We'll take the bike. Especially since you're looking more badass than usual in this wifebeater." Her finger followed the scoop neck of the skintight ribbed tank top. Her fingers migrated to the deep cut of muscle in his biceps. "I really like when you show off your impressive arms."

"Don't get used to it. I was in such a hurry to get to you that I switched out my gi pants for jeans and forgot about my upper half."

"Why don't you wear this kind of shirt more often?"

"Because I feel exposed." He kept stroking her jaw. "Sounds weird coming from a man who prefers his partners naked. But I grew up wearing a gi from morning until night. Having my body covered is natural to me. I only wear short-sleeved shirts when I know it'll be hot or if I'm working out. I only strip off my shirt when . . ."

We're alone.

Amery realized that's how Ronin leveled the playing field when the ropes came out. He hadn't removed his shirt during the scene at the club, but he always took his shirt off with her. And for him, that was akin to being as naked as she was. She turned her head and kissed his wrist. "Ronin."

"So now you know," he said softly. "Let's go."

Amery did like the wind tousling her hair. But not as much as she liked the feel of Ronin's bare skin against her cheek as she wrapped herself around him on the back of his bike.

No surprise they garnered attention—or rather Ronin received predatory looks from several women, despite the fact that he'd draped a possessive arm over Amery's shoulder.

They chose a table away from the jazz guitarist and his groupies. After ordering food and drink, Ronin was sweet and attentive. Almost as if it was a date.

Lulled by the soft music and the ease of being together, they lingered. "This is nice."

"Told you. I—we haven't done this in a while."

"So why'd you back out on me tonight?"

"Why didn't you ask me that when I called you?" she countered.

"Too pissed off to form a coherent sentence."

Shocking that he'd admitted it. "That's something you'll have to work on, Master Black, because your curt response gave me the impression you didn't care what I did."

Ronin locked his gaze to hers. "I cared too much. So quit hedging. Why'd you really call and cancel?"

Amery stirred the dregs of her Moscow mule and drained it. "Because I got waxed today."

Pause. Then, "Come again?"

"I got a full bikini wax today for the first time ever. And it might make me a pussy"—she smirked—"but I'm beyond tender around my lady bits. I knew body friction would irritate my skin, so I canceled our plans."

He leaned forward. "Why didn't you just tell me that in the first place?"

She offered a cheeky smile. "You didn't ask."

"You're sidestepping the issue, but I'll let it slide. Why did you think we couldn't get together tonight?"

She threaded her fingers through his. "Ronin. Master Black. Sensei. Sir. You are many, many things and I appreciate every facet of you, but tenderness isn't in your arsenal of seduction. Within five minutes of being alone together, we're naked together, and that couldn't happen tonight, so I opted to avoid the situation."

"Which caused an issue between us, so nondisclosure was obviously the best choice," he said dryly. "I'll point out we can be together without it always leading to sex."

"But why would we want to be?"

Her flip comment annoyed him rather than amused him. "Sounds like it's past someone's bedtime." He pushed to his feet and held out his hand. "Shall we?"

The night had cooled off and the short bike ride left her chilled. She didn't protest when Ronin informed her he'd tuck her in.

He followed her into the bedroom and began to unbutton her blouse, pressing kisses down her chest as he did so.

"What are you doing?"

"Helping you get ready for bed. Lift up." He curled his hand around her knee and lifted her leg to tug off her boot. "Other side."

She clutched his shoulders as he removed her other boot.

As soon as Ronin was upright, his mouth landed on hers. The slow kiss belied how fast his fingers worked the button and zipper on her jeans. Despite the fabric being skintight, he easily peeled the denim down her legs.

He nuzzled her temple and brushed his lips across her cheekbone. "Let me show you."

"Show me what?"

"That I can be tender." He strung kisses down her throat. "So very, very tender with you."

"Ronin. You don't have to."

"I want to. I need to."

She about melted into a puddle of goo.

"And you don't have to worry that I'll rut on you afterward." He unhooked her bra and removed it. "Take off your panties."

His sweet but commanding tone sent a shiver through her. When she reached down to grasp the lace band, Ronin's fingers were there, helping her slide them off.

Then he dropped to his knees.

Amery blushed head to toe. It was far from the first time he'd been up close and personal, but she'd literally never been so bared before.

His hands started at her hips and his thumbs swept over the smooth sheen of her mound. His fingers skated down the crease of her thigh and then up the inside edge of her slit. Ronin made that long sweeping caress several more times, not speaking, just staring.

Just when she didn't think she could stand another second, he said, "How can you be so pale and yet so perfect?"

Her breath stalled when his fiery gaze met hers.

"Spread your legs, baby. I need my mouth on you."

That quiet, sultry demand caused her knees to buckle and her butt hit the mattress.

Ronin didn't miss a beat. He scooted closer to the edge of the bed and pushed her thighs apart. Way apart.

He covered every inch of her denuded flesh with butterfly kisses. By the time he dipped his tongue down her slit, she'd gone slick and slippery.

"The way you taste is addictive." And he proved it by licking, lapping, and sucking her juices. Never aggressively, but with a tender need she'd never experienced with him.

And Ronin didn't threaten to bind her hands if she touched him while he went down on her. So she sifted her fingers through his thick, unruly hair. Her fingers swept over his eyebrows and cheekbones and even the shell of his ear as he worked her over with his mouth.

His eyes were closed, but every once in a while those thick lashes would lift and she'd find him watching her, watching him.

Sexy. Hot. Sweet.

When he focused on her clit, the detonation against his mouth was instantaneous. Delicious. Perfect. Especially when he didn't relent and immediately drove her up and spun her into orbit again.

Amery could scarcely hear over the blood whooshing in her ears. She slumped back on the bed, reveling in every hard throb against his firmly sucking mouth. Every unerring flick of his tongue. Every soft smooch on her swollen flesh. She also reveled in his fingers digging into her inner thighs. Ironic that his intent to show her tenderness would leave a mark on her? No. And she wouldn't have it any other way.

She yawned. "Now I'm tired."

"Sleep."

A kiss on her forehead. Then he tucked the covers around her. "I'll lock up."

She whispered, "Thank you," as sleep beckoned.

"No. Thank you."

"For what?"

"For reminding me I can lower my guard around you. For letting me be what you needed tonight."

Her last thought was she'd been mistaken about Ronin. He knew exactly how to be tender. He'd just needed someone to allow him to show it.

CHAPTER TWENTY-THREE

WHEN Amery realized Molly was already on a call on the other line, she picked up the ringing receiver and answered, "Hardwick Designs."

"May I please speak to Amery Hardwick?"

"This is Amery."

"Ms. Hardwick, this is Maggie Arnold. I'm happy to finally get in touch with you."

Great, another telemarketer. She'd opened her mouth to decline whatever fantastic special this woman planned to offer when she said, "I assure you this isn't a sales call. I oversee the North American district for Okada Foods. Have you heard of us?"

That was some kind of Asian food line if she recalled correctly. "It's vaguely familiar."

"Good. Okada is in the product development stage for creating healthier frozen entrées. Since these foods will launch an entirely new product line, and will only be offered for limited distribution, we're looking for a younger, hipper, fresher packaging design. We received your name and were intrigued by your ad designs for local organic food outlets, such as Wicksburg Farms, Grass Roots, Fresh Start, and the farm-to-table restaurants like Nature's Bounty and

Juniper's Garden that specialize in the type of audience we hope to target."

That piqued her curiosity. "Your company is entering the organic food market?"

"We're dipping our toe in the water. We've chosen a few areas of the country to test-market and we're restricting the product line to higher-end grocery markets. Would you be interested in looking at some specs?"

"What type of specs?"

"An outline of what we'd need for FDA packaging requirements, including details of each specific food item, the deadline, a budget, and samples of existing products in the Okada line."

"Sounds like an interesting project. I'd love to see the specs."

"Excellent. First we'll send a nondisclosure statement for you to sign and ask that you don't discuss this potential project even before you receive the packet of information."

A tiny kernel of excitement built in her. "Not a problem. When should I expect it?"

"Tomorrow morning."

"That fast? From overseas?"

"No. I'm based in the Seattle office. My contact information will be with the nondisclosure statement, and if you'd be so kind to drop me an e-mail after you receive the packet tomorrow, I'd appreciate it."

"Will do."

"Thank you. We're looking forward to the possibility of working with you, Ms. Hardwick. Good-bye."

Amery stared at the receiver after the woman hung up. Odd to have something like that come from out of left field. Really odd. Wasn't it? Then again, the woman had mentioned Amery's biggest clients, so she had done her research. Maybe she'd even contacted a few of those clients to get a recommendation.

"Amery?" Molly prompted. "Are you okay?"

"Yeah. Why?"

"I said your name, like, three times."

"Sorry. Just lost in thought." She tapped her pen on the desk. "This is a weird question. But have you gotten any strange phone calls lately?"

Molly frowned. "Like how weird? And how recently?"

"In the last couple of weeks."

"Not that recently. But the week after the break-in I got a call from someone asking for information on you. It started out with general questions and then it got personal. That's when I told the caller I was uncomfortable with the direction of the conversation. She thanked me for my time and hung up. The number was unlisted and I figured it was someone with the insurance company checking to make sure you weren't the type who'd trash your own building and file a claim on it."

Amery's eyes widened. "Why didn't you tell me this?"

Molly fidgeted and pushed away from the doorframe. "Because it was confidential and I'd forgotten about it until just now." She paused. "But I think you should know that same person contacted both Chaz and Emmylou, asking them the same kinds of questions about you and the business. They were asked to keep it confidential too."

That kicked Amery's memory. Her mother had mentioned getting a phone call pertaining to Amery's personal and professional life that same week. That pissed her off. She'd made an insurance claim one time and the company questioned her integrity? Behind her back? Harassing her coworker, her office mates, and her mother?

"I'm sure it's just standard procedure," Molly said diplomatically. "Especially since the cops were involved."

"Maybe you're right." But something about it didn't sit well with her.

"So, who called that made you bring this up with me?"

"Doesn't matter now." Although Molly would eventually work

on the Okada project if Amery landed it, and she'd already signed nondisclosure agreements with Hardwick Designs, Amery didn't want to discuss the potential project because she didn't want to jinx it. "Who were you talking to?"

"Nancy at Grass Roots. They're having some kind of members-only sale in three days. And she's sorry for the late notice . . ."

Par for the course with Nancy, so Amery didn't even blink. "What does she need?"

"An ad that goes out in an e-mail blast to their newsletter subscribers. And Q codes for the twenty products they're putting on special."

"What else?"

"Each store will offer twenty sale items. Fifteen are standard, and then five items are sale items unique to that store."

"Which means multiple newsletters."

Molly nodded. "A master, which will go out to everyone. And then another one for whichever store they're registered at."

Amery tapped her fingers on her desk and tried to sort through it. "Can't we just list everything in the master for all eight stores? There are fifteen things that will be on special on all six locations. And then under that can't we list the five unique items to each store? Like the Lakewood store is running a special on spelt flour, kumquats, organic beets, gluten-free crackers, and chemical-free dishwasher soap? And the Castle Rock store is running, X, Y, Z, A, and B?"

"That's what I thought too. But Nancy swears their sales numbers can back up that a general ad blast, and then a targeted ad blast increases their sales by seventeen percent."

"She's got the data to back it up, and if that's what she wants . . . she is the client."

"Yep." Molly smiled. "Plus, we get paid more, since it'll be more work for us and we can't afford to turn any extra jobs down right now, can we?"

With the downturn in business, Molly hadn't asked if her position was at risk, but she could see the writing on the wall if things didn't pick up. "No. So how detailed are her spec sheets?"

"Same as usual. She's sending a courier over with the stuff you need to take pics of. And she warned me, like, three times not to unpack everything because it's sorted and bundled according to store."

"Fine. You're working on the newsletters?"

"I'm loading the templates and I'll start with the master."

Amery had done a lot of work for Grass Roots over the past six years. The stores featured organic food from produce to meat and dairy. It was similar to the big organic national food chain with the exception that it was locally owned and the company of eight stores supported Colorado-grown produce, Colorado-raised meat, Colorado dairies, and other products made in Colorado. Most companies wouldn't take actual pictures of the items and produce available in their stores; it was much easier to use stock images. But Grass Roots wanted their newsletters to be an honest representation of what their stores offered. So Amery's photography skills were put to the test, taking shots of everything from Romanesque broccoli to free-range chicken carcasses.

She stood and grabbed her empty coffee mug. As she passed Molly's desk, she said, "Want a refill?"

Molly handed over her cup without looking away from her computer screen. "Might as well load us both up because it's going to be a late night."

AMERY finished the last shot for the newsletter around ten o'clock and sent Molly home. Since she got to keep the items she photographed, she sorted items she didn't need, like organic dog food, into donate and save piles. But after a long day she only had the energy to refrigerate the perishables.

Around eleven Ronin texted he was at the back door. Yawning, she hefted herself out of the chair and cut through the back room to let him in.

The man was on her even before she closed the door. She twined her arms around his neck and held on, letting the energy that always pulsed from him restore hers.

He broke the kiss and said, "I missed you last night."

"Same here. I was just finishing up."

"Anything I can do to help?"

She pecked him on the mouth. "Keep me company." As she locked the door, she said offhandedly, "I should just give you a key." When he didn't respond, she backtracked, "Not that I'm making it into a big thing, I just thought—"

Ronin spun her around and framed her face in his hands. "It *is* a big thing. Next time you come over I'll give you a key card and the codes to my place." He pressed a kiss on her forehead. "I'm not doing this just to give you free swimming privileges—you know that, right?"

"Right." Smiling, she took his hand and led him to her small studio.

He bent down and peered at the props on the table. "What are those? Turnips?"

"Golden beets. They're milder than regular beets but still good."

"I might have to try cooking with them." Ronin's gaze took in the piles everywhere. "Looks like you've been busy. Does that mean things are looking better on the business front?"

They hadn't talked about her business struggles at all in the weeks since he'd offered her a loan. While she still appreciated his generosity, taking his money—no matter how much she needed it and how well intentioned he was in offering it—would drive a wedge between them. Not only because of her pride, but it'd just add another layer to their already complicated relationship.

"All this"—she gestured to the piles—"is for a Grass Roots

newsletter. As far as adding new business . . . it's been pretty slim pickin's." She thought back to the phone call from today. That could be huge. So huge she couldn't wrap her head around it, or why they'd approached her.

Then Ronin was in her face, resting his right hand against her cheek. "I recognize that look. Did something happen today that's worrying you?"

How could he read her so easily and she couldn't read him at all?

She latched on to the first random thought that popped into her head. "It didn't happen today. It's something I've been putting off, which isn't smart when I need the work, but the project is out of my usual realm." She frowned. "Out of my realm photographically speaking."

"What do you mean?"

Amery dropped into her chair and propped her bare feet up on the edge of her desk. "Several weeks ago this author contacted me, asking if I'd be interested in creating a cover for her next digital book. At first the whole thing tripped my warning bells because that was a day after the night I ran from you and your magic rope tricks."

A smile ghosted around his mouth.

"Anyway, it struck me as coincidental that this erotic author I didn't know wanted a specific image for her cover."

"And what image is that?"

Her gaze hooked his. "A woman in bondage."

His expression didn't change.

"I thought you'd put her up to contacting me, expecting I'd ask her a lot of questions and during those conversations I'd get a handle on the mixed feelings I was having about you and your rope proclivities."

"And?"

"And she did give me a different perspective, for which I owe her.

I agreed to work on her cover. She's not under deadline, and neither am I, so in my spare time, I've been thinking about how to create the image she wants—a woman in bondage that's tasteful and sexy, yet doesn't show any of her girl parts." Amery twisted her ponytail around her finger. "The thing is, if I do a good job, it could open up a whole new income stream for me. I won't get rich creating custom digital book covers, but any projects that keep me in business are worth attempting. So I can't figure out why I'm dragging my feet."

Ronin remained quiet. But he paced, which wasn't like him. After a couple of minutes she got tired of watching him. She tipped her head back into the headrest and closed her eyes.

She'd just started to drift when warm lips pressed into her forehead. "Don't crash on me now when I have a solution for you." Then his lips brushed over hers half a dozen times before he sank into her mouth for a panty-dropping kiss. Then he pulled back abruptly.

Amery opened her eyes. "Were we done kissing? Because it sure didn't feel like it."

"I just wanted to make sure you were awake."

"Now I'm wide-awake and ready to strip off my clothes so you can fuck me over my desk." She moved everything to the side, creating a large empty spot in the center. "See?"

"Another time."

"Fine." She set her feet on the floor. "What is your solution?"

Ronin spun her chair around and placed his hands over her forearms on the armrests. "You need a picture of a woman in bondage. I'm a bondage master."

"And?"

"And you should be the model."

Her mouth dropped open. "Are you insane?"

"Hear me out. You want it tasteful and anonymous? Set up the camera with the right lighting and angle and all I have to do is press the button. You've got your artistic bondage cover."

"Ronin. Didn't we discuss that I'm all right with you binding me as long as it's not in public?"

"Yes. But this is private. A shadowed photo of you is much different than me binding you in front of everyone at the club. And the bonus? You'll get to see how absolutely stunning you look when I have you bound."

She stared at him, in shock and yet . . . not. "How would you bind me?"

Pure pleasure warmed his eyes. "With your arms behind your back in a dragonfly sleeve. I'd use red rope. It'd be a gorgeous contrast against your pearly skin."

Maybe she was sleep-deprived or just curious, but she found she wanted to see herself as Ronin saw her: her naked body as a canvas for his artistic tying skills. "Okay."

Ronin kissed her quickly, but their teeth clacked together because he wore a big grin. "I'll grab my bag."

"You just *happen* to have a bag of red ropes with you?"

"I like to be prepared."

In the small studio, Amery chose a different backdrop and adjusted the umbrella lights. She rarely did portraits because she didn't feel she had the artistic eye for it. But in this case only her back would be visible in the shot.

Ronin hadn't returned by the time she was ready to take a few test shots. After removing her shirt, she hooked up the remote button to the camera on the tripod. Using a roll of masking tape, she marked off a spot, stood on it with her bare back to the camera, and snapped a pic. Then she returned behind the camera and scrolled to the digital image. Too close. She backed up the camera, stood on the X, and clicked off another shot.

Better. But the light glared off her shoulder blade. After adjusting the backlight, she threw a diffuser—just a piece of darker opaque fabric—over the top of the light. She found her mark on the X again.

Before she clicked the remote, Ronin said, "Arch your back and turn your head to the right instead of looking forward."

"I don't want anyone to see my face, remember?"

"Only your profile is visible and you can darken that after you get the shot." When he closed in behind her, his body heat warmed her and his presence soothed her. He tugged the ponytail holder free, running his fingers through the long strands. "There. Now take it."

Amery angled her head and pushed the button.

When she whirled around, she expected to see Ronin behind the camera checking out the shot, but he remained off to the side, letting her do her job.

"You're right," she admitted. "That is much better." She tested a couple more, adjusting the zoom a fraction. After repositioning the tapes, she inhaled a deep breath, waiting for Ronin's instruction.

Then he was behind her, that deliciously deep voice in her ear. "You ready for me to start tying you, beautiful?"

"Yes."

He placed a soft kiss on her shoulder. "Arms at your sides."

Amery lowered her arms and closed her eyes.

She heard him behind her. The rustle of fabric as he removed his shirt and became Ronin the rope master.

His bare skin brushed hers as he swept her hair aside. Then he unhooked her bra and slid it off. He brushed a kiss between her breasts as he unzipped her jeans, tugging them down her hips and to the floor. When she attempted to kick them free, he said, "No. Keeping them around your ankles will hold you in place."

Just another way he chose to bind her.

His finger leisurely followed the lace edge of her panties hugging her lower curves. Then his lips thoroughly tracked her spine from the dimples above her ass to the nape of her neck.

Although her pulse raced and her blood seemed to pump hotter with anticipation, she focused on her breathing.

Ronin slipped rope over both of her shoulders. She felt a quick pull, and sections of rope brushed the inside of her arms as he secured the first knot. More rope slid up her wrists and over her elbows to cross her upper arms. Another tug, another caress on her skin beneath the knots. His soft, steady exhales drifted over her damp flesh.

Goose bumps spread just from the nearness of his mouth to her skin.

Callused hands were busy behind her, rarely jerky, never clumsy. At times the rope would swing across her calves, giving the impression of his fingers teasing her there, even when she felt his fingertips on her spine.

The more knots he added to the rope configuration, the closer her arms got to touching. This pattern didn't restrict her breathing like some of the chest harnesses he'd crafted. Yet Amery found herself floating into that same headspace, where his fleeting touches set off little pulses beneath her skin.

He held her wrists and placed several thick loops in the center of the rope that kept her wrists from touching.

Amery knew when Ronin finished. He stepped back to scrutinize his creation, much like an artist. Then he'd make minute adjustments to the ropes. Sometimes he'd circle her, looking from all angles. But this time he stayed behind her.

And his voice was so perfectly modulated it never abruptly brought her out of that trancelike state when he spoke. "Amery."

She didn't have to answer him; he just needed to know he had her attention. She barely moved her head in acknowledgment.

"You are stunning bound in red. I'm grateful you'll get a chance to see the pure beauty that shines through you." Then Ronin's hands were on her once again, circling her hips as he snugged his body in behind hers.

"Stay in this heightened state and tell me what I need to do to capture the picture."

Amery fought against the pull that would yank her out of

blissful nothingness. "The remote button is attached to the camera. Press it when you have the shot you want."

There was movement behind her and Amery managed to stay still.

He adjusted her arms higher. "Hold like that."

The shutter made a whirring click. Then another. And another. So many she lost count.

Ronin didn't suggest she change poses. She understood his gaze wasn't behind the lens, but entirely on her.

"Will you let me try something?" he asked. "I won't move you, I promise."

"Yes."

"Stay still no matter what I do to you."

That meant he planned to touch her.

Stretching out the anticipation was Ronin's specialty. He'd never kept her hanging on the jagged edge for long. Yet knowing he could keep her there indefinitely, that she had no control in how or when he chose to send her soaring into pleasure, added another layer to their play.

His gi pants teased her bare toes when he dropped to his knees in front of her. He kissed the skin below her belly button.

The same time Amery released a little gasp of surprise, the shutter whirred behind her.

Ronin's breath drifted over the damp spot he'd just kissed and she bit her lower lip as the camera clicked. His warm mouth slid a fraction lower.

Click.

Another inch put his mouth right on the lace band of her panties.

Click.

But the sneaky man didn't kiss her there; he dipped his tongue beneath the lace.

She jerked and her head moved out of position.

"Don't move." Those rough fingertips were on her hips and he tugged her panties down—not off—but far enough to prevent her from widening her stance.

Click.

Amery felt the hot wash of his breath over the rise of her bare mound. No. He wouldn't.

And then he did.

Ronin burrowed his tongue into the top of her slit and licked down, then back up. Zeroing that flicking tongue directly on her clit.

Somehow she held the position as he used that wicked tongue to drive her out of her mind.

She thought she heard the camera clicking, but she wasn't sure she wasn't hearing the muscle in her jaw popping from clenching her teeth.

No teasing. No slow buildup. Ronin just tongued her insistently until that breathless moment right before the orgasm slammed into her. Amery couldn't help dropping her head back in ecstasy and sucking in a few gasping breaths as she gave herself over to the pleasure.

Once the fog lifted, she let her face dip down, almost in supplication.

Several more shots clicked.

"Amery."

Her heart rate picked up.

"Look up for a second."

As always when he bound her, she followed his instructions.

"Good. Now turn your head and glance over your shoulder."

Her hair hung her face and she tossed her head to clear her line of sight.

Click.

The flash startled her, but she stared right into the camera lens.

Click.

"Beautiful, baby. Now relax."

She allowed herself a small smile but didn't otherwise move.

Click.

Then Ronin's hands were on her face and his mouth captured hers in a combustible kiss. Although her heart still thumped like mad, she existed in that post-orgasmic haze.

"Need to have you like this," he murmured against her lips. "Step out of your jeans."

As soon as she kicked them free, he herded her backward to her office.

Ronin turned her around and bent her over her desk. She hissed in a breath when her nipples and belly connected with the cold surface.

The head of Ronin's cock nudged her hot, wet center. He jerked on the rope dangling between her wrists. "Arms up and keep them up. I want to see your ass shake as I'm fucking you."

Amery pressed her cheek into the cool wood and lifted her arms. The silken cord dropped between her butt cheeks.

Ronin said, "Jesus. I can feel the rope teasing my dick."

He did a pelvis twist and plunged inside her cunt fully. Wrapping one hand around her hip, he repositioned her to keep her hipbones from banging into the desk. Then he twisted the rope in his other hand, pulling it as he fucked her.

Each steady stroke fueled the fire between them. Ronin's quiet intensity as he plowed into her kept her on the edge as she waited for him to detonate.

When that moment arrived, he stopped slamming into her and shuddered as his cock emptied. The combination of her restraint and his passion set her off again. Her pussy clamped around his cock as it pulsed, milking every last seed.

Then he lifted her up and cranked her head around to meet his avid mouth, kissing with such sweetness she melted.

"Stay still," he said gruffly. As he unwound the rope from her arms, his fingers brushed over the marks. "Still red even after the red rope is gone," he murmured. "But they'll fade in a few hours."

Why did she have a twinge of regret that they'd fade so soon?

He held her for a long time and she relished the skin-on-skin contact. Then he played with her hair, twirling it around his fingers. He wrapped a thick chunk around his palm and brought it to his mouth, rubbing his lips across it. Each caress on her cheek and tender kiss on her forehead brought her back to herself. She felt secure that he knew exactly what she needed without her having to ask.

"Better?"

"Much. Thank you. For . . . all of it."

"I'm humbled by the trust you place in me." He nuzzled her temple. "I'll never take that for granted."

Men, in her experience, in the afterglow of great sex, would say anything in hopes of a repeat performance. But Ronin was different since he'd backed up his words with actions on more than one occasion. She could fall for him so easily.

Don't be a fool. You've already fallen for him.

"Are you ready to see yourself on film?"

"No. I'm afraid to look."

"Why?"

"I don't like pictures of myself." Understatement. Amery hated pictures of herself. "I always look goofy. Like the redheaded stepchild who gets shoved into the background hoping no one notices her."

He pinched her chin between his thumb and forefinger. "Then you'll be surprised by how breathtaking you look bound by me, won't you?"

It'd kill her to see his disappointment when he witnessed proof of how unphotogenic she was.

"I don't want you deleting anything until we've gone through them all," he warned. "It sounds as if you can't be objective when it comes to photos of yourself, let alone half-naked photos." He kissed her nose. "Grab the camera and let's take a peek."

"What if they're all bad? You've already untied me, so it isn't like we can do a reshoot."

"First of all, I can have you retied in five minutes. Second of all, my fear is that you burned up the camera with your smoking hotness. Especially when I went down on you. If the image could capture the sex noises you made, tied up for my pleasure and coming on my tongue, the images would easily sell for hundreds of thousands of dollars."

Amery wiggled out of his hold. "Now you're just being ridiculous."

"Am I? Get dressed. I'll be back." He snagged his shirt off the floor and ducked out.

She put her clothes on before she unhooked the camera from the tripod.

Ronin rolled her office chair into the studio. He lowered into it and patted his lap. "That way we can both see."

Meaning he wouldn't let her escape and he'd know if she tried to delete something.

The camera had a decent-sized viewing screen. She selected the first shot of the session and held her breath as she enlarged it.

The binding was intricate, making her body look delicate and malleable, yet strong in her submission.

"Keep going."

Ronin didn't comment . . . until the pictures where the angle of her head had changed. When he'd put his mouth on her.

Holy. Shit. The arch of her back, the way her hands had tightened into fists, even the bend of her neck screamed *woman in the throes of passion.*

Amery couldn't believe that sexy woman was her.

"Told you," he said smugly. "I'll bet they're all like that."

So maybe she was a little more eager to view the remaining shots.

The subtle changes toward the end when Ronin had taken advantage of her orgasm-scrambled brain suggested movement. When they reached the last three images, Ronin's hands tightened around her biceps and his body went rigid.

"What?"

"That one." He pointed to the picture of her glancing over her shoulder, her hair in motion, her eyes sultry, her lips parted. "Is mine."

"What?"

"That look belongs to me because I put it there. It's mine."

His possessive tone wrapped around her like a silken ribbon.

"I want a copy of that one for myself. No one else will ever see it."

She leaned back, turning her head to kiss beneath his jaw. "You promise?"

"Yes, baby, I promise."

CHAPTER TWENTY-FOUR

"I cannot believe you talked me into an IKEA trip on a Saturday," Ronin complained.

Amery returned the green glass vase to the shelf. "I bet you've never been in this store, regardless of which day of the week it is."

"My place is furnished. Why would I need to add more to it?"

"You can go into a store and just look at things without buying them."

With a perfectly straight face he said, "If I need an item, I go into the store and buy it. Why would I waste time going into a store if I didn't need to buy anything?"

"For sheer shopping pleasure? The joy of being a consumer?" she offered.

Ronin continued to give her a blank stare.

No wonder his apartment was so minimalist.

"Do you even know what you're shopping for?"

"Yes." She smiled and said, "Doodads."

That earned her a sigh. But he did follow her to the next room display. Everything looked so hip and put-together. Amery had the pang of self-awareness that any funky cool vibe in her loft was strictly by accident.

Ronin asked, "Do you like this?"

"Yes. I wish I could create a room this chic and modern. My decorating style is castoffs, garage sales, and the occasional piece headed for the Dumpster. I can spend hours looking in here and leave without purchasing a single thing."

"Hours?" he repeated.

She couldn't help laughing. "I won't torture you today. Spending hours in IKEA is something you work up to."

"For the first time ever I hope to have zero stamina."

"Come along. Let Master Hardwick teach you all the tricks about being a ninja shopper."

They stopped at the next display and were discussing form and color when a female voice said, "Sensei Black?"

Immediately his posture changed and that blank mask slid onto his face before he turned toward the woman.

"I thought it was you, but I never thought I'd see Sensei out shopping."

Amery scrutinized the Asian woman who spoke in heavily accented English. She in turn scrutinized Amery.

And Ronin didn't seem inclined to introduce them.

Then she refocused on Ronin. "Is this your new girl?"

Ronin switched to Japanese. His tone seemed sharp, but the language inflections were so different that Amery couldn't be sure.

The woman snapped back in Japanese, her eyes flinty, her gestures choppy.

Definitely an angry reaction. Which got her no reaction from Ronin besides a shrug.

She attempted to get in Ronin's face.

All he had to do was hold up his hand; she stopped in her tracks. But her mouth kept running as she rattled off something that sounded like a verbal smack-down.

His response was clipped.

Which didn't deter her. Her voice took on a low, almost seductive bent. When she didn't get the response from Ronin she expected, she switched to a one-sided diatribe and the words came much faster. When she finally quit speaking, she gave Amery a once-over and sniffed.

Ronin had struck the defensive stance Amery recognized from class. He leaned closer to the woman and spoke so quietly Amery could hardly hear him. But she did make out one word loud and clear: Naomi.

Holy shit. She knew Naomi was Japanese and this woman's pouting tone suggested she and Ronin had shared an intimate relationship at one time.

The woman walked away without looking back.

Ronin stared after her, his face still blank. But when the interloper disappeared into the crowd and Ronin's eyes met Amery's, she saw the anger burning there before he banked it. "If you're done browsing I'd like to go now."

"Ah, sure."

Amery swore IKEA changed the exit point every time she was in the store, so it took ten minutes to escape.

They were zipping downtown when she couldn't stand the silence a moment longer. "So, that woman you had words with . . . was that Naomi?"

"No."

That was all she got for an answer? Bull. "Then who was she?"

"Naomi's friend Kiki."

Silence.

"What did Kiki say?"

"She blathered on with a Naomi update, which I warned her I didn't want."

"What was the update?"

Ronin said nothing. He just cut in and out of traffic as if they'd jumped onto the autobahn.

"Ronin?"

"That Naomi was coming to Denver."

"When? Does she want to see you?"

"Doesn't matter. I won't see her."

Her mouth opened. Closed. When she opened it again to ask him a question, Ronin shook his head. "End of discussion."

That was a little high-handed. And another example of him holding back on her and just expecting her to accept it.

Why are you surprised?

"Where to now?" Ronin asked.

"Home."

"I thought you had more errands."

"Nothing that won't keep."

Ronin frowned. "You sure?"

"Positive." Amery didn't fill the void with chatter. In fact, she didn't look at him at all.

He pulled into the alley. "I'll find a parking place and be right up."

"Actually, I'm tired and I know you're exhausted after your mysterious all-nighter, so let's call it a day."

"It's only two o'clock in the afternoon."

"Just means you can nap longer."

"I don't nap," he said curtly.

Maybe you need one. "Whatever. Later." She started to open the door, but Ronin stopped her.

"Tell me what's wrong."

"Think about it, Sensei."

"Jesus. Don't act like this."

"Like what? Pissed off you pull that *end of discussion* bullshit and expect me to accept it?"

"I tried to head off a pointless argument, which obviously was a waste of breath because you want to fight with me today."

"Wrong. I wanted to talk. You refused."

"That's it?"

"Isn't that enough?"

"No. Why didn't you introduce me to Kiki?" *Are you ashamed of me?*

"She's a snake and you're better off if she doesn't know who you are."

"Or maybe you don't want her blabbing about me because you still have feelings for Naomi and that's why you won't talk about her."

"That's laughable. You should know—"

"I don't know anything about Naomi or your relationship with her besides the bare bones. Anytime I ask questions, you shut me down. I'm tired of you making me feel like a jealous hag about it, especially when it's clearly not my issue, just because I had the audacity to ask a question about her." Amery inhaled a calming breath. "So I finally get it, okay?"

"Get what?"

"You've proven to me time and time again that you want to keep this casual. We're hookup buddies. Hot sex with a few bondage games thrown in. That's it."

Ronin pinned her with his hard stare.

Amery wouldn't back down. "So, call me if you literally want to tie one on. But not tonight. I've got plans."

"With who?"

"Chaz and his friends."

"Why didn't I know about this?"

"Because you didn't ask." Amery opened the door and slid out. "And that right there is the difference between us, Ronin. I ask you a question and you don't answer. But you can't even be bothered to ask me any questions in the first place."

SOMEHOW Amery got everyone's attention over the deafening noise in the restaurant. "Tonight we're celebrating a milestone in our beloved friend Chaz's career; his glorious artistic work will be showcased in the launch of a groundbreaking new series in the U.S, graphic novels featuring homoerotic story lines."

Clapping and wolf whistles followed.

"So let's toast." She lifted her martini glass. "Chaz, may the contracts keep rolling in, brother. We're all proud of you and no one deserves this success more than you."

Hugs, congrats, and a few tears were shared among the dozen friends gathered at the table. Then the wait staff cleared the plates and passed out glasses of champagne at Chaz's request.

Champagne reminded Amery of the night at the sports gala with Ronin.

Everything reminded her of Ronin.

But nothing about that realization made her happy.

"Why the sad face, doll?" Vincent asked when he reached across her for the coffee creamer.

"I'm not sad. Why? Do I look it?"

"A little." He squeezed her forearm. "You okay?"

"I'm fine. Just thinking about the last time I had champagne. I made a few questionable choices."

"Is this a juicy story?"

Amery laughed. "Not really."

"Pity. I had perverted hopes you'd dish out a sexy story about you and the scrumptious Ronin Black." He leaned closer. "Is it true what I've heard about him?"

"Depends on what you've heard."

"That he's into . . . all sorts of . . . things."

She sipped her champagne and studied Vincent, Chaz's tailor and longtime friend. "Can you be more specific?"

Vincent fussed with the sleeve of his shirt. "Just that Mr. Black doesn't list all his services on his dojo's Web site. But if you know who to ask, what to ask, and have the means, he's available for hire."

"For what? As a clown at kids' birthday parties?"

"Hilarious. No, silly. For personal protection. Yes, he offers training, but for the right price he'll also sign on as a bodyguard."

She relaxed, relieved Ronin's real proclivities weren't the subject of rumors. "Now, where did you pick up that information, Vincent?"

He waved his hand. "I'm tailor to Denver's elite. It's amazing what one overhears when customers consider you part of the furniture. I'd forgotten a conversation I'd overheard until Chaz mentioned his concern about your involvement with Mr. Black."

Why had Chaz talked to Vincent about Ronin?

"I can see Chaz didn't share the information I shared with him with you."

"Probably because it wouldn't surprise me that Ronin hired out his services. He's an advocate for self-protection and he's highly trained in all areas. If I needed a man to guard my back, he'd be first on the list."

"But doesn't that scare you?" Vincent pressed. "That he might hurt you without meaning to?"

"Ronin would never hurt me. The man has unparalleled control in any and all situations." Amery remembered Ronin's icy coolness the night they were attacked—both during and after. Then her mind went back to how much he knew about stripping down and discarding a gun.

"Interesting." Vincent stirred his piña colada. "Well, I'm glad to hear you trust him, because frankly, I never expected you to be attracted to that sort of man."

"What sort? Hot? Older? Exotic?"

"A thug. A highly trained thug, but a thug nonetheless."

Amery's jaw dropped. "Wow, for a gay man who deals with preconceived ideas, you're pretty goddamn judgmental."

"And what would sweet, naive Amery call a man who teaches violent tactics and sometimes uses them himself for profit? Isn't that the very definition of a thug?"

She hated his pseudo-reasonable I'm-talking-to-a-child-tone.

She drained her drink and stood. "Excuse me. I need to use the facilities." *And get the hell away from you.*

In the bathroom, she replayed the conversation with Vincent. The problem with her friends and the groups they hung around with? They intellectualized everything. They wouldn't look beyond Ronin's brawn to see his brain. If he capitalized on his skill and expanded his income base, it didn't make him a thug for hire; it made him smart.

Despite her frustration with him, she missed him.

Back at the table she took a seat at the end opposite Vincent.

Chaz made a beeline for her and sat on the arm of the chair. "Amery, the girl who always brings her A game, what's up?"

"Not much. Just enjoying your par-tay."

"You could've brought Master Black, you know."

"Might be awkward for him, with your prissy friends judging him."

Chaz crouched beside her. "Ignore Vincent. He's a flaming asshole."

"I just don't understand why you talked to him about your concerns regarding me getting involved with Ronin."

"Well, sugar cube, Vincent is my friend. I talked to him around the time Emmylou had me freaked out. That's all."

"You sure?" When Chaz hesitated, she knew that wasn't all. "Tell me."

"I just hate the secretiveness that's grown between us since you started seeing him. Don't jump on me, because I'm not blaming him, okay?"

Chaz did have a point. She didn't talk about her relationship with Ronin. "Okay."

"Seriously, where is he tonight?"

I don't know. "Contrary to what you and Emmylou believe, Ronin and I do lead separate lives."

"I'm glad because that means you're here with me. I'm selfish enough to want you all to myself to help me celebrate tonight." He took her hand. "So we okay?"

Amery smiled, suspecting it looked as bogus as it felt. "Of course. We going dancing?"

"You know it." He stood and hip-checked her. "But no bitching because it's a gay club," he warned.

RONIN texted her at two a.m. I'm at the back door.

She debated ignoring it. She started a snarky response about him forgetting his key and deleted it. She typed K and rolled out of bed to let him in.

The metal door screeched loudly. After he stepped inside, she said, "Why did I bother to give you a key?"

Ronin responded by wrapping his hand around the back of her neck and pulling her mouth to his. Kissing her softly, but thoroughly. He broke the kiss to press his mouth up her jawline. "Goddamn, I missed you so much tonight. I was an ass earlier today."

It wasn't exactly an apology, but at least he acknowledged his bad behavior toward her. She tilted his head back and stared into his handsome face. Such tired eyes. "Ronin, you're exhausted."

"Pretty much."

"You never did tell me what you did last night that kept you from sleep all night."

"A favor for a friend. Now we're square."

Amery frowned at the shadow beneath his jaw. "Is that a bruise?"

"Probably. Some favors are unappreciated."

Vincent's nasty comment from earlier echoed in her head. *"He's a thug. A highly trained thug, but a thug nonetheless."*

No, he was just a man. She kissed the mark. "Let's get you in bed."

"Love to hear you say that. Although all I'm up for tonight is sleep."

She stopped and pointed at the back door. "If you're not going to fuck me at least three times, you might as well get the hell out."

Ronin laughed, as she hoped he would. "Let me get a few hours of shut-eye and I'll be all over you."

"Well, then. I *suppose* you can crash with me."

CHAPTER TWENTY-FIVE

RONIN woke her when the faint orange glow of dawn teased the edges of the curtains. He said nothing; he just brushed his mouth over her ear until she offered him her throat. He placed a soft kiss on her jawline and nuzzled his face against her neck.

At first she loved the prickliness of his facial hair abrading her skin. But when he rubbed in the same spot on her throat and then the tops of her breasts, it became uncomfortable.

As soon as she tried to touch him, he knocked the pillows to the floor, pinned her arms to the mattress, and trailed sucking kisses from one side of her neck to the other. Over and over. Then he did the same scraping sweep from one breast to the other. Keeping a firm grip on her wrists, he settled between her thighs and thrust into her. He moved with such desperation. Fast and hard, with no time for finesse. No time to catch his breath in the race to the finish line. He swiveled his hips and Amery arched up, reaching for that moment of pleasure. She came quietly, panting against his neck, and his silent climax followed hers.

Amery was a little taken aback by his impersonal actions, because Ronin wasn't a selfish lover. Ever. Not even when he had her bound. She broke his hold on her wrists. Touching his back, running her hands through his hair, hoping to get through to him, because he seemed to be in a daze. "Ronin?"

He started to lift up and she thought she'd finally gotten somewhere with him. But he rolled onto his side, away from her, and she heard the deep rhythmic breathing that indicted he'd fallen asleep.

She slid off the bed, grabbed her robe, and crept out of her bedroom, completely disconcerted. Something hadn't been right with him. She didn't mind aggressive sex, but she suspected Ronin hadn't been conscious of his actions.

What? He was sleep-fucking you?

That did sound ridiculous.

She poured a glass of water and noticed the red mark on her wrist. On both her wrists. Finger-shaped marks. Where else had he left marks on her? She dropped the robe and stared at her reflection in the mirror, shocked at what she saw.

Her neck was covered with patches of beard burn interspersed with red suck marks. Same with her chest.

Amery looked away from the marks and slipped the robe back on.

He's a violent man. Aren't you afraid he'll hurt you?

The irony wasn't lost on her. Ronin hadn't hurt her in anger; he'd hurt her while making love to her. Had he even been aware of his actions in his exhausted state?

You're making excuses for him?

She jumped when a loud knock sounded on the door. "Amery?"

"If you need to use the bathroom, try the one downstairs."

"I don't need to use the bathroom. Let me in. I know something's wrong."

"Just give me a minute."

"No. Open the goddamn door or I'll kick it in."

There's another example of his violent streak. Are you really sure you know this man?

She shrank against the wall.

No sound came from the other side for several long moments. Then he said, "Please."

Amery found herself unlocking the door and walking past him into the kitchen. Hands shaking, she poured a glass of juice. Her heart raced when Ronin moved in behind her.

"What happened? Help me out because I don't remember a goddamn thing."

She faced him. "You don't remember anything at all?"

"I vaguely recall coming here late last night and crashing next to you. Then about five minutes ago I woke up alone, surrounded by twisted sheets and your taste on my tongue." His gaze dropped to her hands, and how tightly she clutched her robe. "Amery. Did I hurt you?"

She stared at him but couldn't give voice to the *it's not so bad* excuse.

"Let me see."

"I'm afraid to."

"Why?"

"Because of what you'll do to yourself when you see what you did to me."

That gave him pause. "Jesus. I hurt you and you're worried about me."

Yes, because it wasn't really you.

"Let me see it. Now."

Fed up with her self-recrimination and frustrated by his hot and cold behavior, Amery let the robe fall to the floor.

Ronin clenched his hands at his sides as his gaze mentally catalogued every inch of her. "You are brightness and beauty in my life and your trust in me is something I treasure . . . and I did this to you?"

Amery didn't say anything; she just watched him. The horror on his face ripped at her.

"Where does it hurt the most?" He briefly closed his eyes. "If you say you hurt worse inside than outside . . ."

And like usual, she rushed to reassure him. "The beard burn stings. Arnica gel will help, but first I need a shower." Maybe steam would clear the cobwebs in her brain and the heat would loosen her tensed muscles.

When she exited the bathroom thirty minutes later, Ronin stood in front of the living room window. In two steps he erased the distance between them. "Baby. Let me put this right." He nuzzled her temple. "Please." He kissed her. Not tentatively as she expected, but with surety that felt like comfort and love.

Love?

That's when she feared she'd forgive him anything because she loved him. It frightened her as much as it thrilled her.

When he finally released her mouth, she tilted her head back and looked at him. She noticed Ronin had dark circles under his eyes. Every line in his face read *exhaustion*. She let her fingers drift across his baby-smooth face. When had he shaved? Had he done it out of guilt? "Ronin. You're not okay and it doesn't have anything to do with me."

"You're all that matters to me right now." He placed his hand over hers. "Come on."

She let him lead her into the bedroom. The scent of orange blossoms and ginger perfumed the air from the candles on the dresser. Soft strains of Norah Jones tunes drifted from her old CD player. He'd put on fresh sheets, her favorite ones, pale pink cotton emblazoned with cherry blossoms. The whole space had a warm, comforting vibe.

He kissed the back of her head, and his hands moved to untie the sash. Then he slipped the robe from her body. "Sit in the middle of the bed."

Shivering, not only from her nakedness, Amery positioned herself cross-legged in the center of the mattress.

Ronin cocooned her in fleece. "Warm enough?" he asked as he brought her damp hair on the outside of the blanket.

"Yes."

"Close your eyes. Let me know if I'm hurting you." He scooted in behind her with his legs stretched out in a V; then he spread her hair out.

Was he really . . . ?

Yes. Ronin was brushing her hair.

At first, it seemed weird. But then she blanked her mind to everything except the sensation of the bristles lightly digging into her scalp. The brush tugging down the long strands. His hands smoothing the untangled tresses. Ronin's need to atone for his carelessness with her touched her on so many levels.

"Such beautiful hair." He brushed it straight back and gathered it at the back of her head. "I'll braid it so it's out of my way."

"You know how to braid?" tumbled out.

"Same principle as braiding rope, right?"

"I guess." And he'd know all about that.

Ronin's warm breath drifted across her ear as he loosened the blanket. "Stretch out on your back."

Her heart beat faster—not from fear.

His hands caressed her shoulders, her arms, her sides, her belly. He placed tender, warm kisses on every mark. Ronin continued to stroke her as he applied arnica gel to the areas that needed a salve stronger than the loving touch of his mouth.

Amery kept her eyes closed. Her thoughts scrolled back to the night he'd shown her in the mirror how she looked bound by him. She remembered the dreamy quality of sitting perfectly still and feeling his hands on her everywhere. His fingers caressing her as he worked the ropes. Even when he'd unbound her, she'd still felt the pull, as if the ropes were digging into her skin.

She felt that same type pull now—as if Ronin were burrowing beneath her skin. When she reached up to touch him, she saw the bruise on his jaw had darkened. Her gaze moved over his face. Was his bottom lip swollen? Why hadn't she noticed the scratches on his neck?

"What? You're glaring at me."

"Where were you last night that you ended up with marks on your throat?" Now that she thought about it, he'd been fully dressed when he came looking for her. And the entire time he'd been touching her—he always took his shirt off. So what other marks was he hiding? And why?

"It's nothing."

"It's not *nothing* to me. You didn't have those Saturday morning when you pinned me to the bed and fucked me."

"Amery—"

"Did you go to Twisted?"

Ronin scowled. "No. I told you—"

"You haven't told me anything. So you'd better come clean about where you were last night or you can leave and don't come back. I'm not kidding."

He sighed. "I know you're not." He pushed back onto his haunches and studied Amery for a long time before he spoke. "The only time I've slept in the last seventy-two hours was when I crawled in bed with you. After my twenty-four-hour surveillance gig, I came here and we went shopping. Seeing Kiki . . ."

A knot in her chest tightened.

"I'd signed on to ref ten matches in an amateur MMA event last night. The last guy's opponent didn't show, so I stepped in."

"Wait. You fought last night? In an actual match?"

"Yeah." He jammed his hand through his hair and she noticed his knuckles were shredded. "I saw the chance to alleviate some of my aggression from the previous forty-eight hours and I took it."

When his eyes met hers, she recognized the challenge. *Go ahead and judge me.*

"Before you ask, yes, I won. But he managed to kick me in the head, which rang my bell pretty good. The fight went all three rounds, so the fans got their money's worth."

The casual way Ronin relayed all this raised red flags. "How did you hear about the event?"

"It was my event. I set it up."

Why didn't she know that about him? Was that part of the shady business dealings others had mentioned? Was that why he didn't talk about where he'd been or what he'd been doing some weekend nights? "You do that often?"

"Often enough. And no, it's not something I advertise through Black Arts."

Vincent's warning surfaced again. *"Mr. Black doesn't list all his services on his dojo's Web site."*

"The only reason I'm telling you this is that the kick to the head scrambled my brain. I hope you know I never would've done what I did this morning if I'd been in my right mind." He curled his hand over her cheek. "I shouldn't have shown up last night, but I can't stay away from you."

Somehow that didn't bring the relief she thought it would.

"I'm sorry I hurt you."

"I know you are."

Ronin stretched out beside her and snugged his body behind hers. "I could use a nap."

Even before she could jokingly warn Mr. I Don't Nap not to sleep-fuck her again, he'd fallen asleep.

FOUR hours later they sat at the kitchen counter finishing the salmon salad Ronin had made for lunch. Things had seemed normal between them after he'd tended to her, and she didn't want to wreck the moment. But she had questions that couldn't wait any longer. "We need to talk."

"I know."

"What happened between you and Naomi? Just talking about her yesterday affected you and now that's spilled over onto me, so I have a right to know."

He shoved his plate aside and ran his hand through his hair. "I met Naomi six years ago at a club."

She didn't have to pussyfoot around and ask what kind of club. "Did you use bondage on her?"

"Yes."

"Right away after you met her?"

"Yes."

So he hadn't sprung it on Naomi as he had on her. "Did you demonstrate erotic bondage on her and then fuck her in front of a roomful of people?"

Ronin gently wrapped his fingers around her jaw. "Are we going to talk about this, or are you just going to hurl jealous accusations at me?"

Amery closed her eyes. "I'm sorry."

"I am too. Can you please look at me?"

She shook her head, but she didn't shake his hand off.

"Why not?"

"I know you cared about her and I can't look into your eyes when you tell me about her. Even though I'm the one who's making you do it."

"Sweet baby." He softly kissed her lips. "Come here." He led her to the couch and settled her between his legs with her back resting on his chest. He strapped one arm over her belly, holding her in place.

Why did his tight hold on her make her feel . . . secure?

"When I met Naomi she told me she was thirty when in fact she was twenty-six. That's just the first of many lies. She claimed to be familiar with shibari and kinbaku—also a lie, but she convinced me she'd be willing to try it. Within a few weeks we became involved outside of the club.

"We'd been together two years, in a relationship and she was my exclusive rope partner, when she asked if instead of adjourning to a private room after a kinbaku scene to have sex, we could add it to the scene."

"So you had her naked, tied up in provocative poses, and never fucked her during a demo? Not once in two years?"

"No, because we were in public."

"You never had sex in public? With any of your bondage partners?"

"No." Ronin bent closer and brushed a kiss across her temple. "I'm a private man, Amery. For me sex is as private as it gets. But I'm a foolish man sometimes because I agreed to try it."

His voice was filled with so much regret she squeezed his forearm.

"Took me a month to map out a new complicated suspension scene—mostly because I didn't want to do it. At the end of the demonstration, I fucked her."

The harshness of his response meant it hadn't gone well.

"Afterward . . . it didn't leave me in a good place. I went home and downed a fifth of scotch."

"Did Naomi come with you?"

He absentmindedly stroked the inside of her wrist. "No. Should've been my first indication things were wrong. She wanted a repeat performance at the club the next time and I said no. She threw a tantrum. No one undermines my authority at the dojo, or during a demo or at the club, so I forced her into a hojojutsu punishment scene."

Amery's pulse jumped. "What happened?"

"No matter how much she begged and cried, I refused to punish her in private. I bound her in a pose called humiliation, which includes neck ropes. Then I gagged her and used a paddle on her. After I'd broken her, I fucked her but didn't allow her to come."

She turned her head away. That didn't sound like him at all.

"Rather than it upsetting her, she got off on it. I rarely use humiliation in the dojo as a teaching tool, because it doesn't work. I was completely unprepared for her reaction and my disgust with myself. I quit going to the club."

"Ronin."

"Then Naomi stopped showing up at my place, unless she was drunk, crying, and a mess. I always took her in. At the time I hadn't known she'd still been going to the club and she'd become a submissive to several Doms. A few months later the club owner asked me to come back and give a shibari demo, but Naomi refused to be involved unless I fucked her during the scene. I found another rope model. Naomi went a little psycho after the demo and started threatening me. So I had her banned from the club." He set his chin on top of her head. "She told everyone I ruined her life and she returned to Japan."

Amery let that sink in before she spoke. "She was responsible for her choices. You did what you had to, to protect yourself and your reputation."

"It is my fault. She was young and I pushed her to the edge and she liked it."

"And you ended up at war with yourself for giving her what she wanted."

"Yes."

Amery turned and kissed his jaw.

"Needless to say I joined a new club—the same one Knox belongs to. The women who agree to be bound by me know my rules. I rarely deviate from them."

"So the woman at the club who ended up with Knox . . . ?"

"The club auctioned off a rope session with me for charity. The woman's husband gave it to her as a birthday gift. They requested Knox as the demonstration closer."

"I didn't stay for that part."

"Good. You should know that Naomi is also the reason I built the practice room. I thought if we had a designated place she wouldn't need to go to the club. It didn't change anything. And that room has been unused since then, until I met you."

She closed her eyes. She'd heard men talking about being fucked up by an ex. But what Ronin had dealt with Naomi? Epically fucked up. And she suspected he hadn't told her everything. Maybe he never would. It scared her to think Naomi had damaged him to the point he'd never trust her enough to open up completely.

THE next morning Amery scrutinized the marks on her body. Some had started to fade, but makeup wouldn't cover the hickeys and scrapes on her neck. Was it ironic she chose a scarf that Ronin used to bind her to cover up the marks?

She opened the office, started coffee, and got to work.

Molly dragged in an hour late. The girl looked horrible.

"Are you all right?"

"Not really." Molly bit her lip as if trying to hold back tears.

"You want to talk about it?"

"Not yet. It'll help if I focus on work."

"Being the über-organized boss I am, I e-mailed the updated daily task lists first thing."

That earned her a smile. "Über-organized. That ages you, boss. No one says über anymore."

"Get to work, whippersnapper."

At lunchtime, Molly came into her office and shut the door.

Looked as though she'd decided to talk. They'd gotten a lot closer in the past few months. Whether it was because they'd passed the martial arts class together, or was due to Molly's newfound confidence—either way, she'd opened up. They'd gone out for dinner and drinks several times, and their conversations hadn't revolved around work. Amery had hung out with Molly more often than Chaz or Emmylou. "What's up?"

Molly slid into the chair in front of the desk. She stared at her hands for a moment and blurted, "I cheated on Zach last night."

Not what she'd expected. "Okay. How'd it happen?"

"Zach and I were supposed to go to a movie last night, but he called and canceled again. It's happened so many times because Master Black makes Zach do jobs outside the dojo. Jobs he can't talk about and he's keeping really weird hours."

Amery frowned. Ronin had been keeping odd hours too and hadn't been forthcoming about what he'd been doing either—except he had come clean about jumping into the ring. But prior to that, when she'd asked why she couldn't get a hold of him, he'd given her that scary "back off" vibe, so she hadn't brought it up again.

"Anyway, this has been going on for weeks and last night I'd had enough. I went to a sports bar with my new friend Nina and she introduced me to one of her guy friends." She sighed. "A really cute guy friend, who was funny and charming and he was way into me. One thing led to another and I went home with him." Her cheeks turned crimson.

"Have you ever had a one-night stand before?"

Molly peeked up at her. "It's probably hard to believe because I come across as shy, but yeah, I've done the walk of shame a couple of times. I like this guy, we had fun, and he wants to see me again."

"So what's the problem?"

"What if the only reason he wants to see me is that he thinks I'm a slut? And what about Zach? He's really sweet and I like hanging out with him, but he's taking things so slow. I don't know if it's because he thinks I'd have anxiety during sex because I was attacked or what, but we've never done anything more than kiss. Even when I let him know I want more, he says stuff like *no rush*. So I'm back to the same worry that I'm some kind of slut for wanting sex from one guy one day, and another guy the next day."

"Molly, as long as you're having safe sex and your partner or partners are enjoying it too doesn't mean you're a slut. It means you're a normal college girl with a healthy sex drive. And that's not something to be ashamed of; that's something to be proud of."

"Really?"

"Really. I've struggled to reconcile my feelings of guilt about sex, wanting it and having it, since I was in my teens. The way I was raised is a pretty powerful deterrent to accepting and embracing my sexuality."

"Even now?"

Especially now that she was involved with Ronin and all the layers of kink he'd added to the mix—kink that didn't seem dirty, bad, or wrong when she was in the moment with him. But she still had an uneasy feeling if she thought too much about how other people would react if they ever found out what she liked and what she did behind closed bedroom doors.

"Amery?"

She glanced up. "Yes, even now."

"I'm not glad to hear that, because those feelings suck, but I sort of am because it lets me know I'm not alone with some of these hang-ups." She smiled sheepishly. "So thanks."

"Anytime."

"So what do you think I should do about Zach?"

"Break it off with him. He had his chance; he blew it. Hang out with the guy who wants to spend time with you. No pressure. Just have fun." Amery grinned. "And if he's good? Girl, hit that hard every chance you can."

Molly smirked. "Now that the woman who's banging the hottie known as Master Black has given me sex advice . . . I plan to."

"Good."

"And there's one other thing I need to talk to you about." She threw her shoulders back and lifted her chin. "Are you planning to let me go because business has dropped off?"

She'd hoped to have this conversation later, possibly even never. "I won't lie. It's not looking good. The new clients I've picked up still aren't making up for the loss of income from Townsend's. And I've been out on every call, no matter how small the job . . ."

"What about the secret project you've been working on? Does that have potential?"

Amery's eyes narrowed.

Molly rolled her eyes in response. "Come on, Amery, I work here. I'd have to be blind and stupid not to notice the packages and phone calls from Seattle. Why is it so top secret?"

"I signed a nondisclosure agreement with them. And I've got that *don't talk about it and jinx it* superstition too—I'm not sure anything will come from it." Which would be too bad because she'd really enjoyed the challenge and the creative freedom of working on something completely different. The client had assured Amery she'd welcome all ideas and designs that focused on thinking outside the normal frozen food box. So she'd worked up several concepts after-hours while Ronin was torturing his jujitsu students and doing his mysterious nocturnal things. Maggie said she'd hear Amery's full pitch in Denver sometime in the next month, which put extra pressure on Amery to have it ready soon.

"Earth to Amery."

She looked up from the doodle she'd drawn on her printout. "Sorry, I'm zoning out today."

Molly leaned forward. "Let me help you work on this project."

"While that's sweet—"

"Hear me out. I'll work on this project for free."

"Why?"

"Because if Hardwick Designs doesn't get new business soon, I'm going to be out of a job anyway. So there's an incentive for me to bring my best. And I've already signed a nondisclosure with you, so if you bring me onboard I can't discuss it with anyone."

Amery tapped her pen on her desk, studying her eager employee. "Extra work for no pay won't put you in a bind?"

"No. Look, my grandma is so elated I finished college and I'm pursing an MBA that she's funding my living expenses. What I earn here goes into my savings account. Besides, a lot of students in the grad program spend their summers and even part of the school year in unpaid internships. At least you pay me. If it makes you feel better, we can call this an apprenticeship because I'll bet you're not getting paid either unless you land the project. What company is this?"

"Okada Foods. They have roughly thirty percent of the overseas market in Asian food and they're looking to expand here in the U.S."

Molly's eyes nearly bugged out of her head. "Are you fucking kidding me? No offense, but how did that happen? They're huge."

No idea. "I guess they saw my ad work with my other organic food–based clients. Maybe lady luck is finally smiling on me."

"You have to let me work on this project with you. Please."

"You sure you want to do this now, Mol? The extra hours will cut into your social life."

"The reason I love this job is that I get to use the creative side of my brain, not only my business side. It balances me."

That tipped Amery into the *yes* camp of bringing Molly onboard. Ronin had mentioned the same type of thing: a need to express himself creatively outside of his normal routine. Who was she to deny Molly that chance?

Plus, she loved that she'd have someone to talk to and bounce ideas off for this opportunity.

She grinned. "Order us some Jimmy Johns and I'll bring you up to speed over lunch."

CHAPTER TWENTY-SIX

One month later

"AN hour?" *Take a deep breath.* "Absolutely I can be there. I'll be meeting with Maggie?" She felt her hopes plummeting. "No. I understand. Of course. Please tell her I'm looking forward to it. Thank you." She hung up the receiver and said, "Fuck."

Molly poked her head in. "What's wrong?"

"I'm pitching the Okada project today. In a freakin' hour."

"Amery, that's great!"

"No, it's not because I'm not pitching it to Maggie. The VP of Okada is here and I'm meeting with her."

"The VP of the North American division?"

"No, the big VP. She answers directly to the president of the entire company."

"Oh, man. What can I do?"

"Pat yourself on the back that we finished by the skin of our teeth last night." She pointed to the studio, where they'd spread the design paperwork on the floor. "Get everything together. Check it. Double-check it. *Triple*-check it. Then put it in my portfolio and type me up a list of what's included. I have to change into a power suit and get my game face on." She scaled the stairs to her loft two at a time.

Amery tore through her closet. Where the hell were all of her dress clothes?

Dirty. She'd been so tied up in the Okada project and pounding the pavement for new clients that she hadn't done laundry in two weeks.

Tied up. There was a play on words.

Her gaze landed on the coil of black rope on the floor. Strange, Ronin never left his ropes behind. But last night had been . . . intense. Even more intense than usual. Maybe he'd been as scrambled as she'd been this morning. She looked around and smiled. But he had remembered to take his gift.

Ronin had shown up late last night. After wrapping up the Okada project, she was wired. Like really wired. As soon as he'd ditched his overnight bag, she was on him. Kissing him crazily. Slipping her hands beneath his tank top and running her fingers all over his muscled torso. Biting and sucking on his neck with complete abandon.

"I take it you're happy to see me," he said, pushing her face back into his neck when she stopped sucking on his favorite spot. "More and harder."

"I don't want to leave a mark."

"With you this restless tonight? Baby, I don't care. I'll wear your mark as a gift."

She sucked on him until he hissed and she eased back. "Speaking of . . . I have a gift for you," she whispered in his ear.

"For me? What's the occasion?"

"Just because. Hang tight and I'll get it."

She'd made it halfway across the living room when she heard him say, "Strip for me."

Amery turned and looked at him. "Don't you want your present?"

"Yes. But you'll give it to me when you're naked."

She whipped off her clothes. "Happy now?"

"Yes. Seeing your bare ass jiggle is a gift in itself." He grinned at her. "But yeah, go ahead."

She'd hidden the wrapped package in the linen closet. The brown paper wrapper wasn't fancy, but she'd gone online and watched a video on how to tie decorative knots. So the twine was similar to the plain jute rope he used on her sometimes.

For some reason she had a bout of shyness when she returned with the package. But Ronin's uncharacteristic "Gimme" made her laugh.

He studied the knot, as she'd hoped he would. When he looked up at her, pure pleasure shone in his eyes. "Someone has been studying up on knot-tying techniques."

She shrugged and smiled.

He didn't untie the knot; he said, "I'm keeping this as part of the gift," and slipped the twine off. He tore the paper away and went motionless as the pieces fell to the floor.

"Do you like it? I know it's probably bigger than what you were expecting, but I figured that no one else is going to see it but you." She'd enlarged the picture he'd declared as *his* from the bondage cover photo shoot and framed it in an Asian-inspired red-and-black lacquered frame. It'd taken her a few weeks to find the courage to take it to a printing shop. Even then she'd chosen a place on the outskirts of Denver, given the clerk a fake name, and paid in cash—not that she'd ever confess that to Ronin.

The longer he stared at the explicit image without speaking, the bigger her fear became that he hadn't really wanted a picture of her bound. "If you don't want it . . ."

Those golden eyes met hers. Must've been a trick of the light, because for a split second she swore she saw a shimmer of tears.

Then he said something in Japanese.

"What does that mean?"

"It has no literal translation, which is an indication that I've got no words to give you for what this means to me, Amery." Then he bowed to her deeply.

Which was weird even when part of her realized he'd just paid her a high compliment.

Ronin carefully wrapped the twine around the corner of the frame and carried it into her bedroom.

After a minute or so when he hadn't returned, she followed him.

He stood beside the bed, bare-chested, wearing white gi pants. Even if she hadn't seen the black rope in his hand, she recognized he'd slipped into rope master demeanor when he'd slipped on his uniform.

"Beauty given from the heart should be rewarded."

Her entire body quivered.

"Come here."

She took two steps, stopping next to the bed.

"Stand still."

His body brushed against hers.

Amery trembled harder.

His hair tickled her cheek and her neck as he kissed her temple and nuzzled her jawline to the tip of her chin. Warm, soft lips followed the cords straining in her neck, down the hollow of her throat, over her breastbone, and between her breasts.

"Sit on the bed."

She perched on the edge, knees open, never taking her eyes off the man before her. Ronin's wicked mouth landed on her sternum and zigzagged down her belly, pausing to lightly skim the sensitive area between her hip bones. After gracefully dropping into a squat, he pressed kisses over her bare mound, softly suckling her clit. Then he dragged his tongue down the seam of her sex and plunged deep into her cunt. He made the growling noise that sent additional shivers through her.

Her skin beaded, electrified by every touch of his lips, or his fingers, and even the soft lash of his hair.

His hands were on the inside of her thighs pushing her wider open yet and pulling her forward until her lower back pressed against the edge of the mattress. Ronin's liquid gold eyes were on hers. "Every part of you is sacred to me. Every. Part." He swirled his tongue around her anus.

Amery gasped even as she blushed. She never imagined that something so . . . dirty and forbidden could feel so good.

"I will have you here. Every part of you is mine to worship." He lapped at the rosebud several more times and pushed his thumb against the tight pink muscle. His teeth grazed the fleshy outer edge of her pussy and he soothed the sting with soft kisses.

After more long drugging kisses from her clit to her anus, he set her feet back on the floor.

"Stand up, spread your legs wide, and grab your ankles." He toyed with the black rope as she got into position.

Then he very calmly started binding her right wrist to her right ankle.

With her hair hanging down, obscuring much of her vision, she couldn't tell if it was an artistic wrap or merely a functional one. She basked in Ronin's sexual energy. By the time he finished his handiwork, she was dripping wet.

He took another length of rope and let it dangle through his fingers as he caressed her chest, preparing her for the next section of her body he intended to bind. When he finished the chest harness, she'd transitioned into shallow breaths, the white bliss of subspace teasing the edge of her awareness.

Every time he bound her, he checked every strand of rope to ensure that it was properly placed and any pinching sensation was intentional.

Ronin cupped her face in his hands, pushing her hair back to peer into her eyes, and straight into her soul. "Gorgeous. I would like a picture of you like this, black rope against your pearly skin.

Showing your eyes as you struggle to understand why your being bound for me appeals to you."

She remained quiet, hoping to find that dreamy space where she could hear Ronin's broken breaths in the same tempo as her own. Where their blood pumped thick and hot and slow in perfect synchronicity. Where they were two entities bound together by one rope.

Ronin stroked the inside of her thigh with his entire palm. "See how when I use my fingers here"—he lightly pinched the section of skin where her thigh curved into her butt—"how beautifully your skin quivers? It's a drug, Amery, how perfectly you react to my touch. I want to feel that quiver against my lips. I want to feel it on the outside of my thighs as I'm fucking you."

His words settled in her like a seed and she knew he'd coax her to bloom beneath his hands.

He turned her and lifted her onto the bed as if she weighed nothing. As if she were an object to be moved at his whim.

She twisted her shoulders, trying to find a better balance point.

"Stop." Ronin was right there calming her, petting her. "The harder you struggle against the bonds, the higher the chance of marks."

"Don't you want to mark me? Isn't that part of the appeal for you tonight?"

"I wanted a mark from *you*. I demanded one. And I'll ask you before I leave marks where others can see."

The warmth filling her had nothing to do with his mastery with ropes, but how he'd mastered reading her.

"Let your thoughts go. Give yourself over to me."

Ronin literally kept her balanced on the edge of the bed. He gripped the inside of her thighs as his mouth covered her pussy. Suckling her intimate flesh strongly, resting his teeth above her clit, almost as if he was about to take a big bite.

Amery fought the urge to buck and writhe. She focused on her breathing. The delicious worship Ronin gifted to her cunt. She could feel the stickiness flowing from her sex and spreading across her inner thighs as Ronin ate at her like a juicy peach.

Then Ronin began sweeping the pad of his thumb across her anus. Tender sweeps that heightened her arousal. So when his thumb pushed past the ring of muscle, she gasped.

Did he plan to fuck her ass tonight as he'd warned her?

The wet whip of his tongue on her clit brought her focus back to that buzzing tingle building at the base of her spine.

He was persistent in pursuit of her orgasm. As soon as that first spasm hit, he thrust his thumb in and out of her ass in time to the blood pumping into her clit. Every swirling plunge of his thumb brought awareness to the nerve-rich tissues. The added sensation prolonged her orgasm—she cried out and lost herself in the moment of pleasure.

Ronin drove his cock into her and she immediately felt another orgasm gathering steam. He wrapped his hands around the place where her ankles and wrists were bound together. The gentle caress of his fingers over hers while he was pounding into her so furiously was a perfect dichotomy—so perfectly Ronin. When he whispered, "Let go," she did.

The sweet, sweet throbbing took on a sharper edge with the violent movement of his pelvis. This time Ronin didn't come in silence. He came with a roar, after demanding, "Look at me."

In that moment she knew his passion for her was the real beauty.

And her passion for him had turned into love.

Tell him.

His mouth brushed her ear. "Tell me what?"

She tried to remember if she'd blurted that out but her thoughts were still muzzy. "What are you talking about?"

"You said, *Tell him.* Tell me what?"

Her stomach had knotted with nerves. Instead of confessing

her true feelings, she tossed off a breezy lie. "Just that I should give you gifts more often."

He'd laughed then. He'd laughed so hard the bed shook.

But now she regretted that she hadn't told him the truth.

Amery snapped back to reality. Shit. What was wrong with her? She didn't have time to moon dreamily over a coil of rope. She had a presentation to give in . . . fifty minutes.

But that memory had kicked a memory of something else that Ronin had once told her about Japanese customs. Every time he trained in Japan, he brought a gift for his sensei. At the beginning of a business meeting, before any business discussions were done, the person who required the favor always presented a gift.

Since she needed Okada to hire her, she needed to present VP Hirano with a gift.

Dammit. Amery was fresh out of gifts with no time to buy one.

Except . . . she had picked up a small token at the downtown Renaissance Faire a few weeks back. A small tintype of a Japanese Zen garden she'd planned to have mounted and framed for Ronin's office.

Sorry, Ronin, I'll get you something better, I promise.

She dug it out of her pajama drawer, hastily rewrapped it in a piece of brown paper, and tied it with twine. If she had time, she'd tie a better bow, but after her flashback to last night's bondage games, she had ten minutes to make herself presentable.

HER courage from the pep talk she gave herself on the drive to the Ritz-Carlton vanished when she stepped foot into the hotel's luxurious lobby.

Uh, yeah, this opulent place was way out of her league. On so many levels.

And she still hadn't figured out how this pop pitch to the Okada Foods VP had come about, when she'd been dealing with Maggie Arnold in Seattle exclusively. But guaranteed she'd get to the bottom of it today—for better or for worse.

She adjusted the strap on her leather portfolio as she waited at the front desk.

"How may I assist you?" the clerk asked.

"I'm Amery Hardwick and I've got an appointment with Okada Foods. I'm to ask which room we're meeting in."

The clerk's fingers clicked on her keyboard. "Yes, Ms. Hardwick. I'll need to see a photo ID for security purposes."

Security? Amery dug out her wallet and flashed her driver's license.

"Thank you." The young female clerk picked up the phone, poked a few buttons, and waited. "This is the front desk. Ms. Hardwick has arrived. I'll tell her. You're welcome." The clerk smiled at Amery with a practiced hotelier smile. "They will meet you on the eleventh floor. The elevators are around the corner."

"Thank you." Amery hoisted her heavy portfolio again.

On the eleventh floor Amery didn't have to guess who'd been tasked to escort her. The man standing just outside the elevator bay could've passed as a sumo wrestler.

His eyes met hers and his face was devoid of expression. "Ms. Hardwick. She has requested you meet her in the penthouse suite."

Penthouse? Sweet. She kept cool. "That will be fine."

Sumo Guy punched the elevator button. Inside the car, he swiped his key card and poked the code for the top floor.

Amery studied his thick neck and broad shoulders. For the sheer size of him, his body held that same stillness that surrounded Ronin. She wondered if eighth-degree black belt Master Black could take down a sumo wrestler in hand-to-hand fighting. She bit back a smile. Talk about an interesting conversation starter.

Her escort didn't face her when the elevator doors opened to the penthouse. He cut down a short hallway to a set of double doors, knocking twice before entering.

She followed even when she wanted to gawk at the carved

marble columns, vivid artwork adorning the linen-covered walls, and the domed glass ceiling over the entryway.

"Jesus, Amery, don't act like such a rube."

Nice timing for a memory of Tyler's snotty voice, but it did the trick, snapping her professional persona back into place.

They entered a small conference room with a large table in the center. The front wall was composed entirely of glass and faced the Rocky Mountains. A slender woman stood in front of the windows with her back to them.

She appeared to be Amery's height. Hair as glossy as polished ebony fell in a straight line to her hips.

Sumo Guy said, "Do you require anything else, Madame Hirano?"

"No. Thank you, Jenko."

He left the room and closed the door behind him.

Amery didn't move. Didn't speak. She definitely felt like a lesser being as she waited for Madame Hirano to acknowledge her.

Finally the woman spoke. "I'm Hirano Shiori from Okada Foods. I apologize for what must seem like rude behavior. I arrived from Tokyo a few hours ago. The difference in altitude has given me a vicious migraine."

"I'm sorry. Would you prefer to reschedule?"

Ms. Hirano turned and offered a wan smile. "I'm afraid that won't be possible. So you'll have to forgive me for wearing sunglasses indoors. But they help with the light sensitivity."

"No problem. I once had a client wear a kilt and a bagpipe and speak in a Scottish brogue during our meeting. I'm used to dealing with eccentricities in this business."

"Good to know. Please have a seat."

When Ms. Hirano walked to the conference table, Amery admired her business attire. Cream silk pants and an embroidered tunic that managed to be sleek and trendy. Killer shoes. She carried herself with grace, which only accentuated the overall impression of beauty and power.

After she'd glided into a high-backed chair, she said, "Shall I order tea or coffee?"

"None for me, thanks." Amery began pulling folders out of her bag and extreme nerves made her babble. "I'll admit I got a little overzealous with this project. I created several designs that keep the Okada Food logo prominent, but I didn't study your existing product lines too much since you're looking for a fresh approach. I also—"

"Ms. Hardwick. Please slow down. And sit down. You don't have to start your pitch within five minutes of walking in." Ms. Hirano waited until Amery dropped into a chair. Then she picked up the phone and spoke rapidly in Japanese. After she returned the receiver to the cradle, she said, "They'll bring us refreshments shortly. I'm a few cups short on my daily tea intake."

Amery forced her hands into her lap, away from the urge to shuffle the folders. "I'll probably forgo the caffeine."

One pencil-thin eyebrow rose above the sunglasses frame. "Are you always so energetic, Ms. Hardwick?"

"Yes. And please call me Amery."

"So, I'm curious, Amery, as to how you ended up running your own graphic design business."

"You sound as if that's a novelty."

"Perhaps. Small American businesses fascinate me. Especially businesses with a woman at the helm."

Grateful for the chance to discuss her work, Amery shared the abbreviated version of her career. She finished just as two raps sounded on the door and Sumo Guy rolled in a cart loaded with pastries, fruit, and beverages.

"Help yourself to whatever you'd like." She paused. "Or would you prefer to have Jenko serve you?"

The slight stiffening of Jenko's shoulders indicated he wouldn't be down with that at all.

"I can serve myself, thank you."

Ms. Hirano lifted a slim shoulder and spoke to Jenko in Japanese. Amery and Jenko stood side by side as he filled his boss's plate and she arranged hers. She opted for a nonalcoholic mimosa—orange juice with a splash of 7up.

When she returned to her seat, she felt the woman staring at her.

"While we're taking a break, tell me about yourself. What you do outside of work for fun."

This was getting weirder, but maybe it was a Japanese thing, so Amery played along. Talking about her interests and her friends without giving too much away was much harder than she imagined.

Ms. Hirano sliced a chunk of mango and speared it with her fork. "You're not in a relationship?"

She stomped down the urge to snap *none of your damn business and can we please keep this focused on business?* The thing between her and Ronin wasn't the type of relationship she could explain. Amery wet her suddenly dry lips. "No. I'm currently single."

"A woman who likes to play the field. I admire that."

But that wasn't what Amery had said. This woman had twisted her words and Amery heard another alarm bell go off.

Another bout of silence fell.

Something wasn't right. Amery continued to covertly scrutinize the woman, but big round lenses kept more than half of her features hidden.

Why was she playing so coy? Why had she started asking such personal questions? Why had Amery sensed a thread of hostility coming from her?

An odd thought clicked into place. Could this woman be Ronin's ex, Naomi? Kiki had warned Ronin that Naomi would be returning to Denver soon.

Her stomach pitched. She tried to remember if she'd been contacted by Maggie at Okada Foods before or after the run-in with

Naomi's friend. Which brought her back to her original question: why had an international Japanese food conglomerate requested Amery's small company to prepare designs for a new major campaign? Then after a few weeks of clandestine phone calls and secretly working on project specs, she was invited to a last-minute meeting with the company's VP, not her usual Okada contact? A business meeting, which takes place in a private suite? A meeting in which they'd not discussed business at all, but the VP had grilled Amery on her personal life?

This was total bullshit.

"Is there a problem?" Ms. Hirano asked.

"Yes." Amery hoped she wasn't making a mistake. "Who are you really?"

"Excuse me?"

"Who are you? This last-minute meeting with the company bigwig doesn't make sense. Neither does the fact that none of your other business associates are here except for Jenko, who I'm assuming is your bodyguard since he didn't seem comfortable serving tea. And there's the fact that you can't even deign to look me in the eye. So you can understand why I'd be concerned this is some sort of scam."

"I assure you Okada Foods Conglomerate is not a scam."

"I know that. I did my research. I'm saying your being here doesn't make any sense and I wonder what you really want from me."

"A little paranoid, aren't you, Ms. Hardwick?"

Amery shrugged. "So prove me wrong."

"How?"

"Take off your sunglasses."

"Why is that necessary?"

"Because playing the cool, mysterious food magnate hidden behind unflattering cheap sunglasses doesn't ring true for you."

She cocked her head prettily. "How so?"

"Nothing about you is cheap. Or unstylish. You bought those

sunglasses for one reason only; they're big enough to mask more than half of your face. So why do you want to hide your face from me?"

"You read that much into this? How is it you think you know so much about me thirty minutes after meeting me?"

Amery pointed to the purse on the opposite end of the table. "Your handbag is from Hermès and runs about twenty-five thousand dollars. The diamond-encrusted watch on your wrist is easily in the hundred-thousand-dollar range. Your shoes? Roughly ten grand. I don't have any idea which designer you're wearing, but I'll bet a month's rent that suit is not off the discount rack from a Tokyo department store. Your scarf, also Hermès, set you back around fifteen hundred bucks. So the cheap sunglasses don't fit. Besides, if you truly had a vicious headache, you wouldn't take a meeting with me."

She smiled. "Very astute."

"I don't know what game you're playing, but my gut instinct is warning me to walk out."

"Walk away from a project that could potentially pay you six figures?"

Don't think about the money; think about the principle. Amery raised her chin a notch. "Yes, ma'am. Who are you?"

"Who do you think I am?"

Ask if she's Naomi.

No. She didn't even know Naomi's last name. "You ditching the shades or not?"

"How like him you are," she muttered. "Believing eyes are the windows to the soul and all that crap."

Who was *him*? Was this woman completely bonkers?

Just as she'd decided to cut her losses and run, Ms. Hirano lowered her head and removed the shades.

When she glanced up at Amery, Amery's entire body seized in shock. In recognition. Looking into those amber-colored eyes, she knew. Only one other person she'd ever met had eyes like that.

Ronin Black.

"They are a giveaway, aren't they?" she murmured. "You can see why I felt the need to mask them."

"Yes," Amery managed, relieved this woman wasn't Naomi. But facing a member of Ronin's family when she knew next to nothing about said family . . . not fun either. She couldn't be certain yet how this woman was related to Ronin. "You are Ronin's . . . ?"

"Sister." She gave Amery that same seated bow she'd seen Ronin do a hundred times. "I'm Shiori Hirano."

Ten billion questions bounced around in Amery's head, but she couldn't give voice to a single one.

"You're not what I expected, Amery."

"To say that I wasn't expecting you, Ms. Hirano, is an understatement."

"Please. Call me Shiori."

She pronounced it *she-o-ree*. "Where's the Hirano come in? The whole Japanese family surname first, and then the given name last confuses me."

"Hirano was my married name. I opted not to change it back after the divorce. In Japan I introduce myself as Hirano Shiori. When dealing with people in Europe or the West, I switch it to the Westernized version Shiori Hirano. My headache is such I neglected to do that today."

Amery couldn't help but stare at Ronin's exotic-looking sister.

"I know Ronin and I don't look alike—except we both have our mother's eyes. Although we do have the same parents. Our father was an eighth Japanese."

Amery frowned. Had Ronin ever told her that about his father? No. "Does Ronin know you're here in Denver?"

Shiori shook her head. "Curiosity about you got the better of me."

He'd spoken to his sister about her? "What did he tell you about me?"

"Nothing. He circumvented my involvement by dealing with Maggie. He demanded that we hire your firm, sight unseen, for a major product launch for the family business. Naturally that caused a major red flag."

"What family business?"

Shiori's gaze sharpened. "You really don't know? When you can rattle off the retail price of every item on my body? You know exactly what Ronin is worth. I'm observant too, Ms. Hardwick. Don't try and snow me like you've snowed my brother."

Snowed her brother? What the hell? "The Ronin Black I know owns a dojo. That's it. There is no snowing the man. Ever."

"Ronin isn't only some two-bit dojo sensei, teaching classes and putting together amateur mixed martial arts fights. Ronin Black is heir to the Okada Food Conglomerate. An international company currently valued at five billion U.S. dollars."

After a moment of stunned silence, Amery said, "What? Are you fucking kidding me?"

"No, I assure you, I am not kidding."

Not happening. Ronin would not do this. He had too much integrity to lie to her on such an epic scale.

But he didn't lie; he just wasn't completely honest. He wasn't honest with you about a lot of things. Why are you so shocked by this?

Because she'd *trusted* him. She'd believed he was just a jujitsu master living his life according to the tenets of his discipline.

She had to keep her teeth clenched to hold back the roar of fury threatening to escape. Her face and neck became fire hot, which was odd when she'd felt the blood drain out of her face and her entire body turned ice-cold.

Shiori leaned over the conference table. "You had no clue about who he is, did you?"

"None at all."

The man was a fucking billionaire.

The sick feeling spread from her gut straight up to her heart. He'd lied to her about who he was from the start. While she'd bared everything to him. Everything—her mind, her body, her will. And what had she gotten in return? Hot sex, kinky sex. Not the same type of soul-baring disclosure. He'd kept his place in the international billionaire's club a fucking secret.

"I wasn't wrong in my assumption that you two are intimately involved?"

"We've spent time together the last couple months."

Shiori gave her a skeptical look. "You didn't use the fact that you were *spending time together* to demand that he give your company the new Okada food line project?"

"How could I have demanded anything from him when I had no goddamn idea he had any tie to Okada? When I hadn't even heard of the company . . ." Until a couple of weeks after she'd mentioned her financial struggles to one Ronin Black. She exhaled. "He set this whole thing up. He set me up." Amery wanted to beat her fists into the table. "I was flattered when my little graphic design company garnered interest from a big corporation. Naive of me to trust it, but I had so much hope that playing in the big leagues would turn things around for me. Now to learn it's all been a lie?" She shook her head. She'd never bounce back from this type of betrayal. Never.

"I saw your financials. It's been a rough year."

Of course she'd scoured Amery's financials—a company like Okada wielded a lot of power. Which probably meant that Ronin was also aware she had two grand in her checking account, the exact amount of her outstanding mortgage payment and how much she'd socked away in her 401k. Pitiable amounts to billionaires, for sure. Her face heated again. "I never asked Ronin for money."

"He most likely considered this a favor to you?"

"A favor? A favor is helping your friend move into a new

apartment. Or taking a self-defense class with a friend to bolster her self-esteem. A favor is not secretly demanding your billion-dollar family business take pity on your flavor of the month and tease her with the possibility of a multimillion-dollar contract."

Shiori studied her. "How long have you been . . . ?"

"Several months. So when he demanded you hire me, did he ask you not to tell me?"

"Like I mentioned previously, I haven't actually spoken to Ronin about this. He instructed Maggie to find a project for your company and hire you outright. She contacted me, letting me know what my brother had demanded. I decided to intervene."

"So you came to Denver to see if I was some gold-digging hustler."

She lifted a slim shoulder. "It's happened before."

Amery frowned. "To Ronin?"

"No. To me."

Why was she being so forthright? Because it sure as fuck didn't run in the family.

"You seem surprised I'd tell you that."

"I'm used to your brother's nondisclosure."

"I'd point out it's a Japanese thing. But it's mostly a Ronin thing."

"Didn't you do a background check on me?" Amery demanded.

"I didn't need to." She nonchalantly sipped her tea. "Ronin had you checked out shortly after you two met."

"Checked out how?" And how had Ronin's sister found out about it?

"Having the investigative company Okada keeps on retainer call your known associates, your customers, your neighbors, your friends, and your family."

That bastard. It hadn't been the insurance company after all. Another wave of anger rolled over her.

"So you know nothing of our family's background?" Shiori asked.

"None," she said flatly.

"Our grandfather married an English nurse who treated his injuries after World War Two. She was assigned to Japan during the allied occupation. She was quite a bit older than him, but they married anyway. Evidently my grandmother had been exposed to chemicals during the war and with a weakened immune system, she died during an influenza outbreak a few years later, leaving my grandfather a widower at age twenty-two with a year-old daughter. In his grief he threw himself into his food supply business and ended up building an empire.

"Our mother fled his control and married an American soldier. After our father's death, our mother chose to bring us to Japan. I was five and Ronin was eight."

While Amery appreciated the family history, she wasn't sure why Shiori felt the need to tell her. Simply because Ronin hadn't? Nothing she'd said had helped Amery understand why Ronin had kept so much from her.

"Earlier when I asked you who you thought I was, why did you hesitate?"

"I wondered if you were Ronin's ex, Naomi. I don't know much about her beyond that she's Japanese. Someone told Ronin a few weeks ago she planned to visit Denver. I imagine since she and Ronin were together for a while you knew her."

"I was at the club when Ronin met Naomi. In fact, the only reason he went there that night was me. Did he tell you about it?"

Ronin's sister was aware of his club activities? Or maybe she was fishing for information. For some stupid reason Amery wanted to protect Ronin's secrets.

Because you're in love with him.

And right about now that made her the biggest idiot on the planet—how could she possibly love someone she didn't know?

When she realized Shiori was still waiting for her response, she shook her head.

"I'd just been granted a divorce and I came to the U.S. with a friend. She wanted to go to the Denver Japanese Social Club and I was afraid she'd hook up with her old boyfriend and ditch me, so I begged Ronin to accompany me. He hates those places, but he agreed and that's where he met Naomi. She was involved in international finance and was in the U.S. to oversee her father's business interests. They hit it off. For a while anyway. Until Ronin found out . . ." Shiori looked uncomfortable for the first time. "Sorry. I talk too much."

But Amery's mind had already latched onto the fact that Ronin hadn't met Naomi at a sex club as he'd led her to believe, but at a social club.

Was there anything he hadn't lied to her about?

His lust for her.

"So knowing all this . . . what are you going to do with the information I gave you today?"

Something in Shiori's tone seemed off. Amery turned the question back on her. "What did *you* hope to gain from telling me this?"

"An insight into my brother's frame of mind."

"Through me?"

"Yes. And I'm afraid I can't say any more than that."

"You don't have to." Amery stood. "You've said plenty."

A panicked look flashed across Shiori's face. "Wait. You're leaving?"

"No point in staying here and listening to more of the Okada/Black/Hirano saga since it no longer affects me."

Shiori's eyes narrowed. In that moment she looked so much like Ronin that Amery's chest tightened. "How does this not affect you?"

"Okada Foods dangled the carrot and I bit. Shame on me for being hungry. But now that I found out it wasn't a real carrot, I won't make that judgment error again. You got the answers you wanted and so did I."

"You're not pitching the project?"

No fucking way. "No."

That shocked Shiori, but she recovered quickly and tossed off, "Petulance doesn't make good business, Ms. Hardwick."

"Neither do lies." Amery picked up her portfolio and dumped all of the design work on the conference table. As she reached inside for her keys, her fingers brushed crinkly wrapping paper. She pulled out the package and all but threw it on the table. "Oh, I almost forgot to give you this."

"What is it?"

"A parting gift, a cheap token of my affection, a meaningless gesture I'd brought in good faith. Take your pick."

Amery walked out with her head held high.

CHAPTER TWENTY-SEVEN

AFTER the meeting with Ronin's sister, Amery found herself at loose ends. She drove aimlessly for an hour, knowing once the shock wore off, her wrath would kick in again—full force this time—and she'd go off the rails.

She had no one to talk to. Although she and Emmylou had mended fences, her friend hadn't revised her opinion on Ronin Black. She'd just accepted that the man would be in Amery's life. So showing up to cry on Emmylou's shoulder, about Ronin's lies, and deliberate omissions, would make Amery look like a naive idiot for blindly trusting him and not heeding any of her friends' concerns about him.

Was saving face really more important than unloading all the heartache that was threatening to choke her?

Yes.

She couldn't go to Chaz either. He'd been marginally more supportive about Ronin than Emmylou, but Chaz defined materialistic. He'd be wowed by Ronin's status as a billionaire heir. He'd encourage her to forgive Ronin for misleading her about his true colors—which were apparently green, the color of money. Then he'd toss off a comment that he could think of a *billion* reasons why she should just let this issue go.

Yeah, it sucks to be involved with a gorgeous sex-god billionaire.

But Amery wasn't that shallow. And she couldn't give a damn about Ronin's financial status—until she'd learned that he'd withheld the truth about it.

What burned her ass, scarred her soul, and shredded her heart was that Ronin hadn't trusted her enough to tell her anything about who he really was. But he'd demanded full disclosure, body and soul, from her.

A sick feeling started to take root.

That wasn't really true. Ronin had never demanded anything from her. She'd just been so crazy about him, so happy that he'd helped free her from some of the moral confines that'd held her back her entire life, that she'd given him every part of herself without question. She'd willingly handed herself over to him physically, emotionally, sexually because she'd trusted him, because she'd believed he was being equally honest with her.

Not so.

Even after his rope proclivities came to light, he'd basically said *take me as I am.*

She had.

But that wasn't who he really was.

And that made her question who she was.

AMERY showed up at the dojo and rode the elevator to the second floor. Not many classes were held this time of day, but she didn't give a damn if the entire dojo was in attendance. She'd say what she had to.

She found Ronin Lee Black, otherwise known to her now as Rich, Lying Bastard, in the largest training room. He remained at rest in front of the class of black belts. Amery paused out of view and watched two men grappling until one guy plucked up his opponent and slammed him into the mat.

What she wouldn't give to be able to do that to Ronin right now. She didn't know if her heart had ever pounded as hard or her blood had ever pumped as fast and hot and angry as when she stormed in.

Every student turned to see who was dumb enough to interrupt his class.

Amery didn't wait for him to acknowledge her. "Sensei. A word please. Now."

Ronin spared her one quick glance. "The 'no observation' policy is in effect all day, every day. Return to the main room."

"I'm not leaving until I talk to you."

"I am teaching."

"And that time is sacrosanct?"

When he looked at her, his face betrayed nothing. "My classes take precedence over everything, Ms. Hardwick." *Including you* went unsaid.

Putting her in her place and then he all but dismissed her? Screw that. Screw him. He spoke to the wide-eyed students as if she weren't seething in the doorway.

She interrupted him with, "Would you prefer to discuss the meeting I just had with your sister in front of your students? Because I'm good with that too."

Without meeting her gaze, Ronin said, "Everyone out. Five minutes. Don't go far."

After the students were gone, she said, "I'm thrilled you can spare five whole minutes for me."

"Which I won't waste on pointless bickering. Tell me where you were that you just happened to run into my sister."

"I didn't just happen to run into her. She sent for me. Okada Foods ringing a bell?"

He glided toward her, his expression devoid of emotion. "Conference room."

Amery followed him, feeling like a naughty child about to be punished by the headmaster. Seeing the conference room at the end of the hall, she hustled past him to reach it first. She stood at the far side of the table and watched as he closed the door and blocked it with his body. That's why she'd chosen her spot first. She had an exit behind her.

"Talk."

"Shiori Hirano is your sister. She's also vice president of Okada Foods, the multibillion-dollar conglomerate, which also happens to be your family business."

Ronin said nothing.

Not that she'd expected anything different. She laid it out for him brick by brick. "Weeks ago I received a phone call from Okada's North American director. She'd gotten my company's name— gee, I wonder where—and asked if I'd be interested in doing design work on a new healthy frozen food line. I'll admit it was a big ego boost when I got the call. The client confidentiality nondisclosure meant I couldn't talk about anything, which is why I didn't tell you. Still, I'd thought it odd that this ginormous international corporation would contact little old Hardwick Designs. I finished the specs, sent them off, and was told to proceed with my design ideas.

"Imagine my surprise when I learned that Okada Food's VP was in Denver today and had requested a meeting. With me."

His jaw tightened.

"There's a sign of life. Didn't your darling sister share her business travel plans with you?"

"No."

"I wasn't supposed to ever deal with her, was I? You'd gone out of your way to demand that Maggie at Okada hire me sight unseen. Which tipped off the VP—aka your sister—that something wasn't right. She was curious about my company and my connection to her billionaire heir brother."

"I'm sure my sister told you that with absolute glee."

"Actually she seemed shocked you hadn't shared that tidbit with me."

Not a spark of guilt showed in his eyes.

"When did you plan to tell me about being a billionaire baby? Ever?"

"That's not who I am."

"So that's your logic for not sharing that you're an heir to one of the twenty largest corporations in Japan?"

"You knew when you met me that I'm a very private person, Amery."

"To the world at large, yes. But to me?" She shook her head. "I thought I was different. I thought—rather mistakenly, it appears—that we had something together."

"You're using the past tense."

She ignored his flat statement and looked for a glimmer of anything besides apathy on his face. "I opened up everything to you: my body, my thoughts, my feelings, my fears." *My heart.*

"I didn't demand that of you," he pointed out.

She felt as if he'd thrown her on the mat and knocked every bit of air from her lungs. She didn't recognize this man at all. "Which is what makes it so much worse."

No response.

"I trusted you." She curled her hands into fists. "My friends were right. I am naive. I should've heeded their warnings about you. Only their warnings about you being a dangerous man didn't even come close to the real truth. I can't believe you investigated me through my family and friends the week after we met! And yes, they all told me about the invasive phone calls, but I didn't know you were the one who initiated it. God. If you thought I was such a sketchy person, why did you even want to get involved with me?"

"What did your friends say about me?"

Amery met his gaze after he'd sidestepped yet another question. "That you were a thug. Your past was suspect. No one knew anything about you until you just showed up in Denver ten years ago and set yourself up as a jujitsu master in a building you couldn't possibly afford. Some suggested you got the building on the cheap from TP. In exchange, you owed him favors. Which he collected, demanding you root out vagrants and criminals in this area so he could buy other real estate cheap and then cash in on urban renewal funds to get them up to code."

"Who's your source?"

"Then someone else hinted," she continued without pause, "that with your martial arts background, you hired out as muscle for the Russian mob and handled TP's management problems."

"Anyone tie me to the Yakuza?"

At any other time she would've laughed at his mention of the Japanese Mafia; now she just wanted to cry. "After we were attacked in the alley, the fact that you knew just how to ditch a gun put me in the camp that you were a street thug who'd made good. Your secrets, or maybe I should say your nondisclosure and layers of protection, made sense. I accepted them. I'd hoped that given time, you'd let me in.

"I did get to you a couple of times, but then those walls came right back up like they'd never been down. You *know* you got to me with your sexual expertise, with those times you were so sweet . . ." *Don't cry. Jesus. Keep it together, Amery.* "I actually bought into your sincerity." She closed her eyes. "God. Could I have been any more moon-eyed over you? Especially when you gave me that whole bullshit story about the stupid scar on my arm being the same symbol for your name and it being a cosmic sign."

"Amery—"

"Now I have to wonder why you took it so far. Was I just a game for you? Toying with the . . . what did you call me? Wholesome? Toying with the *wholesome* North Dakota farm girl because she provided a different challenge than the usual skanks you met at the various clubs? Get her to open up, get her to sleep with you, get her to let you practice bondage on her, get her to spend all her free time with you until she's crazy about you. Then act like it could be a long-term relationship by offering to lend her money to help her struggling business. I bought it all.

"And while I was beating myself up on the way over here, about why you didn't trust me enough to tell me about your true station in life, I realized the Okada 'reveal' was part of your master plan. So you took it as far as you needed to. Go, you, Master Black, master manipulator. You win."

"Part of my plan?" he repeated.

"It stings that I didn't see the signs. Gorgeous penthouse. Check. Expensive cars. Check. Relationships with the bigwigs in this town. Check. Your devotion to an art not dependent upon income from it to thrive and survive. Check."

"Not going to throw anything in about me being a spoiled rich kid who expects women to accept my sexual kinks?"

"No, but I'll add that you discard your partners when you get what you want from them and they no longer please you," she retorted.

"Where'd you hear that?"

Amery looked at him. "Deacon. He repeatedly expressed surprise that your current flavor of the month—me—had lasted an entire summer."

"Deacon wasn't speaking of my lovers, Amery; he meant that in the rope partner sense."

"That's comforting. Does Knox, closest thing you've got to a friend, know that you're a closeted billionaire?"

"Yes."

"Deacon?"

"Yes."

"Your sister told me Naomi knew too."

"Why do you think she stuck around as long as she did?" he said testily.

"You led me to believe she was some poor waif who used you and needed more kink than you could provide. I had no idea she was an international businesswoman you met at a social club."

"She wasn't an international businesswoman when I had her bound. And how did the subject of Naomi come up?"

"I figured out the meeting with the Okada VP was a setup when the exotic Asian woman started asking me personal things. I thought she might be your ex trying to get to you, given the hush-hush nature of the project and the last-minute meeting. Plus, the woman wore sunglasses until I asked her to take them off. When I saw her eyes I knew."

"That's the only way you'd know, because my connection to Okada is not common knowledge. And yes, that is intentional."

"In this day and age where information can be at your finger-tips in a nanosecond . . . why doesn't everyone on the planet know who you are?"

"Who'd care? I'm not a celebrity."

"So there'd be no interest in a story about Denver's hidden Japanese billionaire?" she taunted.

That's when he cracked. "You plan to out me in the *Denver Post*? Or is this just the threat of exposing me where the real money is?" he snapped. "Think I'll pay you to keep quiet about my family ties and my kink? Think again."

Once again she felt as if he'd kicked her in the teeth. Once again she looked at the man in front of her, the man she thought she'd loved and she saw a stranger. "You actually believe I'd try and extort money from you? Wow. I've already been lumped in with Naomi as a total backstabbing bitch. Now that I know what you really think of me, I'll go."

Ronin laughed harshly and it was an ugly sound. "You're leaving now? Bullshit."

"I've said everything I needed to."

"Except for one very important thing."

Yes, I fell in love with you. Yes, I'm going to suffer for that for the rest of my life. "What?"

"Did Okada offer you the project today?"

"That would get you off the hook, wouldn't it? You had your fun and games with me and you're throwing me a bone to alleviate your guilt."

"That's not an answer."

How's it feel, asshole?

"It doesn't matter what my sister said to you. One phone call to my grandfather and you'll have the Okada project." He angled forward. "Because yes, I do have that much power. I'm just selective on when I choose to use it."

"Save yourself a phone call and don't waste your power on me. There's no way I'd ever take the job after this. No fucking way."

"That right? A struggling company like yours turning down a contract worth several million dollars? One job with Okada could put you on the map for the rest of your career."

"I don't care."

"Don't be stupid."

She hated being called stupid. "You don't know me at all if you think I'll stand here and take your insults just because you have—"

"Money?" he supplied. "That's what it always boils down to, which is why I never goddamn talk about money." Ronin stared at her, the anger pulsing off him. "So you really want to punish yourself by saying no? You'd be losing a lot."

"If not for us hooking up, Hardwick Designs wouldn't be on Okada's radar at all. So I haven't lost anything, because I never truly had it."

"I thought you were a smart businesswoman." He looked at her as impassively as a bug. "Apparently I was wrong."

That stung. "Apparently I was too. About a lot of things."

"You don't know what's really going on. You only have half of the story."

"Doesn't matter. I never knew what was going on with you and that's the way I'll leave it—as clueless about who you really are as I was when we met months ago."

"You know who I am."

"No, I don't. Is this where you promise to explain everything to me if I just trust you?"

"Is this where you storm off?" he countered. "And expect me to run after you with apologies and explanations?"

Another direct hit. "When have you ever done that?"

"Every single time we've had a problem," he bit off.

"Wrong. And it's just another example that we've never seen things the same way."

"That's because you only see what you want to see."

Goddammit, she wouldn't cry in front of this man. She grabbed the door handle.

"You don't get to walk out on me, Amery."

"Watch me."

"I mean it," he warned. "Don't you walk out that door."

Amery turned and looked at him, her heart heavy, her nerves shot, feeling as though part of her world had caved in. But *she* didn't cave in. She met his golden-eyed gaze with as much dispassion as she could muster. "Or what? Are you going to tie me up to make me stay?"

Raw vulnerability flashed in his eyes and he flinched as if she'd slapped him.

Don't fall for it; next he'll close himself off like he always does.

Then it happened, the mask dropped back into place.

"That's what I thought. Don't bother running after me with the excuses you consider apologies or offering more lies masquerading as explanations because we're done this time. Done."

CHAPTER TWENTY-EIGHT

Ronin

The door slammed hard enough to rattle the glass.

Ronin remained frozen in place as if staring at the door would make her walk back through it.

Go after her.

But his feet didn't move even when everything inside him was screaming at him to chase her down, and yes—tie her up if he had to. She had to listen to him. He had to make her understand. . . .

Why you lied to her? You brought her into this fucked-up family situation without any warning—that is all on you.

He was such a cruel, arrogant bastard. Twisting her words around and forcing her to defend herself because he had no other offensive position.

So go after her.

It wasn't pride that kept him in place but fear. Debilitating fear. His years of defensive training tamped down anything resembling real emotion as the *don't show fear* mantra he'd lived by his entire life echoed in his head until he felt as if it would explode.

Find the eye of the storm and center yourself against it.

Ronin counted to sixty.

No change. His rage still fought to get free.

Again. Look deeper for the calm.

He counted off sixty more clicks on the clock.

Then sixty more.

And sixty more after that.

When he reached the three hundred mark, he'd lost any semblance of control.

Ronin picked up the closest chair and hurled it against the window. Glass shattered and the wall shook from the force of impact. But the explosion of sound quieted the fury that'd overtaken him.

Good. He'd found a coping mechanism. He grabbed another chair and threw it into the wall. Harder than before. It bounced off the counter, sending the coffeepot crashing to the floor.

He'd reached for the next chair when the door behind him opened.

Knox said, "Jesus, Ronin. What is going on?"

"Get. The. Fuck. Out."

The next thing he knew, Knox had broken his grip on the chair and had shoved him against the wall, wrapping his hand around Ronin's neck in a submission hold.

For once, Ronin didn't bother to fight back.

Knox snarled, "There's nothing to see here," to someone who'd entered the room. "Get back to class and shut the goddamn door."

Normally Ronin would worry that one of his students had seen his loss of control, but right now he didn't give a shit.

After the door closed, Knox hissed, "What the fuck is wrong with you?"

"If you ever want to use this hand again, you'll remove it from my throat right fucking now, Shihan," Ronin snarled.

"Convince me you won't go on a rampage, *Sensei*, and I'll back off."

"I can't. So why don't you just beat the hell out of me?" Ronin grabbed Knox's wrist, forcing more pressure against his own throat. "And you'd better make it count because I won't go down quietly."

Knox didn't back off. In fact, he increased his choke hold. "Don't tempt me. But since I know your preferred method of dealing with pain is to get the shit kicked out of yourself, I'm gonna pass." He let go of Ronin and stepped back, but blocked him against the wall. "The better torture for you is to make you talk. So what happened?"

"Amery."

"What about her?"

"She walked out."

"Why?"

"She found out . . ." Jesus, he needed to get some modicum of control. He inhaled and let the air out slowly. "My sister set up a private meeting with Amery and revealed my family connections to Okada Foods."

"Your sister is here in Denver?"

"Apparently. I'd like to wring her neck. Send her back to Japan with a clear message for my grandfather."

Knox opened his mouth. Shut it.

"What?"

"You're blaming your sister for Amery leaving?"

"Who else am I supposed to blame?"

Knox raised his eyebrows. "Yourself? Since you should've told Amery months ago about your family? Then it wouldn't have been such a huge shock."

"Fuck off." Ronin jammed his hand through his hair, dislodging the elastic band holding it back. "For three and a half years I've refused any direct contact with my family's business. Three and a half years," he repeated. "And the first time I tried to do something to help someone, they immediately start meddling in my goddamn life again."

"Then fix it. Track Amery down and talk to her. Then deal with your family shit. You've been avoiding it for too long."

"I can't go to Amery now."

"Christ, Ronin, you are the most stubborn—"

"Look at me." Ronin held out his hands. Normally so steady, even after hours of working out, but right now he shook violently. "I can't trust myself around her when I'm like this. I don't have any control. The last time I felt this way and I ignored it?" He finally met Knox's gaze. "I ended up hurting her. I don't leave a fucking mark on her when she's bound, but the one time . . ."

"After the match in Fort Collins?" Knox finished for him.

He nodded. "So I can't even be in the same room with her until I'm calmer."

Maybe it wouldn't be such a bad thing, showing Amery how her leaving affected you.

"Along those same lines, you're done teaching today." Knox pointed to the destruction in the room. "Clean up your mess. Before you do anything else."

"I plan on it."

But Ronin wasn't talking about broken windows and dented walls. He'd fix this mess with Amery—no matter what it took, no matter what it cost him.

And don't miss the conclusion to the *Mastered* series
by *New York Times* bestselling author Lorelei James....
UNWOUND
will be available in late March!

One man's need for control is tested
by the woman he'll risk everything for....

WHEN sensei Ronin Black first encounters Amery Hardwick, the
fire in her eyes ignites a sexual spark a thousand times better than
the primal rush he used to get from mixed martial arts matches.
She accepts his darker edges and admits to him that her desires
aren't as wholesome as he believed. And before long, Ronin is grappling with emotions he's never felt before....

Yet despite demanding Amery bare her body and soul to him,
Ronin holds a part of himself back. When she learns Ronin's secret
and walks out, his life begins to unravel. To regain her trust, he must
let go of his pride and prove to her that it's more than passion binding
them together.